In search of a Soulmate

Swapna Rajput

Invincible Publishers

First published in India in 2017 by Invincible Publishers

ISBN: 978-93-86148-24-7

Invincible Publishers
F-55, Sushant Lok II, Hong Kong Bazar Lane Sector 57,
Gurugram-122003

Opposite Kasturba Ashram, Radaur Distt Yamuna Nagar,
Haryana- 135133

Digitally Printed at Replika Press Pvt. Ltd.

Acknowledgement

* * *

Thanks to almighty for blessing all the best gems in my life.

Thanks to my parents, my loving husband Amitsingh, who always support me and my cutest blessing, my baby Vedanshi, who brought all the happiness in our lives.

Thanks to my siblings and cousins who are more like friends and with whom I share the extreme happiness. Thanks to my entire family.

Special thanks to my school friends, I'd experienced many things in real which are described in this novel. Each friend's character in this novel is real and mixture of many of my friends. Thanks to all my buddies who came in my life since my childhood till today, without whom I can not imagine my life. Love you all!

Dadi (Padmavati, it is real name of my own Dadi) is somewhat combination of my own Dadi and bit of my Nani. Miss you and Love you both. Sudhir (Father of Sandeep) is almost matching to my Papa, Late. Shri. Subhash.Hajeri, miss you Papa! You guys always live in my heart and will be live in this novel forever.

Thanks to Mr. Ajay Setia for his constant support throughout the publishing process, Mr.Abhijeet Singh and Ms. Malvika Solanki for editing the novel, Ms. Sneha Agrawal for designing the lovely book cover and the complete team of Invincible Publishers for their support.

Many of the events in this novel are based on real life experiences...

ONE

'Awww... Look at you! You are the most handsome groom in the world! I always feel you are an incarnation of your Dadaji, he was also as handsome as you. I am very happy today... Finally you are getting married! Love you *beta*...God bless you (kissed my forehead)' she walked out of the room in her slow pace with a big smile on her face.

Yes, that's my Dadi (Paternal grandmother) Padmavati Singh. She has only two important things to do in this world. Watching all the English soaps and bringing smile on everyone's face. She is my best buddy at home, I never hesitate to share the most complicated things with her.

Well, I glanced into the mirror after Dadi walked out. 'Hmm, I am really looking good in this *Sherwani*. Wait a minute, what am I saying!? I am getting married!! Oh, No!! Why the hell I said yes!?? No man! What have I done!!

Suddenly, the door opens with that same old cranky voice 'Hey Sandy, *Saale*! You didn't even throw a bachelor party on your wedding! My throat is thirsty for liquor man!' That's my friend Sumit who barged in my room urging for alcohol! The one thing that he perpetually seeks for since the day he turned 18. He is good looking, tall, fair, and a healthy guy in our group. Following his family tradition he became a banker, and is the most pampered son of his family.

'Hi Sandy, don't listen to him, he just got a bit emotional on your wedding day! (Laughed, patting my shoulder)*Arey haan...ek baat bata! Baaratiyon ka swagat pan parag se horaha hai na*? (laughed again) That's Shaun, who loves talking with famous Indian commercials taglines from school days. A dark, attractive chap, who loves to flirt with girls, just like me. He works in an MNC but has an ambition to do stand-up comedy ever since childhood. He does perform some acts with his troop of theatre.

Aarzoo and Preeti came with beautiful bouquets in hands and with the same old line, 'Hi guys, what's up?' Aarzoo embraced me and wished luck for me, that wonderful fragrance of perfume, which she gets from her Dubai based uncle was hypnotising. Coming from well-educated rich doctor's family, she is a doctor as well. Recently; she completed her MD from UK and shifted back to city couple of months ago and is practicing in the multi-speciality hospital along with her parents. Preeti used to be champion in all the sports at school, we played badminton together in the inter school sports. At present she is an IPS officer in the city, she also followed her family tradition and joined defence. Both the girls looked beautiful in their traditional dresses.

I smiled on everyone's reactions and all started interacting with each other, except for me, I just wanted to go inside my shell! Preeti was quietly observing me with that cute smile of hers. I glanced at her while raising my eyebrows asked 'What?' She smiled, nodding her head, she said 'Nothing, I am so happy for you guys!' I nodded and whispered myself 'All are happy except me!'

Out of the blue, Shreya arrived with her 1 year old boy Akhil. Everybody rushed towards her and started talking and pampering the adorable baby Akhil but Aarzoo, she didn't say a word to Shreya, and she kissed the baby and didn't look at Shreya and asked me

'Where is the bride'?

'Third room from left' me and Shreya both said in unison! Aarzoo intensely looked at Shreya. Shreya smiled innocently and said 'I just met her'. Aarzoo didn't say a word and rushed out. Shreya smiled at me bizarrely, I smiled back, and it was a pale smile with no happiness from both the sides.. Shreya is the most talented girl in our gang. She has the special gift of sketching and painting but ever since she married, her art has disappeared somewhere in her routine life. She has an interesting story with Aarzoo which keeps both of them in silent mode whenever they meet.

Preeti and Shreya started chatting with other guys, I was not at all in a mood to say a single word. Sumit showed his concern asking 'What happened? *Nervous hai kya*?' (Are you nervous?) I smiled and shook my head. Shaun said 'Of course he would be nervous yaar! After all spending whole life with a single 'unknown' girl is a big time risk!!' And they all started laughing again. 'Shut up guys, stop pulling his leg.' Preeti said playfully patting the boys. 'He is getting married, so show some seriousness!' Shreya added her point. Baby Akhil started crying all of a sudden, 'I have to take him to washroom, excuse me guys...' said Shreya, she went inside bathroom holding her baby.

Meanwhile, Preeti said 'I will see whether our bride is ready or not'. And she walked out of the room. 'Let us know, if she is ready we will also come to meet her' Sumit uttered. Shaun got busy with his mobile. Sumit asked me with his cunning look 'Any last wish?' Ignoring him 'Shut up! *Meri fatt rahi hai*! (I am scared) I am getting married!' I said. 'Yeah, we got the invitation! So we are here!' said Sumit mockingly. I kept quiet. Shaun kept his mobile in the pocket, looking at my stressed face he cheered, 'C'mon man! We all know what you are going through, we discussed it many times and you are not looking at the best part! You are marrying a person who knows you better than yourself! She will understand your feelings and certainly co-operate with you.' I was still quiet. 'Now cheer up! And don't show this tedious face to the bride and others outside. She must be happy to marry you and doesn't know how you are feeling, so please... Smile!' he added.

Sumit cheered me by looking at his mobile 'He is right.! Chill *maar*! It's the best day of your life! So don't spoil it by thinking rubbish...' Meanwhile, Preeti called on Sumit's number saying the bride is ready. 'She is ready, we'll go meet her.' said Sumit and they both went out by patting my shoulder.

Everything is happening so fast. I feel like yesterday I went to school with these guys and today I am getting married. Missing Mandar and Gourav, they couldn't make it to attend my wedding as Mandar is in USA because of his new job, he's working as Software Engineer in a MNC there and Gourav is out of town as his wife gave birth to their baby boy in Mumbai. Gourav handles his family business of sweet shops. On this important day, my all-time best friend Mansi is three rooms away from me, getting ready to marry me!

Uh, it's hard to digest! I am marrying my best friend! I was drowning in to flashback, suddenly, my Mom Asha and sister Ramya came in my room and muttered '*Chalo* (Lets go), its time, Panditji is calling you.'

I walked out with them; few of my cousins joined me on the way. All of us went in wedding area the so called *mandap*. Panditji did some rituals, he made my mom to sit in the entrance of wedding hall, I drank milk from her hands, her saree *pallu* covered my face while drinking, and it felt like I was back in my childhood. Somewhat I remember, she used to carry milk bottle wherever we went out and fed me when I was hungry by covering my face with her saree in public places. I used to drink milk with bottle till the age of five. Panditji's mantras dragged me back to the present, it is a Hindu ritual which states, '*Man should not forget his mother, who gave him birth and fed her milk to him, after arrival of his wife!*'

After that we started for *baraat*. Full sound of *band baaja* started when I went outside with family and friends. I climbed on a fully decorated horse of my *baraat* and it started moving towards the temple. The band started to play the music, the title song of old Hindi movie Don '*Arey deewano...mujhe pehchano*'. Till now, I never understood why this song is an anthem for *baraat*? Is it a groom going on horse or a Don? Suddenly, my aunts and uncles jumped on the road and started dancing! And there goes a basic step of *nagin* dance and *tumkas*! Everyone just enjoys this part of wedding! Band played some Suraj Barjatiya film songs and slowly all my cousins, kids and friends joined the dancing troop. Shaun is a good dancer and he enjoyed dancing with my cousin Vaidehi, from top of the horse, I could observe that this rascal was trying to impress her. Sumit was dancing as well, he hated dancing but for the first time he was dancing with his heart. My Dad brought Rs.10 brand new notes, he circled the bundle of notes over my head and started distributing the notes to the band troop and the horse man. My male cousins, who were still hungover, showed there *nagin* dance in the *baraat*. The fragrance of jasmine flowers from my *sehra* was the only thing that made me relaxed. It took an hour of street dancing and traffic blocking to reach the temple of Lord Ganesh, which was just 15 minutes away from the wedding hall.

I entered the temple, my family and friends came along. After all the worship and prayers, we started to move back to the hall, again I had to face the street dancers but thankfully one of my uncle hurried it and the same dancing show finished quickly and we reached the hall in 30 minutes, adding some traffic. I looked my watch it was 12 pm, thank god it was not peak hours for traffic, as it's hard to handle the traffic in Bangalore during peak hours. And the weather was fine as sun was not harsh on us, since it was the month of February.

I am Rajput by caste but Mansi is a south Indian, Kannada girl. My Mom's only condition was to perform this wedding as per Rajput rituals and Mansi's courteous mother agreed on it. Our wedding rituals are bit different from the South Indian weddings but in any case, end of the day we were about to be declared as Man and Wife.

Finally, we reached the venue. While entering the hall Mansi's relatives welcomed our family members with beautiful garlands at the entrance. Mansi's aunt and mother welcomed me doing aarti and later her aunt pulled my nose. I don't know why do they do it? May be because after marriage the son-in-law would always be present for pulling their noses! One of my aunt was instructing them to perform all the rituals according to Rajput caste.! Poor Mansi's mother, who knew nothing about our customs, was doing everything like an amateur. Mansi's relatives held a cloth like a curtain in between us, covering Mansi inside the door, on the other side of cloth. Suddenly, everyone started throwing flowers on my face from the other side, my aunt covered my face with her hands and strong rain of the flowers started blowing from both the sides. I didn't get a single glance of Mansi in that florid crowd and so did she! And this whole flower rainfall called *Sajan Bhet* (Meet the spouse!).

With all family and friends I started towards the *Mandap*, the entire crowd present in hall were eagerly watching me by widening their eyes and with big smiles. I felt like am a celebrity walking on the red carpet! I thought of waving my hands and throwing fly kisses to everyone, after all, you get this one day of your life where everyone will keep watching you, wants to take pictures with you, wants to shake hands with you! May be that is why it's called big day!

I crossed the crowd of 500 people, who made way for me to reach the *Mandap*. Panditji was waiting for me, after some *shlokas* and *mantras,* he asked the elders to call the bride. And there, I saw Mansi walking towards me. She was looking tremendously gorgeous in her bridal suit, red and white combination *lehnga* dress, her *ghoonghat* and dazzling make-up altogether enhanced her beauty. I was unable take out my eyes off her, it wasn't the first time for me to like Mansi, and she always attracted me with her beauty and sweet nature.

She came gracefully and stood before me, the whole crowd was watching us. Again the drape of cloth came in between us but not for long time. Soon after Pandit finished his *mantras* the cloth was removed. Pandit asked us to pour rice grains on each other's head and later he asked to decant the garlands of flowers around each other's neck. Mansi took a garland from her cousin's hand and suddenly, my cousins and friends lifted me up. Mansi was shy and blushing, soon her cousins came and lifted her up and she quickly positioned the garland around my neck. Everyone started laughing, it was a victory for Mansi and I joined the club as well. Later, I placed the garland easily around her neck. She was looking so elusive, I felt that heavy flowers may harm her.

After 1 hour of rituals (which I hardly understood), I applied *sindhoor* on Mansi's forehead and tied *Mangalsootra* across her neck. We took seven circles of *hawan kund* (popular *Sath phere*) holding each other's hand. Mansi's mother's eyes were filled with tears but she did not cry to spoil the happy moment. My Dadi also got emotional at that moment but I saw the happiness on everyone's face. All our friends were busy taking selfi's during the *pheras*. Mansi's hands were wet with sweat the hold was not strong but still I felt good somewhere in my heart. Finally, the marriage was over.

I was fully tired with previous 3 days back to back ceremonies but it was not an end. We had to touch the feet of all the elders present in the hall one by one and that took another half an hour's time. Thanks to my Dadi! Who fast forwarded it and rushed everyone towards the buffet.

I was damn hungry, though it was a ritual not to eat anything before marriage but my Mom fed me glass full of milk and plateful of Idli's without coming under notice of the relatives, who could oppose that explaining the importance of rituals. Nevertheless, she is a mother and cannot see her child hungry, moreover she understands my hunger and knows my temper in empty stomach, and she packed that hot food when the banquet cooks began to prepare breakfast for everyone. All the rituals are useless if your stomach is empty, as they say in Hindi, *Bhooke pet bhajan na hove* (Prayers are not possible with an empty stomach). However, that was at early morning 6.30, it was hard to fill anything at that time but I had no option to fuel my stomach since I knew, I won't be getting anything for hours from then.

It was 1.30 PM and from there we went to changing room. My Mom and Ramya came along with me, Ramya took out my brand new blazer from cupboard and asked me to change. I was feeling like a ramp model, a restless hungry model, who was tired of 3 days ceremonies and sleepless nights. They say before marriage you won't get sleep with excitement but I wanted to sleep! I felt relaxed after removing the heavy *sehra* from my head and garland. I fell on the bed but Ramya dragged me up complaining, 'What are you doing Sandy, get up!! Still many hours left to sleep! Get ready before Mansi comes out there'.

I went to washroom and got fresh, Ramya didn't allow me to rest a second and made me to dress up again. I wore dark blue Armani, which really suited my complexion. Ramya did some more touch up on my face, looking at my reflection into mirror, 'That's my handsome bro!' Ramya complimented me patting my back.

Ramya is my elder sister, married and has a 2 year old beautiful princess, Anvika. My brother-in-law Goutham is a computer guy! Another Project Manager in the house, apart from my sister. No wonder my 2 year old niece Anvi is expert in operating any brand smart phones and laptops!

I came out from the room after drinking a glass of water, I felt that water moving through my neck towards my stomach. God! I was so hungry! But with no option, I moved up on the stage where the special decorated couch was placed for the couple to sit. I saw a big banner behind it on the decorated wall 'Sandeep Weds Mansi' covered with hundreds of flowers, the whole banquet was decorated with flowers. We Indians spend so much on weddings! And world calls us financially developing country!! I placed myself comfortably on the couch for few minutes and Mansi came after changing her dress, she looked stunning in that orange bridal suit. She came over gracefully and sat beside me. I wanted to sit for a while but the crowd started rushing towards us with their wishes, bouquets and gifts!

We both shook hands with hundreds of people and posed for photos! And in the middle we sipped a juice together. I had to share the juice with Mansi for snaps. We posed as if we never shared anything before! Slowly, the crowd started disappearing after sometime, some were in dining hall and some left after having their lunch. The aroma of food was irresistible, I couldn't control two things, my anger and hunger, and that day I had no other option but to suppress both! Soon the clock hit 4pm! I called Ramya and said 'I am feeling damn hungry'. Mansi heard that and blushed. She knows me very well, so I was not awkward in front of her. Ramya smiled and said 'They are making arrangements for your food wait for 10 more minutes'.

Finally, the time arrived and we moved to the dining hall. They decorated the dining table for us with flowers. We sat together, soon the waiters started putting all the dishes on the thali. Variety of sabjis, rotis, rice items, sweets and many more. Wow! I was in heaven. Again the photographers were standing before us for snapshots. To start with, I fed some sweet items to Mansi and so did she. It was awkward to pose like that when you are hungry, once they vanished, I ate all the items in my *thali*, just like a hungry tiger snatches it's pray without caring for anybody.

Fifteen days, I didn't have single word with Mansi, while having food, I observed she was eating very little with small bites. I whispered 'Have food. You must be hungry too!'

She didn't say a word, and she blushed. Looking at us everyone started pulling our legs with their naughty talks.

In the end, the time came for separation! Not ours, it was separation of Mansi from her family, *Bidaayi* time. Everyone started crying, Mansi lives just two blocks away from my home, yet it was hard time for her. She is the only child of her parents. Her mother was speechless, she was crying so much like a small child. Mansi was crying a lot, she was missing her dad, her dad expired few years ago, her mother and grandma took care of her. Her grandma cried a lot by holding Mansi. It was very uncomfortable for me, I felt upset with that entire scene. I looked at my mother, who was also crying. For a fraction of second I felt, am I going out as *ghar jamayi!?*

My dad brought our brand new XUV in front of the hall, which was fully decorated with flowers! He wanted his daughter in law to come home in a brand new car, that's why he took a delivery of it just a day before the wedding. Mansi got into the car and I followed her and sat beside her, Mom and Dadi joined us and Dad started the car. Sumit, Shaun and Shreya said bye from the wedding hall. Arzoo and Preeti were coming to our home. Everyone left slowly from the hall. Mansi was sad, I looked at her and held her hand to console her. She didn't look at me as she had mixed feelings at that time. Dadi noticed it and she smiled looking out of window. Back side of XUV was filled with Mansi's luggage, my parents were strictly against dowry, I felt god knows what on the earth she was bringing in those big bags to live just 2 blocks away! However, Dadi also filled some other items and our bags as well in the car! Thank god this time at least she left the seats empty for us to sit. Otherwise, whenever we plan trips, she fills the car with food items and bags in such a way that many times we end up travelling by sitting on the bags, which were placed on seats!

The entire family members were standing in our fully decorated house lawn to welcome us. My Dad built our duplex bungalow two years ago. My mother welcomed us with *aarti*. Pending rituals were performed partially by me and fully by Mansi like bringing together the two diyas, carrying utensils without making sound etcetera. So much laughing was going around, relatives fully enjoyed teasing us, making noises to distract Mansi so that if she makes sound from the utensils they can pass their valuable comments on the new *Bahu* (daughter in law), my mom said ignoring the comments 'Stop it all of you, if she makes sound then also its fine, after all utensils are made to make sound, apart from cooking!'. Wow! What a comment! This dialogue would have vanished all the *saas-bahu* TV soaps!! I must appreciate that Mansi did everything patiently. Poor girl, after separating from her beloved had to perform that circus.

After the rituals, Aarzoo and Preeti accompanied by Ramya took Mansi in my room in the first floor. I went to the guest room and took bath, it was refreshing, wore brand new kurta and pajama and came out. One best thing about marriage is you get all brand new things. There are clothes for every occasion and every ritual.

Before dinner, once again I had to play some silly games with Mansi, which I quietly enjoyed, untying the knots of sacred thread from each other's wrists, which were tied before marriage. Finding the ring in a big bowl filled with red water and so on.

After dinner Aarzoo and Preeti left for their respective homes. Thankfully it was not 'First night'! Of course, every man will eagerly wait for that night after the wedding, after all, people get married to have sex! But for me it was more like entering a suffocated jungle in the fire, where I can't figure out the exit! I was not at all prepared to face Mansi for that thing! She is stunningly beautiful and I always liked her but that time I had no face or right to touch her! I went to the guest room and fell on the bed. My brother- in- law and cousins were sleeping in the same room. I was so tired that I fell asleep right away after closing my eyes.

TWO

Next morning, when I opened my eyes, Jeej (my brother- in-law) was holding hands of my sister Ramya and dragging her towards him to kiss her, I uttered 'good morning!' by closing my eyes. Ramya ran out from there, Jeej rushed into bathroom, I smiled. Ramya and Jeej fell in love after they got engaged! People say all the romance goes away after one year of marriage or after a child, researchers say many software professionals are getting separated after marriage due to work load, stress and blah blah... but in my sister's case it's completely wrong. Both are software professionals and both go on official foreign trips couple of times in a year and more over it was an arranged marriage yet they are beautiful love birds even after 4 years of marriage. I must say they are the living example for those who create the myths.

Jeej came out after taking bath, 'Just another two days of separation jeej' I said, blinking my eye. 'Saale, same to you!' patting me he said. I blushed and went to the bathroom, wearing another brand new Kurta dress, I got ready for *Satyanarayan puja*. I came down. Holding a glass of milk in front of me, my Dadi said 'No breakfast till the pooja gets over'. I gave a pale smile. 'You are looking handsome! Cheer up! It will hardly take 1-2 hours,' she added. I looked into my watch, it was 9.30. Approximately 12, I calculated the breakfast time; rather I could say brunch time and drank the milk from the glass in my hand.

House was filled with kids and relatives running here and there, it was exceedingly much for our 4 or 5 member's bungalow. Last I witnessed this crowd in Ramya's wedding. Mom and Ramya were busy getting Mansi ready. Priest was starting the *pooja*, my Dad signalled me to sit in front of the priest for performing rituals, he uttered 'Asha...' calling my Mom to check whether Mansi is ready. 'Haan...We are coming down.' Mom replied loudly from my room. Mansi came down in living room and sat beside me for performing the rituals. She smelt wonderful. The entire clan was present in home, so I could not look at her face, if I did, again they would have started passing naughty comments for us. But I glanced at her red saree, while performing rituals, I looked at her face, it was mesmerising. I never saw her so beautiful before, like I saw her in those two days. I know her since childhood, she always used to be cute. But never imagined that she could look this beautiful. Her fair complexion complimented red colour and her perfect figure carried the saree so well that she looked like an idol sculptured on the temple wall. Her hair dressing was done as per South Indian style with lots of flowers. Hands covered with lots of bangles and designed with mehndi till her elbows. *God she is so beautiful* my inner voice uttered! I looked good enough though, but she did not take a single glance at me due to shyness. I heard many relatives talking about us that we look wonderful together. My aunt from Mumbai came to us and complimented *'Ram banayi jodi hai, khush raho'* (couple made for each other, be happy). She turned some hundreds of rupees around our heads and gave it to the servants. After the lunch, many of the relatives left for their homes and some were getting ready to join us in travelling to our ancestral home in Vijaypur Kuldevi mandir. Jeej was sleeping in guest room, he asked me too, to rest for an hour. I could not sleep, Mansi's beauty was sheltered all over my mind and heart. I walked out of the room, all the ladies were busy chatting everywhere in the home along with my mother. Ramya and Mansi were in my room packing and chatting as usual. Men went out and some were sleeping in the rooms down stairs. Many of the relatives left for their homes though, still it was not an empty home. My cousins were playing cards on terrace. I went to my Dadi's room, kids along with Anvika were sleeping there. Dadi was resting in balcony on her long chair. Usually she takes a quick nap on her long chair in the afternoon. I sat near her feet and laid my head on her knees. She woke up with my touch, caressing my hair she asked 'What happened?' I shook my head and smiled. She smiled, 'Isn't it calm here?' she asked. Twisting my lips and raising eyebrows, I took a long breath and nodded again saying yes. '*Dulheraja* should go in search of his *Dulhan*, to add some sweetness of romance!' by blinking her eyes she said and laughed. She removes her artificial dentals while sleeping. I always loved her that cute wrinkled face and laugh without her teeth. Dadi is most mischievous person in our home. Keeping my head on her knees, I said 'I can't do that, I don't deserve her'.

'Hmm, things will change *beta*...try to forget everything. I can see that you like her, so just go with the flow and follow your heart. After all, you are married with this wonderful girl, who is as beautiful as her heart. I still insist you don't need to tell the truth...it's better to hide the bitter truth when you know it will hurt someone'. She added showing her concern. I kept quiet. It's the most difficult thing of my life to confess to Mansi. Anvika woke up and came to us smiling. My Dadi took her on her lap. I smiled and asked her 'Hey my lil princess how was your *nindi*'(Sleep)'.

'Barbie came in my dream!' adorably she replied. She is expert in making stories, started telling her dream. Dadi was in full swing of playing with her. Those innocent chats relaxed my guilt. After some time Anvika asked 'I want to go to mamma'. Dadi signalled me to take her in my room, where Ramya was with Mansi. While I was going out of the room with Anvi, Dadi said 'Sandy beta, Cheer up!'

I smiled and raised the stairs to my room with Anvi. My heart beats were mounting, I was not sure whether it was for glance of Mansi or the guilt residing in my heart. The door was semi closed, I knocked the door but before that Anvi opened it and rushed in to the room shouting 'Mamma!' I stood on the door, looking at her knotting my hands against my chest. Ramya and Mansi were sitting on the bed with coffee mugs. Ramya hugged Anvi with a smile and asked her 'Hey, when did you wake up?'

Mansi was smiling, looking at the love between mother and daughter. She took a quick look at me and her face became red like an apple. I was still on the door, Ramya taunted me 'It's your room, you can come inside!' I smiled and said, 'No! You girls carry on with your chit chat! Actually I need coffee…' I appealed. 'Mamma, I want milk' demanded Anvi. 'Come on my sweetie, I will get you milk' Pampering Anvi, Ramya got down from bed and started walking out of the room. Mansi got up from the bed 'You sit Dee, I will get her milk and coffee for…' there she paused before saying my name.

'It's ok dear! Sit, anyhow, you still have time to get in to the kitchen!' said Ramya blinking her eye. While going out, 'I will get coffee for you, till then you can chat with her but be disciplined!' Ramya said mockingly and walked out.

I smiled, looked around, no one was there, I entered the room. Mansi hesitated to sit on the bed, she stood there holding a table. 'You can sit.' I said showing my hand towards bed but she stood quiet. 'Does everything change so much after marriage?' I asked her. She was still quiet but she looked at me, this time it lasted for few seconds. 'It's been more than 15 days, I haven't heard your voice, your phone is also off…and…' I was continuing but when I looked at her, she was blushing with her eyes down, I smiled and stood still looking at her. 'So…you are saying that you missed me?' she asked. I smiled, 'Of course I missed you! I didn't know that marriage will split two best friends…in these couple of months everything changed…look at us! …we hardly met and spoke since we got engaged… We are behaving like strangers!' complained with agony. 'That was just for a few days, from now on we are going to be together…for life…' Softly she replied with her head down. That was a relief, to hear that last line from her, I uttered in my mind 'Amen!' I didn't want to reply on that, so changed the topic asking her 'Anyways, how did you like it here?' She smiled and asked 'You changed the bed room interior?' 'Hmm…It was all Ramya's idea…

You liked it?' I asked. 'It's beautiful' she said with her cute smile. 'Welcome home!' I greeted her with smile. She blushed and said 'Thank you very much!' I wanted to tell her that she was looking stunningly beautiful these days. By that time Ramya arrived with a mug of coffee, by knocking the open door. I took the coffee mug from her hand. She asked mockingly 'Should I go back?' I smiled and said 'Do you wanna go? Coz… jeej is sleeping alone in the guest room' blinked my eye. She pat me, by widening her eyes she said 'Shut up!' Mansi blushed. I was unable to resist my stair at her, I never felt like this before, I was confused is it marriage or infatuation on her beauty or care or something else? I knew it's not that old feeling for a friend. Then what is it? Is it love? If it is… then I am a dead man! *God why you brought this situation in my life?* I was lost in my thoughts looking at Mansi.

By that time, Mansi and Ramya started chatting again, Anvi arrived in sipping milk from her sipper. I realised even I have to sip my coffee. I walked out of the room silently sipping my coffee and thinking how much these girls talk. They don't even have etiquette to ask me sit in my own damn bed room!! What happened to these other guys, all of them have no courtesy to call me back. I grabbed my phone from pocket and started calling everyone…one by one. Sumit didn't answer, I got a message 'In a meeting, will call you back!' I called Shaun, his mobile was not reachable, don't know where he kept it away from his reach! Aarzoo is a busy doctor she never answers phone. Shreya is a married girl, who rarely takes any call in her busy life of raising her baby and juggling with family. Dialled Preeti's number, she answered quickly 'Hey pretty boy, how come *dulhe miyan* called me on the very next day of marriage? *Biwi se bore hogaya kya?*' She never stops flirting with me. 'Aayee…Missing you baby, when are you coming to meet me? I asked mimicking old Hindi film villain Ranjeet. She laughed and said 'you guys are going out tonight, will come after that, why? Is everything alright?' 'Yeah, everything is under control officer!' I replied to the IPS officer. 'Ha ha! very funny! How is Mansi, I wanted to talk to her but busy right now, will catch you guys later, ok? Sorry *da*…you guys enjoy the trip.' She disconnected without hearing my reply! Yeah, that was a rude act from all of my friends.

All were busy. I am also busy though, I run my father's business of real estate and construction, but take out time for the friends every now and then. Those good old full day chats and fun are suppressed in small whatsapp chats and few forward messages. Hardly anyone comes online, if one does, then someone gets off from the chat. Couple of friends are facing some issues in their lives, they can discuss the problems to find the solution but they are just surviving by ignoring them. Wait a minute! I am also doing the same. In fact, I am in a big problem now, I messed up my life as well as Mansi's! My thoughts were never ending. I took a long breath and saw my Dad, who was busy making some list in the living room. I came downstairs and kept the finished coffee mug on the dining table beside the stairs and walked to him.

Looking at me he stopped his paper work and smiled. 'Do you want any help Papa?' I asked. Most of the time he communicates with his eyes, he showed me the seat beside him on the sofa and asked me to sit. 'I was just making some lists…' he said looking at his papers. I sat beside him looking those papers. 'We are leaving by 10, so that we can reach early in morning by 6, Ashok and his family made all arrangements of water and beds everything in the house there. So, no need to worry about anything. He also arranged for cook and Pandit. Our family, Chacha's family and your Buwas (Aunts-Father's sisters) are coming with us. Total 23 people, so I arranged an AC Volvo bus. I was just calculating the amount.' He explained the travel plan. I shook my head. My Dad is expert in making planning's and executing them successfully. He is cautious in spending money but not a miser, it is natural though for a man who was raised in underprivileged conditions and struggled a lot to build his own empire of this real estate and construction business. Our family was always well to do till my Dad lost his job in a private company. He entered in this real estate business few years back by mortgaging his 2 bedroom house and my mother's jewellery, today with his intelligence he is a successful businessman in the city. It all came from his hard work and smart mind. He is just a 12th pass with 3 attempts! But he has more knowledge in every aspect then me, who is an MBA graduate! However, as they say time always changes! These relatives, who are filled in our home like a sheep house filled with sheeps, never came to help us when my father needed. But today everyone is roaming around my Dad.

Dad was talking about the expenses and travel plan. I heard everything he said by nodding my head. Sometimes it's irritating when he sits with his accounts but he works hard, so I value that by listening carefully. Soon the clock hit 6 in the evening, all the relatives were speeding up, packing and getting ready for the trip.

Night, sharp by 10 the bus arrived in front of our home, we all had our dinner by that time and everyone got into the bus. House was locked by Dad and before leaving he made Raju incharge for the security of home. Raju lives in our out house, 23 year old boy, who was brought by my Dad from Vijaypur seven years back, he works in our office. Trustworthy and loyal guy, to describe in bollywood style he is a *Sevakram* (Old Hindi movie servant name) of my Dad. My family is more like, families in Suraj Barjatiya movies. Everyone is perfect, loyal and easy to mingle nice people. Sometimes, I feel like I don't belong to this family because of my brat nature and anger.

I was happy that I was sitting beside Mansi in the bus. It was a night journey, so many of the members slept immediately after the departure. Some of the cousins played Antakshari for a while and all the songs were love songs and somewhere I felt butterflies in my stomach with the songs and Mansi's touch. Yes, I was very close to Mansi, her arms were touching my arms, and it felt good. Within an hour everyone slept the in bus but me and Mansi. The lights went off. Her fragrance was wonderful, even I smelt good. She was looking out of the window, the weather was chilling outside and inside the bus. I felt like holding her tight but controlled my feelings. There was a silence in between us, I wanted to talk to her but did not understand from where to begin the conversation. I wasn't sure whether to start the conversation or not, she must be tired too with the intact wedding. She might also need some sleep, I thought of maintaining the silence as she was quiet. It was a calm, long silence with uninterrupted snoring competition between my uncles and aunts! It was dark in the bus but the moonlight was all on our face and she looked bright. After five minutes of bearing the sounds, I dared to look at her, she looked at me as well. I laughed and she laughed too! But it seemed like no one got disturbed with our laughing! Controlling each other we said 'Ssshhhhh' at the same time.

'You didn't sleep?' I whispered. 'No.' nodding her head she replied. 'You haven't seen Vijaypur right?' I knew she did not, but still to continue the conversation I asked. 'Did you ever take me there?' Sarcastic answer came from the other side. I looked at her, moonlight from the window was sprinkling light on her face, and she looked attractive. She also looked at me, our eyes met for few seconds, my heartbeats were rising like Sensex points on a Monday morning. Inner voice was screaming *'kiss her you idiot'*. She blushed and looked out of the window. Again the silence surrounded with snoring sound. I laid my head on the seat. I did not want her to sleep this night.

'You spoke to your Mummy?' I began the conversation once again. 'Hmm' she muttered.

'You should have asked her to join us today.' I asked. 'She can't travel that long, due to her arthritis' she replied looking out of the window. 'It's beautiful outside isn't it?' I asked.

'Indeed, yes' She said smiling. 'You remember school trip? We travelled as it is like in bus during full moon night.' With an excitement I asked.

'Hmm...' She smiled looking out. I was quiet for few minutes. I looked at her, I never imagined in my life that I may see this day or night probably, in my life. I am with the most beautiful friend of mine, who is my wife now. She knows every tit and bit of my life. Who would be as lucky as me or as unlucky!

She was looking out of the window. I knew she was thinking that why am I not doing anything romantic with her? She must be surprised that schools biggest playboy, who never lost single chance of flirting or romancing with the girls is not even holding the hand of his wife. She must be jealous of all the girls I dated in the past, it's not like I never dated Mansi. We both dated for few months but she was always a close friend, my heart beat for every girl in the class, so I had to let go the 'girlfriend Mansi' to welcome the other girlfriends and decided to be with best friend Mansi in school.

It was 1.30 AM and I was feeling sleepy, so was she. 'Within 4-5 hours we'll reach, you sleep for some time now. I am also feeling sleepy' I said by yawning. 'Hmm' she muttered softly and closed her eyes.

Early morning at 6.30 I opened my eyes, the bus was passing through the rough roads. We reached Vijaypur and our home was 20-30 minutes away. Mansi was sleeping by resting her head on my shoulder, her hand was in my hand, I softly tightened the grip. Her hair had covered her face, I slowly moved them behind her ears without waking her up, even in the early morning her charm had not faded. Still many people were sleeping. I thought of kissing her but suddenly, Jeej walked beside our seat, he didn't notice us and went towards the driver to give him the directions for the house, Dad also followed him. Mansi woke up with voices of my Dad and Jeej and she took off her hand from my hand and pushed her hair back her ears looking here and there. I smiled.

We reached the home, after three years I was coming here. The house was fully decorated with decorative lights and flowers. All the credit goes to Ashok uncle and his family. Who looks after the house as their own house. Ashok uncle's wife Bhadra aunty welcomed us with aarti. There were 4 rooms in the house with veranda, bathroom and toilet. Some relatives rushed to the toilets. Bathroom crisis raised for everyone, Ashok uncle had already arranged for it in his house and in a neighbour's house. And some of the relatives took bath in Ashok uncles home. We all had upma and tea in breakfast and got ready for the rituals. Once again we did the same procedures of rituals as we did in past 2 days. By the evening all the rituals were over. My Dad decided to stay one more day there. We visited Gol-Gumbaz in the evening with entire family. I wonder about the architecture of that structure since childhood. I visit there every time I come here, still that feels great. Mansi liked the entire ambience. My Dad told her the story of building the Gol-Gumbaz. Some relatives, who were against this wedding due to inter-caste, were getting close to her by now. Her charming nature attracted everyone.

Next morning, Ashok uncle called me and Mansi along with Mom, Dad, Ramya and Jeej. He presented gifts for all of us. My Dad was against that but he strongly insisted everyone to take them. Ashok uncle and Dad are childhood friends. He does farming and has many acres of land there. He recommended Raju to my Dad, who is living with us now. Raju is an orphan and a relative of Ashok uncle.

After the lunch we visited some of the neighbours. Few of the relatives and neighbours who came with us from Bangalore, actually live here. They came to attend my wedding, they stayed back in Vijaypur. We started for Bangalore by 10 PM after the dinner. Again the things repeated. Everyone slept after the same old time pass of *Antakshari* and some other games performed by my cousins and other relatives, which was not too long this time though. I took a long breath, had no guts to look at Mansi. She must have been expecting some romance. It is natural, every person enjoys these moments but I am the only idiot who was avoiding those situations, it was damn hard for me. Newly wed, beautiful wife sitting beside me in a bus filled with all the relatives, lights were off and moonlight was peeking from window and giving the feel of spot light on our faces. But I was sitting like dumb. For the sake of formality, I asked her 'Are you feeling sleepy?'

'No' she replied looking at me.

'....'

'Do you want to say something?' She asked promptly.

'I don't know where to begin...It's all very different yaar...!' I spoke my confused mind.

'Look, I understand that it's all hard for you, this marriage, accepting me as wife.... I don't want to force you for anything and you can take your time for everything.' She helped me by speaking up with those lines.

I wanted to say something else to her but ended up saying. 'Thanks...I knew that you will understand.'

She smiled and after few seconds she said 'By the way, my phone was not broken from last few days. I kept it off.'

That was surprising! Blinking my eyes, I asked 'What? Why????'

She smiled, jumped her shoulders and said 'I wanted to see that you miss me or not! And the other day you said that you missed me.... (Paused and looked at me) I felt good after hearing that.' She finished and our eyes locked.

I felt good too. 'You are my best friend, certainly I will miss you if you are away from me.' By holding her hand I said.

She looked at my hand, I quickly took it back and she blushed. I blushed as well. After few minutes, to change the topic, I asked her 'How did you like my native? Bit hot here.'

'Its fine, not that hot. But the people and everything is very nice, it's overwhelming.' With that cute smiling face she replied. 'Hmm...good, since my Dadi moved in with us, we rarely come here. But before that we used to come every year and celebrate Dashehra and Diwali here.' I said remembering those days. 'Yeah, I know:' she said.

'You know, this place is very bad with water, we used to fetch water from wells, Ahh...those good old days! The municipality water used to come after every 4-5 days, we used to fill each and every utensil in the house after filling the tanks and buckets. The neighbours used to make fun of us saying that how come you guys have left the spoons!' I said with excitement. We both laughed. 'But now I didn't see any shortage of water.' She asked. 'Yeah, Dad had dug the bore well and also renovated the house, it was not this posh before, it was just 4 room house, which was built by my great grandfather 70 years ago...somewhere in 1940's!' I gave her the info. 'Oh, ok. He built it very well using such a small place so wisely...Who lives here now?' She asked after complimenting my Dad's architecture. 'Ashok uncle's relatives live here for rent. Though my Dad never wanted to take rent but they insisted. Our relatives wanted to move in their but my Dadi did not allow them. Those are the ones who never came to help us, even now Dadi and Mom never talks to them, it's just Dad who entertains all of them. Ashok uncle takes care of the house very well.' I said.

'Hmm, those are the relatives who stayed back?' She asked. 'Yup, they are Dad's chachaji's (Paternal uncle's) son and family and our step uncle and family. They are all well to do, have a house yet spread hands for money, my Dad gave them their share before constructing the house but... Anyways, Ramya and I do not get into these matters, so you also don't worry about them. If you face any problem with them in the future just try to ignore and if they get in to your nerves, you can always tell me or anyone in the house. But there is nothing to worry much about them, Thanks to my Dadi and Mom they never comes to us.' I advised her.

'Okies' she said with smile. However, I knew she handles every situation very smartly without hurting anybody's emotions but she was new to family, it was not like influencing her but she should be aware of the people whom she will deal with from now on, so I had to do my job informing her about the positive and negatives of the family. After all every family have some pieces like them. 'Let's sleep now, its 1 AM' I said.

Morning we reached home by 6AM. Many of the relatives were going back to their destinations today. My first *Buwa* (peternal Aunt), uncle and cousins Vaidehi and Sangram were from Jaipur, my second *Buwa* and her family of 2 children and husband were from Mumbai, they all left by catching evening flights. Both the uncles and Buwa's work in nationalised banks. The house was comparatively empty in the night. Some of my Mom's relatives, who live nearby were going next morning.

Jeej went to office in morning from our house. Ramya had few more days off, she stayed back, she lives in the same city but in far far away locality! She hardly visits us once or twice a month. She lives with her mother-in-law, who also has two jobs in the world. Attending the Satsangs and giving the pravachan to others! Anvi imitates her granny very well. I feel only my Dadi is modern in India, who watches fashion TV, Hollywood movies, and soaps like Sex and the city, Desperate Housewives, Two and half men etc.,

THREE

After the dinner I was lying alone in the guest room. It was still a mess after the departure of Buwa's. Ramya came in asked me to take bath. 'Why now? I want to sleep!' I replied without moving from bed. 'Shut up! And Get up! Don't ask a single question! Go and take bath! C'mon fast…!' she ordered. 'C'mon yaar!! Another ritual? Not again!! Not now yaar please!' I requested. She didn't hear a word of excuse and dragged me out of the bed and forcefully sent me to the bathroom. I took bath in 5 minutes and came out. Ramya arranged a new set of Kurta and Pajama and rest of the clothes on the bed. I wore them and got ready. Ramya came in a few seconds later and sprayed perfume all over me.

'C'mon yaar, what is this now?' I asked. 'Come I will tell you…' by holding my hand she took me towards my room.

I was stopped on the door by my cousins, Ramya joined them as well, they blocked me outside and asked for entry fees! I remembered all these steps of an Indian marriage because I was present in Ramya's and all my cousins' weddings. Instantly, my mind alarmed me '*Fuck!! It's THE first night*!' Piercing the crowd of ladies my eyes looked inside the room and I saw Mansi sitting on the fully decorated flower bed, covering her face with *ghoonghat*. Such an embarrassing situation! Practically thinking I am paying my sisters to have sex with my wife! *Ohhh…shit man!! What the fuck!* I felt ashamed of my thoughts. I did not bargain much and agreed for Rs.10000. Which I got from my Dadi in the same evening! I didnt realise this, when she gave the money by saying, 'Give this to your sisters in the night!'

They let me go inside and locked the door from outside by shouting 'ALL THE BEST!! HAVE A GOOOOOOD NIGHT!' It was awkward, I took a pause. In few seconds, I locked the door from inside and slowly went towards the bed. I waited for the sound of Alarm! We hid alarms everywhere in the room during Ramya's time. No sound! That was a relief. I looked around, they transformed my room in to a flower shop! The bed was decorated with roses and other flowers. Mansi was sitting in the middle of bed wearing red saree, covered face with *ghoonghat*. The room smelled awesome with aromatic candles everywhere and the lights were arranged romantically. 14 years of friendship with Mansi and for the first time I was unable to say a single word! I felt like an idiot standing in the middle!

'Ahem…' I cleared my throat. She sat quietly, keeping her hands on her knees, was shivering a bit, it was obvious to be nervous during such time. I moved towards the bed, hesitating, 'Soooo, yo...you....you knew that....ummm...this is gonna happen today?' I asked to start the conversation. She shook her head, it was a NO. There was silence again. I took a long breath and at a stretch I said 'I need to talk to you Mansi'. She was still looking down. That ghoonghat was distracting me to observe her, 'Just remove that ghoonghat! I can't focus, it's...disturbing.' I said. 'Umm, you are supposed to do that...as we see in movies...' she said with a touch of cynicism. 'What the F...' I shut myself scratching my forehead.

I made up my mind and sat on the bed hurriedly and removed the ghoonghat from her face. And there I was speechless again! I was stunned! This was for the first time in past 3-4 days I was seeing Mansi's beauty so closely. Of course the bus was first instance but that was in moonlight but there in my romantically decorated room we were all alone. Her striking eyes were looking down, her face was glowing, and those beautiful rose petal lips were so attractive that I felt like kissing them straight away. She was not wearing much jewellery but her hair was tinted with jasmine garland and that fragrance was hypnotising. My hand automatically moved towards her face, I held her chin up and said 'You are stunningly beautiful!' She blushed and covered face with her hands, she felt shy. That rang a bell of school days, there have been moments like this. I felt hundreds of butterflies in my stomach, *she is gorgeous! And she is mine!* I said to myself and smiled. Suddenly, my guilt came in front of me and I got up from the bed saying 'I cannot do it yaar!' I turned back without looking at her, it was the most difficult part of my life to face her that time. I walked towards the balcony and said 'I am sorry Mansi...' She got down from the bed, I heard the sounds of her bangles and anklets, and she walked towards me and muttered 'Ahem...'

'I am sorry Mansi...I know this is rude...I...I ...' my confused mouth was uttering. She quickly held her hand against my mouth and said 'Ssshhh, its ok...I already told you, I understand.' She was so calm and generous. Her husband was not giving her all the rights she deserved yet she didn't have had a single touch of moan on her face and in her words. I felt to embrace her for her patience and good behaviour but I didn't had the guts to touch her. 'It's not that yaar, I just don't deserve you...' my repent came out in my words.

'Why do you keep saying that? I know you since our childhood...I know every part of your life...I have no problem with anything you did in the past...I wouldn't have married you if I'd felt like that, and you know that. So stop saying that....' She said calmly.

'Mansi I...' I wanted to say that but I had no guts to speak the truth I stopped. She took a long breath and said 'Actually, I am feeling sleepy... you know...from so many days we didn't sleep properly due to marriage stuffs...Can we go to sleep now?' she asked innocently. That brought smile on my face, I agreed to what she said. She moved to bed and said 'you sleep here, I will sleep on the couch.' 'Is this a TV soap?' I asked. She looked at me smiling. 'Obviously not, then why this sleeping on the couch and bed and all? I do not want you to sleep on that congested couch. We'll sleep on the bed.' I commanded her.

My mother is addicted to Hindi *Sas-bahu* serials, I often see them while having dinner along with her. They show similar scenes in every serial, they have one heroin with three to four heroes and one hero for four to five heroines and still they are identified as Lord Ram and Seeta, I feel WTF!! They show this bullshit in the idiot 'flat' screen (as no boxes exist now!)! I always felt one thing is most ridiculous in Hindi soaps...Hero and Heroine get married and never have sex! And guess what? That actually happened in my life!!

'OK... If you don't have any problem, then I don't mind.' She said with her cute smile.

I took the load from the couch and placed that in the middle of the bed and said 'This is my area and that is yours.' in return, she laughed by holding her hands on her mouth and

I smiled. I knew it was silly but I didn't trust myself and didn't want to take any risk. I felt already I have made a mistake by marrying her, I cannot go further anymore, and it will be a sin if I touch her without confessing the truth.

She took out some clothes from her bag and went to the bathroom for changing. I had made space in my closet for her clothes and stuffs but maybe she had no time to unpack her clothes. I laid on the bed closing my eyes, kept on thinking, *how to tell the truth, her family suffered only because of me, I am the culprit of her messed up life in the past! She moved on after we got engaged and if I tell her the truth, she will go again into her shell of depression. She likes me...in fact she loves me! Should I hide the truth for life and sleep on it as Dadi said or...No I should tell her, as I decided. But I think I am falling for her now...and if she leaves me then I cannot take that pain... Aahh...Its killing me!!'* My thoughts surrounded me all over and the bathroom door opened. She came out folding her saree. There I saw another avatar of beauty! She was wearing sky blue colour night dress, no makeup on the face and yet gorgeous! That's it...I cannot control anymore!! Quickly, I went inside the bathroom and before she looks at me I closed the door.

I came out after 15 minutes finishing my fascination and saw divine beauty sleeping on my bed. I went on the bed and slept beside her, I muttered myself looking at her *'I may not be able to touch you, kiss you or hug you...but the fact that you are mine makes me happy'*. I fell asleep staring at my sleeping beauty.

Next morning, when I opened my eyes Mansi was not around. Thinking that she must be in bathroom, I glanced at my mobile, it was 8 AM and my mobile was flooded with hundreds of text messages and pictures of best wishes, I did not open any message and kept the phone aside, knocked the bathroom door but the door was open and no one was inside. I went in, got fresh and came out after taking bath.

I was in the towel and Mansi entered the room, she turned back immediately after looking at me in towel and said 'I came to wake you up... good you are already up...Gourav is coming to meet us now and Dad said some more guests are coming. So, get ready and come down Mr. Ranbir Kapoor...' she giggled and went out without looking at me. I smiled, she was wearing saree, again! I looked up and asked God, 'Is it some trap? You already made her so beautiful, she looks gorgeous in anything but in sarees she is irresistible for me!! Why you dragged me into this?'

I grabbed my casuals and went down in the living room. Gourav was waiting there, he hugged me wishing 'Welcome *Dulhemia*! Congrats buddy! Sorry I couldn't make it for the marriage.' 'Thank you! Finally you got time to meet us....Did you meet Mansi?' I asked him. Mansi came out from the kitchen, holding tray filled with tea and snacks. 'Yes, we met already. Here, have some snacks and tea.' She offered us with smiling reply. Ramya was feeding Anvi on dining table and I did not see Dad, Mom and Dadi around. '*Arey* why all these formalities *yaar*? I already told you I had my breakfast just now in home and came here.' Gourav said to Mansi. '*Chal na*, I am hungry, have some with me.' I said taking tray from Mansi's hand. She smiled and handed over the tray to me, I controlled myself staring at her face. 'Good to see you guys married yaar...you both are looking very nice together. Remember? I said this years ago in school...you guys make the best couple.' Gourav complimented us. Mansi blushed. I felt good inside. 'Thank you, have tea' I said. We met Gourav after months. Gourav has branches of his Sweets shops all over Bangalore. After the death of his father, he hardly gets time to call any of us. At the time of our marriage he went to Mumbai. His wife was in labour, he was blessed with a baby boy. Today he brought kilos of sweets to celebrate both the occasions, his fatherhood and our wedding.

Mansi asked me 'Did you wish him? He is a proud Papa now!' and smiled. 'Yeah I totally forgot! Congrats Papa! How are both, Bhabhi and Baby?' I asked with an excitement. 'They are fine. Wait I will show you the pics.' He took out his mobile with same anticipation and showed us the pictures. We all saw the pictures of cute baby, Anvi loves kids and she started kissing the pictures in mobile by snatching it from our hands. We all had a great time with Gourav. He is the only son of his Marwadi family of 2 uncles. He handles the business as well as family of 13 people. Since childhood he is a less spoken and low profile guy, he was always dominated by his sisters and cousin sisters. He was brilliant in studies, especially math, he should be because he comes from a business family. He used to sit in shops since school days. He always took out time for us from his busy schedule. He personally supplied tons of varieties of sweets on our wedding. He was not even taking money from us, of course, he is a Marwadi! But for him friendship is always important than business. However, my father made the payments for wedding sweets.

After half an hour chat he left for his shop. The Trinity of my Dad, Mom and Dadi arrived within minutes after the departure of Gourav. They went to see off all the relatives and came with the news of arrival of more guests' in the evening. I thought now we are going to get relaxed but the marriage ceremony has become a never ending TV serial!

Dad gave me some accounts work to finish. I was doing his job on my laptop and Dadi went in her room and called me inside. I entered the room she was sitting in the balcony on her favourite chair, she asked me to close the door. I did as she said and went towards her. Her balcony comes in the back yard of the house closed with glasses, so its more like a secret chamber for confidential chats!

'How was it?' the quick and straight arrow hit on me.

'Nothing happened' I said with pale face.

'What? Why?' surprised she asked.

'How can you ask that, after knowing everything...' I raised my question in return.

'Hmm, so you have decided that you will tell her everything.'

'Yes'

'Do you know the consequences?'

'Yes'

Few seconds silence and she said 'Your Dad booked a honeymoon package for you both in Phuket, the flight is tomorrow night.'

I looked at her, she was smiling. I gave a strange look, she said 'I told him!'

I maintained my silence looking at mobile.

'Today, after the departure of guests, she is going for *pag phera* to her mother's place, will be coming back tomorrow evening. You start your packing for tomorrow, Ramya will help you both in packing.' She said looking at my facial reactions. I stood like a stubborn man. Whatever she said, I got only one line which disappointed me that she was going to her mother's place! In those 4-5 days, I had only one task that is to search for Mansi and keep staring at her. Hearing one day staying apart was a miserable feeling. Yet, I was quiet. Actually, I was scrolling Mansi's pictures on mobile, which I'd captured in those four-five days without anybody's knowledge.

'Bring scotch for me from Thailand. I heard that tastes better.' She asked with her old smile to change the topic. I smiled and said 'I will bring some good brands for us partner.' She meant for liquor, my Dad stopped drinking after his first heart attack few years ago. But my Dadi drinks beer once in a while. In fact, she is my drinking partner after the guys from the gang. It is not that we regularly drink or addicted to it. Dadi is a bold woman in this modern era, who always wants to live her life with full extent and never stops anyone for anything as far as she feels it's acceptable.

I spend most of my time with Dadi at home. Mom is always busy cooking in kitchen and feeding all of us and rest of the time watching her TV soaps. She is bit withdrawn in expressing her affection for us. She rarely talks to Dadi because if she does, then Dadi will point out other meanings in her words. They always have conversation by taunting each other. But she hates people who gossip about my Dadi and it's same with Dadi. They both love each other but never show that they content together. Strange duo of *Sas-bahu!* We never interfere in between and let them be on their own. I did not have any more conversation on honeymoon.

'She is beautiful isn't she?' Dadi asked, she observed my facial expressions while scrolling Mansi's pictures. I was standing away from her, where she could not see my mobile. Still those aged eyes caught everything.

'How do you guess everything so perfectly?' I expressed my curiosity.

'I can see the love on your face while scrolling her pictures.' She said and I hugged her.

'Don't worry she is a nice girl and one day she will understand everything.' She said patting my back.

My mobile started ringing and it was Sumit. I picked the call. 'I am sorry da, I was busy that day so didn't answer your call...So how is newly married life? How is Mansi? I hope you did not bother her much...' he asked all the questions from the other side, before I said 'Hello', his unstoppable mouth started uttering. 'Everything is fine.' I said. 'Such a pale answer, what happened buddy?' He asked. 'Nothing yaar...just getting used to things...' I replied casually. 'So what is the plan for honeymoon?' he asked. 'Phuket' I replied. 'Thailand is meant for chill-outs, gogo bars and massages and most importantly without 'wife'!' he said mocking from the other side. 'TYFI (Thank you for informing)! Dadi planned for it' I said, smiling at Dadi. 'Huh...No more comments! When are you leaving?' he asked. 'Tomorrow' I said. 'Ok. Enjoy *Maadi* (*Maadi* means 'do' in Kannada language). We all are planning to meet you both, we'll meet after your 'Thailand honeymoon' after a pause 'And yeah! Make sure you won't take any special massages or enter into any gogo bars!' He said cynically. 'Are you encouraging me to do so?' I taunted him. 'I said it, it's up to you to take it in whatever way you want...ha ha...*Chal*, bye will catch you after coming back.' He said in his wicked style. 'Bye' I disconnected.

Anvi was playing around and heard our conversation of Honeymoon, she rushed and asked with that cute little excitement 'Maamu, where are you going with Maami? Even I want to come with you.' The two year old is expert in talking fluently. I smiled and kissed her forehead with a reply 'Ok, we all will go. Now you play, I need to finish my work.' Dadi called her to play with her.

I finished the paper work which my Dad gave me and took the printouts from the printer in study room by commanding from laptop in Dadi's room. Thanks to the advanced technology, where we can take printouts operating on laptops and tablets from anywhere in the house or office. Earlier we had to sit before the desktop for hours to take printouts of our school projects. Even these smartphones made life as easy as making a milkshake. Earlier in phones we had to type the numeric three to four times to get the exact alphabet! The struggle was double if it gets deleted after typing 3-4 pages, we had to take a new start! I handed over the printouts to Dad. 'Go Green' is a tough task for Dad, he never believes in soft copies, as he thinks the person can change anything anytime with soft copies, so to play safe he always carry hard copies and takes attestation and acknowledgment from the opposite party. I gave the papers to Dad and he left with them.

In the meanwhile, Ramya called me and I went to her. She came close to me and muttered. 'Mansi is unpacking her clothes you go and help her, you have all the privacy, I am with Mom in the kitchen.' She smiled. I looked up at my room and started to go towards the heavenly beauty. By then I realised, it was not lust and certainly love, Ramya held my hand and pulled me over and asked 'Hey, wait...' I stopped and looked at her asking 'What?' 'How was it last night?' She asked with blinking an eye. 'Did I ever ask you how is it from last 4 years? You tell me first, then I will tell you with each and every detail.' I replied mockingly. She left my hand 'Shut up! You idiot, its pointless talking to you…now run!' with shyness covered with artificial anger, she said. I smiled and ran towards my room.

I entered the room, it was full of mess with 4 big opened bags of clothes and stuff spread all over. I asked Mansi 'Do you need any help?' 'No, its ok I will manage.' She said with smile, she was sitting on the floor, organising her clothes. 'Here, let me help you' I said, by taking some clothes from her hand. She did not refuse hence she knew it's a tough task. She started giving the clothes by sitting on the floor and I organised them all in the closet. I told her about Sumit's call and she did not react much, maybe she was thinking about something else. We didn't speak later, while organising the clothes, I couldn't stop myself staring at her, she was busy taking out the clothes from bags and folding them appropriately to fit in the space left. I thought they will never fit into my closet but hats off to Mansi for folding them according to the available space in the closet. 3 big bags emptied and I kept the bare bags under the bed storage. It took 1 hour for us to arrange the clothes. I must appreciate my family for not disturbing us in this tenure. At last, only one bag was left. I placed that on bed and opened it, she suddenly rushed towards the bag and stood before me covering it, and said 'I will keep these clothes myself.' I glanced at the bag, some straps were peeking outside, and I understood that there are special clothes inside that small bag. I smiled and said 'Ok, if you need anything call me.' I said and started walking out of the room as a gentleman. 'Thank you so much for helping me so far!' she said. 'You are always welcome.' I said with smile, I never say this to anyone but this time I meant it with my heart. 'Sandeep…' She called me with my full name. I was surprised to see that she didn't call me with my nick name, because she was shy after the wedding. I immediately turned back asking 'Sandeep…haan…' For the first time she said my name after our marriage, in fact from last few months I never heard my name from her mouth. It felt good, I wanted to hear my name again and again from her mouth. She looked down shyly. I went close to her, and said 'Yes Mansi…tell me.' She looked bewildered, I did observe she was thinking something from long time while unpacking. There was a pause from her side. 'Do you want to talk about something? Actually I observed that you are thinking something from long time…What is it?' I asked to break the silence. 'No…it's just…I was wondering that, am I bothering you?…I mean we had a discussion on this before but last night…' she stopped, her sad face looked down. I went slowly towards her, took her hand in my hands and said calmly 'Mansi, it was never you…It's me who is wrong in this whole ceremony of relationships. You are the most perfect girl in this world. I really got lucky to have you as my life partner. I need to tell you something…but it's not the right time.'

'I was just thinking… is it about my family? I mean you know…' she muttered.

'No…please don't take all this in that way…I would never ever think on that… and you know that…' I whispered. She stood quiet.

'Sandy…Mansi…Come down beta.' my mother uttered from downstairs.

She hurried to go, I stopped her holding her hand, our eyes met. 'Let's go!' blushing she whispered. 'Never ever blame yourself or your family for anything.' I completed my sentence. She looked at me, I actually saw the respect she had for me at that moment. And in fraction of seconds the thought surrounded my mind, when she will hear the truth, this respect will turn into disgust. She left and I stood there for few seconds thinking about my past and then I followed her.

Mansi's mother and Dadi were eagerly waiting to see their newly wedded doll. Mansi ran into her mother's arms, they all hugged each other. Her mother's eyes were filled with tears. Though they live only two blocks away from us but it was an emotional moment for them. They did not visit since marriage, her mother believes in orthodox customs of not visiting the daughters home after her marriage. They are here to take Mansi away from me. Perhaps, it was only for a day but I felt sad.

Some more guests arrived in the meantime, they all wished us luck for our future. We received some complimentary gifts and designer envelopes filled with Indian currency. It was Mansi's first day in kitchen and she prepared *kheer* for everyone. All of us had lunch together.

Evening after the departure of guests, Mansi also got ready to go with her family. Her mother hurried to get ready fast since it's a ritual not to send daughter-in-law after sunset. I was in the living room when she went upstairs to get her bag. When everyone was busy talking to each other I took an opportunity to go in to the room. Mansi took a small bag, which she packed in the morning itself and came out of the room to go with her mother. I stood before her. She looked at me and muttered shyly with her head down 'I will wait for you tomorrow.' 'Hmm…Hope you will keep your phone on today' I expressed my sorrow in a taunting way. She blushed and got down from the stairs without making any eye contact with me. I stood motionless, my heart was squeezing, I saw her till she reached the door, everyone was waiting for her in the lawn. I was expecting that she will turn back and look for me, like in a Hindi movie and she did it! Everyone was outside, and when she reached the door she turned back and looked at me waving her hand. I said bye and it was painful to see her going away from me. Till now I was damn sure that I love this girl.

Raju dropped Mansi and family to their home and my relatives came inside with there never ending chit chat. Everyone was praising Mansi's beauty and her soft nature, some were praising with heart and some were jealous on our luck to have a girl like Mansi. Basic human nature, especially popular in India, where people cannot see success and good things happening to the known and next-door person. When I see these people, I feel lucky to have bunch of friends and family members without any dash of jealousy for each other. Rest of the guests went after having evening snacks and tea. Jeej arrived after the office to take Ramya and Anvi with them. My mother requested him to keep them back for few more days. Hence the house will be totally empty if they also go away. Jeej agreed and went alone after the dinner, Ramya extended her leaves for 2 more days and decided to stay till we come back from Phuket. However, it was Wednesday and she had weekly off on Saturday's and Sunday's.

Soon the clock hit 10.30 PM and everyone went in their respective rooms to sleep. I thought of calling Mansi but kept the phone down thinking that she might be busy talking with her mother. My phone rang and I quicky answered it without looking at the screen thinking that it might be Mansi. 'Hey handsome, whats up?' it was Aarzoo on the other side. 'Hello doctor! Not feeling well' I replied. 'Ha ha …I knew that...there must be pain in the heart, uneasiness, loss of appetite etc., must be the symptoms…' she giggled. 'Yeah, it looks funny to you, haan?' I asked. 'Take it easy lover boy, she will be back tomorrow.' She consoled me. 'Wait a minute! How do you know she went today?' My curious mind made me ask her. 'Duh…I just spoke to her…' she said. 'Is she alone?' I asked. 'Nope! Her mother and granny are home!' she laughed again. 'Shut up yaar, I mean is she alone now, so that I can call her.' I asked her. 'Stupid, that's why I called you…call her. She didn't say but I am damn sure she is waiting for your call…good night…have a nice talk.' She disconnected. I smiled and said good night looking at phone. My friends never wait for my line before disconnecting the call. I felt like I won a gold medal, without wasting a second I called Mansi.

'Hello' the soft voice answered the phone. 'Hi, just now Aarzoo called …' I said idiotically like a person goes on stage without his speech. 'Are you going to talk to me only to inform who have called you and who has not?' She asked sarcastically. I smiled and said 'No, actually… I was wondering that you must be busy chatting with your Mummy. So did not call you and Aarzoo told me that you are free now...' I stopped talking. 'So you will not call me if I am busy with something?' again an arrow of taunt. I was quiet this time. 'C'mon...from when you started becoming so sober? You used to drag me for your mischievous games on teachers or movies, when I used to prepare for tests and exams...and that naughty person is taking permissions to talk to me!!' She said. 'Hmm...right' I said. No answer from the other side. 'Had dinner?' I asked to begin the conversation. 'Hmm...You?' she asked. 'Yes...' There was a silence for few seconds. Strange! We used to chat for hours before all this and now we are speechless.

'I have done my packing for Phuket, you want me to do yours or you'll do it after coming back...' just to re-start the conversation and to know her reaction on honeymoon talk I asked her. 'I will do after coming back' she said. 'So, you knew that we're going to Phuket?' I asked. 'Hmm, morning Ramya told me about that. Actually, Dad took my passport before marriage and he told us that he needed that for Visa to Thailand.' She said. I had no idea about that, Dad had asked me to sign some papers 2 weeks back, I didn't see they were Visa papers.

'Oh, ok...Actually I didn't know about this...Today Dadi told me that we are going to Phuket. I signed some papers couple of weeks ago but did not ask Dad what they are...'

'I know you...' She said and I smiled.

'So, how is it back in your *Mayka* (Mothers home)?' I wanted to say that I am missing you, I love you! But ended up with those words.

'Yeah, its nice.'

'Hmm..so...what else?'

'Hmm...Nothing' she said, I could feel little disappointment from the other side for no affectionate conversation from me.

I was quiet.

'I am feeling sleepy' she said in few seconds with an attitude.

'Ok...good night!' I said without any reaction.

She disconnected the call to maintain the legacy of my group, disconnecting the call before saying or hearing the last words. *'I love you Mansi'* I whispered myself. I knew she is angry on me for the reason that as a newly married couple we must be saying those magical words to each other and chat romantically. But I didn't do anything like that. *'I am stuck with my guilt Mansi, I cannot do anything without revealing the truth to you.'* I said myself. It was 11.30, I went to sleep thinking about Mansi.

Next morning I opened my eyes with so many beep sounds of messages on my mobile. I grabbed the mobile from side table to see who is dying now!! Everyone texted me from the group but Mansi... there was no single message on the group but all were personal messages! I started reading them all one by one.

Sumit- Asshole! What is the matter with you! (angry faces) You haven't done anything yet? You didn't even tell her that you love her! Whyyyy??? (Bang) because she is your ex- girlfriend and present wife!

Shaun- *Abey* what is this? *Yeh bechara kounse kaam ke boj ka mara*? You are a devil! You never left any girl in the class and college now what is the matter with you?

Kuch quotes bheja hai...send them to her. pictures and quotes...

Aarzoo- I told the guys that you still did not do anything, Idiot!!! She felt so bad yesterday! She called me and she was crying man! I didn't want to tell you this but she loves you man...and I hope you know that!! What is the matter with you? She has no problem with your past and you are still regretting that? C'mon man...now at least act smartly in honeymoon. We all will surely meet after you guys come back. And we want to see you both happy ok...and don't take it otherwise.. I know you will not but saying...

Shreya – Hi dear, I got messege from Sumit. I just want to say that you guys are made for each other and I want to see you both happy together. If you have any problem you can always discuss with all of us.

Gourav- Hi bro! What am I hearing. It's all right...its normal to be nervous. Even I was nervous with your Bhabhi for the first time. I didn't tell anybody but telling you....took a week to start...I told the guys as well not to bother your privacy.

Mandar- Hi bro! Congrats man. I am sorry for late messages. Love is a great feeling man. And I know you both love each other. Since school days I liked your pair and wished that you both be together forever. Is this like you taking time to adjust to the things or something else. Take care...I will be coming to India soon.

Preeti- Is it like you love me from deep inside and married to Mansi!? Ha ha... just kidding...I know you are very smart man and act properly according to the situations. Just keep in mind that she loves you.

Fewwwww!! It was like serial bomb blasts! I felt like killing Aarzoo...The volcano was waiting to erupt inside me. I threw the phone on bed and went into the bathroom. I took a nice shower and I realised that there was nothing wrong in all those messages. Perhaps, I felt bad thinking that Mansi cried last night just because of me.

I came out of the bathroom, I called Mansi immediately. She answered the phone after 6-7 rings. 'Hello' she said, her voice was rough like she did not sleep whole night.

'Good morning' I said

'Good morning' she replied.

'Are you ok?' I asked.

'Yes' she said

'Mansi, I know everything...just got the messages from everyone....Trust me...everything will be fine soon. Please keep in mind it's not because of you...' I consoled her.

'....'

'Mansi, say something'

'Mummy is calling me, will call you later' and there goes again... she disconnected the call without hearing my reply. I was really stuck in this, things would have been different if I'd told her the truth 3 months back.

FOUR

3 *months back.*

Our business was at its peak from a couple of years. I was totally involved in business and rarely had a chance to meet friends. That day, I was passing through Mansi's house, thought of stopping by, I saw a car parked out of her house. While walking inside, her neighbours saw me with strange look, I thought I am at an interrogation but they started gossiping.

Meanwhile, some well-dressed people were leaving from Mansi's house. Mansi's uncle accompanied them till their car, he gave me an angry look while going. The guests had a question in their mind about me, Mansi's uncle seemed like resolving the question, as I heard some of their whispers.

While he was busy, I went inside and heard the entire story from Mansi's mother. They came with a marriage proposal for Mansi. The groom looked older than Mansi, he was in his mid-thirties and bald as well, immediately, I opposed the proposal. Her mother asked Mansi to bring a glass of juice for me and requested me to stay away from their family matters. I sat quietly on the sofa, Mansi gave me glass of juice and requested me to leave after having it. I got upset when she said that and came out of the house angrily. I was moving out quietly and her uncle stopped me asking 'Still you come here?' I felt awkward and asked him 'Sorry?' 'What sorry? Leave our girl alone! Don't you dare to enter this house again!' he angrily uttered on the door. I'd already lost my temper when Mansi asked me to go out, and when her uncle spoke to me in that tone, I didn't like it. 'What are you talking about? She is my friend and I can come anytime to meet her, it's none of your business!' I answered loudly. Mansi, her mother and grandma came out of the house hearing our loud voices. 'Hey! Who are you to ask me stay away from this! You already messed her life? Stop coming here or I will break your leg if you come here again.' Uncle warned me loudly. Hearing that was annoying and I raised my hands, holding his collar I uttered 'Hey...Don't you ever talk to me like that! Or else I will break all your bones!' Mansi rushed and stopped me by snatching out my hands from her uncle, her mother came in between and asked me to leave him. Her uncle got scared a bit when I raised my hands on him. Neighbours were watching the free show, one of the lady took a chance and muttered 'He is her boyfriend that is why he is getting angry on her marriage proposal!' I was astonished hearing that and I looked at Mansi. She requested 'I beg you to leave, please!' I left from there without saying anything. That incident made me uneasy and I called Mansi in the night but she disconnected the call and switched off her mobile. I was very anxious and thought of speaking to Dadi about the incident and I went to her. After hearing everything calmly, Dadi asked me to take her to Mansi's house next day.

The next day, we went to Mansi's house, exempting uncle, all were home. They welcomed both of us blissfully and after the formalities of tea and snacks, Dadi asked them 'What is the matter? Sandeep told me something yesterday.' There was a silence, they looked each other and kept quiet. Dadi forced them to speak out and then Mansi's grandma started talking 'As you both know, my son Manoj committed suicide for loss of his office money. He invested all his fixed deposits in share markets and lost everything in that. Office staff knew that and when the money was stolen, they thought, he used the company money for fulfilling his losses. They presumed that he himself stole the money and was making the stories, without a second thought they suspended him and sent him notice to pay the amount or he will be sent to jail. He didn't want to lose his prestige and he lost his life, thinking that we could pay the amount to the office with his life insurance claim amount. But insurance claim was rejected as it was suicide, we were at complete loss. But fortunately or unfortunately, after his death, we found that lost money under the bed. We all thought that Manoj must have kept the money and with some reason the bag must have slipped under the bed. We all cried a lot after finding the money.' Their eyes were filled with tears. Dadi and I looked each other, Mansi's grandma continued after a pause, 'Mansi went to her father's office for handing over the money and to ask the office staff to forfeit the blame on her father's character. But on the contrary the office staff didn't believe that money was found in the house, they asked her…' she paused and started crying. Mansi with strong will held her grandmother's hand and stopped her saying anything more she continued from there, and said 'They took the money. The company didn't even pay the settlement of my father. Anyways it doesn't matter now, it's all our fate.'

I got angry, tightening my fist I said 'I will sue the company on your behalf, how could you keep quiet on all these things. They have to pay you, it's your right.' Dadi asked me to calm down, and Mansi's mother said 'Mansi's uncle is trying on that. Anyways…forget all that.' She tried to change the topic and I changed it soon asking 'What about your neighbour? Why she said that yesterday?' I asked Mansi. Mansi kept quiet looking down. Her mother said 'Sorry son, we never wanted to drag you into this. That is why, I asked you to stop coming here. I trust you both but the neighbours were talking gravely about you and Mansi. They even told these fake stories to our relatives, when they visited here, and the rumours spread all over as a fire in the jungle. I wanted Mansi to get married and relieve her from all this but due to these rumours nothing is working out and after yesterday's incident, I am thinking it's enough of being a joke in the society. I thought of selling this house and go away somewhere else and later we can look for a groom for Mansi.'

'That's really bullshit, why should you leave everything for these rubbish people.' I said angrily. 'Sandy!' Mansi muttered softly to stop me by nodding her head. Dadi and I felt guilty after hearing everything, Dadi said 'Why didn't you people come to us? We did not know anything about all this. Mansi, at least you should have spoken to Sandy about it…after all you are best friends.' Looking at Mansi she asked.

'What is the use, as I said, we never wanted to drag you into this, Mansi was against all this, she was right however, as people would spoil your family name as well, so we kept mum on this.' Mansi's mother said. I looked at Mansi, she was quietly standing behind her mother. I looked at Mansi's mother and said 'I am sorry Aunty, just because of me you all suffered so much.' Dadi held my hand and signalled me to say nothing.

'No son, it's not your fault, what can you do for our fate. Her father lived with respect all his life and died in the fear of losing it. But even after his sacrifices we are living every bit of life with the question on our self-respect. Many a times we feel like eating poison. But don't know what stops us.' She expressed her grievance. Hearing that, I rushed towards her, and held her hand 'Aunty please, don't ever think that!' I said. Mansi kept her hand on the shoulder of her mother and looked at me, it seemed her respect for me amplified.

After consoling them for some time, we left from their house. While stepping out of the house, Dadi decided something in her mind and said 'We will come back tomorrow evening.' I sensed something was already decided by Dadi.

Dadi called an emergency meeting in her room. We all went inside and I took a seat on the bed, Dadi was seated on her long chair, Mom and Dad sat on the couch. Dadi explained the entire scenario to Mom and Dad and presented her wish in front of them. *It was my marriage with Mansi!* Everyone including me was surprised on her wish. Mom immediately acted and asked 'I don't understand, it's their personal problem, why should we interfere in that. I mean, we can search a better boy for Mansi or help them financially but marriage! And more over they are not of our caste!'

Dadi answered calmly, 'I don't believe in these caste and all! I feel she has all the qualities to be a life partner of Sandy and part of our family. Moreover, people have spoiled that poor girl's name, saying she has an affair with Sandy. It's impossible to find a good groom in their caste now, all they are either divorced or widower or old, that poor girl does not deserve them at all.'

'Affair!? And you are making that true with this proposal??' Mom interfered in the middle.

'Shhh, Asha.' Dad shook his head to mind the tone of Mom.

'It's all right Sudhir! Look Asha, we can't change what people think, they'd talk in any condition, I am not worried about them. Only thing bothering me is the question on that poor girl's character, yet they didn't come to us even after suffering for so many years. And to be precise, I have selected Mansi because I feel she is the perfect girl for our Sandy. He will be very happy with her.' Dadi spoke out with a firm voice.

I was speechless in this matter, for the first time my anxiety and temper were under control in the family discussion on my life, otherwise it was always a mess. Dad didn't say anything, he had full trust on his mother as he knew, a woman who handled the family in worse situations and raised her own children as well as her rival woman's children when needed can never make any wrong decisions. He knew she cannot think of anything which will turn into disaster in my life. He wanted Mom to clear all her doubts in this matter and kept watching their discussion quietly.

Mom asked me 'Is there really something between both of you Sandy?' There was a pause from my side, I looked at Dadi, apparently she smiled. 'I asked you something' Mom reminded. 'Mom, there is nothing between us now.' I said. 'Now? It means there was something before?' she caught the point immediately.

'....'

'Speak it out Sandy!' She asked again.

'Mmm, Yes, but back in school days...now we are just friends.' I said looking down.

'There you are my boy! That's the reason ...So rumours are not false! Oh my god!! I always thought that you both are so innocent, caring friends. I never thought that you guys could do something like this! Does she have other boyfriends as well?' She asked.

'Mom, please! Don't say anything like that about her, she is a nice girl, if anyone is wrong in this, it's me, who broke up with her to get into relationship with Bindu! And Mansi didn't see anyone after me.' I muttered.

Mom and Dad were astonished after hearing that.

'Shit' I whispered for the flow of the truth, even devil on my shoulder was laughing at my situation that time.

'You…! We sent you to school and college for all this? Do you have more girlfriends?' Mom shouted.

'It's complicated' I mumbled.

'What? I am not asking your Facebook status you idiot! You are doing these things from school and god knows what all you did? Oh my god!! There are so many diseases spreading with those things and …' her worry spoke out and she kept on mumbling something for herself.

'Please Mom! I…I haven't done anything with Mansi and … Ahh, it's so difficult! Mom…don't worry I didn't do anything wrong that I'd get those diseases. I … I am sorry' I apologised scratching my head as that was really embarrassing.

'Oh great, you are sorry now? Sudhir, why aren't you talking?' She yelled again looking at me and Dad. Dad didn't say anything but he kept on staring me by knotting his hands against his chest.

'Asha, things don't fall in place if we keep on discussing this matter. We are here to make a firm decision to sort out Mansi's family problem.' Dadi consoled her by bringing her back to the point.

'But he is too young to handle the responsibility of marriage.' Mom defended with her point again.

'He is having girlfriends since school, he is 25 now and it's the right time for marriage.' Dadi answered.

I looked at Dadi by widening my eyes. I was speechless, I wasn't ready to get married but I had nothing to defend. However, Dadi had still kept my secret with her.

Mom kept on mumbling about views and comments of the relatives and society on this inter-caste arranged marriage and we all quietly looked at her. Suddenly, Dad got up from couch saying 'Enough of this discussion, I think he has made everything obvious. We should go ahead with what Maa has decided.' he finally spoke with certainty. I got up from bed, and stood there still, with no clue of single defence, Dad looked at me. 'I am sorry Dad. But marriage now is like…' I wanted to take an escape but paused with my eyes down, when he stared angrily at me.

Dad shook his head 'You both, especially you made so many mistakes since childhood and I never asked you any questions or slapped you, EVER! Because I trusted our way of upbringing, I believed that you both will prove to be good human beings. Your sister proved that but you, you disappointed me and failed our upbringing. You already did many things to upset us, better you don't repeat it henceforth. We are going ahead with your marriage proposal with Mansi tomorrow. I don't want any more drama on that.' He said and walked out of the room. Mom was staring at me knotting her hands. I went close to her and said 'Mom, I am sorry, it was all past. I…I …' before I say anything, she got up and went out of the room.

I looked at Dadi, and mumbled 'Why?' She calmly looked at me and said 'Ask yourself!' I went close to her and sat on the table before her and said, 'I can't do that! You know everything…I am a sinner!'

'That is why, you have to pay for your sin.' She replied sitting on the chair calmly.

'But she doesn't deserve me, she deserves someone just like herself. I already messed her life but marrying her will be wrong Dadi!' I said remembering the bitter past.

'No its not, now only thing to patch it up is to support her and her family, stand with her in good and bad times, no matter what others say, but I know you are a good person and you will prove to be a good husband. Moreover, looking at the present situation, she won't get a better person than you.' She said.

With a fake smile, shaking my head 'That will be cheating Dadi, we are taking advantage of her situation.' I said.

'No, that is the solution for all the problems.' She defended.

'Whatever Dadi but I can't marry her without telling her the truth, after all I am responsible for what she is going through.' I said.

'Go ahead, and tell her the truth but be prepared for your father's health and her mother's health as well.' She warned me. I was bowled over. 'Uhh, it will be a life time punishment for me, I will die in a guilt.' I said keeping my head on Dadi's lap. Caressing my hair, Dadi said 'I know it's hard to forget and you are guilty. This is the only thing how you pay the mistakes done by you. Trust me boy, after some years you won't remember these things. Furthermore, ask yourself, don't you like her? You always respected her, you said so yourself and you proved that, by taking me to them after yesterday's incident. I have seen the same respect and love in her eyes for you. Don't look at this as a punishment, it is a best gift for you. You will never get a better partner than Mansi.' Dadi made her point.

There was a pause from my end, I closed my eyes on her lap and I saw Mansi's sweet innocent face, smiling at me. Holding my shoulder Dadi said, 'Sandy, that's all I had to say, still if you have any problem, then we'll tell your father tomorrow and cancel the plan. However, your mother will be happy with that, as she can enjoy looking out for some dumb girl from our community for you.' she giggled. Hearing that, I smiled.

The whole night I didn't sleep. Mansi's cute but glow less face, her mother and grandmother's lean bodies with worried faces, struggle which they had gone through all these years just because of me was hammering me. I made up my mind and decided to go ahead with Dadi's decision. As I thought that was the only key to disburse my guilt.

The next morning, Mom wanted to ask the priest about the *mahurat* (auspicious time for important things) but Dadi did not agree on that, she saw the favourable time in the *panchang* (Hindu calendar) and ordered us to get going by 6.30pm. Mom called Mansi's mother and informed about our arrival in the evening.

In the meanwhile, Dad called Ramya and told her the entire story. Ramya came over in the afternoon by taking half day leisure from her office, Anvi also accompanied her as a bonus. I came back from the office and was working on the presentation in my room, Ramya came to me. Smiling she said,

'Congrats!'

'Shut up' I laid on my pillow by keeping the laptop aside.

'C'mon, you are doing a great job. I always wanted that you should marry a girl like Mansi, she is a nice girl. I am happy for you.' She expressed her feeling genuinely. I smiled in the reply.

'So, Mom and Dad spoke to you after yesterday's drama?' She asked mockingly.

'Nope' I said.

'Hmm, it's hard for them, they thought you are Ram but you turned out as Krishna!' She laughed.

'Ha ha…very funny' I said with fake smile.

'C'mon, cheer up! Things will fall on place soon. Let's get you ready pretty boy.' She said and took out formals from my cupboard.

Evening, we all went to Mansi's home. We all got out from our car, some of Mansi's neighbours saw us going inside and started gossiping with each other. We entered their home, Mansi came on the door to greet and receive us, her mother and grandmother followed her. Mansi had taken half day off from her office, as Mom requested for her presence to Mansi's mother in the morning. Mansi was in her salwar kameez, she went inside the kitchen right away for preparing snacks for us. Obviously, they all had no clue for what we all went there. Looking at our whole family with so many fruits, flowers and *shagun* they were all astonished and confused.

Mansi brought juice for all. I was in an awkward situation, I had no idea who will start the conversation and what will come up from Mansi's family. Mansi looked confused, and she was shaking a bit looking at my whole family in her home. We all had juice and Dadi sighed Mom to start the conversation. Mom looked at Dad and he sighed her as well to start it by herself. Mom took a long breath and said.

'Maa told us about everything yesterday, and we are really sorry for all you've gone through.' Mom took a pause, and Mansi's family looked each other. With firmness, Mom spoke again, 'We had a discussion on this yesterday and came to a final decision' she looked at everyone and everyone had eye on her next words.

By taking a long breath 'We came here to ask you Mansi, for marriage with our son, Sandeep.'

Hearing that Mansi dropped the empty tray from her hand, everyone looked at her and she got embarrassed, 'I...I... am sorry' she said and rushed inside the kitchen. Her grandmother's jaw dropped and her mother looked at Mansi running inside and thunderstruck lady looked at us.

My Dadi smiled and said 'Don't think that we are showing sympathy to you all with this proposal, to be specific, we like Mansi and feel that she is the best girl to be our Sandeep's life partner.' Mansi's family was still speechless, they had no hint on how to react. Dadi understood their hesitation and she calmly said 'We know it sounds strange and it's a tough decision to make. Our caste and cultures are different and there will be questions in the society. But frankly speaking we don't believe in caste and community.'

'How is that possible, we have to answer the society?' Mansi's confused mother said after few seconds.

'This is the answer to the society. People will shut their mouth after this.' My father said, I felt proud of my family.

After few minutes of debate between Mansi's family and my family, Mansi's mother and grandmother agreed for the proposal. Mansi's mother was nervous as well as happy that finally she was getting a good family for her daughter. As we all were so close together that there wasn't any space for formality, Mansi's grandmother asked me and Ramya to solicit Mansi's opinion on the matrimony.

We both walked towards the kitchen, I was feeling awkward in all that, I stood outside the kitchen and Ramya rushed inside, she saw Mansi was crying by sitting on the floor. Mansi stood up suddenly when she saw Ramya and wiped her tears. Ramya hugged her. Mansi didn't know my presence outside. 'Are you ok?' Ramya asked her. 'I never thought that I would get a chance to hear this in my life?' Mansi said by holding Ramya. I was astonished to hear that, she still loves me! I cursed myself, if there was a competition on selfishness, I would be the winner. I never realised her feelings and never really cared for asking her how she was after that break up.

'Well, that's wonderful, I came here to ask your opinion on this and here I got my answer!' Ramya said with her smile. 'I will tell everyone out there' and she started walking out from there. Mansi's face became red with shyness, and in a hurry, she stopped her by holding her hand back and asked her 'Wait, I always wished for Sandy's happiness and I hope he is happy with this decision.' Ramya smiled in reply and said 'That, you ask him.' she dragged me inside by holding my hand, Mansi got surprised looking at me. Ramya said 'Sandy, answer her. I will go out from here.' Ramya walked out with a smile, neglecting Mansi's request to stay back.

It was again awkward situation for me to face Mansi. 'Hi…mm… that must be quite a surprise?' I said by clearing my throat.

'You always come with them.' Mansi said with her head down.

'I don't know what to say. Well, Dadi knew about us long ago and it was Dadi's decision after yesterday's incident.'

Her facial expression changed after hearing that. 'She knew about us?'

'Yeah, I told her long back. And looking at the current situation she felt this is the best solution.' I replied casually.

'So, it's all because of my problems and you are here only to solve them?' she asked with sarcasm.

'NO...Not like that…you are taking it in a wrong way, I don't know you heard my Dadi's conversation out or not…everyone in the family feels that you are the best girl for me.' I said.

'And what do you feel?' she asked looking straight into my eyes.

And this time without any hesitation I looked at her and said 'You are always best Mansi. The truth is…I don't deserve you.' I shook my head.

There was a smile of relief on her face, blushing, she walked into her room. I stared her walking out from there and joined the family club in the living room. Dadi asked Mansi's mother to get Mansi ready for the *Shagun,* Ramya accompanied her. After few minutes Mansi came out from her room wearing a saree. I didn't observe her properly as she was surrounded by ladies. My mother gave her all the things which she'd brought for Mansi. We had snacks prepared by Mansi and walked out happily wishing each other. We sat in the car, and immediately Mansi's grandmother called her neighbours and told them the story in her full volume that we could hear all from our moving car. My Dadi laughed like a small girl hearing that, which made everyone laugh.

Preeti called me in the night, it was Mansi who had messaged her. I picked the phone and before I said 'hello', a yell came from that side 'Stupid, idiot! You didn't tell me!! I am feeling like killing you...OH MY GOD!! I am so so happy!!! Congrats! Congrats! Congrats.....!!!' she uttered without any pause.

'You already got the news? Your sources are faster than anyone elses...' I smiled.

'Yes, they are...! Stupid, why didn't you tell me before?'

'I don't know...actually, I am kinda not sure about things happening in my life these days!' I said.

'What do you mean you don't know... anyways...I don't want to hear anything...it is surprise and great surprise...you know I always wanted you guys to be together. Really hats off to your families...this happened only because of them. Specially your Dadi, give my love to her. I will try to come and meet you guys this week.' She said.

'Sure.' I said and we hung up.

I started calling one by one in the group with the big news, in between I was getting calls from Shreya and Aarzoo, I saw the mobile and thought myself, *these girls still think together and act together. It's so difficult to get a perfect life, the girls who are madly in love with each other couldn't get along with each other, because of the society.* On the contrary, my family is ready to face the society with our marriage but I wasn't feeling anything for Mansi.

Fifteen days before marriage, our families were in the mall, busy with the last minute shopping for the big day. While everyone was busy buying clothes and stuff, I got a chance to take Mansi along with me to the coffee shop in the same mall, Ramya helped me. We ordered cappuccino and some bites, as I was damn hungry with nervousness. For the first time I was feeling anxious in front of Mansi. I wanted to make a confession but wasn't sure from where to begin. By gaining some energy I began to speak 'I wanted to talk to you about something very important.'

'Mmm, hmm..' she mumbled looking into my eyes.

I gazed at her, and my mind said *'Wow! She is beautiful'* she was wearing green and yellow colour combination chudidar and kameez, that attire perfectly fitted her body, covering all her curves, but perfectly showing her figure. After our break up in the school, for the first time I stared at her for so long. Teenage cute and cuddly Mansi, turned into stunningly beautiful young girl, the tiredness of work and worry about past issues created some dullness on her face, yet she had all the beauty that can amaze anybody. No wonder few people kept on staring us in the mall. With my pause and gape she looked down with shyness that hit my mind to the present.

'Ahh....Sorry...I got distracted...! Anyways...You know...about... the things you have gone through...mmm...I...*Damn it* (mumbled and tightened my fist)' That's all I said, I didn't had any guts to come up with the truth and I paused.

'You can ask anything.' She said, looking at my fussy face.

'No, I...I...don't wanna ask anything...I want to ...' I was uniting all the strength in my heart for the confession but got distracted by the waiter in the coffee shop, he placed our order on the table and backed off.

'You were saying something.' She reminded me, after the departure of waiter.

'Yeah...mmm...can we eat first?' I asked pushing the saliva back in my throat.

'Ok' she smiled.

We both had snacks and coffee which was kept before us. I ate everything in panic and she took some bites gracefully like a lady. By the time we finished, my phone rang and it was Ramya. I picked up the call and voice came from the other side 'We are done with the shopping here and going to jewellery shop, Mansi has to be there.' Ramya spoke as per the order of Mom.

'I will drop her on my bike.' I said.

'Ok, don't be late. I will text you the address of the shop.' she said.

'Fine... and yeah, Thanks.' I said with the smile, Mansi blushed with her head down.

'You owe me!' Ramya said and hung up the phone.

I smiled, looking at Mansi, kept the phone in my pocket.

She looked at me, expecting me to continue the talk.

'Yeah, I was saying...mm..' stopped again, with all the guts, I took a long breath and said 'Mansi, you are a good girl. I am really sorry for whatever happened to you...just because of me you suffered a lot and...I awfully feel bad...I am living with that guilt and...its killing me every moment...' I paused again and looked down keeping my hands on the table. She kept her hand on my hands and softly mumbled 'It's ok. It was past, why are you recalling it. I told you many times that I forgot everything. I know you, and I understand your nature, just forget it and live the present. We are together and our families also wants us to be together, that is what matters now.' Touch of her soft hands passed the current in my body, I looked up in her eyes, her eyes were shining, and I fell deep in those beautiful brown eyes. Those people were idiots, who rejected her. Any man will stand on one toe to marry this beauty but she is going to be mine, who never deserved her. I remembered what Dadi said to me few days back,

I was regretting the past, and she said *'Don't think that you are marrying her because all this happened. May be that all happened to keep both of you together forever.'* She was so right, I was such a jerk, broke up with this wonderful girl without any reason.

'Hello?! What are you thinking' she waved her hands in front of my eyes, I woke up from my thoughts and suddenly said 'Haan, I was thinking that you are looking beautiful.'

She blushed looking down. 'But I don't deserve you.' I spoke again.

'Enough, if you say that again. I am not gonna talk to you.' She said strongly.

'No, its not right yaar…this whole thing is fake…its all…'

'That's it Sandy! Ok, forget whatever happened, just tell me why are you marrying me?'

'….'

'I need to know, you are marrying me with the sympathy for whatever happened in my life or you really like me and want to marry me?' She asked me looking into my eyes.

'I don't know…I am…I am confused…What I am thinking, what I am doing and what I am saying …nothing is matching with each other these days.' I said with uncertainty.

'Its just simple, you love me or not?' She asked looking into my eyes.

'Mansi, I was thinking just now that, you are one wonderful girl, I was an idiot to break up with you…I said it many times before and saying it now as well…'

'Just answer me, why are you marrying me?' she asked again.

'I don't know…' I said looking down.

'OK, if you are doubtful about the decision then let us stop everything, because I don't want to be a compromise for you, Sandy.'

'No, you are not. Just forget it…forget this…this whole thing ever happened. Let's go to the jeweller.' I got up from the chair and walked out from there, she followed me. Certainly, she was upset, she didn't talk to me the rest of the day.

In the jewellery shop, she spoke with an artificial smile to keep everyone happy. Her mother and grandmother seemed the happiest, same was with Dadi. Slowly, my mom also joined the happy gang. Mom tried almost all the sarees and jewellery on Mansi and chose the best ones for her budding daughter-in-law, both the families were totally excited with this marriage but Mansi, who was upset with our conversation in the coffee shop. She switched off her phone for the coming days till the wedding. I couldn't meet her before wedding as per the customs and I went back in my shell of guilt, waiting for the chance of confessing it in front of Mansi.

FIVE

I came out of my thoughts and got ready. It was more than fifteen days I did not look in to the business due to wedding. Dad asked me to go to office that day while having breakfast, and I obeyed. We got the new contract of construction of a township in the outskirts of Bangalore, which will hike the financial standards of our company in the market. Dad believed it's because of Mansi we got this contract, he says, she brought good luck along with her. We went to the site, spoke to engineer and dealt with the material issues. It would take a year and half to complete the construction if everything goes well with the labour and finance.

After the lunch, Dad went to office and he asked me to stay back at home, hence I had to go to Mansi's home to bring her back. Mom asked me not to sleep in the afternoon for the reason that, if I fell asleep I would not get up on time. Meanwhile, the photographer came home to sort out the photos clicked in the wedding. We all selected the photos to be placed in the wedding album. Ramya initially gave him the list of the songs to be added in the wedding video. He promised to get the album and video CD in the coming week.

By the evening we all went to Mansi's home, except for my Dad & Dadi. Dadi went to meet a sick relative. When we reached near her house, I saw Mansi standing on her terrace waiting for us. I saw her from the car, Ramya looked at her and waved her hand out of the car window, and teased me with her naughty eyes. I felt good to see Mansi after a gap of 24 hours. Mansi's mother and grandma welcomed us with pleasant ambience. Mansi arrived with tea and snacks. She was wearing green and white combination saree but she looked fidget. I did not stare her for long in due respect of all the elders.

We came back home along with Mansi, after all the formalities and rituals. She looked upset to leave behind her mother again. After coming back Ramya and Mansi got busy in packing for Phuket. Dad confirmed the flight timings, it was at 11 in the night.

Dadi was tired after her visit to relative, she did not come along with us to airport. Mom never leaves anyone without having food, though we were not hungry but she prepared quick snacks and fed us forcefully. We hurried to airport by 8 and caught the flight on time. We hardly spoke anything other than formalities of travelling during those flight hours. I ordered a glass of juice in the flight and slept hard after drinking it. She slept as well.

We reached Bangkok airport and got a connecting flight to Phuket from there. We reached Phuket airport and met our travel co-ordinator. She took us to the hotel, it was a 5 star hotel with all luxurious ambience. We got a studio apartment on 20th floor of the lavish hotel with the beautiful view of sea from the balcony. I placed the bags on the side table and was about to fall on the bed, Mansi stopped me instantly saying 'No No No… stop it yaar, remove your shoes and get fresh.'

'C'mon its not home! It's a hotel room' I made my lazy point.

'Yes, but we are going to stay here for next 4 days! So please…' she showed me the way to bathroom.

I grabbed the towel from the bed and went in to bathroom. Opened the knob of hot water in bathtub and laid in it immediately after removing my clothes. It was an awesome feeling after 9 hours of travel. I came out after 25 minutes of bath wondering how come Mansi did not knock the door. I saw she was unpacking our clothes by placing them in the cupboard.

'Still doing the same thing?' I asked.

She saw me in a towel and in seconds turned her face towards the cupboard and gave my clothes but the undergarment, which was missing. I went close to her, she stepped back with her face down. I searched for my undergarment.

'Ahem… I have still not taken out all the clothes from the bags.' She said with hesitation.

I looked at her, after all the travel and tiredness her eyes were fluffy yet the face was as bright as usual. I looked into bags only my undergarments were left in them. I gave a slinky look at her, she was blushing. I took them all and placed in the cupboard where she'd arranged my clothes and went into bathroom to wear my outfits. She was ready to go inside the bathroom when I came out. I ordered breakfast and some snacks by calling the room service by the time she came out of the bathroom.

After the breakfast I slept, though it was not jetlag but I felt sleepy. Mansi called both the families to inform our safe arrival in the different country. I woke up by the lunch time and saw Mansi reading a book on the couch, she looked like an angel in her pink dress. The climate was cloudy outside, the balcony was open, allowing the cool breeze inside that was fragrant with the scents of the ocean, the breeze ruffled the hem of her dress, touched the warmth of her cheeks and caught her loose hair hanging on her back, for a second I envied that breeze it was touching her body so gracefully. I felt to hold her in my arms and kiss her.

We hardly spoke in last two days. I thought of starting the conversation, which should not feel awkward or worthless in this romantic atmosphere. 'Hi....You didn't sleep?' I asked. She looked at me 'No, I didn't feel like, it's a beautiful view outside...I went down and took a walk near the pool for some time and reading now.' she said. I smiled and said 'Oh ok... nice...I slept hard'. 'I saw that...that's why I didn't wake you up.' She said.

'Thanks...'

She smiled in a reply.

'Shall we order lunch here or go down to the restaurant?' I asked

'It's better we'll go down...' She insisted.

'Ok, I'll get fresh and we'll go then...' I went to bathroom saying that.

There were hardly ten people in the restaurant when we entered. Barely anybody had lunch in the hotel restaurant, it's obvious that rest of them were busy in their sight-seeing and others have it in their rooms. As per our itinerary we had plans of sight-seeing from next day. The menu had many such items, which Mansi had never heard before. I came to Thailand once before along with my family, after the marriage of Ramya. It was Ramya's honeymoon! In which we all enjoyed our holiday! Though, the couple went to Malaysia and Singapore after Thailand but we all gave them company till Thailand. These Asian countries have become favourite travel spots for well to do Indian families in last few years. Indians increased their travels abroad after the airfare and other expenses have become cheaper. We've visited Pattaya and Bangkok previously, I wanted to go to Phuket as well but due to Dad's business commitments we had to rush back. May be that's why Dad arranged for Phuket trip now. Thankfully the family was busy this time, so we didn't get any company. I had all the 5 days to come up with my secret in front of Mansi.

Mansi ordered pasta since she did not want to try anything new when she was hungry. I ordered Pad Thai along with fish fry. After finishing the lunch we planned to take a walk on the beach. The sea looked crystal clear with beautiful green water, the beaches were clean and well maintained, some people were lying on the deckchairs and mats, on the sea shore, some were half naked and some barely had any clothes expecting sun to peak out of those dark clouds. Mansi was feeling awkward between that bunches of naked foreigners. We walked bare foot sensing the crispy sand, we didn't speak anything in that calm atmosphere, and the company of each other was enough with no words. After walking a mile the naked gathering disappeared, I asked her to sit on deckchair under the umbrella.

I ordered for coconut water, the vendor delivered immediately. Hawkers started approaching us for foot massage, I looked at Mansi she wasn't interested, neither was I. After few minutes again a young lady offered a foot massage, I couldn't say no to her. Mansi gave me that old naughty look by twisting her eyebrows. I blushed scratching my forehead. After 20 minutes of massage it felt like I am in the heaven. The lady offered the massage to Mansi but she rejected.

'It's amazing, try it' I insisted

'No I am fine…' She said with a sip of coconut water.

'Just try it' I said again. She agreed. The lady started massaging her foot. She felt relaxed and after 5 minutes she closed her eyes. The sea had all the beauty in front of me but the gorgeous mermaid beside me looked more beautiful. I could write countless poems to portray her attractiveness if I were a poet. The girl who was massaging her foot smiled at me and asked 'Wife?'

'Yes' I replied with a smile.

With my reply that sweet smile appeared upon Mansi's face after a long time, I knew she wasn't asleep. She must have also noticed that I was staring at her.

It was 5, the young girl finished her massage. I paid her and the deckchair vendor for coconut water.

'Let's go, we'll be late for evening Cabaret Show.' I said.

She nodded without looking at me and said 'Fine.'

We caught a Tuktuk to reach hotel after a relaxing foot massage. Tuktuks are open vans move around in the cities of Thailand, which takes minimum amount for pickup-drop on sharing basis. Within 5 minutes we reached our hotel. While entering the hotel, 'Sandy…' she called me. I turned back, she stood there looking at me. 'Yeah…you need something?' asking her I went close. She nodded looking down and said 'Nothing… lets go.' It was the most romantic atmosphere and I was the most idiotic person roaming around with beautiful wife in my honeymoon without any romance or even a single good conversation.

We got ready and went to the show. It was wonderful, Mansi enjoyed it although I was busy looking at her happiness and I was sure she must have observed that hence nothing can be hidden from wives. After the show we came back to hotel had our dinner at the restaurant, the crowd was proportionally higher than that in the afternoon. Mansi wanted to talk to me about our relationship, which I could make out with her body language. When we entered the room it was decorated as honeymoon suite. My heart stopped for a while, because I didn't wanted her to get any ideas after my staring throughout the day. I wasn't prepared to tell her the truth yet and didn't want to get close to her without the truth. She hesitated a bit with the decoration and immediately rushed to the bathroom grabbing her night gown from the wardrobe. I felt relaxed, I didn't want to spoil her holiday by telling the truth. She enjoyed the show and we were yet to go for Safari and Phi Phi islands trip in next two days. I changed the clothes in the bedroom itself and went inside the bathroom when she came out. I didn't even dare to look at her because this time I may not control my feelings for her. It was awkward and foolish. She slept on the couch without a single word. I didn't dare to talk to her and slept on the decorated bed alone desiring her beauty.

Next morning, we got ready to go for Safari, the whole trip was full of silence. Any woman could lose her temper by this time by nagging her husband's mind with thousands of questions, Mansi was safe, and she has immense quality of patience and tolerance. Rest of the day and night just passed like a wind. Coming day we went to Phi Phi Islands. The speed boat ride in the blue beach felt wonderful, the beach on the island, the floating mountains in the middle of the sea confirmed that we were in heaven. I was drunk, 3 bottles of beer filled my dehydrated stomach. We had our lunch and relaxed on deckchair. Mansi looked wonderful in her yellow dress, I asked her for slow boat ride in the sea between the mountains, she refused at first, but I forcefully pulled her for it. I was drunk so much that it was awful for her to handle me. I grabbed one more bottle of beer and filled that in my big tank.

Our boat was floating in between those green mountains on the crystal clear sea, I was a foolish drunken monster inside it with my fair lady Mansi. We were standing together watching the mountains, she was taking pictures, the beer got active inside me and I held her hands grabbed her around my arms and said with my wobble tongue 'I love you! I am madly… intensely… extremely… and…and deeply in love with you…I can't tell how much I love you…' I did not notice her face in my drunken phrase. But I felt like it was uncomforting her, maybe the smell of alcohol or my tight hold or whatever was going on, she had not expected that it would have been turned out like that. And in a fraction of seconds, I kissed her in the middle of a sea, totally drunk with no knowledge of the situation and public present in the boat. Suddenly, I collapsed on her, as far as I remember we both fell in the boat.

I opened my eyes, I was on my bed in the hotel room, scratching my eyes I looked into my watch it was 9 in the night. My head was bursting with pain and I smelled horrible. I looked around for Mansi but she wasn't there. I quickly got up from the bed looking for her. Meanwhile, heard the sound of the door, she entered the room with a book in her hand. That was a relief for a second. She came in, I tried to stand still, she took a glass from the table and headed towards me.

'Here, lemon juice...it will help you to get rid of hangover.' she said holding the glass in front of me, her eyes were looking down. I realised I was shirtless, I took that glass and drank the entire juice from it. 'Thanks' I said. Without saying anything, she went in the balcony. I grabbed a pair of clothes and went to bathroom as my mouth was stinking so much that I could make her unconscious with that! Brushed my teeth and gargled with mouthwash again and again to get rid of the smell, later took a shower to freshen up myself. I got ready in few minutes and went to accompany her in the balcony, looking at the sea in the dark with some ship lights here and there, 'What happened...I don't remember anything...How did we come here?' I asked her to begin the conversation, which I knew was going to end with a fight.

'How do you feel now?' she questioned back with concern.

'Better...Thanks for the lemon juice...how did you know that I was having a head ache?' I asked her with a prompt reply.

'Guessed it...' she looked at me.

I looked into her pretty eyes searching for her questions on whatever happened in the afternoon. She looked down shyly and asked 'You remember nothing?'

'Nope' I said.

'You really want to know?' she asked me and I shook my head with yes. 'You took a hell out of me today!!...Thanks to the travel co-ordinator, what's her name (Tried to recall)? Aahh... anyways...!! She took everything under control... That girl and the driver dropped us safely till our room. You puked 4-5 times in the van and even after entering the room. The room service helped me in removing your dirty clothes and they cleaned the room...and even they washed the van!! One simple question?? Why did you drink so much when you cannot handle it???' She raised a question after finishing my deed.

'Mansi, I know I must have embarrassed you today...I am sorry... if I said something or did something which hurt you...I am really sorry...I actually didn't mean it all...I didn't planned it like this...I thought of something but I ended up doing something else....I...I...' I was struggling to explain the show, which I did few hours ago. 'Its OK' she said and stood quietly watching the sea. I sat on the chair, scratching my head. 'Wait a minute...did I hurt you? I mean I know I must have hurt you emotionally with my behaviour but...Did I hurt you physically? Or did I hurt anybody??' I asked her. 'No' reply came from her. 'Oh, thank god!' I said to myself. After few minutes of silence she asked 'Do you want to eat something?

You must be hungry…'

'You must be hungry as well…' I said looking at her. I imagined she has waited for me to wake up without having her evening snacks and dinner. 'Hmm, I will order 2 sandwiches and 2 glass of juice, do you want something else?' she asked. 'No, that's enough…' I replied.

She sat on the couch after ordering for food and started reading her book. There was a silence in between. I watched her by sitting in balcony. Watching TV was useless, hardly any channels we know were telecasted in that, there was only Hindi channel Zee TV and English HBO were available. I grabbed the camera from dressing table and played the slideshow of the pictures clicked that day. The room service arrived with the food. I was famished and ate the double size sandwich like a dinosaur, it suppressed both my hunger and headache. She had her sandwich slowly as she always does. After the juice I went to the balcony with struggling mind of coming up with the truth, I didn't even know what drama I had done in the afternoon in the middle of puking. She came and stood beside me and smiled. 'Sorry….' I apologised again with a smile. 'It's ok…Actually…I am not understanding whether to curse that beer for taking hell out of me today or to thank it for taking out the hidden love inside you for me…' she said shyly looking down. That sentence made me go bizarre, I looked at her and asked 'What?'

She blushed and said 'Today you must have uttered hundreds of times that you 'Love me…'

'Aaahhhh….did I?' I asked awfully!

She was shy after saying that, she turned back and nodded her head with yes.

I hit my forehead with tight fist and asked her 'Andddd…what else I said?'

She walked towards the other side of balcony, without looking at me she said 'Sandy…, do you remember I told you? You were the first person to kiss me in school? I kissed nobody after you…And today…we kissed again…' she said turning towards me, she was shy staring the floor. 'Of course…We did!' I said without any expression, I know my slippery, characterless mind, which never hesitated to take advantage from my all ex-girlfriends, I wonder how it took the longest pause for Mansi after wedding. 'What is the matter with you Sandy? You were never like this before, we are not only friends but also we're in a relationship…What is that truth you are hiding from me and cannot touch me before confessing it?' she came on the point after complaining. 'Truth!... What truth?' I asked wondering what else did my drunken mouth uttered.

'You were saying this all time from afternoon, even while asleep you were mumbling these words.' She said.

'.....'

'Sandy, you know that I don't care anything about your past, all that matters is we are married now and…till now I was thinking that you don't love me and that's why you are keeping distance...But today it's clear that you…love me (smiled shyly)…and …trust me that's enough for me…I don't want to hear anything else…' she said.

Still a pause from my side…I didn't know from where to begin or whether to say it or not to. She waited for my reply for few seconds and came close to me, holding my hand in her hands, she softly whispered looking into my eyes 'I LOVE YOU SANDY!…There…I said it…! I had a crush on you from the very first day I saw you…I loved you madly when we were in a relationship, I missed you and cried every night when we broke up but still loved you…my happiness was endless when your marriage proposal came for me…And I am falling more for you day by day.' and she hugged me with that line. Her soft touch was wonderful, for a second I thought of holding her tight in my arms. But the guilt alarmed me from inside, holding her shoulder, slowly I pushed her back and I whispered looking into her eyes 'I LOVE YOU TOO MANSI! There is nothing which can hold me back from loving you…I was always attracted towards the pretty girls…it was always infatuation and lust. Before our marriage, when you stopped talking to me for fifteen days, I missed you a lot…I recalled our relationship episodes in school days. Those fifteen days the way I felt for you, I never felt for anybody…and from the day I am married to you I am falling in love with you every moment…I am in love with your beauty, soft voice, patience, loving nature…your sarees, your dressing, your hair, your smell, your presence around me…I love everything about you…' her cheeks became red blushing, she covered her face with her hands. I continued…'But I don't want to start our relationship with this guilt inside me…' She took off her hands and looked at me, her eyes were searching for answer in my eyes.

I took a long breath and said 'I AM THE ONE, WHO STOLE THE MONEY FROM YOUR HOME!

'What?' she stepped back with the question. 'Yes, you heard me. I stole money from your father's bag.' I said again with no pause and hesitation. 'What?! H…How… Why?' she asked broken questions.

The hidden truth started coming out of my mouth. '5 years back, I was coming from college, some of my batchmates were up to booze party, those were the days, when I was depressed with Dad's financial crunch and his heart attack, I wanted a change. I went along when they asked me. I took Dad's car to party and dropped everyone to their home after the party. While riding back home, suddenly a man hit my car with his bike, it wasn't my fault he came from the wrong side and it was so dark that I didn't see him coming from the other side of road. I stopped my car immediately and everything happened in a fraction of seconds that I wasn't able to think anything. I got out of the car and saw the man unconscious, I was scared. The road was totally empty and dark without any street lights, I thought of escaping as no one noticed me. But I heard the voice of that man muttering for help. I couldn't escape from there, I took him to the hospital. The doctors asked for police verification, cops arrived in an hour. I hid the car and truth from the police. I said, I was riding my bike and saw this man lying…Doctors operated him and police informed his family. The man belonged to lower middleclass family, he had two children and wife to look after. They didn't look like paying single rupee to hospital. I told doctors that I will pay all the expenses. Thankfully, my pocket was filled with Dad's credit card. I swiped it to pay initial bills, Police had no witness other than the man himself and he was unconscious. His family was not prepared to launch any complaint in the shock. I got the car repaired in a single day, luckily there was hardly any loss in car other than small dent in the side, nobody could make out that the car met with an accident. I was stuck in tedious circumstances, I wanted to save that man and help him for his family's survival until he recovers. But Dad had crunch in business and he was recovering from his heart attack, confessing the truth to him was impossible that time. Dadi had gone to pilgrimage along with Mom and Ramya. I couldn't reach Sumit, Shaun and Mandar as they all had gone to bullet ride to Himalayas, Gourav had no powers of handling money in his family that time. I came to your home to ask your suggestion in that. While I was on the door, your father was talking to someone on phone, saying that he kept all the 5 lakhs in the bag and will be waiting for the person, I saw from window, your father kept the bag in cupboard and went inside the bathroom, I didn't see anybody around. The door was open, many thoughts surrounded me in that single moment and I made my mind to steal the bag. Without any hesitation, I took the bag from the cupboard and rushed to hospital!

(Astonished, she kept her hands on her mouth. She was speechless.)

Police started investigating on the case, within few days the man recovered but he had multiple fractures. He didn't recognise me but he understood it was me, who did all that. His family explained him how I saved him and helped them in the hospital. He realised that it was his fault while driving. As a token of gratitude, he did not say anything against me to the police on the contrary, he accepted that it was his fault while driving. From your father's money, I gave him two lacks for the survival of his family until his recovery, paid hospital bill of rupees two lacks and paid one lakh credit card bill, which I'd spent on him in the hospital. I took all the measures for not giving any hint to Dad about the credit card swipe and I blocked the card.

I was guilty, I came to your house after that, to confess in front your father. He was alone at home, and he said you went to Shirdi along with your family. He didn't speak anything about the money, I had no guts and was scared to tell him that I am the culprit. He seemed fine, I thought he must have arranged something else and I left from there hiding the truth. I had no guts to talk to you or anyone in the gang about that. I told Dadi after her arrival from pilgrimage. She slapped me instantly after hearing that. Next morning, she had withdrawn her fixed deposit which she saved for the worst times and gave me the money to hand it over to your Dad with confession.

Dadi accompanied me to your home. We came to your home but it was too late! Your Dad committed suicide on the same morning! From the crowd we came to know that he killed himself with a disgrace of stealing office money. I didn't even know that he was suspended from the job. We were speechless, I felt like a murderer. I was afraid to speak anything about it to you or your family. I slowly went inside and kept the bag in your Dad's room under the bed while the crowd was busy. Which you found after few days, I never knew that money would kill your father after saving that man's life or mine...I am sorry Mansi...' I finished my confession and looked at her, she stood still in a shock, I touched her hand to hold it, she stepped back by throwing my hand, I went close to her saying 'Look I didn't do anything intentionally...I...I'

'Shut up!' She uttered.

'Mansi....I...'

'Don't say anything!! You are a murderer! You killed my Papa... How could you Sandy?! How could you!?' holding my t-shirt she jolted and started crying. I could feel her pain inside me but I was helpless. All the love for me she expressed few minutes ago, has turned as volcano of hatred. The whole night vanished in a sorrow.

Next day, was our trip to Bangkok, Mansi cancelled the Bangkok trip and we headed back to Bangalore by catching an early flight. There was no conversation between us. I tried to initiate some talk but she ignored me every time as if I was a stranger. Dad sent Raju to the airport to receive us.

We arrived home and heard the loud voice 'SURPRISE!!!' The whole gang was present in our home with a cake to welcome us, it was my birthday! They all came to wish me. I saw Mansi's mother standing in the crowd, with all the happiness in her eyes. Mansi gave artificial smile to everyone and rushed towards her mother, embracing her mother, she started crying. Everyone thought she must have missed her mother, except for Dadi, who judged the situation perfectly and distracted everyone saying, 'Let them talk for a while, she must have missed her mother in all these days.' She sent Mansi and her mother in the room.

My mother felt a pinch of doubt, looking at whatever happened. Rest of the people turned towards me, asking how wonderful our trip was. They all wished me again for the birthday. My attention was all at the room, in which Mansi went along with her mother. I was worried about the consequences by then, I had no guts to lose Mansi or face Mom and Dad or anything else, I was in a mess. In the meantime, Aarzoo whispered in my ear 'What's the matter?' 'Haan…no... nothing' I said by waking out of my thoughts.

After few minutes Mansi and her mother came out of the room. My eyes were waiting for their reaction. Her mother looked normal, Mansi also pretended as nothing happened and that was a relief for me. I cut the cake along with Mansi as everyone insisted so. After the dinner everyone left for their respective homes.

While in the room, I thanked her for not revealing my secret to her mother and my family. 'I already lost my father and don't want to be the reason for any problem in both the families. That is why, I did not say anything to my mother. You can break any number of hearts with your acts but I can't!' She said sarcastically. I was upset, 'Ok, I will sleep in the guest room, you sleep here.' I said and started moving out. She stopped me by saying 'Don't make that decision, it will create new scenes in the family, we will sleep in the same room. I don't know the future of our relationship but I can't forgive you!!' I got angry when she spoke to me like that but didn't say anything as she was right in her angle. Mansi slept on the couch and I laid on the bed thinking about her, I could feel her detestation for me in her body language, and she wasn't like this ever before. I fell asleep, from that day, as Indian TV soaps we slept in the same room but in separate places.

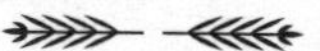

SIX

14 years back (Without narration)

Fifth grade, Sandeep was absolutely horrible in maths. His mother, Asha hit on every wall of house to teach him maths, Ramya left all the hope then his father Sudhir decided to send him for tuitions. He spoke to a school teacher a block away and sent Sandeep for tuitions.

Sandeep entered the tuition class for the first time, it was a big hall just like a classroom, decorated with benches all over the hall and a writing board and teachers table and chair on one side of wall, world and India maps, numbers, fruits etc., pictures on the other walls. All the benches were occupied by kids. Only one place was left beside a fair cute girl in a pink frock, who looked like a Barbie doll. Teacher asked him to sit beside that girl. Sandeep hesitated, hence he never sat beside any girl till that day. Teacher reminded him to take a seat and open the book immediately. The girl smiled at him with her missing front tooth and offered a seat to him. Sandeep smiled back and opened the book.

After the tuitions, everyone came out of the class, Sandeep looked back for the girl, she was talking to some other students, disappointed by that, he moved towards his bicycle with his head down. He was unlocking his bicycle and a soft voice came from his back. 'Hi, I am Mansi, and… you?' the same girl was standing behind him. He turned back and smiled at her. Sandeep always had a charming personality, he had many friends in his school. He was always popular between his friends yet a bit shy to initiate an approach for friendship. Sandeep wanted to talk to that girl since the moment he sat beside her and he felt nice when she spoke to him first. 'I am Sandeep, everyone calls me Sandy.' Replied with his charming smile. 'Sandy, nice nick name. I don't have a nick name…everyone calls me Mansi only.' They both giggled and started walking. 'Where you live?' he asked her to keep the conversation on with his new friend. 'Just a block away from here… and you?' she replied with a question. 'Same, a block away from here…actually I am very bad at maths and science, so my parents decided to send me here.' Sandeep replied. 'Oh ok. By the way, Dev sir is pretty good in teaching both, you will be expert in these subjects soon and don't worry, I will also help you, if you get stuck somewhere.' She approached her helping hand. 'Thank you. That's so sweet of you, you don't seem like from our school.' 'I go to SDS, my Papa will be taking my admission in Xaviers next year…He tried this year itself but the seats weren't available.' she replied. 'Wow cool! I am from Xaviers! So, we will be classmates from next year.'

Sandeep said with his excitement. 'Oh that's nice...umm...this is the turn of my house. Do you see that blue colour gate, that's my house.' Pointing at her house she said. 'OK. Nice. I will have to go this side...will see you tomorrow...bye.' He rode his bicycle towards the opposite side.

That was the first meeting of Sandeep and Mansi. Sandeep had a group of friends in school Sumit, Shaun, Gourav, Mandar, Aarzoo and Preeti. Sandeep was an average student, good with sports and cultural activities. While coming to the studies, book worms Mandar and Aarzoo were always there to back-up everyone in the gang. But Sandeep rarely used to talk about studies with his school friends.

Days passed, Sandeep and Mansi became close friends in tuition. In the meantime, he started improvising his studies, his grades improved gradually with the coaching of teacher and help of Mansi. His parents were happy to see B's in his report cards after long time C's. He loved to go to the tuition, just because he was getting chance to meet Mansi, at the age of ten there was nothing like love or crush, he simply liked the company of Mansi. He introduced her to everyone in the group.

Year ended with 'A' grade in Sandeep's report card, his parent's happiness was touching the sky. Ramya was always a brilliant student, all they were worried about was, Sandeep. His mother threw a party inviting all the friends of Ramya and Sandeep, on the occasion of Ramya's birthday and both the kids good score in studies. The house was not as big as present duplex bungalow, it was a small house but Sandeep's mother made all the refreshments and cake cutting arrangement for kids on the terrace.

Coming year, Mansi joined the same school and same gang happily. Mansi didn't have any friends in her previous school other than Shreya. Shreya took admission in the same school after one year and she was also welcomed by everyone in the gang. They all named their group as '9 gang'. As the days passed everyone came close to each other.

8th grade

They were all 14 now, except for Mansi and Shreya, they both were 13, they got admission one year early in their previous school. These years, Sandeep and Preeti became inter-school champions in badminton doubles. Sandeep also won prizes in imitating the movie stars along with Shaun. Shaun was good in doing stand-up comedy, his humour was always ultimate. Sumit won prizes in singing, Mansi and Shreya won prizes in drawing, Aarzoo and Mandar were scholars and won spelling contests. Gourav lived in low profile all the time, he loved to accompany his father and uncles in their sweet shop, he had only one hobby and that was making money, just like all the other Marwadis.

These years changed many things in kids. They were not kids anymore, all were going through puberty, it was a time for dramatic changes in hormones, as a result girls turned out beautiful day by day and boys started fantasising about the girls, they all were stepped into their adolescent years. Sandeep's charm wasn't lost in his teenage years like the other boys. He always had an athlete body with good looks and attracted many girls in the school. Other boys were shy in expressing their feelings to girls but Sandeep became a champ in that in no time. Soon he became heartthrob in the school with his confidence, good looks and sports. He was first attracted by Arushi, a cute girl in his class, Arushi was a dumb girl but very attractive. He started dating her after the school, they used to spend hours in school garden. The gang always saved him from his parents and teachers with made up stories.

Sandeep used to catch all the eyes on him during the sports days. Preeti was always a last option for guys, not because of her average looks and athlete body but she comes from a defence family, her father was a police officer. Guys are always afraid of these family backgrounds. Shaun and Gourav never attracted any girls with their lean body. Mandar never felt anything for any girl, he was always in love with his books and he turned out to be a complete geek these years. Aarzoo also loved to study and spent hours in library, apart from being attractive, she never came up with anything on boys. In the interschool competition a handsome boy from other school approached her but she rejected his proposal. Sumit concentrated on singing classes since he was attracted to his sexy music teacher. Shreya was keen only on her studies, a shy girl always expressed her feelings in her sketches, and her sketches were never understood by anyone other than Aarzoo and Mansi. Mansi developed secret crush for Sandeep but always hesitated to express her feelings to him, she envied Arushi for dating him yet helped Sandeep in his loving days. Sandeep couldn't bear Arushi's dumbness for long and he broke up with her soon after sports day. And started dating Soniya a scholar from other class, Soniya was a smart girl with beautiful long hair. Sandeep's slipping eyes for other girls ended their relationship as well. After Soniya he dated two more girls and broke up with them as well. That year was filled with jealousy for Mansi.

9th grade

One month was left for the sports day. Girls were studying in the library during the leisure time. 'I am fed up yaar! Sandy is not coming for practice from last two days. PT sir is also on off and we have only a month left for the interschool tournament.' Preeti said aggressively throwing books on the table. 'Ssshhh, its library!' Shreya whispered holding her index finger on her lips. 'Sorry...but you only tell yaar, what should I do?' Preeti urged in soft voice. 'He must be in the canteen or in garden with Ankita...go and drag him to the court!' Aarzoo said smiling. Shreya and Mandar chuckled without making sound. 'I searched him in both the places...he is not there.' Preeti said dragging a chair and sat on it, keeping chin on the table. Mansi was quietly listening them. 'Mansi why don't you talk to him yaar...' Preeti said looking at her. 'What should I say?' she asked peeking in her book. 'C'mon...he is close to you, maybe he will listen to you.' She made her point again. 'Yeah...he is close to me...but I cannot reach him.' Mansi said at a halt, looking into her book, with sorrow filled in her words. 'Hey, are you ok...' Preeti asked holding Mansi's hand. 'Yeah...I am fine...it's just...I have to check other books...not finding proper info in this one...' by getting up from her seat she said. 'I will go and search for Sandy.' said Mandar, he went out of the library by leaving girls to talk.

Mansi's love for Sandeep was hidden deep inside her heart. Everyone but Sandeep understood that Mansi likes him. 'These algebra formulas are never gonna help us in the future... still have to learn them!!' Shreya said distracting everyone to cheer up Mansi. 'I am bored of history...' Aarzoo accompanied her. 'Mansi will help you in that yaar...' Preeti said looking at Mansi. 'I am fine girls...No need for all this...' Mansi said with her smiling face. Everyone looked at her. 'Seriously...I am lucky to have friends like you guys...I don't have any complaints for Sandy...I am fine...' she made her point. 'Remember, one day Sandy will realise that you are perfect match for him.' Preeti said holding her hand. Aarzoo and Shreya hugged Mansi agreeing with Preeti. Within few minutes, everyone started making fun of the maths teacher, who always sleeps in the library.

Meanwhile, there was another rare love story which was ready to surface in front of the gang. Shreya showed her new sketches to the girls, as usual Preeti did not understand her modern art. Mansi loved that and Aarzoo correctly judged the meaning of the picture saying 'The kid is searching for his mother and found her in the nature.' Hearing that Shreya got emotional and asked her 'How could you always understand my paintings so perfectly?' With that question, Aarzoo smiled and said 'Because I know you better than yourself.' Everyone giggled without taking it seriously but Shreya and Aarzoo gazed deep in each other's eyes. Unknowingly, the unspoken love was budding in both the hearts. And that was the first time when Mansi and Preeti realised that the silent love was not only concealed inside Mansi for Sandeep but also it made place in the hearts of Aarzoo and Shreya for each other.

In the intervening time, Sandeep came uttering at Preeti 'What are you doing here? Only one month left for the match and you are chit-chatting here??' He looked at everyone. 'Ssshhhh!! Where the hell were you? I looked for you everywhere! And BTW! You are late not me!! I waited for you half an hour in the court for practice.' Preeti defended, muttering after showing him the 'Silent' board in the library. 'Ok..ok..Sorry! Let's go for the practice…bye girls, catch you all later.' Sandeep whispered and went out of the library. Preeti followed him waving hands to the girls. Rest of the girls stared at each other and looked back in the books.

While on the way to the badminton court Preeti initiated the chat asking Sandeep 'Where were you?' 'I was with Ankita on the terrace!' he said winking his eye. 'What? You were planning to jump off from there with her or drop her from there!?' Preeti disapproved mockingly. 'Ha ha… very funny' he mocked. 'No seriously! You deserve someone better than these dumb girls!' She justified. 'You are indirectly asking me to hook up with you?' he teased her. 'Shut up!' she patted him. 'C'mon yaar…we are teenagers! I am not going to marry or something with these girls…they are looking for fun with me and so am I…just chill…' he said mockingly. 'We've come here to study! Not for all this time pass! And if you seriously enjoy this, then join the company of a smart girl, who cares for you!' she made her point. 'I am in the company of 4 smart girls and 4 smart boys! You all save me and help me every time I need! What else a person require?' he said with his charming smile. 'Forget it! There is no point in discussing with you!' Preeti muttered. 'Wait a minute! What happened? Why are you nagging like a wife today! Is there any problem?' Sandeep asked teasing her. 'Eeww! First of all, I am not a wife! Second of all…I just want you to concentrate more on studies, games, AND all of us, who really love you!! You are not at all connected with us from so many days…in fact months! Look at you! You've become like a playboy of this school and also other schools!! You dated girls from other schools too!! You are dating all the girls who follow you on sports or praise your good looks! We are just 14, and this is not the time for all these things…think!!' Preeti sneered at him. 'God!! What is the matter with you today! These girls really like me! And I enjoy being with them…and it's not like I am totally into it... I am doing my studies as well as sports!! Only today I came late for the practice and you are hammering me!!...fine from tomorrow onwards I will be on time…and be with you guys too!! Ok?' He said with courtesy. 'OK' Preeti did not stretch the conversation and concentrated on the game.

A month passed, Sandeep and Preeti won the doubles. Preeti also won the girls singles which Sandeep lost in boys singles. Sandeep got runner up medals in throw ball and archery, whereas Preeti won in all the games. After realising that his performance was going down without proper practice, he broke up with Ankita. After sports he didn't spend time with his so called girlfriends, instead, he spent most of the time with the gang and also studied well with the help of Mandar, Mansi and Aarzoo.

Meanwhile, during the sports Aarzoo spent her time in the library. Shreya accompanied her all the time in school, their innocent minds were confused about their relationship beyond friendship. But both were sure that there is something in between, attracting them to each other. Aarzoo invited everyone for celebrating Ramzan festival at her home. But being an upper caste pure vegetarian Hindu girl, Shreya did not get permission from her grandmother to visit her home. Shreya's mother expired when she was five, she was brought up by her father and grandmother, who were very orthodox by nature. She always missed her mother in her life, thus, most of her sketches were based on that emotion.

Aarzoo got disappointed for Shreya's absence in the festival but she understood her situation. Although, she would have offered her special vegetarian food, prepared by herself along with her mother for all the vegetarian people.

Next day in the school, Shreya was waiting for Aarzoo at the corridor, she was upset because of not attending Eid at Aarzoo's home. When Aarzoo came to school, she consoled her explaining the situation. Aarzoo, a big hearted girl did not mind it, on the contrary, she held her hand and said 'It's ok. Actually, I was upset yesterday, but I understand your situation, so forget it…don't make this sad face…I want to see you happy always…' With her soft statement Shreya's heart melted. She never felt so much cared and loved before. She doesn't remember her mother's face and her love. The care and affection she was searching in her relatives, was found in the eyes of Aarzoo. The feeling for Aarzoo, which she was confused all this long, was love! She closed her eyes and heard the voice from inside '*She is the one*'. Aarzoo smiled at her and asked 'What happened?' Shreya opened her eyes, tears were filled in her eyes, she looked down blushing and slowly she took her hand off from Aarzoo's hand and mumbled 'Nothing…' and ran from there towards the class. Aarzoo felt butterflies in her stomach with Shreya's reaction. She grinned and followed her.

Mansi saw that from pillar beside the corridor, she felt happy for both of them, and why not? Love is blind, it can happen with anybody, anytime. She has also fallen in love with Sandeep at the age of 13! There are phases in life for everything, Mansi had a hard core crush on Sandeep, which was beyond any attraction. And then, she liked him not only for his looks but for the way he treats everyone with respect, made her to fall for him.

Aarzoo knew that there was always something special about Shreya. But she wasn't sure whether it was love or phase of attraction. She comes from a well-educated modern family of doctors. Her parents were Doctors, working in a well-known hospital of the city. She is the only child, her parents poured all the love and attention on her, she lives in her bungalow, located in a very posh area of the city. She has a pretty face with fair complexion and nice long hair, she had everything which a person wants in life. Many boys wished to date her but the hormones in her body never gave any attention to male gender. She liked to watch the girls in ad films and movies. And the first time she had any attraction was for her cousin's beautiful wife! She totally neglected it thinking as it must be some hormonal imbalance period of life.

On the contrary, Shreya never received love or affection from anybody around. Her father is a clerk in PWD, working from nine to five and reading paper rest of the time, only things left for him in his life, after the death of his wife. He did not marry second time, thinking that the woman may not provide love to Shreya which she deserves. He rarely spoke with anyone, so showing the affection for his daughter was next to impossible for him. His mother and Shreya's grandmother was a strict old woman, who lives on the rules of her caste and customs, she tied the robe of rules for everyone. She never allowed any of Shreya's friends inside her home, even for exchange of books. The girls were allowed to meet her on the gate but boys had no chance for that. Old lady used to sit on the door at the time Shreya returns from school. Shreya is an attractive girl with soft voice as well as soft and shy nature. Excessive control of her grandmother on every activity of hers, made Shreya shy, less spoken and reserved. She knew that the way she felt for Aarzoo, she never felt for anybody, she would never express her feelings in the fear of losing her or misunderstanding between them.

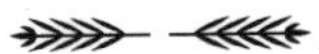

SEVEN

School Picnic

Days passed and school arranged for picnic to near by hill station for a day. Everyone in the gang got permission from their parents to go for it. After convincing her father Shreya also got the permission to attend the picnic, which was against the wish of her orthodox grand mother.

They left for the adventurous picnic at 8 in morning. Immediately after the bus started, children started playing Antakshari. Mischievous boys started making pranks on everyone in the bus. Sandeep was the leader of all the pranks as usual, he had hid the dummy lizards and spiders under the seats of students and as well as on the food items and scared everyone. He hid the costly camera of the teacher under the seat and took a heck out of teacher.

They all went for trekking from the place where the bus stopped. While trekking Mansi was continuously slipping off on the muddy way, Sandy was supporting her. She felt good with the company of her beloved friend. Preeti started teasing her by winking her eye. In that slippery mud soon Mansi sprained her leg, cautiously she was taken to the camp by a lady teacher with the help of Preeti.

After sunset, all the students were enjoying the games sitting around camp fire. Teachers were on high alert watching the boys and girls for no mischievous behaviour, some teachers kept on checking tents on regular intervals. They arranged separate tents for boys and girls, guarded by the teachers in each one of them. The trip organiser arranged all the amenities including hygienic food and separate clean toilets. The camp was set in a beautiful atmosphere of jungle beside the lake. Every one had great fun in playing games around the fire. Shreya sat beside Aarzoo while playing games, Aarzoo happened to touch her hand which brought all the butterflies in Shreya's stomach. Aarzoo felt good, deep inside her heart said, there is something special about Shreya and her friendship. She asked Shreya to go with her to toilet. Both of them walked taking permission from the teacher. Preeti and Mansi smiled at each other when they left.

Aarzoo halted near the toilet. The place was calm and lonely, lights were good enough to see the faces of people around. The crowd was away but voice of students was heard mildly in that place. Shreya's heart beat increased with the sudden stop of walk. She didn't say anything and waited for Aarzoo's words. 'I wanted to talk to you about us...but...don't know what to say…or from where to begin!' She said hesitatingly. Shreya didn't say anything, scratching her eyebrows, she looked down her feet. Aarzoo came close to Shreya, both heart beats increased. She held the hands of Shreya and said 'I don't know whether it's right or wrong…but I think I love you!' Shreya was expecting this from her, she took a long breath of relief and closed her eyes. Aarzoo asked in a confusion 'You…you …understood what I meant?' With her closed eyes, she nodded with yes. Aarzoo whispered 'Say something!' In reply, Shreya embraced her first love tightly and whispered 'I have been feeling this for you from months…never had guts to say this!' That was a relief for Aarzoo she smiled and held her tight in her arms. She lifted Shreya's face by holding her chin, hesitatingly she went close to her lips but some foot steps sound alarmed them and Shreya pushed herself back from Aarzoo and mumbled 'We…We should go now.' And started walking. Aarzoo stopped her by holding her hand and whispered 'Wait…' By that time some girls walked towards them and they moved back to the camp. Mansi and Preeti were waiting for them near the camp. When the love birds arrived with a smile, Mansi understood what has happened. She winkled her eye at both of them and asked 'So…' Shreya walked from there with her pretty shy face, Preeti stopped her by holding her hand, Aarzoo's smile was so bright in her charming eyes. All four of them laughed. Every one moved in their camps to sleep after the dinner around the bonfire. The teachers checked all the camps before sleeping. In each camp, one teacher slept for the safety of the students.

While asleep Shreya felt a hand on her waist, she woke up suddenly, before she could act a hand covered her mouth tightly and a soft voice hit her ears 'Ssshh, its me! Don't shout!'

That was Aarzoo. 'What are you doing in my bed!?' astonished Shreya whispered. 'I wanted to talk to you!' Aarzoo whispered. 'I think you should go to your place' said Shreya. 'Relax! Everyone's asleep…can you hear the snore of Shetty Miss!' said Aarzoo. 'So, what you want to do now!?' Shreya mocked. 'I just want to be with you! Tomorrow we all will be going back …I won't get this night again.' She whispered.

There was a silence everywhere, except the snoring sound of Miss Shetty. Aarzoo held the hand of Shreya. Both the pretty faces were glowing in that dim lamp light.

'You are beautiful' whispered Aarzoo.

'So are you' said Shreya softly. Both smiled.

'I feel very happy with you, never felt like this before' said Aarzoo.

'Same here' said Shreya.

'Are you just gonna repeat my lines?' asked Aarzoo mockingly.

'You are saying everything I feel!' softly she replied.

'You didn't say yet...'

'What?'

'Those three magical words!' Mockingly Aarzoo smiled.

Shreya smiled and said 'We should sleep!'

Aarzoo mocked angry face, Shreya smiled. There was a pause from both the sides for a while. 'I don't remember my mother. Grown up under the strict rules of my grandma, with some unknown fear. Appa(Father) is always busy with his work and stuff. Ajji (Grandmother) loves me of course but her rules and anger makes me feel like living in a jail. I had no friends other than Mansi, and I changed the school with her. After coming here, I got all of you along with Mansi. I always expressed my feeling with my paintings and sketches, which you always understood. All the boys are nice in the school, and in our group all are darlings. But never felt anything for any guy. Whenever you were close to me, my heartbeats were always increased, now also its high...Few months back, I realised there is something special with you. I was scared to say anything in the fear of rejection, I never wanted to be treated as a joke...but the feeling for you always remained the same and it increased day by day....when you guys convinced my Appa for the picnic I felt like I am on the top of the world, because I was getting the whole 2 days time to be with you...I don't know what is our future or what has to be done after this... but today when you expressed your feelings...I felt this is it...if my life ends here I have no complaints...I know all this sounds silly...but Yes...I LOVE YOU TOO...' Shreya whispred all her feelings. Aarzoo quietly heard all she said and caressed her cheeks, soon they both kissed. It was a long beautiful first kiss of the girls.

'Ahem...' the sound came from the other side. 'We didn't see or hear anything...' soft whispers came, that was Mansi and Preeti. 'Idiots!' Aarzoo whispered with anger, Shreya covered her face with her blanket shyly. Mansi held the hands of Shreya and Aarzoo and said 'Very happy for both of you.' They all blushed. Aarzoo slept beside Shreya rest of the night. The girls were under the control of their physical emotions and nothing happened between them.

Meanwhile, inside the boys camp, every one slept immediately after laying on the bed. The snoring sound of Prakash sir was hundred times louder than Miss Shetty. Sandeep wasn't getting any sleep. His heart started beating for Mansi this time. He made distance from all the girls after the poor performance in sports and unit tests. It was more than 2 months he stayed away from his girlfriends, and he spent all his time with his group. During the day, while trekking up on the hill, when he was close to Mansi, his heart felt the tickle again. When Mansi sprained her leg, he was the person more worried about her. Sandeep was always a sensitive boy, he watched her every step while walking up with the help of Preeti and teacher and felt the pain she was suffering. At the camp, his eyes were kept on searching for Mansi. He even offered a massage to her while the teachers were away for checking on the cooks. He noticed shy face of Mansi with his interest in her, she denied his offer with the hesitation and the fear of teachers. She was always a sweet friend for him, he hugged her many times when she helped him solving maths problems or saving him from someone but he never felt this way for her before. The whole night Sandeep kept on recalling the pretty shy face of Mansi. He remembered each and every moment he spent with Mansi from the day one he met her. Her helping nature, her co-operation in studies, her sweet smile, saving him from teachers, lying for him, everything about her flashing one by one infront of his closed eyes.

The next morning immediately after waking up Sandy rushed towards the girls camp. Preeti was standing in the queue for toilet. 'Where is Mansi?' He asked her. 'She is taking bath' Preeti replied holding her natural pressure. 'Do you have any idea, how long is she gonna take?' he asked her again. 'Dude, I am in an emergency right now...so leave me alone...' she muttered holding her stomach. 'Ok.. ok... just tell me from how long she is in?' he urged again. 'Sandy! Just get lost with your useless questions...or else I will kill you!!' irritation with pressure spoke out loudly from Preeti. In the meantime, both the doors of toilet and bathroom opened...Preeti rushed inside the toilet immediately after the girl came out from there. From the bathroom, Mansi slowly came out crippling and wiping her hair, she was amazed to see Sandeep outside.

'Hi' said Sandeep, gazing at her beauty after bath. It was the first time when Sandeep saw her like that, she was wearing yellow t-shirt and blue jeans, open wet hair all over her shoulder moist some patches on her t-shirt. She walked crippling with sprained leg, he rushed and held her hand. Some girls were standing in the line, smiled at the duo. Mansi hesitated to give him hand but Sandeep did not care for the girls, he held her hand and walked with her towards the camp. Her soft hand was moist after the bath. 'What are you doing here at this time? Its 6.30 and you woke up so early.' She asked him. 'Actually I didn't sleep all night... how are you now?' he expressed the truth. 'Yeah better, the swelling is down, I don't think I could go for trek today...woke up early so got fresh to avoid the crowd for bathroom...' she said. 'Hmm, you better take rest...' he said. 'Hmm' she mumbled. Both smiled and reached the camp. Most of the girls were still asleep. Even some teachers were asleep. The dawn surrounded with deep fog all over the greenery. The camp fire ended with smoke. Fog was so thick that even distance of a foot was also not clear. Calm and beautiful atmosphere with fresh air mesmerised. Sandeep was still holding her hand just to be cautious in that foggy climate and smudged floor. Mansi's heartbeats increased with his closeness but she wasn't making any illustrations with his behaviour, since she knew his caring nature, thus, made up her mind thinking that it's nothing but a friendship hand from his side. There was a silence for few seconds. 'Mosquitoes?' she broke the silence. 'What?' he asked astonished. 'You just said that you didn't sleep last night…so, because of mosquitoes?' she asked. 'No, I had applied the repellent cream… no…Not because of mosquitoes.' He said with a pause. 'Then?' She asked, expecting some funny answer from him as usual.

'I was…mmm…forget it…You slept well?' He hesitated to express and laid the different question. 'Yeah, we had a talk for some time, the pain killers made me sleep well. Girls were still awake… Hey…Do you know…' She thought of saying about Aarzoo and Shreya but stopped, thinking that it wasn't the right time to speak about them or may be it wasn't right to tell the guys and others about their relationship. 'What?' he asked. 'Nothing… you didn't answer me…why didn't you sleep?' she asked him again. 'I told you na…forget it' he said. 'Ok… who is it this time?' she mocked. She knew that he gone through this almost every month thinking about the beauty of the girls he dates. 'If I say…Aah…leave it…' he hesitated again, it was the first time when he was hesitating so much in front of his love interest. Before this, he used to express it very easily to all the girls. He was finding it difficult in the fear of rejection as well as losing the friendship from his best friend. 'So, now you don't want to share your new story with me… haan?' She pretended to be angry, she always supported him in his affairs by hiding all her pain. 'It's not like that yaar! Those were all outside from our group…and…' he paused. Her heartbeats increased with that sentence. She understood that this time it's some one from the group, she was afraid to know the name, it must be anyone…She jumped in her thoughts, *'Aarzoo or Shreya…what if he comes to know about their interest? I know his weakness, he likes beautiful girls and both the girls are beautiful. Or it's Preeti? Because she spends most of the time with him during sports and he broke up with last girl after the sports. Preeti is wheatish but atrractive athlete girl. Or…or is it me! no…no…I doubt that, he would never do that even if I am the last left out girl in the world. No matter how good I look, till today he never saw my beauty. He is always busy observing the random girls.'*

'Hello!! Where are you?' he distracted her by waving his hand infront of her eyes. 'Yeah…I…I am here only…' confused words came out of her mouth. 'Look Mansi, I know what you are thinking…I am the guy who doesn't deserve any good girl…because of my lose character and flirty nature…but I don't know…this time I am feeling different…I've never hesitated like this before…look its up to you…I don't want to lose our friendship because of this…I want to be friends with you for life. I love you all… you all come first in my life before all these incoming-outgoing girls…' he was speaking out of his mind continuously. 'Wait…wait…wait…what is your point!?' she interrupted hearing some strange lines pointing at her. 'It's you!... There…I said it!' he said it firmly looking into her eyes. Her heart stopped! She never expected this, she never thought that he would ever say these lines for her, she stood still. 'Hey, I know you must be thinking that I am kidding…but trust me…I am serious. I was thinking about you all the night…I wanted to see you in the night itself but controlled my feelings till morning and came searching for you. Look, I don't know what you feel and I don't want to force you for this…I just expressed my feelings and that's it…I hope this will not harm our friendship…and I…' he was talking without any halt, 'Shut up! Sandy you…' She stopped him to say something but by that time teacher came out of the tent, she did not notice them in the fog but Mansi realised her presence with her voice of yawning. 'You go now, Shetty miss is here, we'll talk later.' She whispered. Sandy walked out from there with hope of meeting again, and she slowly crippled towards her tent.

While inside, she saw Aarzoo and Shreya sleeping together with hand in hand. Preeti entered the tent behind her, after brushing her teeth and departing natural calls. Mansi woke up the girls. Both woke up and in the presence of the girls, Shreya recalled what happened last night, she felt shy and rushed to the bathroom. Mansi and Preeti smiled. Aarzoo blushed with their reaction.

'Why our Romeo was here to see you so early in the morning?' Preeti asked Mansi. Mansi was speechless and she blushed. Aarzoo and Preeti stared at her and they understood the scenario by her body language, both uttered with soft voice 'Ooooo!! To see his Juliet!' 'Ssshhh' Mansi whispered pointing out at sleeping girls and teacher outside. 'What did he say?' Aarzoo asked with curiosity. 'The clow is on to me this time…' Mansi said with fake smile, there was a disappointment in her voice and that was, fear of dumping. She always loved Sandeep from her heart, never expressed her feelings because she knew his Casanova image. Just like in a toy store, a person picks one toy with clow and leaves it for another. Sandeep's flirty nature was not hidden from anybody, she knew that if he chose her this day, once he is fed up of her or found new girl, he will surely dump her as he dumped other girls, and he never dates the same girl back again.

'Shut up! You are not a random girl...You are Mansi and Sandy would never dump you...It's just he realised it late...' Aarzoo said distracting her. 'Yup, she is right...I will kill him if he hurts you...' Preeti said mockingly. Mansi blushed. 'Now tell me what happened? What he said and what did you say?' Aarzoo asked again with same curiosity. 'Nothing...he said it and Miss came out of the tent and I sent him back.' Mansi replied with soft voice. 'Awww...Ok will make a plan today' said Preeti.

By that time it was 7 and girls started waking up. Shreya came inside the tent after getting fresh. Aarzoo was staring at her and Shreya felt shy infront of the girls. 'Ahem, you girls enjoy the staring business...I will take bath and get ready for breakfast.' said Preeti picking up her clothes from bag. 'I will check if the breakfast is ready' Mansi started moving out by winking her eye at Shreya. 'No, you stay here. You must be having pain in the leg...I will check it and bring your breakfast here.' Shreya said holding Mansi's hand. 'Yeah, you stay in...anyhow I am going to the bathroom.' said Aarzoo with blinking her eyes at both the girls. Shreya wasn't aware of Sandeep's morning action. She helped Mansi in dressing her sprained ankle. And Mansi told her about Sandeep. Shreya felt happy for her close friend. Mansi spoke her fear as well. Shreya consoled Mansi, not to get second thought on that.

Sharp at 9, breakfast was ready and all the students got ready with the plates near the buffet. Shreya got the breakfast plate for Mansi back in tent. Every one started for trekking after having tasty Upma and a cup of coffee. Shetty Miss asked Mansi to stay back at the camp because of her sprained ankle. The camp was safe since there were some female workers and cooks stayed back around the tents, only an old watchman was present in male category. Teacher left Mansi alone in the camp instructing the female cooks to look after her. Aarzoo, Preeti and Shreya wanted to stay back but Mansi sent them all saying not to lose there enjoyment just because of her.

The cooks were got busy in washing the breakfast utensils and preparing the lunch for the whole unit. Their chit-chat in local Kannada language was going on loudly while working. Mansi zip locked the tent from inside and grabbed a book from her bag and started reading it lying on her bed.

After some time the women stopped their conversation, human sound vanished completely and the jungle started to speak, birds were twittering, the wind was shaking the tents. Mansi got worried with the deep jungle sound and no human talk for more than 30 minutes, she took a long breath and concentrated in her book ducking the panic inside. Suddenly, she observed the tent zip which she locked from inside was being opened by somebody from outside, the panic increased in seconds and she grabbed the tennis racket beside her and slowly got up from the bed. The zip opened fully and she shouted 'Aahh….stop there or I will hit you!' Sandeep entered inside the tent, holding his hands up 'HEY.. HEY…easy… it's me…' he said. 'God!! You scared me!' she said, throwing the racket aside she held her hands on her mouth and with relaxed tone. 'I am sorry! I didn't mean to scare you!' saying that he walked inside the tent. 'How come you are here? Trekking is over, so soon?' she asked. 'No…its on…I just ran here…' he said. 'Oh…why? I mean nobody saw you coming?' She was astonished by that sentence. 'I told them that I am going for toilet' he juggled. 'And… did you go?' jumping the eyebrows she asked. 'Ahh, I am not feeling like to go!' he laughed. 'Then why are you here?' She asked turning back with a soft voice. 'Don't you know?' He came close to her and asked her. She paused. He started talking 'Look … I shouldn't have said that all…you know… I came here to say that, just forget everything and just be friends as usual…it doesn't matter…I should have never said that…I don't know why I started feeling like that for you…its silly…I …I am sorry…you must be feeling like I am a jerk…I…I don't wanna hurt you…I always want to be friends with you…and with this thing…I…' he kept on talking. 'Its always about you…isn't it?' she asked, by stopping his talk in the middle. 'What?' he asked. 'Yeah…its always about you…no matter what others feel…' she said again. He stood still. She turned back, looking into his eyes 'You said what you wanted to say and what you felt…and now before hearing my opinion you are asking to forget it! It doesn't matter what I feel or think… isn't it?' She asked with firm voice. 'No, it's not like that…you are getting it all wrong…I…I felt like…Look, whatever I feel is not important…there are many girls for whom I felt the same way…but you are one of my best friend and I don't want to lose you for this new feeling…that's it…and you know me very well, how I am…I...I can change my mind any time!' he said hesitatingly looking down. 'For God sake will you SHUP UP for a while and listen to me?' She uttered. He was astonished and looked at her. 'You said whatever you wanted to…now listen to me… I know what you are and how you are…I know you can change your mind anytime…but do you know that I LIKE YOU TOO?' she paused. 'WHAT?!' he was shocked to hear that. 'Sshhh…let me finish…(taking a long breath)Yes, I like you… I had a huge crush on you, I don't know since when but whenever I dream about someone…only your face comes in my mind…it was always you…

no matter how many dumb girls you dated or the stories you told about them…my feelings never changed, I always felt the same for you…I never expressed this...not because I am afraid of getting rejected or getting dumped one day like other girls…but just because you never liked me, in that way…and I didn't want you to compromise for me in anyway…' she finished staring the floor. 'Wait…wait…what!? You like me too?' he asked with a smile. Pause from the other side. He went close to her, her eyes were filled with tears. He held her hand and said 'Hey, you are crying? Please… don't cry…you know I can't see anybody crying…' She covered her face with her palms and sat on the bed and bursted crying. He took off the hanky from his pocket and held it in front of her to wipe her tears. She took it from him and wiped her eyes yet the tears were snapping out from her eyes. He sat beside her 'Mansi…I am sorry…I am an idiot…I never realized what you felt for me…I am sorry…please stop crying first…I cant speak if you cry…' he said softly. She wiped her eyes again. There was complete silence for seconds. 'If you want, you can clean your nose as well…' he grinned. She looked at him and blushed. 'Sorry…I couldn't control my emotions' she returned his hanky. 'It's ok...Actually, I am sorry…' He said by keeping the hanky back in pocket.

'Can I say something now?' After a second he asked. 'Yeah' she said. 'You are the first girl with whom I am this close…I mean ofcourse, Preeti, Aarzoo and Shreya are there but I don't know how come I always felt to share some things only with you…You are really a good girl Mansi and I don't want to hurt you…I know there are girls, who were hurt because I dumped them…of course, some of them dumped me… I don't know what I am talking…But I think this time its something different, because I liked 'you'…and I don't see any reason to dump you…or getting dumped!' he chukkled. She blushed.

He moved close and held her hand, she took it back with a hesitation and said 'I…I am not prepared for your moves…so…' she paused shyly, he grinned and said 'Relax, I am not doing anything…I just want to see you…from this close…' Their eyes met, her heart melted, Sandeep slowly moved towards her lips, there was nervousness first from her side but she got lost in his magic and they kissed for the first time. He surrounded his arms around her and embraced her tightly. After dating so many girls Sandeep was an expert in kissing but for Mansi it was her first kiss, she was hesitating, Sandeep held her face in his hands to comfort her. After a minute, she pushed herself back shyly and stared the floor, he smiled licking his lips. He enjoyed seeing her shy, there was a silence for few seconds. Her heartbeats were fast with his closeness, she wanted to change the topic to avoid futher moves, 'How did you open that tent zip from outside…it was locked from inside…' she asked. 'James bond' he said. 'What?'She looked astonished. 'I saw that trick in one of James bond movie, opened it with magnet.' He took out the piece of magnet from his pocket and juggled it infront of her. She looked at him and said 'You are such an …' and paused. 'Yes I am…come here.' he smiled and hugged her. She pushed him back slowly 'Where are those women?' she asked. He stared at her for pushing him back 'They were sitting near the lake. No one was here when I came.' He replied. 'I think you should go now…what if someone finds us like this.' She said with a concern. 'Guys will take care of it' he said and came close to her. 'What? Who all know that you are here' she asked him. 'Everyone in the gang' he smiled. 'God! I will die with shyness now…everyone will tease me now…' she said covering her face in her palms. 'It's fine…they will tease me too…' he grinned. 'You go now…those ladies will be here any moment.' She said pushing him, he grabbed her again and his heart warmed to see her face melting, she closed her eyes shyly and he kissed her on forehead, 'You are beautiful…You know that?' he said caressing her cheeks. She melted, 'Go…please.' blushing she said. 'Ok..ok…I am going but… I LOVE YOU.' he smiled and moved out of the tent, within seconds he disappeared in the mist.

Mansi was on the top of the world. She wanted to jump in excitement but her sprained leg didn't allow her, she muttered 'Oh my god!' several times. Her heartbeats were still fast. Her crush and her first love was in love with her. She experienced a kiss, the first kiss, she always dreamed about her kiss with Sandeep, and it was her dream come true, she pinched herself to check the same. Her joy was endless, she fell on the bed thinking about her love.

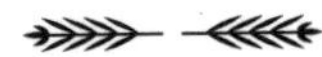

EIGHT

On the other side, Sandeep walked in the smog to reach the trekking point, he felt like walking on the clouds. He always loved to enjoy with his girlfriends but this time, he was not intended to have fun with Mansi. There was something special about her, for the first time he saw her innocent attractive shy face, and he desired to see her again and again. He had kissed many girls, yet he felt good kissing Mansi. That blush and happiness on her face was for him and he loved that feeling. Throughout the way he was smiling. He reached the trekking point, the gang was eagerly waiting for him. While climbing the rock mountain, boys showed curiosity to know what happened back in the tent but he maintained the dignity of Mansi and did not reveal anything to them. Even the girls loved to hear the story from him, Sandeep did not disclose anything to anyone to uphold the respect of Mansi. He always hid many personal things from everyone to maintain the respect of the girls he dated, so far he had disclosed some intimate things to Mansi to take her tips and advice, Mansi with the broken heart, gave him suggestions, which helped him to get close with the girls.

After trekking everyone had lunch in the camp, Sandeep kept on staring Mansi and she couldn't look at him in shyness. The gang didn't leave single chance of teasing them. Before the dusk they started walking down the hill towards the bus. The trip got over with everyone in a jovial mood. Sandeep's new love interest spread like a fire in the jungle and the girls who dated him earlier, were jealous on Mansi. On the other hand, Mansi found her love. Shreya and Aarzoo also expressed their feelings with each other and comprehended the new phase of love. However, everyone wasn't aware of their love apart from Preeti and Mansi. Soon the darkness covered the muddy roads. Shetty miss started blaming Ramesh sir for his idea of resting after lunch, she wanted to start immediately after lunch to avoid the darkness. Sandeep took care of Mansi in the crowded walk of the jungle, in his care, her ankle pain wasn't bothering her anymore. Looking at his love and care she whispered 'My hero.' He heard that and started blushing 'Hero wants to sit with you in the bus' he muttered. 'What!' she was amazed with that line and looked at him. 'Yes, I told Preeti to exchange the seats when everyone will sleep in the bus…it will take 3 hours to reach the city and everyone will sleep by that time in bus…' He said. 'Are you mad? No way…' she muttered. 'I am not asking your permission, so shut up!' he said firmly.

Everyone got into the bus after a walk of 1 hour. Aarzoo and Shreya sat together holding each other's hand. Shreya's heart stopped when Aarzoo tightened her hold, she looked at her. Aarzoo smiled and whispered 'I love you.' Shreya looked into her eyes and said 'I love you too' and rested her head on Aarzoos's shoulder. 'Shreya, tomorrow is a holiday and I can't wait for 1 whole day to see you, can you come to my place?' She blushed, closing her eyes on Aarzoo's shoulder, she nodded with yes. Aarzoo smiled and closed her eyes.

Meanwhile, due to tiredness of trekking everyone fell asleep in the bus but Sandeep. He waited for that moment and exchanged his seat with Preeti, who was sitting beside Mansi. Mansi wasn't allowing Preeti to get off from her seat in the shyness but Preeti smiled and whispered 'Easy yaar, he is not gonna do anything more in this bus...You won't get these moments again…so just chill and enjoy.' She went back on his seat. Sandeep jumped in with the victory of sitting beside her and said 'Hi.' Mansi did not reply, she looked outside the window and blushed. Sandeep took her hand in his hands. She closed her eyes and tightened her hold and whispered 'I am scared'. He asked 'Why?'

'I don't know' she muttered. He smiled and kissed her hand. She looked at him and rested her head on his shoulder. They didn't do anything else in the bus other than that. And within half an hour, the city lights were visible from the bus and he went back to his seat but before going he kissed her cheek and muttered 'Love you'. She melted in shyness.

Bus reached the school by ten in the night, parents were present there to pick their children except Sandeep and Shreya's parents. Mansi's father told Sandeep's family that he will pick him up along with Mansi. Shreya's father was sick and Grandma couldn't come in her old age. Before leaving, teachers promised her father to drop Shreya safely at her home, Shetty teacher was about to drop her. Meanwhile, Aarzoo insisted her father to drop Shreya on the way, he agreed and asked Miss Shetty for her permission. Ms. Shetty called Shreya's home and informed the same to her father and permitted Dr. Shaik to drop Shreya to her home. On the other hand, Mansi's Dad picked her as well as Sandeep from the school. Looking at the situation, Preeti said 'Who says you won't get what you want!' Mansi, and the girls were amazed with her line. But luckily nobody got the meaning except the girls. While going back Aarzoo held Shreya's hand in the back seat of the car. Aarzoo's father kept on asking how they enjoyed and Aarzoo said 'We had a great time Daddy! I wish the day never ended. And the night as well (whispered slowly)' Shreya blushed with her answer. 'Good, you guys should go for the trips next time as well…' Aarzoo's father Aarmaan Shaik said. 'We'll surely Daddy!' She said by winking her eye at

Shreya. Meanwhile, Sandeep didn't get any chance of romance in the Auto, having Mansi's father in between them.

Next day was holiday for school. Holiday was declared by the teachers, since the students weren't tired with trekking, at least both the couples were excited to run towards the school. Shreya couldn't go to Aarzoo's home as she'd promised. As usual, the old lady did not allow the bird to fly out of the cage. Aarzoo understood her situation and they had a talk on phone for few minutes.

Days passed and ninth grade final exams approached, everyone concentrated on the studies. Sandeep was also serious with studies this time after his bad performance in sports and all his tests, he got strict warning from his parents as well as teachers for his declining performance. The scholar students Mandar, Aarzoo, Mansi and Shreya scored good marks in studies. Sandeep, Gourav, Preeti, Sumit and Shaun achieved first class marks with hardly some hard work. Soon, exams phase got over.

Holidays started, whenever Shreya desired to meet her love, the poor girl couldn't make it because of her orthodox Grandma. She was treated more strictly by the old lady during holidays, Shreya used to do complete household work from washing clothes to cleaning the house and helping Granny in cooking, she got little time for her hobbies and was hardly allowed to meet or talk to any of her friends. To make it worse, Shreya got news from her Grandma about her marriage! Old lady fixed Shreya's marriage with her paternal aunt's son Arjun, he was a pampered son of Granny's beloved daughter. Marrying cousins is normal in south India. After hearing that news, Shreya lost her interest in life, her cousin cum fiancé, Arjun was doing his second year in civil engineering that time. His greedy family was enthusiastically ready to take Shreya as their daughter-in-law, since she was a single heir of her father's ancestral land of 10 acres in the village nearby, 500 grams gold of her Granny, and well-built house in the prime location of the city. Most importantly, her father was a well-known government officer, who could help Arjun in getting civil contracts and job in the future. For them, all those things were on priority and later Shreya's beauty and soft nature. It was simply a jackpot for them, even a fool can't reject that proposal. And the old lady was satisfied that her beloved cage bird would remain in the family. Shreya's father had no opinion on anything as usual. After knowing this news Aarzoo got devastated. She asked Shreya to reject the proposal and she was right, Shreya was just 15 and her family had no right to decide her wedding at that age without her opinion.

However, they decided the wedding after completion of her education, the old woman made this decision after her piles operation, as if she was dying next day due to piles! She became a pile on Shreya's life. Shreya had no guts to oppose that and as a result, it created a distance between Aarzoo and Shreya. Mansi decided to reunite them, she tried everything from her end with the help of Preeti but nothing worked out. After all the trials, finally the girls decided to tell the truth to the boys. Gourav and Mandar were always busy with their shop and studies respectively. Sumit was totally infatuated with his singing teacher and involved all his vacation time in music classes, whereas Shaun was least interested in girl's matters, they targeted Sandeep as he was the easiest guy, who would understand their love.

It wasn't safe to converse on the phone hence, Mansi called Sandeep at a garden nearby their home one day, 'You must have observed, there is a cold war between Aarzoo and Shreya. They aren't talking from long time.' she said. 'Yeah…' he nodded. 'I want you to make some plan for their patch up.' She asked him. 'But why? I see they are not interested in each other's friendship, I think it's not good to interfere.' He replied casually. 'It's not friendship' wavering, she said. 'Then what? Cat-fight?' he laughed. 'Why you boys always associate two girls fight with cat-fight?' irritatingly she asked. 'Ok…I am sorry, I was kidding…you continue…' he apologised. 'I don't know how to say…mmm…Have you ever heard about the 'L word' in movies or anything you happen to watch?' she aksed. 'Yeah… sometimes…why?' by winking his eye he asked. 'Don't you understand?' she asked him by jumping her eyebrows. 'What should I understand?' he was confused. 'They are in LOVE, you Idiot!' She said patting his shoulder. 'WHAT?' he was totally astonished and sat on the bench. There was a silence covered with shock for a minute. Mansi sat beside him and explained everything. 'They really kissed?' He asked with his eyes wide open. 'You got only that from the entire story?' surprised Mansi asked. 'Wow…I've always heard of this but never thought that it happens in reality…and in India.' He said. 'Why? Indians have no right to choose their love interest?' She asked with a firm voice. 'No…I mean, Yes...I... I didn't mean that way yaar!…I always saw these things in Hollywood movies…Anyways…what do you want me to do? Act as cupid and hit arrow of love on both of them for patch up?' he asked by winkling his eye. 'The arrow has already hit them, you have to show that to them again.' she said. 'What?' he asked shaking his head. 'You have so many 'what's and 'why's? You are an expert in these things. Do something…take out your magic wand and help them.' she said. 'Hmm…ok…leave it to me…I will do something…but let me tell you…I can't change the old woman's mind…she is impossible.' He warned her about Shreya's marriage decision by her Grandma. 'OK' She nodded.

'And what do I get after the task?' he asked her with a naughty smile. 'That is a surprise.' She blushed. 'I like surprises' he said getting close to her. She pushed him saying 'It's a public place…let's go.' They both left from there with a smile. Though, Sandeep was equally romantic with Mansi as he used to be with other girls but he always took care of her emotions more than other girls and obeyed all her orders.

The coming Sunday was Ramya's birthday and Sandeep arranged a small surprise party at his home, he invited Ramya's friends as well as everyone from his gang. Shreya made it only after Mansi convinced her Grandma. The party was arranged on the terrace of Sandeep's house and decorated wonderfully by Sandeep. Ramya got emotional with her brother's love and thanked him with heart and Sandeep too felt good after seeing his sister happy. Though, his intention was different, he did all that for patch up between his lesbian girl friends. During the party he asked Aarzoo to get some plates from his room and signalled Mansi to send Shreya in the room and his plan worked. He locked the room from outside immediately when the couple entered the room. Aarzoo uttered 'Sandy, what is this yaar… open the door!' She banged the door. 'You guys sort out whatever is between you…I will open it.' He said and walked out from there along with Mansi.

Everyone were upstairs, Mansi and Sandeep were climbing the stairs, taking a chance of privacy, he grabbed Mansi towards him 'My gift?' he asked. 'It's Ramya's Birthday, not yours!' Blushing she said. 'I know but you promised something.' He asked winking his eye. 'Let them come out happily, you will get your gift.' She pushed him back and started hopping the stairs, he got angry and stood there, she turned back at him 'Let's go!' she came down and said. 'I am not coming, you have fun.' he said in fake anger. 'It's your home, what if somebody catches us here…' she paused. 'Oh c'mon! You always give excuse of places…your home, my home, school, garden!! Where on earth we should go to have romance!?' he uttered. 'Shh-hh! Relax…' she calmed him down. 'You know what? You go upstairs and enjoy with everyone. I will wait here, to open the door…' he said sarcastically. She came close to him 'There is always time and place for things…' she said holding his hand. He snatched his hand out and said 'Oh yes! Do you even remember when we last kissed? We've hardly kissed in last 5 months! Your 'time' never came in between exams and your 'places.' He said looking at her. 'Oh my god! Anger always sits on your nose!' she said mockingly. He leaned his back against the wall and stood looking here and there, knotted his hands against his chest 'Yes! I am like that only! You please go up.' He said showing her the stairs. She stood looking at him with her cute smile but he didn't look her. 'I am sorry!' She said softly but he stared her in anger. She looked here and there cautiously, 'Fine! Close your eyes.' blushing she muttered, he didn't close his eyes, instead he stared at her more angrily. 'Please!' she requested making sweet innocent face. He took a long breath and closed his eyes. She slowly moved towards him and kissed his cheeks holding his face, which calmed down Sandeep's anger. Swiftly, he held her waist and grabbed her close, their bodies touched each other, her warmth raised the passion in Sandeep 'Kiss me, on lips!' he asked staring her. She rested her head on his shoulder shyly, 'I…I can't' she whispered. He pressed her waist, she looked him up widening her eyes. 'Kiss me or else I will not leave you…no matter what!' he warned her raising his eyebrows. She took a pause, timidly, she looked here and there and slowly moved towards his lips and Sandeep handled the rest of the romance, they kissed for long time. Mansi heard a sound from upstairs, quickly, she pushed him and hopped the stairs. He smiled looking at her, her shyness always tickled his heart. He waited near the stairs to open the door of his room, playing games on his father's mobile.

Meanwhile in the room, Aarzoo was busy knocking the door, which wasn't heard by Sandeep or Mansi, who were away from room romancing near the stairs. Shreya came close to Aarzoo 'Many times we don't get what we actually want in life…and in our case it's next to impossible.' she said. Aarzoo looked at her 'You can't jump into conclusion before even trying.' She said firmly. 'I can't go against my family…try to understand…and it's not like they are getting me married tomorrow... There is a long time for that…who knows, things may change during that time.' Shreya made her point. 'So, you are just gonna wait for the things to change and don't do anything to make it happen?' Aarzoo asked sarcastically. 'It's not like that Aarzoo, I am not made like that…please try to understand.' Shreya begged her. 'I got it! You are fine with whatever happens in your life, so let it be…I want to get out from here…Sandy, please open the door!' She banged the door again. 'Aarzoo, we are hardly 16…there is no need to react so much on these things. I LOVE YOU and that is what matters. I don't care what my family is doing or planning about me.' Shreya said by holding her hand, which was busy banging the door. 'I can't imagine you with anybody! How can you be so relaxed?' she asked with sad face. 'I am happy to know that my girlfriend is getting possessive over me…' Shreya smiled with her bright eyes. 'It's not funny' serious reply came from Aarzoo. 'What you want me to do? Go and tell my orthodox family that I am in love with a GIRL and can't think of marrying Arjun?' Shreya asked her, looking straight into her eyes. 'I want you to tell them that you don't want to marry him…we all know how they are, you said so yourself about their greedy intentions... finish it before they get any more ideas. Talk to your Dad, be brave.' Aarzoo said staring her. 'Let them think whatever they want to Aarzoo. I told you, I don't care. I just know one thing, you are my love and I am hundred percent sure that I will not think of anybody in the future as well. How come that is not good enough for you?' She asked her. There was a pause for a minute. 'I don't want to lose you...I know it's sounding over possessive or silly at this age...but...I love you.' Aarzoo expressed the pain of her heart leaning her back on the door. 'I love you too!' holding her face Shreya said. Aarzoo looked into her eyes, holding her face in her hands, slowly she pushed her hair back, caressed her cheeks and she kissed her. After the long passionate kiss, 'I want you to be mine, forever.'Aarzoo whisphered. 'I am all your's' Shreya said with soft voice and they kissed again.

It had been more than twenty minutes they were inside the room, Sandeep thought there must be some action of patch up now so he went upstairs and sent Preeti and Mansi to unlock the room. Mansi knocked the door before opening and unlocked the door. Shreya was correcting her lipstick and Aarzoo standing near the door. Both the girls understood what must have happened. They started teasing Aarzoo and Shreya. There was happiness all over the room. Sandeep entered inside and asked 'All ok?' Looking at him Shreya felt shy and she hid herself behind Mansi, Aarzoo blushed as well. He smiled and said 'You two gorgeous girls, had left no chance for any boys who fantasize about you!' With his quote everyone laughed in the room. They all went back to the terrace, where the entire crowd was enjoying the birthday bash. While going back Aarzoo dropped Shreya and Preeti on her scooter.

NINE

Boy's life was moving smoothly, unless they complicate it by themselves. Mandar was the only son of her single mother. His mother had big dreams for him, she was always ready to show off her son's high scores and obedience to the relatives. He was her pride and only hope after losing her husband. In the same way, he was a complete 'Mumma's boy', he had no interest in life other than being with the gang and his books. Most of the time he was physically present in the group but mentally he was in his books.

Sumit started his music classes 2 years back. He got attracted to Neeta, a 22 year old girl teaching music near his house. One day he saw her on the bus stop while going to school and he enquired all the information about her within few days. He started to watch her from his house, every day passing through for her routine outside works. Soon he came to know that she teaches music to children. He demanded to learn music from Neeta, his family wondered to see the guy who rarely watches any movie songs is asking to learn the music. He made all the drama to convince his family. However, his demand was fulfilled as usual, because he was the youngest and most pampered son.

Neeta was a well-disciplined, good looking single girl, who recently shifted to Bangalore from Kadappa (Andhra Pradesh), she lived in a rented house along with her family. For living she used to teach music to the children. In short time, Sumit became close to her, he was a bold boy and attracted everyone with his speech and humour. He created hundreds of LOL moments in Neeta's life. He always felt happy whenever she used to laugh. Just like her voice, her laugh was also melodious. However, he did not disclose his crush on her in a due respect and fear of rejection.

Sumit's family was a banker family, all the elders of his family work for banks. This rare music interest of Sumit left his family in confusion. To make it more worse, the boy started learning the cooking as well. He followed many cookery channels and cooked at home. However, he was getting better day by day in both cooking and music. At all times, he turned the whole kitchen into a big mess after his cooking. His mother was fed up of his number of entries into her kitchen. She used to yell asking him to learn housekeeping as well along with cooking!

Shaun was always busy mimicking the actors. His family was fed up of his acts, they wanted him to be an intellectual student but the boy had no interest in studies. All he used to score was average marks with least preparations. Recently, he developed new style that is to talk with TV commercial tag lines, which was the most funny thing. Many times he made his family proud with his acts in school and family get-togethers but their mentality was different. They used to think that these things are not useful for living, they wanted him to get a respected job to earn good income in the future.

Gourav was the most obedient boy, when it comes to the family and its business. He does not show any interest in girls at school but lately, he became mischievous, he watched hell lot of special films to enjoy his fantasy time in his room. It started, when he was wandering with dull face all around, the boys asked him the reason. 'Well…guys…I notice my inner wears are sticky and wet, every morning when I wake up! I am scared.' He revealed to the boys. That was a LOL moment for all the boys. They rolled laughing for minutes and later they disclosed him the secret, which made this miser Marwadi spend on tissue boxes.

After the birthday party, love was only in the air, they all rarely met. Aarzoo was forcefully taken for the trip to Dubai along with her family. Rest of the guys except Shaun went to their natives. Sandeep was bored to tears waiting and missing Mansi. She went to her maternal grandmother's home to spend remaining holidays.

During those years, Dadi lived in the native itself. The house was 60 years old, built by Sandeep's great grandfather. She lived all alone, the happening old woman had no enemies in her locality. Everyone loved her active and funny nature. Except some relatives, who wanted to take the position on the old house, Sandeep's father had asked her to live along with them but she never showed any interest because of those relatives. If she moves out of the house, they will take the charge on it and she never wanted that.

Sandeep's mother thought of sending him to Dadi for few days. He asked Shaun to accompany him, as all the others were out of the town. After a night journey boys reached Dadi's home. Dadi sent a boy from her locality to pick up Sandeep from the bus stop, he met his Dadi after 2 years. Dadi prepared all the favourite dishes for the boys. Her open minded bold nature got Sandeep very close to her. Until that time, he had never realised that his Dadi was so cool.

It was very hot climate over there, Sandeep and Shaun decided to sleep on the terrace, cool breeze of Neem tree beside his house was no less than any air conditioner. Dadi got water for the boys on the terrace and told them the flash back stories of his Dadaji and childhood stories of his father and his cousins. After an hour of chit chat she started going down.

While going back she uttered 'Keep in mind one thing! Don't mess my chaddars and bedsheets in the night.'

'Dadi we are not kids to pee while asleep.' Sandeep replied by laughing.

'That is why I am saying boy. I raised 3 sons and I know what will mess the bed sheets at this age.' Saying that with a laugh, she moved towards the stairs. Sandy and Shaun looked at each other astonished.

Next day Dadi asked local boy to show them all the historical places of the city. They also went to Badami, Ihole and Pattadkallu along with Dadi and some of her neighbours. All these days, Sandeep loved being with his Dadi. He asked her to go with him and live in Bangalore with everyone but she wasn't ready for that and explained the reason to him.

Dadi asked him about all his friends. With his body language on Mansi talks, it did not take much time for Dadi to understand his feelings for Mansi.

His love life never came up in front of his family yet, but Dadi caught him very easily. She said 'From the day you were born, I always said that you are re-incarnation of your Dadaji, and with your nature you proved it.' Dadi told him the story of his Dadaji. Sandy's Dadaji was just like him, who loved women and proved it with two wives, in whom Dadi was the first and second wife's sons were also raised by Dadi, since she died very soon. After growing up, she gave equal parts in the property to her step-children as well. Still they kept one eye on the old house and some lacks of rupees saved by Dadi. Her strict and bold nature made them to stay behind and not raise any complaints but the greedy minds always desire for more money.

She advised Sandeep to be loyal and not to play with any girl's heart. At that age he did not get the depth of her advice. Those holidays vanished by amplifying the bond between Dadi and Sandeep.

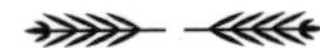

TEN

Schools re-opened with big board 10th studies. Most of the students started involving with their studies seriously, whereas the love birds were at an advantage that they could meet their beloved regularly.

On the very first day of school, Sandy took a chance of meeting Mansi in the library, the lovers have reunited happily, 'So, I want welcome back present.' he said. Mansi blushed, felt the butterflies all over her stomach, she was speechless and covered her face with her hands. Sandy slowly took off her hands and smiled 'You know what? You take my heart away when you do this, I feel awesome when I see you shy…being with you is my present. If I stay more, I may lose control.' He said and turned back to walk out from there. She held his hand, he stopped with a smile. She came close to him slowly and kissed on his cheeks, 'This is your present.' blushing she said. He smiled, looked into her eyes 'It's wonderful… Can I get more?' he asked in his mischievous tone. She pushed him back and said 'That's all for now. Bye' she walked away from there. 'Hey Mansi, wait…' he said stopping her. 'I have to go before someone finds us here like this… bye.' She left by smiling at him. He looked her walking standing from there, her walk wasn't exactly the cat walk but she looked beautiful from back as well, in that blue knee length skirt, her legs were covered with socks and shoes, which didn't show much of her legs, and clean check shirt of school uniform had maintained well the decency of her figure.

Aarzoo and Shreya enjoyed all the time of combined studies in library, sitting together in class by holding each other's hand. Whereas, the others lives were as usual juggling between school and their extra-curricular activities.

Mansi's kiss had mesmerised Sandeep and in the same evening he went to see her. He faced her father in the living room. 'Sandeep, how come you are here at this time?' Manoj asked him in his tough voice. 'Hello uncle, I…I came to take some notes from Mansi, is she inside?' Sandeep asked hesitantly. 'On the very first day of school, you missed the notes?' he asked one more question. But Sandeep was also a champion in rapid-fire, 'Yeah, actually, the sports selection was going on during the periods and I missed the class in that, so am here.' He lied easily. Hearing his voice Mansi ran out from her room towards the living area and stood still looking at her father interrogating him. Sandeep stood there confidently looking at her father. 'Hmm, Mansi get your books here and help Sandeep.' Her father said with strong tone. 'Here?' Sandeep asked shockingly for sitting in front of him. Mansi's mother was cooking inside the kitchen and Grandma cutting the vegetables while watching television. 'Yes, any problem?' Manoj asked. 'Actually TV is on and can't concentrate, that's why…it's ok uncle, I will manage.' Sandeep mumbled. 'Let them read inside the room, I can't watch my serial in their chatting.' The fairy Grandmother said in the favour of duo. 'Hmm, go inside, keep the door open' Manoj said toughly. 'Of course uncle, Thank you!' Sandeep smiled and winked looking at Mansi, she blushed. While entering the room, 'What are you doing here?' Mansi whispered. 'I came to see you.' He said with his cute smile. 'Ok, listen my father has kept an eye on us, so don't do anything which will get us into trouble.' She said with her soft and firm voice. 'Ok…ok…I am just here to talk to you and do nothing.' He said convincingly.

Sandeep opened the book and started writing on his notebook to show her father, who was in living room 'How come your Dad is home so early today?' he whispered peeking into his book. 'Maybe he thought that a mischievous boy will bang in today.' She said and winked her eye. 'I couldn't resist myself to see you' he said. 'Why?' she blushed with question. Staring her 'I wanted some more presents.' He said. 'Shut up and look into books.' she muttered. 'It should be a give and take relationship. So I want to return it with interest.' He smiled and moved close to her. She got up from the chair beside the study table and sat on the bed 'Don't you dare do anything. Papa has kept his eyes and ears here only.' She muttered. 'Relax, you will make him sure with your moves.' he said and sat on the chair comfortly. She kept quiet. 'Don't be so quiet, just pretend that you are teaching me something. Come and sit here on your chair or else I will come on the bed.' He blinked his eye. She got up with her book and sat on the chair. She opened the chemistry book and started explaining him the chapter. He slowly held her hand 'This chemistry is better than that one.' He said. 'Sandy, please.' She begged and took her hands off. 'Ok, ok…I will go home.' He got up with his book. 'Ssshh, don't go so early, he might doubt. Just sit for some more time.' She said softly. He sat on the chair staring her in fake anger. It was seven in the evening, the dusk covered all over. Suddenly, the power went off and taking the chance, quickly Sandeep grabbed Mansi's chair and kissed her.

'Don't worry, I will switch the emergency light. Be seated.' Manoj uttered from outside. His voice did not bother Sandeep, he kissed Mansi, whereas Mansi was juggling to push him back in the fear of getting caught. Before the emergency light spread its beam, Sandeep sat back on his chair. Manoj got lamp in Mansi's room and kept it on the table and went back to the living room arranging for another lamp. There was complete noise by all the members of home outside searching for candles, blaming the electricity board for switching off the power anytime. Mansi's heartbeats had doubled. 'Are you nuts…what if Papa caught us like that? I hate you!' She muttered. 'But he did not, relax.' Sandeep said. Mansi was mad at him but in the same time she was also happy inside with his naughty act and kept quiet. 'Ok, I am sorry, I couldn't control myself. It just happened like I was waiting for this moment. Sorry!' he whispered. There was a silence for few seconds in the room. Sandeep got up from his seat and started going out. Mansi couldn't stop him with hesitation of that moment.

'You finished so early?' Manoj asked him, when he went out. 'Yeah, somewhat. The power went off, so will take the rest of the notes tomorrow in the class.' He said. Mansi rushed into the living room. 'It's dark outside, wait here till the power comes.' Manoj said. Obeying his order Sandeep sat on the sofa. Mansi got one book in her hand and sat in the living room beside her Granny. She kept looking at him in the beam of candles but Sandeep did not look at her. He was angry as he took her cautious behaviour on his ego and Mansi realised that. She wrote something on the notebook and gave it to him by saying 'Here, some notes for you.' He took that book from her hand and opened it *'I am Sorry, I didn't mean to hurt you. I am just scared of my Papa, hope you understand.'* He kept that note and the power came back. Sandeep got up from the sofa and went out by taking a leave from all but he did not look at Mansi. Mansi knew that he was mad at her. She thought that she will handle it next day in school.

But the coming day, everything was about to change. Sandeep was still upset on Mansi. He knew that it was his fault of kissing her but his ego was bigger, which was not letting him to patch up with her. The whole gang was trying to convince him without knowing the situation but he was not ready to talk on that.

Bindu, a girl from 'A' division in 7th grade, who got transferred to Mysore 3 years back due to her father's job, had shifted back to Bangalore this year, she took admission in the same class of the gang and she turned more beautiful in these years. Complete makeover from 'Ugly Betty' to beautiful Bindu has hypnotized all the boys in the class, it was like a movie or a fairy tale for many. Even Sandeep couldn't take out his eyes from her beauty.

Bindu played the role of Sandeep's wife in a school drama during 6th grade, after that she was known as 'Sandy's wife' in the entire school. The girl with braces on teeth and no good looks was happiest to be addressed as most popular boy's wife in school. While entering the class her eyes searched for Sandeep, they stopped on him with a big smile and relaxing breath. She walked fast and sat on the table beside him. 'Hi Sandy, how are you?' waving her hand, she greeted him without giving attention to the class teacher. 'Hi, I am fine, how are you?' he asked. 'SILENCE!' strong voice of Mrs. Fernandise made everyone quiet.

Bindu scanned Sandeep with her eyes. He has grown up, his new hair style was complimenting his handsome face, his fair and attractive looks grown up along with him, his straight and athletic body was good enough to attract any girl in that age, his small moustaches started peeking out on his upper lips, which mentioned that he was turning into a man. His charm wasn't vanished as the other guys in the class, who got pimples and looked ugly in their teenage years, she smiled staring his looks. On the other hand, Sandeep couldn't resist himself staring at Bindu. She looked more beautiful, her figure changed and complexion became fairer. The land of Wodeyars made her look like a princess. They both smiled while the class was on.

Last evening incident gave him a thought that he should get close to Bindu to create the feeling of envy in the heart of Mansi. On the other hand, many girls were jealous of Bindu already. The class got over and Sandeep went to the badminton court for practice with Preeti and other co-players. Bindu joined the team as well since she played for her school in Mysore and won many medals, she started playing along with Sandeep in mixed doubles. Sandeep's personality and good looks attracted her already. She knew about his weakness of girls but she didn't know about his current affair with Mansi. Sandeep was annoyed with Mansi and he didn't give second thought in getting close to Bindu. Preeti observed everything silently.

During the canteen hours, everyone was having lunch together. Sandeep entered along with Bindu and joined the group. Mansi, as well as everyone greeted Bindu, Shaun took Sandeep in a corner 'What are you doing?' he asked. 'Come to have lunch, I guess!' mockingly he replied. 'Why are you getting close to her?' Shaun asked again. 'Relax, we just finished the game and came to canteen, that's it!' Sandeep said. 'Oh, wow… 'That's it?' I have been observing you since morning. You are avoiding Mansi and getting close to Bindu.' He muttered smiling at others sitting away from them. 'Buddy, why don't you find someone for yourself, so that you can get busy…' Sandeep said sarcastically. 'I want to!! But you are not leaving any girl in the class…NO…wait a minute! In the whole SCHOOL! You want everyone here…I am afraid one day I will also become Gay! Without any girl!' Shaun replied ironically. Sandy laughed out loudly 'Well, in that case stay away from me!!' he said. 'Ha ha!!…Very funny!' Shaun made an angry face. 'There are so many girls in the class. You never try! They will get close to you if you try...just by staring at them doesn't work! You are a talented guy, approach them with your witty mind...' Sandy said patting his shoulder. 'They all want to be with 'Sandy'!!' He replied. 'I can't help with that, now... let's go for the lunch, as I am hungry.' Sandy replied by jumping his shoulders and walked towards the table.

Mansi offered Sandeep her lunch box, she carried his favourite carrot halwa in her tiffin but Sandeep did not take a bite of that and sat beside Bindu. That was the beginning of heart break for Mansi. After the lunch Sandeep went along with Bindu and some other students and everyone observed that. 'Did you see that?' Shreya asked. 'Yeah, She is hot!' Aarzoo replied. 'What?' Shreya uttered at Aarzoo. 'What...no...no...I didn't mean that way...I mean...just look at her, she was ugly like *Jassi* before and now she is BEAUTIFUL.' Aarzoo justified her point. 'Oh...Yeah, you find her beautiful?' Shreya asked sarcastically. 'Of course she is, but not my type...' Aarzoo said swallowing the saliva. Everyone laughed to divert Mansi's mind.

It had been more than a month, since Sandeep wasn't talking to Mansi. Initially, he wanted to jealous Mansi by getting close with Bindu but he started liking Bindu. In the same way, Bindu also got close to him. Home visiting, badminton practice, combined study, everything started between the duo. Bindu was a nice girl, with soft nature and humble behaviour. She was never liked by anybody all these years, it was her dream to be with a guy like Sandeep since 6th grade school drama, hence, she was popular in the class over the night, only because she played his wife's character in that drama. Sandeep's closeness created many thoughts in her mind and melted her heart. One fine day, while practicing the badminton in the court, Bindu thought of expressing her attraction to him, it was a good time since no one were around. 'Can I ask you something?' she mumbled. 'Yeah sure.' he said, wiping his sweat after the play. 'Are you seeing someone these days?' she hit a straight question, which rang the bell in Sandeep's mind, he paused and surprisingly, he looked at her. 'I think, I've started liking you' she spoke out before getting his reply. Her eyes hypnotised him and she came close to him. He swallowed his saliva and hesitated to kiss her. She was extremely close to him and was about to kiss him, by that time Preeti entered the court by opening the door, and they got separated within a fraction of a second. Preeti got the idea of what they were up to 'JP. Sir is on leave today, so no science class. If you want to practice more you can go ahead or else, monitor is conducting science questionnaire in the class, you can attend that.' looking at Sandeep she said.

'I will practice for some more time.' Straight away Bindu replied. Sandeep was in an awkward situation in front of Preeti, he felt guilty deep inside 'I will go to the class.' He said and left from the court before both the girls could ask anything to him. 'You can practice with me' said Preeti to Bindu, and stopped her going behind Sandeep. Bindu felt weird by Sandeep's behaviour but concentrated on playing. While practicing she asked about everyone in the gang to Preeti. Bindu wasn't ready to ask about Sandeep's affairs so she did not ask anything about him. Preeti genuinely replied all her questions without any grudge in her mind. The gang had nothing against Bindu, since she was the new girl, who doesn't know the situation, everyone were angry on Sandeep who was avoiding Mansi without any reason.

Meanwhile, Sandeep went to class and he saw Mansi with a book standing near the board, while entering the class. As per the rules, every student should take permission from the class teacher to enter the class, in the absence of teacher they have to ask the permission from the monitor. Sandeep completely forgot that class monitor was none other than, Mansi. It was more than a month he did not say a word to Mansi. Now he was in a complete awkward situation. That moment, whole class looked at him, who was standing outside the class, everyone started teasing him with line, 'Now who's gonna talk!?' Sandeep turned around and thought of going back to the court but he saw principal walking towards the class, he had no option but to rush back in class. 'May…May I come in?' he mumbled. Mansi's heart melted with his voice, blushing she looked at him, without wasting a second she said 'Yes.' For her, it was welcome back invitation for him. He entered the class, the whole class shouted 'Oooooooowwwww.' Sandeep uttered 'SShhhhhh!! Principal is walking this side.' Everyone got back to the questionnaire for group discussion. Sandeep felt relieved after single line with Mansi, he was guilty as well for liking Bindu.

That evening after the school Mansi wanted to talk to Sandeep but before she packed her bag, he went out with Shaun and Sumit. Mansi stood still with a broken heart. Understanding the situation Mandar came to Mansi 'You need any help?' he asked. 'No, I am fine.' Mansi said and packed her bag, he saw the tear dropped on the bench.

He rushed towards Sandeep and caught him in the garden area, 'Just be here, I need to talk to you. I will be back. Don't go!' he stopped him there, and ran towards the class. Sandeep stood waiting for him, within few minutes he brought Mansi there 'She needs to talk to you, do you have 5 minutes to listen to her?' he asked him sarcastically. Mansi stopped him saying 'Mandar, just leave it. Please…' Sandeep watched them, without any word. Mandar said 'No, Mansi, you guys sort out whatever is going on between you. I can't see you guys like this yaar. Everything is messed up after you guys stopped talking to each other. Still 5 minutes is there for the bus to arrive, so just sort it out...' and he left from there.

Mansi stood still, expecting Sandeep to do the talking. Sandeep rubbed his forehead with his fingers, he was confused, from where to begin the guilt talk. She looked at him, taking a long breath 'Is it Bindu?' she asked. 'What' dumbfounded he asked. 'You heard me.' she said staring the floor, hiding her pain. 'Ahem... I don't know.' He said scratching his head. 'Say it Sandy, I have been observing you...first I thought you are doing it to make me jealous but now a days I can see, it's something more.' she said looking at him. 'I really wanted to make you jealous by getting close to her....' He paused. 'Congrats! You did that, I am jealous...I am getting nightmares about both of you and it's haunting me. Now what?' She asked. 'I am sorry Mansi. I didn't mean to hurt you...I...I...' he was speechless to explain his dishonesty. 'I understood. It's not working anymore... Right?' she asked. 'No, I ...I think I am not the right guy...for you.' Hesitating he said staring the floor. She walked from there without a word.

ELEVEN

It was more than 3 months after the incident. Sandeep had no single word with Mansi. The gang was completely separated during these days, every scenario looked like they all were never together. Preeti did not stop talking to Sandeep only for the reason that she could taunt him reminding his guilt, which Sandeep always understood but he ignored her. Mansi knew that she had to see this day before going in to a relationship with Sandeep. She was a strong girl, after many days of crying in the bathroom and sleepless nights she recovered. She always felt that she was better before disclosing her love in front of Sandeep. On the other hand, Sandeep started seeing Bindu after hesitation of a month.

Aarzoo, Shreya, Mandar and Preeti always accompanied Mansi. Preeti asked Mandar whether he likes Mansi. 'Yes, she reminds me of my sister, whom I lost 5 years back. However, I have no interest in all this love stuff.' Mandar said. 'I know Mumma's boy' Preeti smiled. 'That's not the exact reason, I never felt anything for you all. You've always been my best buddies.' He genuinely replied. 'Oh, There is no chance for me as well' Preeti said and they both laughed.

The attachment between Aarzoo and Shreya had improved with the time, all they had was pure love for each other. Sumit got close with his music teacher Neeta. Although Neeta never gave him any signal, yet he loved to be with her in his one sided love.

After few weeks Sandeep slowly started talking to Mansi but only as a friend. This time the friendship was not that close as it was earlier. It was only for studies and notes exchange. Mansi, a heartbroken girl did not complain single time and stopped envying Bindu.

One day, Bindu invited Sandeep when her family was away from home, the reason she told him was to study maths, he went happily. Bindu's mother expired when she was eight, she was raised by her father and step-mother. Bindu never loved her step-mother, who was constantly partial towards her own son. She told the entire story to Sandeep, not to gain his sympathy but she felt good sharing her grief with him. Her step-mother was good with Bindu, only for the intention that she wanted Bindu to be married with her brother, who was doing his MBA and had an eye on her always, Bindu hated him. That reminded Sandeep the story of Shreya, he thought, *what is the matter with all the relatives? They are so much in a hurry to be married in relatives!*

After solving some maths problems, Sandeep got up from his chair to leave. Bindu held his hand and asked 'You really want to leave now?' He looked at her with his naughty smile 'No, but it's already eight, and what if your parents come home and find me here in their absence?' he spoke with concern. 'They are out for a movie and dinner, they will be home only after 10.' She said smiling. 'They went without you, for dinner? They took your brother but you…Strange!' He was shocked. His parents never left him or Ramya at home for movies and dinners. It was him, who denies going with them many times. 'Welcome to my world' said Bindu. 'What you will eat?' he asked. 'Maggi and some fruits or juice' said Bindu with an artificial smile. Sandeep felt sad, he hugged her to console her but within seconds they kissed. Sandeep felt her soft body with all the curves and Bindu wrapped her arms around his neck and felt his chest. They kissed passionately and fell on the bed. He looked into her eyes and recognised her feelings, blazing inside those brown eyes, which were similar to his own emotions. 'I LOVE YOU!' She said passionately holding his face. 'Love you too…and I want you!' He whispered. She nodded with yes, soon they both undressed each other with lightning speed and both stared at each other and were unable to wait a moment to have each other, they grabbed each other. It was first time for both of them, he had done many things with Arushi year ago but did not lose virginity. He never got the chance to do anything with Mansi. He respected her more than any girls he dated and never hurried for anything with her. Their love story ended before the start, only because of his ego and greasy heart, which slipped on Bindu in no time.

Bindu was on top of the world, she made love for the first time in life and that too with her prince charming. Sandeep was happy as well, he had dreamt of doing it with her from a long time. After one hour Sandeep grabbed his clothes from the ground and covered himself. Bindu also grabbed her dress from the ground and got dressed up. Sandeep went inside the bathroom and she cleaned the bed as it was before. He got ready to go, Bindu asked him to stay for dinner, which he couldn't refuse. She prepared Maggi and boiled some eggs, there was much romance in the kitchen as well. They both had dinner along with some juice. Sandeep left from there after few more obsessive kisses. He was happy all the way to home. Bindu went back to the room and cherished the loving moments.

He rode Ramya's scooter to Bindu's home, he parked the scooter and entered inside the house, where Mansi was waiting for him. He was shocked to see her in his home at that time. 'Where were you this long? You said you are going to bring maths notes from Shaun's home! But Shaun's mother said you didn't go there?' Sandeep's mother uttered when he entered the living room. 'I changed my mind and went to library.' Sandeep lied without hesitating. 'Can't you inform us? This poor girl is waiting for you from so long for her notes! We searched all your room for her note-book but did not find it!' Asha (Sandeep's mother) uttered again. 'It's ok aunty.' Mansi softly calmed the angry mommy.

Sandeep rushed towards his room to bring Mansi's science book. He searched all over and remembered he kept it inside the bag to return the same to her in the school and forgot to return. He hurriedly took out the book from bag and came out of the room and gave it to her. 'Sorry, I forgot to give you in school today' he apologised. 'It's ok, actually I wanted to take it from you in school itself, but before I came out from the class, you left from the first bus…And today is Saturday, tomorrow I have to finish new chapter and home work so came to take it back from you now.' She explained softly. 'Oh. Sorry again…and Thanks' he said with a smile. She noticed a special glow on his face but did not dig into the matter. 'It's ok. I will go now. Good night!' she said softly to him and voiced 'Good night aunty!' at Sandeep's mother, who was in the kitchen. 'Have food and go beta.' His mother said from inside. 'No thanks aunty, mummy is waiting for me, have to go.' She said. 'Sandy, drop her to home, it's too late.' his mother ordered him from the kitchen. 'Ok Mom.' He said obeying her order.

While on the way, Sandeep stopped the scooter near the garden, which was exactly in the middle of both houses. He never apologized with Mansi for breaking up with her and on the contrary, he was never comfortable with Bindu when Mansi was around. That day, after making love with Bindu he faced Mansi, and his guilt of breaking her heart made him restless. 'What happened? Why you stopped?' Mansi asked him. 'Mansi, I wanted to talk to you.' he mumbled. 'It's 9.30 already and mummy is waiting for me, I have to rush.' she said avoiding his talk. 'I know, I won't take much time…can we sit in the garden?...just in case….if someone see us here at this time…' he asked. 'Ok, but not for long.' she couldn't refuse. He was silent for few seconds 'I am sorry Mansi.' he said at a stretch. 'For what?' she asked him casually. 'You know, I shouldn't have broken your heart.' He hesitated. 'Oh…That is in the past. I forgot that now.' She said without looking at him. 'But I am still in guilt, whenever I see you I feel like slapping myself. I can imagine how much you were hurt and…' He paused while talking, Mansi interrupted 'Look Sandy, that's all past. I don't want to remember anything, just forget it. You moved on with Bindu and I moved on with my studies. So let's forget it and just be friends like before…I have nothing against you in my heart. I always wished for your happiness and I am glad that you are happy with her.' She mumbled. 'Aahhh, that's a relief! I was so worried…even after we started talking I was always uncomfortable with you...' He said and they both smiled. 'I think we should go now' she reminded. 'Yeah sure, let's go...' he started walking. While starting the bike he said 'By the way, I wasn't in the library all this time.' He said. 'Then, where were you?' She asked. 'I was at Bindu's home and today my dream came true!' he said sitting on the scooter and started it. Her heartbeats raised, 'Oh...great, Congrats!' she said and sat on the scooter, her heart cried and she was broken into pieces inside. Whatever she said in the garden was a pure lie, she never forgot him.

They reached her home, her mother was waiting for her on the door. Broken hearted, she got down from the bike and ran inside the house. He took off saying bye to her mother. Her grandmother had already slept after her dinner. Her father was sitting in the living room. Mansi rushed into bathroom before any interrogation from her parents. She closed the bathroom door and opened the tap, water started flowing in the bucket from tap, and she sat on the stool and cried like a small baby. She cursed herself for falling in love with Sandeep. *'Go away from my heart Sandy!!'* she muttered while crying.

'Come fast Mansi, let's have dinner' Mansi's mother uttered from outside. Mansi washed her face in a hurry and came out wiping her face. She sat on the dining table along with her mother. 'What happened, don't read that much. Your eyes are red' her mother garbled. 'No, something went in my eyes while coming back from Sandy's home.' She said. 'What took you so long?' Her father asked. 'Sandy wasn't home, and his family couldn't find my book from his room...So I was waiting for him.' she said with honesty. 'Oh, ok.' He appreciated her honest reply. 'Good that he dropped you, otherwise now a days it's very bad out there...' her mother said. 'Our area is safe, there is nothing to worry...' her father said. There debate continued on the safety of girls till the dinner got over. After having food Mansi went to her room and closed the door.

She couldn't sleep in Sandeep's thoughts, slipped into memorising those good old days. She met him at his home after the school picnic for combined studies for unit tests. The whole gang was studying on his terrace ground, he sat beside her. When whole gang was busy reading for tests, he held her hand tightly, her heart was thumping. She tried to snatch out her hand from his tight fist but she couldn't, she warned him to leave her hand by widening her eyes. He looked at her with cute smile and nodded his head with no. Mandar saw them muttered 'Concentrate only on studies!' everyone started teasing them. 'I am missing Shreya yaar...I feel like killing that old lady...' Aarzoo said missing her. 'Why don't add some slow poison in her prescriptions, your Dad must know some medicines like that. Once the lady is gone you guys are free birds…her father has no interest in her life however...' Shaun said mockingly and the whole gang laughed. 'Shut up…yaar…' Aarzoo said patting him with her book. 'He is right though, if the lady Hitler is dead…one day her Dad will say *Jaa Shreya jaa…Jeele apni zindagi…*' Preeti said mockingly. While everyone was busy having fun, Sandeep whispered in Mansi's ear 'Let's go!' by holding her hand, he pulled her near stairs. Zero bulb flashed dim light on the stairs, no one was around, Ramya was in her room concentrated on her engineering studies and his mother was busy watching her TV serial. He slammed the door behind Mansi and pushed her up against it, letting his hand over her waist. Their heart beats were pounding, and breathing was fast. He moved his hands upwards from her waist, Mansi stopped his hands moving upwards, she held his hands by nodding 'No' she whispered. Their eyes met, 'OK…one kiss?' he requested. 'What if someone finds us here like this?' she mumbled. 'All are busy, please…' he requested leaning towards her face. She couldn't say no and taking a chance, he kissed her.

Suddenly, the door banged from outside…Mansi woke up from her thoughts. She got up and opened the door. It was her mother, she entered the room with a glass of milk 'Drink it before sleeping.' She said and walked out from there. Mansi took long breath, she made up her mind not to think about him anymore and concentrate on studies.

TWELVE

December month arrived and the school tours were up on them. Mandar and Gourav didn't make it for the trip, rest everyone got ready for the tour but Mansi. Her father insisted her to go, since it was a rare tour of Tamil Nadu with cheapest expenditure, covering wonderful places like Ooty, Rameshwaram, Kanyakumari, Tanjaore etcetera. Mansi couldn't refuse looking at her father's excitement. Meanwhile, everyone were shocked hearing the eighth wonder, Shreya's Grandma had opened her heart this time, she approved for the tour without any pleading. Shreya as well as Aarzoo were the happiest couple that time. The tour was special because the teachers, who were going to accompany the students, were full of fun. However, boys and girls seating in the bus and sleeping places were arranged separately as usual.

The day arrived, bus started from the school at 10 PM. Preeti accompanied Mansi sitting beside her. Sandeep sat on last seat along with other boys. Bindu was accompanied by some random girl from the class. Though, the gang was upset on Sandeep initially for his breakup with Mansi but soon everyone got along with each other just like old days. They were good with Bindu, as everyone knew it wasn't her fault. Sandeep was desperate for Bindu, her beauty and co-operation in love acts hypnotised him. In the mid-night he planned and sat along with Bindu, had whole night of romance with her. Morning by the sunrise he got back to his seat.

Bus stopped at Ooty. Everyone got down at guest house, after bathing and breakfast the troop went for sightseeing at Ooty lake and Botanical garden. Sandeep had all the romantic time to hold Bindu's hand, taking a chance he kissed her behind a tree in that honeymoon city. The troop had fun clicking pictures and roaming around beautiful garden and boating in lake. Aarzoo and Shreya also had great moments to cherish their romance entire night and day. Heartbroken Mansi, strongly handled her mind and been on the spot with Preeti, Shaun and Sumit. After lunch they halted at coffee estate and had a great time clicking more pictures. Sandeep made it to re-unite with the gang by his jokes and innocent face during the day. By the evening they all got fresh in a hotel and after having dinner they started towards Rameshwaram in the night. Sandeep had a great option again in the night to be with Bindu.

In the morning, bus stopped in front of the guest house near the temple. Everyone halted at guest house and changed their clothes. They were instructed to lock their luggage and cameras in the lockers and walk with teachers. First they all went on the beach of Rameshwaram. It was a quiet beach without any waves, teachers hired some priests to perform rituals in the name of all the students. After all the rituals everyone along with teachers, took a dip in the sea and followed the priest. After a walk of few minutes with wet body in chilling cold climate, they entered Rameshwaram Shiva temple. Before taking the *darshan* of lord Shiva, everybody passed through 22 wells inside the temple and took bath from the pious water of those wells. The men standing on the well fetched the water from well and poured it on every student with the buckets, taking a bath with cold water in that cold climate and walking with wet body chilled everyone. All the 22 wells are freshwater wells. The miracle is that each of them taste differently, having little salinity though very close to the sea. Aarzoo being a Muslim and Shaun being a Catholic did not hesitate any moment to visit and show their devotion for Hindu Gods. They performed all the rituals with heartfull of devotion. Shreya was very impressed with her beloved's worldly nature.

After taking bath from all the wells they took darshan of Lord Shiva. The story of this Shiva Linga says, it is made by Lord Rama to take blessings from Shiva for building the *Ram setu* (Rama's Bridge made of stones by his army of monkeys) for reaching Lanka, before marching a war against Ravan. Rameshwaram is one of 12 Jyotirlinga's (12 auspicious Shiva linga's) of India.

After the *darshan* everyone came back to the guest house and changed their clothes, however it's a tradition to donate those clothes to needy poor people and some of the students including Sandeep donated their clothes. They all had lunch after getting fresh, everyone jumped on the food since they did not have anything since morning. After finishing lunch they had some time for shopping. And later they started towards Kanyakumari. Mansi brought home made snacks in her bag and she offered pouches of snacks to all her friends while in the bus.

Bus reached Kanyakumari by the night. Troop rested in guest house, where the cooks got busy preparing *Bisibele bhat* for dinner. Sandeep was hungry by that time, he was getting impatient for food. Mansi understood his starvation, she took out pouch of laddoos from her bag and gave it to him. Sandeep ate all of them and vanquished his hunger till the dinner got ready, he thanked Mansi countless times for laddoos. Some students went for shopping along with teachers. Bindu felt envy on Sandeep's closeness with Mansi, she went out along with teachers and bought some packets of snacks and packed them in her bag for the future starvation of

Sandeep.

Next morning, everyone got ready and had Idli in the breakfast and started for deity Kanyakumari temple. After 2 hours of queue they got the *darshan* of idol and moved towards the ocean. They all caught a ferry to Vivekanad *kendra*, it's a yoga and meditation centre built on the island of an ocean. Beauty of the ocean from that point was amazing. One can see merging of all 3 water bodies into one, Arabian Sea, Indian Ocean and Bay of Bengal's tri-colour view is simply breath taking. Troop was happy that they were all standing on the edge of India from where they can even see a glimpse of Sri Lanka.

While on the Vivekanda Kendra island, Ms. Soubhagya told the story of Kanyakumari to her students. The story says, Kanyakumari, a village deity wished to marry Lord Shiva and she was getting ready for the marriage. But other Gods were against this marriage hence, her purpose was to kill a demon, who got a boon to be killed only by virgin goddess, Kanyakumari. If she marries then her virginity would be lost, thus, they stopped Shiva for marrying her. Broken hearted deity cries and all her wedding makeup drowns into the ocean, that is why they say, the ocean separated in multiple colours. Angry and disappointed goddess killed the demon and stood there forever virgin, that is why she is called Kanyakumari (Virgin girl).

Hearing the story, Sandeep's eyes searched for Bindu and traced her face in the crowd, she was totally involved in listening to the story. Mischievous smile appeared on his face, he whispered 'virginity and marriage are not connected to each other'. Mansi was standing beside him and heard his comment. He was blushing, she understood what he was pointing and unwittingly her jealousy vanished and she grinned.

They all meditated for few minutes in the meditation hall. Sandeep, Shaun, Aarzoo and Sumit could not concentrate even for a second. They came out of the meditation hall and laughed for long without any reason, they cherished that happiness after a long time. After everyone came out they clicked pictures all around with different poses. Sandeep clicked many pictures along with gang and especially Mansi. Bindu was bit disappointed with his closeness towards Mansi.

While on the ferry, Shaun vomited all the idlis he'd dumped in his gigantic stomach, which disgusted everyone with utterings 'Eewwwww' and 'Yucckkkkks'. They all shopped on the port, Bindu bought a shell embossed her name along with Sandeep's. Mansi bought key chains for full group embossing their names on them.

After the lunch they all started for Madurai, bus was filled with all the fun of *Antakshari* and many other games. Sandeep did not involve himself in romancing with Bindu, instead, he utilised all his time laughing with the gang. All the bitterness in their friendship seemed like gone astray. They reached Madurai guest house in the night. Before sleeping everyone played games again near the camp fire. Bindu asked permission from teacher to go back to bus as she'd forgotten her bag in the bus and walked from there, while going she gesticulated Sandeep to come with her. Gladly he followed her, escaping from the eyes of teachers.

Bus was parked in a lonely place behind the guest house, it wasn't locked and Bindu got into the bus, street lamp's dim light was peeking inside the bus through the windows. Bindu stood inside, Sandeep entered in uttering 'Wow!! It's lonely and it's ROMANTIC!' 'Why are you behaving oddly?' Bindu asked Sandeep on a serious note. 'What?' He asked in return for her unexpected question. 'Don't try to be innocent, I am observing you from yesterday, you are totally avoiding me!' She complained. 'C'mon, there is nothing like that, it's just I am having fun with everyone.' He justified. 'Ok, enjoy with them…I am just a girlfriend right? When you want romance you come to me and for enjoyment you are go to them right?' she asked in a high tone. 'What? Are you out of your mind? Do you know what you are talking?' he asked her. She started walking from there, he grabbed her around his arms 'What do you want? Should I stop talking to my old buddies?' he asked softly. 'Leave me Sandy!' she replied angrily. 'Oh, now I understand, you are basically JEALOUS!' he said smiling. 'What? NO, why should I be jealous?' she said with her eyes down. 'Look at me.' he demanded. 'Leave me Sandy, I want to go.' She ordered him. He grabbed her tightly in his arms, pushing her towards the pole, he kissed her, in return she kissed him and embraced her hands around his neck 'I love you!' she said after kissing him, he smiled and hugged her tightly. 'Can we meet tonight?' he asked. 'No way, our rooms are very far and there are so many students in each room.' She mumbled. 'Then stay for some more time here.' he requested. 'No, we should go now...that driver will come here any moment.' she said pushing him back. He kissed her again, after few seconds they went back to the guest house. Bindu walked in first and after few minutes Sandeep joined the group without giving any chance of doubt to the teachers. Everyone in group noticed them but nobody uttered a word.

Next morning, they all visited Madurai Meenaxi Devi temple. The temple has 11 entrances and all of them look similar. Clean and well maintained temple has beautiful idol of goddess Meenaxi. It was built during the period of Pandya kings. The temple's atmosphere is very calm and peaceful inside. Shreya held Aarzoo's hand inside the temple, she was mumbling some prayers, she joined her hands and prayed for long time in front of the divinity. 'You seem different today, what did you ask for?' Looking at her, Aarzoo asked. 'They say we should not disclose what we prayed for.' Shreya replied with a smile. 'And you think goddess will bless you the boon?' Aarzoo asked again smiling. 'She already blessed me...' Shreya said holding her hand. 'And still you are praying!' Aarzoo stared her. 'Hmm, I asked for your happiness!' she smiled. Aarzoo took a long breath and said 'You are my happiness! I am always happy if you are with me.' Their eyes met. Preeti interrupted in the middle whispering 'Don't you dare to kiss now, the whole world is around.' Shreya blushed. 'We know that, Idiot!' Aarzoo said to Preeti patting her. 'Just thought of reminding you!' mockingly Preeti said. They started to Tanjavur from Madurai after the lunch and reached the guest house there. Sandeep had least option to sit along with Bindu in day time travelling. On the contrary, Aarzoo and Shreya had cherished great moments by holding each other's hands and even kissing sometimes while everyone were sleeping in the bus and had endless talks in the long journey. Tanjavur is famous for its Brihadeshwara Temple or Raja Rajeshwara Temple. It was built 1000 years ago by Chola king Raja Raja Chola. They all wondered hearing the story of building the temple and its architecture. Later, they visited Shrirangam, Temple of Lord Vishnu, Trichy and Chidambaram. The richness in temples of Tamil Nadu explains the glory of those ancient empires and their emperor's prosperity and vision. After the entire exploring and enjoyment the trip ended happily.

THIRTEEN

On the very first day of school, after the exciting tour, School board announced that preliminary exams would be conducted within two weeks. Everyone got busy with preliminary exams. Special classes for finishing the portions and revisions increased, Sandeep started reading with full attention, and his meetings with Bindu slowly started vanishing. Bindu wanted to spend some good time with her prince charming, she asked him to come early on coming day at the tutorials so that they can spend some time together before the classes there.

Sandeep promised to meet Bindu in the morning, and he reached class by eight. The corridors were empty, other than a sweeper, there was nobody around. *It is a good place for romance, what is taking Bindu so long!?* A thought came in his mind. Meanwhile, his classmate Vinita ran into him panting and weeping and she went behind Sandeep for protection, quickly two boys followed her. They were strong adults, one boy looked as leader of the other, and they were wearing all expensive accessories like gold chains, bracelets, watches, sun glasses and dressed in denim and t-shirt with jackets. Altogether, they seemed as they belong to a well to do family. Astounded Sandeep stood watching them, while Boss walked ahead and grabbed Vinita's hand and pleaded her to hear him out. 'Please, listen to me!' he requested holding her hand tightly. 'I don't want to hear anything, please go!' uttered Vinita. It continued and Sandeep watched that silently for few more minutes, Vinita wasn't asking for Sandeep's help. Those boys were well built, one knock of a guy could change the diagram of Sandeep's face. When everything was going out of control, Sandeep stood in front of Vinita, 'Excuse me! problem?' He uttered. Sandeep's body was average and he was too young to handle those builder beasts. 'Hey pretty boy! Stay away from this!' other guy warned him showing his finger. Ignoring Sandeep, the Boss was still pleading Vinita. Vinita was always a low profile girl in the school, wheatish complexion, attractive, coming from upper middleclass family, she hardly made any close friend in the school. Sandeep couldn't see that anymore and he held hand of the Boss 'LEAVE HER HAND!' strongly he uttered. The muscular guy pushed him hard and Sandeep fell on the floor and the other guy laughed at him. Sandeep got angry with that push, his temper raised to peak, he looked here and there and saw an iron rod on the corner of the corridor. He kept his bag down and ran quickly to the rod, as the boys were busy with Vinita. Angrily, he held the rod strongly and raged towards the boys, 'Leave her or I will hit you both!' he uttered loudly. 'Hey, easy! You want to hit me? C'mon hit me!' the leader came ahead leaving Vinita's hand. Sandeep was angry, he raised the rod to hit him, by that time 'Sandy, please stay away from all this, they are rascals!' Vinita said. Boss laughed and Sandeep took a quick look at Vinita and grinding his teeth he raised his voice 'Aaaa!!' and lifted the rod to hit the leader, suddenly, other guy pushed Sandeep and his fist loosened but he hit the leader on his elbow. 'You are dead man now! Watch me kicking your ass!' the leader rushed lifting his hand up but quickly Sandeep held the rod in front of him in defence and accidentally the guy hit the rod which hurt him so badly that he fell of the floor screaming. Other boy ran to hit him, Sandeep raised the rod, the boy stood back showing off his hands. The leader uttered 'I am gonna kill you!'

Meanwhile, two men walked in the corridor, they were shop owners of that complex. Looking at them the boys hurriedly ran out from there. Vinita was speechless, she couldn't believe her eyes on the scenario happened there. Leader boy looked at Sandeep in a rage 'Will see you! Bastard!!' he uttered. 'Get lost, Asshole!' Sandeep said. 'What? What did you say?' the leader came back holding his painful hand, and the other boy whispered something in his ears and pulled him back. Vinita held his hand tightly fearing them. 'Asshole!!' Sandeep uttered again to reply him. They both ran from there. The men who came to open the shops asked Sandeep 'Any problem, Son!?' they looked at the boys doubting their identity. The boys ran away from there quickly. Sandeep said 'Nothing Uncle!' and they went inside their shops.

'They live in our lane. He has a mobile shop, every day he follows me wherever I go. Usually, I ignore him but yesterday he had gone too far, I was going to temple and he came in front of me, holding a rose and gifts in his hand. He wants me to be his girlfriend. Luckily, my parents weren't home. Otherwise, they would have scolded me for all that. He has also become friends with my brother and comes home often and keeps on staring at me. He is a son of local businessman and has friendship with some goons. Today, I thought of leaving early so that I wouldn't get to face this monster but he was waiting for me near the class! He started proposing me again and touched me.' Vinita told her story, by sitting on the bench of the corridor.

'Your brother knows about this?' Sandeep asked by sitting beside her. 'No, he will scold me if he comes to know about this.' She said. 'What? Is he mad?' astonished he asked. 'He is like that only yaar. Even my parents are the same… they will stop my education in the middle if they come to know about all this!' she said and paused by closing her eyes. 'What?! I am sorry to say but what kind of people are there in your house? Instead of banishing the bastards like these and protecting their girl they will stop your education!' Sandeep asked her and she started weeping.

Meanwhile, Bindu walked in saying 'Hi! I am sorry! I am late... actually was...' She paused looking at Vinita. Sandeep looked at both the girls and revealed the story to Bindu. 'They may come back again.' Bindu assumed. 'They will! Those boys are dangerous.' said Vinita. 'Let them come, I will see what to do.' Sandeep said looking at the CCTV camera of the corridor. His romance plan became an action packed morning. After the classes he spoke to Preeti, and asked her to call her father who was a police officer. They spoke to him and took his advice. Later, he ran to the server room and requested the admin to give him the CCTV footage of that particular time in the morning. He took the CCTV footage and asked Vinita whether she wants to fight and get rid of the boys or not? For the first time, someone has understood her situation and wanted to help her to come out of her problem. She agreed with the hidden fear.

Sandeep quickly went to Vinita's house. Vinita took the different route in which they don't get to see those boys. Vinita's mother and brother were home. Her brother came angrily when Sandeep entered the house along with Vinita, he raised his hand to hit him but Vinita came in between protecting him. Her mother dragged her hand uttering 'What is the matter with you, come here.' Sandeep was confused to see their reaction, he wasn't getting any idea about what was happening. After few minutes of pulling hands and shouting, Sandeep uttered loudly 'Stop it! Would you please tell me what's happening here?' Everyone got silent. 'Oh! You want to know what's happening. I will show you.' Vinita's brother came ahead uttering, Sandeep stopped him by pushing him back. 'We will tell you boy but after breaking your leg.' The boys walked inside, grinning.

They were the same boys, with whom Sandeep fought that morning. Looking at them Vinita hid herself behind her mother. Young Sandeep understood the whole game of the boys. He felt pity on Vinita's family, for trusting the scoundrels instead of their own girl. 'Oh! I understand. Welcome, I was about to come to you boys.' he said beaming at them. Vinita's family wondered when Sandeep wasn't afraid of anybody, he stood alone in the middle of everyone smiling fearlessly. He looked at Vinita's mother 'Aunty, I want to use your DVD player, may I...' without waiting for her reply, he went to the TV and inserted the disk into DVD. The boys were surprised as well to see what he wanted to show to everyone. Vinita's brother came forward 'What the hell are you doing?' he asked. 'Wait a minute... you will see.' Sandeep said with calm voice and played the CD.

It showed the clipping of the morning, from the entrance of class till the action. How the boys followed Vinita and how they were torturing her by pulling her hand and touching her body. They all saw how Sandeep defended her singlehandedly. When the clipping got over Vinita spoke out gaining all the guts in her voice, 'This Rocky is following me from months. He comes home for staring me.... ' the brave girl explained the entire story to her family. She added that Sandeep is her classmate who hardly spoke to her but today because of him she was saved by those monsters.

Vinita's family understood the situation and her brother was raged on the boys later. Before those boys could escape from there, police came inside and arrested them. Police asked Vinita and her family to launch a formal complaint against the boys and left from there with the culprits taking a copy of the CD from Sandeep.

After their departure, Vinita expressed her gratitude to Sandeep. Her mother and brother were embarrassed for their previous action. They were all wondering how come the police have come on time, Sandeep explained how he planned everything with the help of Preeti. Vinita's mother accepted her mistake, she added that Sandeep behaved like Vinita's own brother by saving her from those idiots. That was little disappointing for him, he opened his big eyes widely gulping the saliva, apart from his own sister Ramya, he never visualized any good looking girl as his sister. Vinita knew about his nature, she beamed looking at his weird expressions.

By the end of January, prelims got over. It was last year of school and friends were about to move on different paths of their future in the coming year. Sandeep thought of arranging a party for the gang before the farewell from the school, his birthday was perfect for that, the day was 14th of February. Sandeep requested his Dadi to come for it but she couldn't make to travel that long due to her joint pain. The day approached, it was special for Sandeep and Bindu, as well as Aarzoo and Shreya. Shreya's grandmother wasn't stopping her for anything from last few days, she gave her permission to go for Sandy's birthday, which was a question of surprise in Aarzoo's mind. His parents arranged for the party on the terrace for their beloved son, they made wonderful decoration and arranged for dinner as well for his friends.

Everyone brought special gifts for the birthday boy. Bindu gifted him the sea shell, which she got from Kanyakumari, engraved both their names on it. Mansi gifted him an expensive pen, from the savings of her pocket money. The party blew out everyone's mind, all had nice dinner after dancing and cutting of cake. Sandeep took the opportunity to spend time with Bindu in private while everyone was having dinner, he took her in to kitchen asking her help bringing water.

In the kitchen, they kissed after a long time and holding her tight in his arms 'I missed you so much!' Sandeep muttered while kissing. 'Me too, Happy Birthday…and Happy Valentine's Day!' Bindu whispered and kissed him back. Soon the surprise waited for them, Ramya entered the kitchen while they were kissing and she was stunned looking at them, both the love birds were shocked with her sudden entry. Bindu ran towards terrace and Sandeep stood there, mute. 'Can you explain?' Ramya asked staring him. 'Ahem…we should be going up now…I will take the desert bowls.' Sandeep avoided her question. 'No boy, you aren't going anywhere without explaining what was that or else I will call Mom and you know the result…' Ramya stopped mocking him. 'No...No… Please don't tell Mom, she will make serial drama out of it…I will explain everything after the party…' He begged. 'Promise?' She asked. 'Yeah, Promise!' he assured. 'Ok, let's go now…take the desert bowls and I will get the dishes and spoons.' She instructed him. While on the terrace Bindu was embarrassed to face Ramya. She hardly ate dinner and left from there on her scooty. Party got over, everyone left for their home happily.

In the night, Sandeep was busy opening his gifts and Ramya entered the room. Sandeep showed her all the gifts, 'The pen looks very expensive, who gave it?' Ramya asked. 'Mansi' he replied. 'Hmm, good…she is a nice girl…You know, few months ago I thought that there is something between you and Mansi…but today I saw something else…' she reminded him. There was a pause from his side. 'I am waiting for your explanation…' she asked again to open his mouth. 'Look, we both like each other…and …we are together…' he said. 'You are just 16! Concentrate on your studies. This is not the time to do all these things when your board exams are knocking the door…' she advised. 'I know, and I am studying well…it's just…you won't understand leave it…' he said. 'What do you mean you won't understand? I am 4 years elder to you…I had many situations like these but I never let my concentration to move around other than my books…' she muttered. 'See, I am saying that only, you never did anything like this…just like a racing horse you always kept your eyes on the books…so you won't get it…and that's good! You are good with your studies and you are doing a great job! …but I am not like you…I do my studies but I have this weakness for girls…' he opened his heart. 'Girls? How many girls you are with?' shocked by his statement, she asked. 'Shit!' he whispered. 'Answer me Sandy!' she asked again. 'I…I…I think…6' he hesitated. 'What! 6…my god! You are dating 6 girls at a time?' she was shocked. 'No, not at a time…they are all past…now its Bindu!' he justified. 'This is ridiculous! You are just 16 and you've dated 6 girls! Who are they? Do your friends know about this? How come Mansi never told me this, she has been close to me from a long time.' She started questioning. 'Because she is my Ex-girlfriend.' looking at the floor he said. 'What the...!!' Astonished Ramya sat on the chair.

Sandeep told her the entire story, starting from his first attraction till Bindu. Hearing his story, 'And you did everything with these girls or just had kissing?' Ramya asked him frankly to know how far her brother had gone. 'Ahem…with Arushi I did some extra's but not....mmm…sex. And with Bindu…I…' he hesitated and looked down. She understood his pause and took a long breath, closing her eyes, she sat on the chair scratching her forehead. 'Look, please don't tell anything to Mom and Dad…I trusted you so told you everything…and by the way Dadi also knows my story.' He informed her after requesting. 'What?! Dadi knows?' that was another surprise to her. 'Yeah, I mean…not about Bindu…but she knows till Mansi…after that I didn't tell her about Bindu.' He said. 'Sandy! I can't believe this!! Tell me one thing, are you addicted to girls? She asked him. 'What…no…no…not like addiction…but I like them…I don't know… like…suddenly, my heart starts liking someone…someone's eyes are good, someone's hair, face, and overall someone is good…and they like me as well…and we get along together….' He paused. 'And what all you do apart from dating and this stuff…anything else? And have you done anything wrong with any girl? Don't try to act smart with me…I want the truth!' She asked to understand her brother's habits. Sandeep was astonished with her question, 'What! No…I didn't do anything else apart from this. And I swear…I never forced them for anything… even I kiss them only when they are open with it…and sex…I… did it only once…that's it…rest all only ended with kisses…and I don't do vulgar things with girls…I swear I could never ever think of doing such things. I respect them…it happens with me, I can't help it, I just like being with them…' he explained his weakness. She paused for a while and took a long breath 'I don't know what to say…you know what? Dadi always said that you are copy of Dadaji…and now I think she is right…' she said and he grinned, looking that she patted him. 'Stop it you idiot! I am not praising you…you know how much Dadi suffered because of his 'deeds'? Yet she never complained! You know why? She loved him.' she said. He was paused. 'Look, 10th board is on your head, concentrate on your studies…be serious, these things will not help you in making your career…' She instructed him. 'Yeah, I am serious…and you know that I did well in prelims.' He replied. 'Good, I will keep checking your notes and studies…you better be prepared well…' She warned. 'Ok, done…but please keep this secret with you…' he requested. 'I will not promise but if you do well in finals, I will think on that...' She left the room. He took a long breath of relief.

It was a week after the birthday. Bindu was embarrassed for the birthday night, Sandeep told her about his discussion with Ramya, after knowing Ramya's condition about the exams, Bindu kept distance from him. Sandeep studied day and night with full attention without thinking about anyone, so did Bindu and everyone. Ramya kept one eye on Sandeep, taking time out of her engineering studies she helped him in his studies as well.

Soon the exams started in the month of March, parents were worried about the boards, Sandeep's mother fed him spoonful of curd along with sugar before going for exams, she believed that it is for good luck. Sandeep did well in all his exams, Ramya kept check on his papers. And finally, the exams got over. Everyone got rid of day and night studies and nightmares about the exams. Sandy did not see Bindu even after the exams, Bindu went to her grandmother's place immediately after the exams. She spoke to him couple of times on phone. Sandy wanted to divert his mind from girls and thought of going out from the city. He spoke to Ramya about that and within a week Ramya came up with an idea of 3 days meditation camp out of the city.

FOURTEEN

Camp and fun after the Exams- There was a meditation camp arranged by a famous yoga institution, which was held out of the city in a meditation hall. Ramya thought it would help Sandeep to get rid of his weakness and concentrate more on his future. Sandeep told the gang about the camp. Preeti, Aarzoo and Mandar were present in the city rest of the friends went to their natives and tours along with their family. They agreed to go for it to improve the concentration and get rid of exam stress.

The camp began a week later, Aarzoo's father dropped everyone till camp. The meditation hall was 30 miles away from city, surrounded by lush jungle. Everything was arranged inside the camp from food to sleeping and everything for next 3 days, people from different age groups attended the camp. They all had to wear the clothes provided by the camp. The lose pajama and shirts were given to all the members. All of them had to follow the rules of camp in eating, sleeping and doing tasks specified to them during the day. Important rule was they all had to stop talking as much as possible, they should not talk if it is not necessary.

The day started in morning at 5 am, after getting fresh every one used to come at the meditation hall, starting from all the yogasanas it used to end with deep meditation. They had light and healthy breakfasts after the meditation, and used to do gardening work and other tasks dedicated to them as per the instructor. Lunch, dinner everything was prepared pure vegetarian most of them were green vegetables. Praying and hearing the stories of gods, *Satsang* and moral story sessions were conducted after the lunch. Most of the stories were based on getting rid of habits, controlling the desires, boosting the confidence and improvising concentration. Sandeep felt all relaxation in his body and mind while in the sessions, not because of hearing the stories but feeling asleep during the sessions. Everyone spoke least during all these days.

On the last day before going back to home, they all went on trekking in the jungle, there was a small village near the meditation hall in the mid of jungle. Some tribal women were collecting the cow dunks around, looking at them Sandeep laughed. 'What is so funny in that? Why are you laughing?' Preeti asked. 'No, it's just a thought…' he laughed again. 'What?' she asked him. 'From last three days we are eating only green vegetables, so my potty is also green these days!! What if we do any shit over here in this jungle… god helps those poor ladies, who are picking up cow dunks!' he laughed. 'Shit man!! You are disgusting!!' Preeti said pushing him. Mandar and Aarzoo laughed out loudly uttering SHIT! 'Hey, I have a question, these cows are eating yellow grass still do green potty, why?' He asked Preeti again to tease her with his potty jokes. 'Yuck! Shut up!!' Preeti uttered. 'Aaye... answer me baby...' he asked mimicking old Hindi film actor Ranjeet. 'Go and ask the cow' she said.

They went back home after 3 days of meditation and relaxation of mind. There wasn't much during the vacation. Sandeep's father lost his job two months ago but he did not say anything to the children, he didn't get any job after hunting for 3 months. The savings were getting empty, day to day expenses were getting affected. Finally, Sudhir Singh (Sandeep's father) decided to do the real estate business and he took a small shop on rent by mortgaging his wife Asha's jewelleries. Sandeep's vacations lasted for 3 months after the board exams, he helped his father in the business. Slowly, the business started improving with good amount of commissions after selling the properties. Sandeep and Ramya's college fees accumulated after meeting the day-to-day expenses. After saving some money for few months, Sudhir thought of moving a step ahead in the business and entered into construction line by mortgaging his small house. And his luck worked well in the business due to his contacts and experience, soon he achieved success.

In the meantime, Sandy's results came out and he passed with average second class marks, to accompany him Sumit and Shaun also passed with second class marks. Rest of the gang passed with good marks. Aarzoo, Mandar passed with distinction, whereas Mansi, Shreya, Preeti and Bindu passed with first class. Based on their results they all got admission in different colleges. Mandar, Aarzoo, Shreya, and Sumit all took science as their primary subject in same college. Mansi wanted to go for commerce but Sandeep took admission in Commerce College and to stay away from him, she too took science. She didn't wished to be associated with him in any matter and she got admission in a different college. Shaun accompanied Sandeep in same college but with Science subject. Sandeep was all alone in the college, away from the gang and away from Bindu, her family compelled her to go for Arts in different college, they wanted her to get a teacher job in the future.

He got busy in adjusting the college and studies, as well as supporting his father during his free time. His father gifted him a phone and thus, sms with the group and Bindu was still on. He made some new friends but the new gang wasn't as comfortable as his previous gang, he was missing his friends. He bought greeting cards and friendship bands for all the friends, he felt it so 'gay' while buying bands for friends but when all his friends but Mansi visited his college, especially to tie friendship band and wish him on the day, he felt happy. He tied the bands to everyone, all had fun and chatted for hours after a long time. Everyone went for a movie and cherished their friendship again wandering in the mall, playing games, eating McD burgers, same as old days.

It was 7 in the evening. Bindu got a call from her step-mother, Sandeep accompanied her till parking lot. It was empty and they got few minutes for romance and kissed each other in parking lot. 'I miss you' she said by embracing him with her hands around his neck. 'I miss you too!' he said holding her waist and kissed her again. 'Saturday my parents will be going out, can you come to my home?' she invited him winking her eye. With no single doubt, 'YES' he said and winked his eye. His words brought all the happiness on her face, she hugged him. 'And yes, please come with a protection this time. I was so scared when we did it first time without any protection but Thank God! Everything was fine.' She whispered. 'Ok, sure…I will bring plenty of them' He smiled mischievously. 'Shut up' She patted him 'I have to go now, bye…HONEY' she mumbled, blinking her eyes. 'Ok, DARLING' he said with smile.

She left and he started towards the mall, he saw Aarzoo and Shreya coming down to parking lot. 'You guys leaving?' he asked. 'Yeah, she got call from Hitler, so…' Aarzoo said mockingly, looking at Shreya. Shreya patted her shoulder. 'It's already late dear… will leave now, Bindu left?' Shreya asked Sandeep. 'Yeah, she just left' he said. 'Ok, I will also go Sandy, will drop Shreya first.' Aarzoo said. 'Ok, take care bye…we'll meet again some other time. Keep in touch' he said. 'Yeah, sure…' Aarzoo replied. 'By the way…it was wonderful meeting you all after a long time…I missed Mansi.' Shreya said. 'Yeah, same here.' Sandeep said. 'We got to go, bye' Shreya said and sat on Aarzoo's scooter and they both went on by waving hands to him.

He went back in the mall and spent another half an hour with the boys. They met Sumit's elder brother in the mall, who came along with his friends and they were all having beer and dinner. Sumit's brother offered breezer to the boys, for the first time they all tasted alcohol. Sumit's brother sent them all by paying auto fare and extra pocket money to Sumit for keeping his mouth shut in front of their parents.

Sandeep genuinely missed Mansi that day. He was aware that Mansi was avoiding him, he always missed her and he hated himself many times for what he did to her. Although, when they were a couple, he did not have that independence of romance with her as he had with Bindu and previous girls but he remembered those moments which he spent with Mansi and loved the decent romance with her. Few percent of alcohol made him fantasise the romance with Mansi. He thought of meeting Mansi before going home and he asked the Auto driver to take a turn towards her home.

Mansi's parents were out for the shopping of groceries. Only her grandmother was home and she was busy watching her serials. Sandeep rang the doorbell, Mansi opened the door. She got surprised to see him. 'Hi' he said with a smile. 'Hi' she mumbled. 'Happy friendship day' taking out the band from his pocket he said. She stared at him for few seconds and closed her eyes taking a long breath, after a pause 'You came here to wish me.' She asked. 'Yes, do you want to talk here itself on the door or can I come inside?' he asked smiling at her, she melted every time with his smile. 'Oh, sorry…come inside.' she invited him. Her grandma looked at him 'Sandeep! How come you are here after long time…' she asked. 'Hello *Amma*, came to wish Mansi, friendship day.' he replied. 'Sit..Sit…Mansi give him something to eat.' Grandma said politely. 'No, No *Amma*, I just had snacks in the mall, actually we all friends celebrated friendship day there. Mansi didn't join us, so I came here to wish her.' He said. 'Oh, ok.' saying that she resumed watching her serial.

He sat on the sofa, Mansi sat beside him. 'Happy friendship day to you too!' she wished. He tied the band on her wrist 'I want your friendship back, like the good old days. I know I messed everything but trust me I always feel guilty for that. Can't you forgive me and forget everything?' he whispered. Her heart melted, eyes filled with tears, she went inside the kitchen, Sandeep sat there hoping for her return. Her love for Sandeep was never lost, it was always hidden somewhere deep inside her heart. It was third time Sandeep came apologising after the break up, she made her mind and thought of forgetting everything this time for sure and keep in touch with him as old days. She poured a tetra pack juice in the glass and brought it for him in the living room. Taking that glass from the tray he looked at her eyes, those beautiful brown eyes were dull, he felt responsible for those tears, which were wiped out in the kitchen. Sandeep's eyes caught a band in the tray, she bought one for him, and he wasn't expecting that. He looked at Mansi surprisingly, she took his hand and tied the knot, 'I will always be your friend. And I will promise that I will try to forget everything, this time for sure.' She mumbled. 'Thank you!' He said with full gratitude. They chatted for a while, Sandeep told her about the day. Mansi's parents came after half an hour and Sandeep got ready to leave. They all asked him to stay back for dinner but he left in a hurry as his mother was waiting for him.

That night Sandeep chatted with Mansi for hours. He shared many details about his college as well as his new friends, how he felt in the college, family things and stuff which he didn't share with anyone else in the group, not even with Bindu. She shared her feelings about new college, study etc., with him. After that day Mansi and Sandeep kept in touch on the phone along with the group.

Saturday arrived and Sandy got ready to go to Bindu's home. He bought a pack of condom from a medical shop far far away from his home, confirmed the exit of Bindu's parents from their house by standing on the shop close to her apartment. Once they left he went inside the apartment by writing the wrong name and flat number in the security register, to be safe in case of any enquiry from her parents.

Bindu rushed towards the door when the bell rang. As soon as she opened it, Sandeep rushed in the house. They both kissed embracing each other, both were alone after their first intercourse few months ago. The lust for each other rose to their head so quickly that they undressed each other without wasting a second.

After an hour of happiness, both got up from the bed and grabbed their clothes from the floor and dressed. Sandeep had snacks and coffee from her house, they chatted for a while and he left from their after some more kisses and hugs. That continued for the rest of the year. They met each other in the malls, saw movies together along with the group. Even Mansi joined them for the movies and parties. Sandeep told Bindu about his relationship with Mansi. She did not give any importance to that since she had full trust on him. His friendship with Mansi also improved. Although, Mansi knew about Sandeep's physical relationship with Bindu, she did not feel anything sad later on. Some guys proposed Mansi on the Valentine's Day in college but Mansi rejected all the proposals on a good note. Aarzoo, Shreya and Preeti suggested her to move on but Mansi didn't have any feelings for any guy. She thought of moving on with her studies and friends. The year ended with great performance by everyone in the exams.

FIFTEEN

A year passed, everyone finished their higher secondary education with good marks. The year made girls look more mature and attractive. Sandeep looked more handsome with his gym workouts and fitness regime. Other boys also looked good, their teenage spots on the face and uneven weight vanished and everyone was building into a fit frame. Sandeep stopped staring at other girls and kept himself totally committed to Bindu. It was almost 3 years they were together; it was the longest relationship which he had with anyone. Shaun had a girlfriend in his college as well as Sumit found a new girl after Neeta's marriage.

Neeta, his music teacher never understood Sumit's one sided love, got married and her family shifted back to Andhra a year ago, after her marriage. Sumit cried for a month like a child infront of the group. Everyone consoled him with their funny talks and even gifted him stuff but he just couldn't move on. After few months, he slowly forgot everything and made a new girlfriend on Valentine's Day. Everyone used to watch movies together. Shaun had a cousin, who lived alone in the flat away from everyone's home. Whenever his cousin was out of town, Shaun arranged for everyone's private meetings with their girlfriend's in his cousin's flat. Boys had enjoyed many parties and even slept drunk in that flat.

While in the vacations, Bindu got the news from her father that they will be shifting to Baroda in next 15 days. It was shocking for the couple. Bindu's only happiness in her life was Sandeep and that happiness was about to vanish soon. She requested her father that to leave her back in Bangalore, where she will live in a hostel and complete her education. But her step-mother wasn't ready for that because if she leaves Bindu, she had to hire a maid, as almost all the work was done by Bindu.

Sandeep hid himself in the shell of sorrow. Bindu couldn't even meet him properly as she got busy in packing. One day, all the friends arranged a farewell for her and everyone cried that day, even Mansi felt sad on her separation. Sandeep and Bindu took out the time privately in the party but they didn't do much other than kissing, Bindu cried and opened all her pain in her heart. It was tough for Sandeep as well. Everyone gifted her stuff to memorise their friendship. They clicked plenty of pictures together.

Sandeep was lonely after Bindu's departure. Bindu kept in touch for sometime on social network and phone but after few months she completely took an exit from Facebook as well as other sites and her phone also got switched off. Sandeep sent a letter to her Baroda address but did not get any response.

He took admission in Bachelor of Business Management. Shaun and Sumit joined him in the college but they were busy with their girlfriends. Mandar opted for the line of Engineering as his mother had already decided him to be a future Steve Jobs. Preeti and Mansi went to B.sc, whereas Shreya took admission in Diploma in Architecture. Decisively, Aarzoo took admission in Medical Science and started her MBBS. Gourav discontinued his studies and joined his family business for full time after his 12th. Sandeep spent his time with his new friends and rest of the time assisting his father, after college. Slowly he forgot memories of Bindu.

His bonding was same with Mansi, he decided not to go beyond friendship and even Mansi did not opt for a second chance of getting close to him. Preeti couldn't make any boyfriend as her defence family professions kept her away from relationships, none of the guys had guts to get close to her. She always flirted with Sandeep but never thought of being in a relationship with him. Sandeep with his charm made a new girlfriend Jia. He again spent all the happy moments with Jia.

One year completed, Sandeep's father's business was running with full speed. He gifted Sandeep a new bike, Ramya also got a new job after her engineering and she started giving him good amount of pocket money every month. His life was full of fun and again on track with his girlfriend. He totally forgot about Bindu. One fine day, he was dropping Jia on his bike after the movie. Her parents saw her along with him in the multiplex as well as on the bike. They changed her college after much of drama and that ended their relationship. But the college was filled with many beautiful girls, who were ready to be with a handsome guy like Sandeep. To maintain his record, he met a new girl Archana. They dated for a few months and he broke up with her as well.

Meanwhile, Aarzoo and Shreya's meeting was only possible at Aarzoo's place. Shreya used to visit Aarzoo's home occasionally after the college. They were busy with their studies but took out time once in a while to meet each other and spend some lovely moments together, their relationship wasn't physical other than kissing, the love they had for each other was beyond any physical relationship, the understanding between two was amazing, they were soulmates. Shreya continued painting, she kept all her artworks with Aarzoo, as her family had no interest in her talent. Aarzoo requested a separate room to her father just to collect all the paintings of

Shreya. As she was the only child, her wish used to be granted as soon as it comes out of her mouth. She named the paintings room as *Love's Art* room. Aarzoo asked Shreya many times to exhibit her paintings but Shreya always rejected saying, '*they all are made only for her love*', which used to soften her heart.

One fine day, Shreya visited Aarzoo's home to show her new sketches. Aarzoo's parents were in the hospital as usual and she was all alone at home. She opened the door, Shreya felt shy as she saw Aarzoo for the first time in her shorts and sleeveless t-shirt at home. Aarzoo opened the paintings and admired her talent as usual. And kept sketches along with her other paintings in the *Love's Art* room. Shreya used to feel blessed for having a girlfriend like Aarzoo, who loves her more than anyone else does.

Aarzoo offered her juice, while drinking accidentally it fell on Shreya's dress and the juice spilled all over her chest. Aarzoo took a wet napkin from the bathroom and started cleaning her dress. Shreya's heartbeats increased when she was that close to Aarzoo. They stared at each other, Shreya closed her eyes, 'You look hot in these shorts.' Shyly she said. Aarzoo smiled, she held her hands and moved close to her surrounding her hands around her waist, 'Open your eyes' she whispered caressing her cheeks, Shreya shook her head with closed eyes. 'Why don't you have something HOT after the chilled juice.' Aarzoo asked her with a smile. Shreya stared at her blushing and suddenly looked down shyly, Aarzoo lifted her face up with her hand, their eyes met and eventually they kissed. Aarzoo kissed her neck and all over her chest, she pushed her on the bed while kissing, this time Shreya didn't oppose to go on the bed. Hotness of two beauties aroused all over the room and the most romantic evening appeared in their lives for the first time.

After that evening, they met few times and enjoyed a great time with each other. Gradually, their meetings reduced and they were completely scheduled with their vast studies and practicals and hardly got any time for their sensual moments. Special kisses and hugs happened only on texts and MMS and meeting once in a while didn't attract much due to their pressure of studies.

Meanwhile, Sandeep met a lady in the gym, who was attracted to him and slowly she was getting close to him with all the open invitation signals. She was beautiful, young and rich. Sandeep had a good chance of having fun time with her but as she was married with two children and rich loving husband, who was in USA. He felt it cheap to get close to someone like that, his inner voice uttered NO. After cheating Mansi in the school, he had that guilt of breaking the heart forever and his heart never allowed him to cheat anyone after that.

Sandeep's father Sudhir's business was on top and he mortgaged his house once again to enter in to the construction business. Some funds did not come on time and the work load and stress levels increased for him. He fell badly in the trap of loans and one day he fell unconscious at his site. Luckily, Sandeep was with him that time and he acted immediately by taking him to the hospital. And it was a Major heart attack! Ramya's corporate health insurance played key role and her father's Angioplasty was done for free from her medical insurance. Aarzoo's father Dr. Armaan Shaikh took tare of everything and did not take any extra amount of consulting fees from Sandeep's family.

Dadi came from Vijaypur, Sudhir recovered and discharged from the hospital. Sandeep's family was in awful condition, loss in the business and mortgaged house kept them worried, Asha gave all her jewellery to sell and pay the debts, Ramya helped with her salary and also offered her savings to improve the business, Dadi offered her fixed deposit. But Sudhir was not ready to risk the money of his wife, daughter and mother, he decided to go with the situation. As a matter of fact, he demanded Dadi to stay with them forever, she couldn't reject that time and started living with them. Sandeep took care of business till his father's complete recovery. Young man's intelligence and presence of mind worked, he initiated with small contracts and moved with priority and eventually finished lots of job and gradually business came on streamline. Sudhir felt as he is the happiest man in the world, three women of his life, mother, wife and daughter were ready to sacrifice everything for his life, his young son worked day and night to improve his business.

Sandeep and Ramya's friends visited their home with bouquets and cards of 'Get well soon' for Sudhir. Mansi visited them almost every alternative day and helped the family even in the kitchen without any hesitation. Dadi came to know that Sandeep broke up with Mansi, she got upset for his behaviour, Sandeep apologised to Dadi. His Dad's incident made Sandeep to get more close with Mansi. He shared many things with her, work and studies, his stress reduced after talking to Mansi. Whenever he was stressed he used to meet Mansi.

Few months passed and the accident incident happened in the life of Sandeep. Mansi's family fell into a big trouble, only because of Sandeep and he couldn't face Mansi after that incident. The money which was kept by Sandeep, was found after a month while cleaning the house.

After finding the money in the home, Mansi's neighbours spread the rumour that her father committed suicide because of her loose character. Regular visits of Sandeep and closeness between both was questioned by many. Mansi's mother had full trust on her daughter but she couldn't bear the questions on her pious daughter's character. She asked Sandeep, not to meet Mansi anymore. When Mansi went to deposit that amount of five lacks at her father's office, Boss's secretary took the money without showing any sympathy. On the contorary, that fellow asked her, what did she do to get the money?! Office staff didn't believe that the money was found in their home after a month. All the relatives slowly made distance from them in the time of crisis. Sandeep knew their fianancial situation and he wanted to support Mansi and her family financially but they did not take any help from him. Mansi stopped seeing and texting him. Slowly, all the friends got separated on their way towards their future. Although, many girls got attracted to Sandeep but he decided to stay single after the incident. His will wasn't ready to romance any girl after messing the life of Mansi.

Sandy got more close to his Dadi by sharing his feelings and guilts. Dadi couldn't bring the truth in front of the family looking at the heart condition of her beloved son, Sudhir. She didn't want to spoil the innocent image of her grandson as well. As the days passed, Dadi forgot about the incident and started her normal life, by teasing everyone in the family, pointing out the mistakes of Asha and watching her favourite soaps 'Despirate Housewives' and 'Sex and the City'. Ramya got married to Goutham when Sandeep was in his last year of graduation. The whole Singh family tree was present at that time.

SIXTEEN

Years passed and everyone finished their graduations. Gourav got married soon after, to a pretty girl Anju from a Mumbai's business family. Everyone met lastly at his marriage. Mansi was accompanied by her mother in the marriage, she didn't had much talk with Sandeep at that time as her mother insisted her not to speak with him.

Sandeep joined his father's business for full time after his MBA. The business achieved its peak and Sudhir cleared all the debts on his home and business. He bought surrounding plots of his house and converted his small 2 bedroom house in to a duplex bungalow of 5 bedrooms, a big living room and kitchen with all modern equipment inside. He even got a garage, small out house, beautiful lawn and a garden outside. He also renovated Vijaypur's ancestral house. They bought new office and employed 5 more people in the office apart from Raju. Raju worked day and night for the success of the business, when Sandeep was busy completing his education, Raju became the most trusted man of Sudhir, he treated him as his second son.

Sumit finished his graduation in Business Management and got a job in an international bank and held up his family flag in Bank jobs. Shaun worked for his father's NGO after finishing his graduation for sometime and later he got a job in an MNC company. He did his theatre as well in his free time. Mandar got job in a top multinational IT company and soon he went to New York on his job. Preeti passed the Police exams and started preparing for IAS and IPS. Soon, Preeti got selected after her IPS exams and took charge as new IPS officer in the city. Mansi started working for a small firm after her science graduation and also taught dance to students in a private school. Her mother wanted her to get married soon, so she started looking for a potential groom for her but nothing was working out. Everyone's life was moving smoothly.

Aarzoo's father got her admission in the top Medical college of London for MD. In the fear of losing Shreya, Aarzoo wanted to do her MD in India itself but Shreya was very happy with her growth in studies and she insisted her to go ahead and complete her studies. Shreya got a job in an interior designing firm with good earnings. That made her more confident. The day of departure arrived, Shreya came to meet Aarzoo at her home before departure. Flight was taking off in the mid night, she informed her father about her late arrival, as the old lady went to her daughter's house, and there were no restrictions. Shreya went directly to Aarzoo's home from her office, Aarzoo's parents were busy in the living room weighing her bags for the airport checking and preparing her luggage. Aarzoo was getting ready in her room, she made an album of Shreya's paintings to take them along with her, and was busy packing them. Shreya smiled looking at that and she held a gift wrapped box infront of her. 'Hi! What is this?' Aarzoo asked taking that from her hand. 'Open it.' She said smiling. Aarzoo stared at her and opend the box, it was a locket with pendent engraved with their names. Aarzoo wore it with a smile 'I will keep it only because it has your name on it, and… I have something for you too.' She said and took a box from table. Shreya opend the box it was an expensive watch engraved back side '*mine all the time!*' Shreya smiled 'I am, always!' she whispered. They both hugged each other, Aarzoo whispered in her ear 'Wait for me.' She smiled and mumbled 'Forever!'

They all went to the airport, the love birds didn't leave each other's hand for a single second in the back seat of the car. The boys along with Preeti and Mansi were waiting for them to see off Aarzoo. Aarzoo went with all the warm wishes from her parents and beloved friends.

Destiny had decided something else for Shreya. A week later, the old lady came from her daughter's home. One morning, she was finalising the wedding card design at home when Shreya was leaving for office. She decided the marriage date of Shreya with Arjun without even taking her opinion. 'What is this *Amma*? You didn't even ask me before going ahead with this!' furiously Shreya asked her grandma. 'What is there to ask you? It was already decided and you knew that.' She said looking at the card designs. 'Yeah, but you never spoke anything about marriage from years. So, I thought you dropped the idea…and today all of a sudden you are deciding wedding cards without even asking me!' Shreya said wondering her grandma's decision. 'Oh look at you! Some thousands of earnings made you raise a tone against me.' Granny said sarcastically. 'Where is *Appa*? I want to talk to him.' Shreya searched for her father. 'Look girl, I am not here to answer your questions.' She said angrily.

Shreya went out of the house without further arguments. With certainty, she called her father asking for explaination, her father repeated the words of her grandmother. She was confused and she didn't had her partner Aarzoo to speak about that and she didn't want to involve her friends in the matter as she knew the old lady will not be convinced by anyone. Evening she returned to home and had an argument with her grandma and father. Her father kept quiet and didn't say single word infront of his mother in the support of his daughter. But Shreya didn't leave the battle and she kept on defending and uttered that she won't be marrying Arjun at any cost and if they force her to marry him, she will leave this home. That was a hard pinch for both. 'Whom do you want to marry then?' the old lady uttered. 'I don't know, but as of now, I don't want to marry Arjun.' She said confidently, as she wasn't prepared to come up with her relationship, which wouldn't be understood by them.

Next day they called Arjun and his mother at home to convince Shreya for marriage. Arjun was a short tempered man, he was annoyed after knowing that Shreya rejected him, he went out of the house with his ego. But Shreya's father and his mother stopped him. The old lady opened her big mouth and uttered 'I know, there must be someone from that bunch of monkeys in your group…I have full doubt on that Muslim girl, she must have filled something in this stupid girl's mind…she never leaves this girl and she is always on phone with her and all those useless friends…I shouldn't have listend to you Sumitra, leaving her free with those useless donkeys.' Shreya caught it now, her aunt and Arjun's mother Sumitra was the one who asked grandma to let her be free with her friends. Shreya got annoyed after hearing those words for her close friends.

'Enough *Amma*, I don't want to hear anything bad about my friends. They did not say anything to me about marriage…Its my life and my wish, I don't want to marry Arjun. How can I marry him, when I don't even know him well?' She said.

'Even I don't know you! But I am not going against my family! Because my family is first and most important thing for me…otherwise, there are many girls in the queue to marry me!' angryliy Arjun uttered. 'No offence Arjun, but its better you marry someone who loves you.' she said calmly. 'Stop it Shreya! I am quiet but it doesn't mean that you keep on talking like this. We have decided the dates and even gone ahead with printing of cards. Now you are saying that you don't want to marry my son? We decided your marriage years ago and you knew that, if you didn't wish to marry him then you should have spoken that time itself.' Arjun's mother uttered. 'I was a teenage girl that time! And after that you people never spoke anything about marriage!' Shreya defended. 'That is because your father wanted you to complete your education and if you remember, we said that we will go ahead with the marriage after your graduation.' offended grandma said. 'Yeah but you should have spoken to me before fixing the dates!' Shreya said. 'Enough Shreya! You give me just one reason why you don't want to marry Arjun? What is wrong with him, he is educated and well settled, he has everything to keep you happy.' Her father finally spoke out irriated by the arguments. 'I don't love him *Appa* and he won't be happy with me.' She answered. 'That is all rubbish, people start liking each other after staying together...love and all is busllshit...After marriage you will start liking him...' Arjun's mother said. 'And more on, that is my problem, to be happy with you or not' Arjun said.

'Wait Arjun! Do you love some one else?' her father asked Shreya. 'I...I...I don't know...' Shreya didn't show guts to come with her love infront of them. 'Then the discussion is over! You, young girl, you will be marrying Arjun next month as decided by us and if you take any wrong steps, trust me, I will kill myself. For me, my pride is more important than your childish behaviour.' Grandma warned Shreya.

Shreya collapsed on the chair, Arjun and his mother left the home and her father went inside his room. Grandma went outside to drop Arjun and his mother till their car. Shreya was totally confused. Previous night, she spoke to Aarzoo and she was happy with her new college and atmosphere in London. She wasn't ready to put a stake on Aarzoo's education and career for her personal life. Soft girl faught as hard as she could but she had lost to come up infront of her family about her special love, which won't be accepted by anybody.

Eventually, she ended marrying Arjun. She didn't invite any of her friends for the marriage but Preeti and Mansi went for the marriage but Shreya had nothing to explain them. Aarzoo got the news of Shreya's wedding, her nightmare came true. She got offended and broke everything in her room, and her phone as well and cried for weeks. She lost the trust in love.

On the other hand, Shreya didn't make any physical contact with Arjun after the marriage. Arrogant Arjun also hated her for rejecting him, he was attracted to her beauty and wanted her but his ego never bowed himself infront of her. She cried everyday missing her love, she called Aarzoo but Aarzoo changed her number and also blocked her from facebook and other social networks. She finally made her mind to talk to Aarzoo and went to her home when her doctor parents were available and took her new number from them. Aarzoo's parents were not aware of their relationship. They gave an expensive gift to Shreya when she visited after the wedding. Subsequently, she did not call Aarzoo, as she knew if she calls, she will again change that number.

Shreya continued her job to stay away from her in-laws and husband, made reasons to stay long time in the office to avoid facing them. Day by day, her mother-in-law started getting upset by her late returns. Slowly, the cold war turned into strong fights and daily the atmosphere in the home was getting worse. Arjun used to drink a lot for maintaining his professional deals and one day, he forcefully had sex with Shreya. Shreya cried a lot after that, her mental strength and self-esteem was totally broken. She didn't share anything with any of her friends. She felt like opening her heart to Aarzoo but she knew that Aarzoo won't take her calls, she thought of texting and saw her whatsapp dp, in which Aarzoo had clicked a selfie with a British girl and status showed hearts, it was a second shock to Shreya, she couldn't type a single word.

Things became worse and Arjun started having physical cantact with her devoid of her consent, for him it was normal. Her father and grandma totally broke up relationship with her. They visited her home once in a while but Shreya did not have any concern with them. Her family permitted her to work only for her salary. Every month her mother-in-law gave all the bills to Shreya. One day Shreya thought of taking divorce from Arjun and get lost somewhere out of the city but she found herself pregnant. She left the job and concentrated on the little life which was growing in her womb. Her mother-in-law dedicated all the work in the kitchen and house to Shreya. Pregnant Shreya was treated worse than a maid and Arjun never cared for her. They all wished for a baby boy, and when she gave birth to baby boy everyone changed. Her in-laws and husband took care of baby and her as well. Shreya went to her father's home after her delivery. Her grandma arranged full time nanny in the home to take care of the baby and Shreya. Things came on streamline but Shreya never felt anything for Arjun. Shreya's father gifted a piece of land in the name of Shreya's son. And he also arranged to pass the tenders of some expensive contracts to Arjun from his PWD.

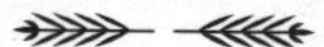

SEVENTEEN

Back from Flashback (With narration)

It was a month after our marriage, Mansi did not speak to me all these days but she comfortably adjusted with everyone and she didn't give a single chance of complaint to anybody in the house. She continued her disciplined life starting her day by 5 with her yoga and later she used to get involved with Mom in the kitchen and other household works. She didn't protest Dadi even for a fraction of second for hiding the truth. She articulated with everyone but me, everybody was happy with her. Dadi knew about the situation between us but she waited for the right time to talk to Mansi. Her avoidance was killing me, I never felt that bad in my entire life. On Sumit's birthday party everyone noticed detachment between me and Mansi. They all sensed that things weren't going well between us. Few days later, Shaun called everyone on his birthday and Mansi did not go for it only to avoid outing with me. However, she was avoiding the gang as well. She hardly spoke to our friends but Shreya and Preeti kept their touch with her by calling her once in a while. Friends kept on asking me whether everything was fine beween us, I couldn't prolong that punishment of abandoning her anymore.

One day, I called everyone and we decided to meet near Shaun's theatre after our work. I told the truth without expecting any solution from them. They were all shocked after hearing my original sin! Sumit asked with curiosity 'The car got repaired in just one day! Which garage you got it done?' everyone's jaws dropped with his silly question. 'Dude! You got only that from everything I said?' I asked shockingly. 'Actually my car is in garage from last one week...Sorry...Anyways. Frankly speaking...I personally feel everything needs time, if she hasn't reacted yet infront of your family, then she is giving time to herself to heal from the pain, which YOU GAVE HER! However, if you need any support, I am there.' He expressed his concern honestly with a pinch of irony. I gave a look at him for his sarcastic punch. Everyone agreed with him, but Preeti had a look of arresting me! Nevertheless, she understood my situation and agreed with the gang.

Days were passing, Mom and Dad smelled something fishy in my married life, as we never spoke to each other while alone, I used to talk to her while around with family, many times she replied by nodding her head and sometimes she soflty reacted with her one-liners infront of everyone. We used to sleep in the same room but separately. One day, Mom noticed Mansi, sleeping on the couch, when I accidentally kept the room door open. Although, they did not interfere in our personal matter. Dadi had decided to keep quiet on it and leave everything on time, she always said *'Time heals everything'*. But Mom was losing her patience on our problem and she went to discuss the matter with Dadi in her room.

Out of the blue, I was passing through and overheard their conversation. 'I do not understand the issue between these two? They both are childhood friends, loved each other, married with full consent and now there is something wrong between both of them. I kept quiet this long letting them to handle it on their own but I think it is not getting over. Are you going to talk to Sandy or should I do it?' Mom said. 'Hmm, you are right, this is going too far, let me talk to both of them.' Dadi replied. 'Ok, Good... you do it, its better...I feel Mansi is a nice girl, there must be some misunderstanding...Sudhir is also worried on this, though he is not saying anything but I can see his concern.' Mom said. I didn't hinder their converstion and hopped the stairs to my room. Mansi was cleaning the room. When I entered, she started moving out of the room. I stopped her by grabbing her hand 'I need to talk to you.' I said. 'Leave my hand!' she mumbled harshly. My ego got hurt instantly when I heard that. I lost my temper and pushed her towards the wall, holding her arms tighly, 'Look! Whatever happened, I can't change it. I am guilty and said sorry for hundreds of times. I would have hidden the truth till my grave but I felt that's wrong! I am ready to do whatever you say but if you keep on holding the grudge, I can't help it. Today my family is worried on our relationship. What is the solution for this? Think and let me know!' I said intensely, and I left from there.

I went to the guest room, and banged the door. Sitting on the chair, I closed my eyes to settle down my temper. Witin few minutes my phone rang, it was an unknown number, I wasn't in a mood to hear out any telephone executive, and disconnected it. It rang again, I didn't answer and kept the phone on the table. In few seconds, I heard a message beep, I took the phone, and it was a messge from the same number, opend the text. *'Hi! It's me Bindu! I got your number from Preeti. Seems like you are busy, not answered the call! CONGRATS! I am really happy for you both! Call me when you are free* (Smiley emoticons)'.

That was a surprise and shock as well. I dialled the number quickly but something stopped me and I disconnected it before ringing. I was confused whether it's right to talk to her or not. But I wanted to know, where the hell she was all these years! I called Preeti to know the truth but her mobile was off. And I couldn't resist myself after few minutes I called her. My heartbeats were high, she answered the phone immediately. 'Hi!...' before I could say *Hello*, she answered the phone anxiously! 'Ahmm..Hi....'

I said softly clearing my throat. 'I was thinking about you only.' She said. 'Same here, after seeing your message.' I replied. There was a pause from both the sides for couple of seconds. 'So...you married to Mansi! Great choice...happy for you both...Congrats again!' she said after few seconds of pause. 'Yeah, thanks...where are you now? Where were you all these years!?' I asked. 'I am back in Bengalooru! I was in Gujrat! Can we meet...I mean if it is ok with you and Mansi.' She asked hesitating, remembering our history. 'Ok..Yeah sure, in the evening?' I accepted. 'Fine, I will text you the place.' She replied. 'Sure' I said. 'Ok...Bye...' she was about to hang the phone, 'Hey...it's nice to hear you after a long time.' I said. 'Same here...' she said with her soft voice and we hung up the phone.

I thought of talking to Mansi about Bindu. I went towards my room, she was sitting on the bed, she seemed upset, thinking about situation that happened few minutes ago. I went inside, she got up from the bed. 'Look, I am not a teacher and you are not a student. So, no need to stand up like this, whenever I come in.' I said to chill her mood. As expected, there wasn't any answer from her. I took a long breath and said 'I over-heard Dadi and Mom talking about us, they are all worried about us. I came to talk to you and you were ignoring me. So, I got angry... I am sorry if I hurt you.' I apolozised in soft voice. She stared me, I gazed in her eyes, they were filled with tears but she didn't cry. 'How many times you will say sorry?' She asked. 'I don't know! I will make a list!' I said with the smile. She closed her eyes and sat on the bed, 'It is my family as well, and I will take care of our family. I will try that they won't be worried about us anymore.' She muttered. I took a long breath and said 'Thanks.' And again there was a pause from her side. I went close with excitement 'Guess what! Bindu called just now!' I said with wide open eyes. I saw a weird reaction on her face. 'She is back in town and I said we'll meet this evening, are you coming?' I asked her. She was shocked to hear that, she stared at the floor, her lips were moving but there wasn't anything to be heard. 'Hello! I am asking you...' I asked again. 'She called you. You are free to meet her... why are you asking me!?' She said looking at the floor. 'Mansi, I don't know what to say...I...leave it.' And I left from there.

I didn't know what impact that made in the mind of Mansi. Ofcourse that might have been edgy for her but I had to meet Bindu, not with the intention of girlfriend but as a friend. I received her text about the venue.

While I was leaving, Dadi called us in her room. Mom went to temple, and only we three were home. As expected she initiated talk on our relationship, Mansi kept quiet. 'You know everything Dadi!' I said to finish the conversation. 'I know, but I also want to clear some points here?' she said. There was a pause from Mansi, Dadi asked Mansi to sit beside her and she obeyed her. Keeping her hand on Mansi's head, she said 'Look Beta! Whatever happened, I am also part of it. I was responsible to hide things from you and your family. I never said this before as we never spoke on this but today I want to say, I am sorry.' Dadi said softly. 'No Dadi, Please! You shouldn't say that, I have no complaints for you.' Mansi said honestly by holding Dadi's hands. 'I know that, yet, I am also equally responsible for everything that happened to you. I stopped Sandy from telling you the truth before marriage, I had been selfish.' There was a pause. Dadi took long breath and looked at Mansi, who sat quietly staring the floor. 'Mansi, you know the first time when Sandy told me about you, he praised you so much that, I saw you in his eyes and his words. He was fifteen or something that time and I imagined that Sandy should get a life partner like you! We old people, always end up everything with marriage. (Laughed). Anyways, when I shifted here, I met you many times, you always made a perfect impression on me, I prayed almighty that *why don't you do something so that Sandy marries someone like you.* I never knew that god will do something like this. You must be wondering why am I saying all these things to you, what is the point behind?'

Dadi asked her, and she looked at her quietly, expecting the answer from her. Dadi continued, 'Sandy is the only son of our family and we always wished perfect life for him. When he came running at me with his confession of stealing. I was completely broke! In this age, I didn't want to lose my son and see my grandson in jail. Though, he used that money to save someone's life, but he committed a crime. I couldn't change the past but as I said I became selfish. To save my family, I took out the money from my bank and we came to your home to request for forgiveness from your father, but destiny wrote something else, we saw your father's funeral! I never imagined that my papmering will show that result one day. I was guilty, I never had guts to visit you all again but trust me, everyday I prayed for your family's strength. The point is, we can not change whatever happened, we both are guilty but I haven't decided this marriage to pity you and your family and compromise with marriage proposal, NO. I always wished you to be his wife, because I loved your nature and knew that you will take care of our beloved Prince, when one day we will disappear from this world.'

She said looking at us affectionately.

'Dadi!' I uttered and sat beside her. Mansi's eyes were filled with tears. Dadi held her hand and continued in soft voice, 'I didn't interfere between both of you. But now, Sudhir and Asha are worried about you both. I am not asking you to forgive him or me, I am asking you to analyse the truth. We both are guilty, and this is the best we did to safeguard the prestige of both the families. And actually, that is what your father wanted, he gave up his life to uphold the respect of your family. I know this is difficult to handle but you can change your perspective and see the positive part of it. I know it will take time to forget things, take your own time but remember, there is always a second chance for everything, I am requesting you to give it a second chance. You are a nice girl and I know you will make a good decision. And keep one thing in mind, I am always with you and with your decision.' Dadi said with her smile.

Mansi heard everything quietly, got up from there and went to our room. I took a long breath and told Dadi about Bindu. Dadi ordered me, not to do any injustice with Mansi again. I went to meet Mansi in the room, she was sitting on bed and seemed as thinking deeply about Dadi's speech. In her blue saree she looked like a beautiful princess caged in the castle, waiting for her prince charming to rescue her. I, a culpable prince, addressed her softly 'Mansi.' She was deeply in her thoughts and did not reply. 'Mansi' I called her name again. 'Haan, yeah…' she said by waking up from her thoughts. 'I, I just came to ask…are you alright?' I asked her. 'Yeah… I am fine.' She said with soft voice. 'Are you coming with me to meet Bindu?' I jumped to the point hastily. She stared at me, I didn't get what her eyes were saying. 'I know this is a wrong time but she is waiting for us back there….' I said looking at her. 'I have some work, you go and see her.' She said taking out some clothes from the cupboard. In that one month, I understood that whenever I go to see her in the room, she gets busy with clothes and in the kitchen she gets busy with utensils to avoide me. I left from there without any word, I knew that she must have been hurt with my meeting with Bindu, I was upset as well, because of her behaviour of avoiding me everytime. So, I decided to meet Bindu.

I went to the Mall and saw Bindu near food plaza. She looked stunning in her western wears, blue denim and designer top, long ear rings, thick bracelet in one wrist and expensive watch in the other, stylish clutch and high heels suited her attire, she rocked the whole food plaza or may be the mall with her beauty. I went in simple casuals of denim and white full sleeve shirt. We both greeted and hugged each other, people stared at us when we met. We weren't less than any celebrity.

'Hi!! Where were you all these years!?' I expressed my concern right away after hugging her. 'Relax, sit down and let me see you first.' She said with her sweet smile, which was awkward to hear at that time. She ordred a coffee for us and asked 'Where is Mansi? Well, I am a bit obvious why she didn't join you here.' She giggled. 'Nothing like that, she was busy with something at home. We will plan and meet all together once.' I covered. After few minutes of chat about here and there and a cup of coffee, we spoke about what we did after our separation, as they say *Ladies first!* She started.

'We went to Baroda, initially everything was going on as usual. But one day, Papa came to know about my relationship with you and he was very disappointed. My step-mother stepped into the matter, it was jackpot for her and she stopped my calls and monitored me everytime, I did my graduation externally from home. I used to do all house works like Cinderella...!' she stopped and stared at me with her sad face, I was shocked and gravely looked at her. All of a sudden, she started laughing, and surprised me, 'Look at your face! Relax...I am just kidding. Nothing happened like that!' Saying she giggled. 'What!? Are you nuts!' I uttered shockingly. 'I am sorry! I saw the concern on your face when you came here so made this story...Actually, after going there, Papa came to know about my step-mother's intentions and he sent me to Delhi to my meternal aunt's home. My aunt showered all the love on me as her own child. I was happy, I wanted to get in touch with you guys but I lost all the contacts. My step-mother's, brother was irritating me on facebook, so deleted my all social accounts. I was scared of him even after that. In the meanwhile, I fell for a guy in the neighbourhood. He approached me first, he was really nice with me, I couldn't say no. Everything became wonderful after that, I missed you though, but was guilty to show up with you after all that. And I knew you will be happy with someone here, so thought of not disturbing you.' She said.

I was upset after hearing that but I had moved on later so that didn't affect me for more than few seconds. 'Hmm, atleast you should have replied my mails. I was worried about you for months. You deactivated Facebook then how you got in touch with Preeti from Facebook? Later, I couldn't find you on FB.' I complained. 'Actually I changed my name it's 'Ritu.Pujari.' she said making faces. 'Why?' I asked devastated. 'Because I didn't want the old name' she said mockingly. I stared, she smiled and said 'I was scared of that stupid man yaar...So...' She said by taking a long breath. 'You are impossible, look at you! You've changed a lot! Both physically and psychologically.' I said staring her from head to toe. 'Yup! Isn't it good change?' she asked. 'Yeah, obviously...good to hear that!' I said resting my back on the chair. 'Thanks...' she said and stared at me. I took my eyes off from her 'And... how come back in Bangalooru?' I asked. 'Ricky...my boyfriend wanted to see South India. We travelled all 4 states. He went back to Delhi yesterday, he has some meeting in Singapore this week. I wanted to stay back and meet all you guys. By the way, I am getting married next year.' She said everything and rested her mouth. 'Ufff!! So many things in 4 years haan… cool…happy for you…So Ricky …nice name, foreigner? Ricky Martine? (chuckled) What does he do? Don't tell me he is a singer and has a music band!' I mocked. 'No! He has a chain of restaurants, actually it's his family business… Ricky Ahuja. He is a typical Punjabi guy, after so many complications, his family agreed for our marriage...' She said. 'Great…Congrats!! Happy for you!!' I said staring at her. 'Thank god! I thought you must be mad at me for completely getting disconnected with you.' she said. 'No! Seriously, I was worried about you…I knew about your step-mother and all blah blah…I actually imagined something like Cinderella story you said before…' I laughed. 'Aww…So sweet of you. I am sorry dear! I knew that you must have thought of something like that...So, I said. It would have become true but thanks to Papa, who came to know about her intentions, he also came to know how she never cooked for me while their outing and all and how she treated me…so he made that decision. You know, I never complained him when I was here… I used to be so happy with you that I didn't even care for her existence…' She giggled and whispered 'Memories!' And she took a pause. I smiled. 'I wanted to thank you for everything! Specially for being with me whenever I needed…You provided me all the comforts and blessed all the things I wished. I became selfish for a while but later I was guilty for not turning back at you and I wanted to apologise on your face, so was waiting for the time. I am sorry! And THANK-YOU for everything!' she held my hand and said with her soft and shaking voice, tears filled in her eyes. I held her hand and said 'Well, it's alright! All is well that ends well! (After a pause) We all would have met your Ricky Martine, why he left early?' I mocked to cheer up the situation. 'I can get him on video chat anytime.' She said mocking with her phone. 'Good, does he know about our past?' I asked to be coutious. 'Yup, I told him about us before signing a relationship with him. Even he has a history and we both didn't mind that.' she said. 'Nice. And…what else?' I asked. 'That's it from my side. You tell me, why you are looking so dull?' she noticed. 'What…I am fine…What in the world can bother me?' I said. 'C'mon! Whom you are fooling? I know every bit of you. Tell me what is wrong?' she asked holding my hand again. 'Nothing yaar! Just stressed, with work, life and all. Today is your day. Let's talk about you. How's your father?' I changed the topic. 'Yeah he is fine! You are a newly married man! Moreover, you married a girl who loves you more than anyone else does… Answer me!' She commanded raising her eyebrows, with a soft voice. 'Preeti spoke to you?' I confirmed before starting the serious talk. 'No, I didn't speak to her, she was busy when I called her. I didn't disturb the 'Indian police' later! I pinged her on facebook and got your number.' she said mockingly.

I revealed the whole story infront of her. She was shocked after hearing that. 'Can I help you with something? Well, I am here for 2-3 days, I can do whatever I can from here as well as from there.' she asked. I saw her concern in solving my problem. 'Thanks! But no Thanks! I have to solve it myself.' I said. 'Yeah but how long are you gonna hold it like this?' she asked. 'I don't know. The thing is…I am falling for her day by day and it hurts when she is upset. So, I don't go infront of her more, as I remind her the bitter past she suffered because of me. I spend most of the time in office and on the sites, made a decision to stay away from her so that she lives happily.' I said. 'That's rubbish! It is not the solution! You are making it worse! You should get more close to her so that she recollects the feelings for you which are hidden under the hatred! I am sure she doesn't hate you, I know how much she loved you!' she showed her excitement to bring ecstasy. I paused staring at her. 'Ahh…Actually! One more confession, I knew about you and Mansi, got that rumour way before we were couple but I desired you so badly that I never cared for anybody's feelings and acted innocent. I am selfish!' squeezing her face with biting her lips she said. 'No! It's alright! It wasn't you…It was always me who hurt her feelings.' I said the truth. 'Hmm, let us get you close to your beloved wife. I have a plan.' She said with enthusiasm. She called Preeti and IPS answered the call immediately. After greeting each other, she told her the plan. Preeti agreed the terms and within a few minutes, Preeti called Mansi and provoked the jealousy inside her heart which loves me. After so much of chat and dinner with Bindu, I dropped her to her hotel and reached home at 11 in the night.

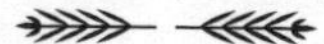

EIGHTEEN

Everyone had slept by that time but Mansi. Evening talk with Dadi and call from Preeti made an impact which I saw when I reached home. She was sitting in the living room waiting for me. 'You didn't sleep?' I asked. She didn't answer and went inside the kitchen to serve food. 'I had dinner.' I voiced little louder to reach the kitchen from living room. She came outside staring at me. 'Bindu insisted to have dinner with her so...' I paused. 'You should have called, I was waiting for you!' She questioned with soft voice. It was nice to hear that bossing question from her for the first time. 'Sorry! I was so much involved with the chat, it didn't flash in my mind. You had your dinner?' I asked. 'Yes!' She said and went upstairs towards the room. I went in kitchen to drink water and saw she was preparing two thali's. I felt bad that she didn't have her dinner. I washed my hands and I served food in plate, prepared thali for her and took it along with water in the room. She was in the bathroom, changing her clothes. I changed outside and wore my night tracks and t-shirt as she takes a bit longer to change.

She came outside wiping her face, 'I brought food for you.' I said showing the thali on teapoy and went inside the bathroom to freshen up myself. When I came out she was standing in the balcony. The thali was untouched. I went in the balcony stood beside her 'You should have had your food. Why were you waiting for me? And why you lied to me that you had food?' I asked. She was quiet. I looked at her, pale face was clearly saying that she had cried. I recalled all that happned through out the day. I wanted to hold her tightly in my arms and say that *'I am with you don't worry!'* But I had no permission for that from her. I walked inside, and brought the thali from the room, holding a bite in my hand 'Mansi, have food.' I said softly. She didn't react. 'Don't show your anger on food.' I said. 'Why? Why are you doing all this?' she asked. 'You know the answer! Please...' I said holding a bite infront of her. She stared at me, I looked straight into her eyes and for a second it was a trip to her heart from her eyes, the heart which was once filled with loads of love and affection for me, had a dark side of hatred for killing her father. She ate a bite, took the thali from my hand and went inside the room, sitting on the couch she ate only one roti and took the thali downstairs in the kitchen. I stood in the balcony, when she went down I followed her, I knew that she would keep all the food as it is. I poured 2 glass of milk and added some portion of health supplement powder in that, held one glass in my hand and offered her the other saying 'Cheers!' with a smile. She couldn't say no to that happy face of mine and took that glass from my hand. We drank the milk, she got busy in organising the kitchen after that. She looked hot in the skin touch night suit, I offered her help but she denied. In the meanwhile, I saw Dad came out of his room and glanced us together and went back to his room, loving elders always care for their children, which I could feel most of the time in my family.

We didn't speak anything in the kitchen and later in the room as well. I felt that she was feeling uneasy about my meeting with Bindu. I wanted to talk to her about our meeting but Preeti and Bindu instructed me not to say anything until she speaks about it. I couldn't sleep and she acted as if she was asleep on the couch. I sat with my laptop, saw the designs of new construction. I was getting distracted when I used to look at her, it was routine for me, my desire for Mansi was increasing day by day, and I went to bathroom to get control over my desire.

Next morning, I opened my eyes and saw Mansi talking to someone over the phone in the balcony. I went to bathroom. When I came out she was still talking, while I was wiping my face, she came to me and held the phone infront of me, mumbling 'Hmm!' I took her phone and she moved out of the room. She was wearing a pink patiyala suit, gazing her sexy figure from back side, I answered the phone with 'Hello'. 'Hi, pretty boy! Is Mansi around?' Preeti asked. 'Ahh..It's you…No, she just left.' I said looking around. 'Great, we have a plan.' She said. 'Wait a minute! We? Who all are there on phone and first of all what were you all discussing from so long?' I asked yawning. 'Good morning sleepy head! I am in.' said Shaun. 'Me too' Sumit said. 'Me too!' voice of Shreya. 'Guys! What is the matter with you all? Early in the morning you are coming up with plans?' I asked. 'It's 9! Not early! I am already in the office.' Sumit said. 'Yeah ok, let me explain! We spoke to Mansi just now, she seemed to be a little worried about your meeting with Bindu and we decided to take advantage of this situation. What say?' Preeti ignited her unstoppable mouth and paused, before the chattering box resumes, I interrupted 'Wait a minute! Last night she didn't ask single question about that, moreover she is upset with many things!' I whispered looking at the door just to be coutious about Mansi's presence around. 'Just listen to us lover boy!' Preeti said. 'Guys I have to hang up, my boss is here…you all let me know what you are planning.' Sumit said and disconnected. Preeti continued. 'Ok, 2 days Bindu is here, and we will create some jealousy in Mansi's mind. We all know that Mansi loves you and we just need to take that love out...' Preeti said. Before she continues, I interrupted again 'Wait…wait …wait…Yesterday I agreed with your point. But that is enough! I can't use Bindu for my personal reason. I know this will not sort out in a day or two...She has come all the way just to meet us and we can't hold her back for our personal reasons. It's my problem Preeti, I can wait for Mansi my entire life...hope you understand.' I ended. 'How long are you gonna live like that man?' Shaun showed his concern. 'I don't know man! But don't want to force myself on her. If she loves me she will come to me.' I said. 'I remember, one day Mansi said this for you! It became true today, but with vice versa!!' said Shreya. I smiled. 'Think on it, you guys had a history, it may hit the bullseye!' Preeti said. 'I know sweety! Thanks a lot for that! I would be happiest person if that happens but it is not right...Anyways, Karnataka police needs you more than me...' I mocked. 'Shut up! Do whatever you want!' she hung the phone with fake anger. She is a light hearted girl, who never takes anything seriously. 'Bindu called us all for a party, she invited Mansi as well and Mansi is coming. I will meet you all there...' Shreya said and disconnected. 'So! Are you thinking something to sort it out or not?' Asked Shaun. 'No! As my Dadi says, I've left everything on time! But frankly speaking it is really hard...' I said. 'Yeah it must be more hard in the night...' he laughed by taking the conversation on fun side. 'It always gets hard for us!' I said and laughed, it was LOL moment for both of us. 'Jokes apart...Why don't you talk to her mother?' Shaun asked. 'What should I say to her? Hello Mummy! I am the murderer of your husband and culprit of your sufferings!' I mocked. 'Aahh... Bad idea! Sorry' he said. 'Anyways, let's catch up in the evening, we all are meeting Bindu in the hotel.' He said.

I was doubtful on Mansi's approach for the party but to my surprise she agreed for it. I didn't analyse whether this change of mind was because of Bindu or because of Dadi's lecture previous day. For me, she got ready to go out with me was more than enough. I stood mesmerised when she came down wearing a grand party saree in red and white colour combination. She was dressed thoroughly and wore all the make up and jewels to match up with her saree. I felt so under dressed infront of her! I was wearing normal Polo T-shirt on my denims. Dadi asked me to change my outfit to match up with Mansi. I wasn't in a mood to change but didn't disappoint her and wore my party wear shirt and blazer on my denims.

We reached the location at eight and had a blast with everyone in the party. Bindu had booked the whole garden restaurant of a hotel only for us. We all presented gifts to her, wishing best for her future, Bindu brought return gifts for everyone. All of them were dressed very well, girls looked hot in their party wears. Surprisingly, my eyes did not follow any girl but Mansi. Aarzoo, who avoided all the parties not to face Shreya, had atteneded this one to value all loving invitations by Bindu. Everyone including Shreya, wanted to sort out things between them, but just like Mansi on our problem, Aarzoo was also not ready to talk to anybody on that.

Soon, Shreya came along with Arjun in the party, their son Akhil was at home along with his grandparents. I observed Shreya staring Aarzoo, I ignored that once but she was continuously staring her. Arjun was too busy boozing with Shaun and Sumit. Shreya wasn't drunk, still looked high while staring her Ex-love. Aarzoo was busy talking with Mansi, Preeti and Bindu, Shreya didn't join the girls for obvious reason that Aarzoo would leave the place if she joins them. After spending some time with all the men present in the party, I glanced at Mansi, she seemed to be happy along with the girls after a long time. I couldn't resist watching her happy, Shaun came patting my back 'Hello Romeo! What's up? You are not drinking?' he asked. 'I am already high on life' I said mocking. 'Hmm, I can see that…coz you are staring at your own wife and not the other girls….' he laughed. 'Hmm, thanks for the information.' that actually reminded me about Shreya, my eyes searched her and she was still staring at Aarzoo by sipping her Pinacolada. I excused Shaun and went to Shreya. Shaun got busy with Sumit and Arjun in drinking. I sat beside Shreya 'Beautiful! Isn't she? I muttered. 'Yeah, as always…' she whispered without noticing me, suddenly, she realised my presence and got embarrassed for her comment. 'I am talking about Mansi.' I mocked. 'Oh...yeah…she…She is looking awesome tonight.' She said juggling with her straw. 'Hmm' I smiled. After a pause of few seconds, 'Isn't it hard to handle that someone whom you love the most is avoiding you?' She asked looking at me. 'Yes it is…but it's not their fault, so can't blame them…' I said. 'Hmm…Agree' she replied. 'You miss her?' I asked. Understanding my point she smiled synthetically. 'Not required to miss her, she is filled all over in my heart.' She spoke her mind unknowingly, after a pause, looking at me 'Just… forget it…it doesn't matter now… you tell me…how come Mansi got ready to come for the party? I mean it's a surprise…is there any other surprise for us?' She asked with a smile. 'I don't know… She is talking to Bindu that is surprise for me…' I said and we both laughed.

Meanwhile, Arjun joined us with his glass of drink and we all had a talk for few minutes. Later, Shreya got up from the chair to go to the wash room. I spoke to Arjun for few minutes, and it seemed as his relationship with Shreya has been improved. I felt good. We were having our starters and the some gravy spilled over my shirt and I went to the washroom to clean it up. While coming out, I heard voices of Aarzoo and Shreya from the lobby, they seemed like arguing with each other. I went out and the girls were involved so much in their conversation that they didn't even realised that I was standing by the end of the corridor, watching them. 'I don't want to hear your explainations. If there is nothing between us then why were you staring at me?' Aarzoo uttered. 'What? I...I wasn't staring at you... How can you say that?' Shreya defended hesitantly. 'Don't lie to me! I saw you from the mirror in my clutch!' Aarzoo made her point. 'What? You... you watch me from your secret mirror??' Shreya pretended to be innocent. 'Don't act so naive...I want the answer.' Aarzoo pushed her towards the wall and asked her with strong hold. 'What are you doing? What if someone catches us like this here? Leave me!' Shreya muttered by fighting to escape from her hands. I was looking at the hot girls like that for the first time, I didn't wish to see more but stood there hiding myself to guard them, perhaps if Arjun walks in, girls would be in a big trouble. Thankfully, every one was busy eating outside and Arjun specially didn't bother for his wife. 'Come back to me...I miss you...I still love you!' Aarzoo said intensly looking in her eyes. They were about to kiss but suddenly, Shreya woke up from her senses and pushed her. 'It's not possible now Aarzoo...I am married and have a son! I can't leave him!' She said. 'I am not asking you to leave your son, you come to me along with him...' Aarzoo said. 'It's not so easy! This is a cynical world....We can't live happily, people will not let us live happily.' Shreya made her point. 'We will make our own world.' Aarzoo influenced her. 'I have convinced myself so long on this...now don't make it hard for me...please!' Shreya begged. 'Accept it! You still love me!' Aarzoo said. 'I will always love you!! But staying together is never possible in this life...I made a decision and I have to live with that for life...I don't have a right to ruin lives!' Said Shreya. 'You already did!' Aarzoo uttered and walked from there.

I hid myself opening the washroom door while she passed from the lobby. I was feeling guilty for hearing their conversation but moreover, I felt sad that these two girls are so much made for each other but can't live toghether. Shreya went inside the washroom again. I went out, my eyes searched for Mansi in the crowd. And there I found my love of life busy with Shaun and Preeti, her eyes looked at me. I waved my hands and called her. She came to me with a question in her eyes. I told her about the incident and asked her to console Shreya in the washroom. Meanwhile, Aarzoo was moving out of the restaurant by taking leave from Bindu. I ran into her to stop but she didn't stop for anybody. Mansi was inside the washroom consoling Shreya. On the other hand, Bindu came to me 'I was so busy talking to everyone, didn't get time to speak to you...So, how is the party?' She asked. 'Yeah that's fine...Party is awesome! It is wonderful to meet all together after a long time.' I said appreciating her hospitality. 'Mansi is looking more beautiful…you guys look cute together.' She said smiling. I smiled 'Thanks…after long time we came out together.Thanks to you!' I said. She stared at me with the pause in same old style. She looked stunning, time has tranformed her into a bombshell. 'You are looking so handsome…you became hot as the time passed!' she said. 'Ahh…Weird!! I am thinking the same for you!!' I said winking my eyes and we both laughed. 'I think we should join the crowd…otherwise history may repeat!' She said smiling. 'Right…let's go.' I was walking and she held my hand, came close to me and kissed on my cheek. 'Happy for you and Good luck! If you need any help, I am always there.' She whispered in my ears. I smiled and bang!! Mansi saw us together! My heart uttered 'O…O!!' Bindu got astonished as well and she went close to Mansi saying 'Look, nothing happened. It is my fault, he turned so hot and I just couldn't resist myself kissing him. I am sorry!' She said holding Mansi's hand and walked out from there, winking at me with a smile. I felt it weird but understood that she said that intentionally to jealous Mansi. One by one, everyone took a leave from the party, where some hearts enjoyed the good old times and some stood broken as usual. I didn't get a time to glance at Shreya as she left with Arjun while I was busy getting a kiss from my Ex-girlfriend.

We got in the car, looking at Mansi 'I was just talking to Bindu and I don't know how that kiss came out!' I explained. She didn't look at me, screening her hand on my face she said 'No need to explain.' Though, she wasn't showing it but I realised that she was jealous. I felt happy inside, it was a sign that she still loved me. In the same morning, I was against the plan of using Bindu. A thought came in my mind, 'Bindu looked hot! Isn't she?' I said adding some more spice into it. 'I don't know, can we just leave from here?' she said looking out of the car window. 'Yeah, ok.' I ignited the car smiling at her.

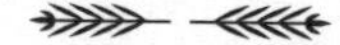

NINETEEN

We drove few kilometers away from the restaurant, the road was empty, and I hardly saw two or three vehicles passing by. It was dark outside and my car head light spread on someones legs on the roadside. I slowed down the speed to check, it was a girl lying on the roadside, and she was injured. Mansi saw the girl as well. We were shocked, I looked at Mansi 'No! What if it is a trap! I read news something like this…there are some gangs who steal people with these types of traps!' She said. 'But what if she is really hurt!' I said and opened the door, 'No!' Mansi muttered holding my hand. 'Let me see, you stay inside and lock the doors' I said and got out of the car and went close to the girl. She was bleeding from her face and from many parts of body. But she was conscious 'Hello!! Can you hear me?' I asked moving close to her. She whispered 'H-e-l-p!!' I slowly grabbed her hand and carried her in my arms, said Mansi to open the door. Mansi hurriedly got out of the car and opened the back seat door, I slowly placed her in the back seat, I searched around and didn't see anyone, but got a hand purse lying few steps away from there. I took the purse and drove the car fastly.

The girl was unconscious, Mansi was worried looking at the girl's condition. I asked her to call Aarzoo, she called her and informed our arrival to the hospital where she works. We reached the hospital, the staff knew about our arrival as Aarzoo called them, they took the girl inside without any formality, nurses and doctors started attending her. Within few minutes, Aarzoo came into the hospital. We waited outside, I asked Mansi to open the purse of the girl, and we found some hundreds of rupees and an identity card in the purse. It was an office identity card with her name, house address and company name and address. The girl's name was Sudha and she lived in Yashwantpur area of Bangalore, she was working in a garment industry. It was strange to see a girl who works and lives in Peenya has fell unconscious on the road near Kormangala, far away from her place.

Meanwhile, I called home and informed about the situation. Aarzoo came to me after few minutes and shocked us with the news that the girl was gang raped and injured badly, she was in a critical condition! Hospital staff called police on this case and within few minute's police arrived. We gave the girl's purse as it is and all the information to the police which they were seeking from us and left from there to our home, leaving the poor girl under the care of hospital.

We reached home and told the entire story to all. My sleep was broken and I woke up around 3 in the morning. In the dim light of bed lamp, I saw Mansi sitting on the couch. I switched on the light wondering that, 'You didn't sleep?' I asked her and she nodded. I got down from the bed and walked towards her. I understood she was upset, I sat next to her on the couch. 'What kind of people are they?' She asked in trembling voice. I had no words, I held her hand to console her in that situation. She started crying 'That poor girl was bleeding allover!! I don't know how her family is gonna hold that situation?!!' she mumbled while crying. I imagined the girl, it was really depressing to see a girl in that condition. Till that day, I saw and read news of rapes but for the first time I saw something like that in real life. I remember once Preeti saying *there are no cases as worse as rape cases, when we see women or children, who got raped, it hurts our soul.* I agreed with her after seeing the poor girl in such a worst state. I kept my arm around her shoulders to comfort her, drowning in the situation, she forgot her rage for me and kept her head on my shoulder, she was disturbed badly and couldn't stop crying. After few minutes, she suddenly woke up from her emotion and got separated from me. Wiping her tears, she muttered 'I got emotional…'

I got up and took a hanky from the closet and offered that to her, 'It's ok. I understand…Even I am upset for the girl.' I said. She took a hanky and wiped her tears. 'Thanks for not listening to me on getting off the car. It's atually you, who first saved the girl.' She appreciated me after months and it felt like after an era she said something good about me. I missed the Mansi, who used to appreciate smallest things, I did in school. Coming back to the situation, I smiled 'Sometimes we have to keep our mind aside and act according to our heart. If everyone thinks like that then there won't be any existence for good people on the earth.' I said and looked at her, she was staring at me, those beautiful brown eyes were filled with tears, perhaps, I saw the hidden love for me in them, she took her eyes off me. I smiled 'Go to sleep, its 3.30, you sleep on bed it is more comfortable, I will be here on the couch.' I Said. 'No, its fine, I am good here. You sleep on bed.' she won't listen to anybody if she has decided something.

I opened my eyes and it was 7 in the morning, Mansi was still sleeping. It was once in a blue moon situation. No matter what, she never misses her Yoga at 5 in the morning, unless she is ill. I went close to her and kept my hand on her forehead to see if she had any temperature. But she was fine, it was last night stress due to which she was dozed off early morning. I went to balcony and made a phone call to the hospital to check the condition of the girl. Hospital reception informed that the girl was still in a critical condition and the police had called her family, who were present in the hospital that time. The day passed with our routine.

Evening we visited the hospital. By that time the girl Sudha's condition was stable and she was conscious, her family thanked us. Police was still in a search of the culprits. Sudha told the story to police, she was waiting for the bus while coming back from her friend's house in Banashankari area. Few co-workers of her company offered her lift to her house in the car and innocent girl accepted as she didn't had an idea about their horrifying intentions. They were 3 men, who were missing after the crime. Sudha's father seemed to be very upset, her family looked dreadfully poor and they weren't able to pay bills of such an expensive hospital. I consoled the family by taking all the bills on me but before I could swipe my credit card on the billing counter, the cashier informed that bills have been taken care by Doctor Aarzoo. I looked back and Aarzoo was standing before me. She smiled and asked 'What? Leave something for us too, I will look after the girl now on...' I looked at her by winking my eyes, I smiled and said 'Be my guest...'

After few days Sudha got discharged from the hospital but we heard the news that her father was not ready to accept the girl at his home. He was worried about the society and the marriage of two more girls at home, the innocent girl Sudha lost both, job and home. We all went to convince her father and the company where she was working but nothing worked out. I was angry on all, people blame the victim and the culprits are roaming freely. It was really upsetting to see the dark side of the society, who don't accept these victims, even after knowing that they already suffered a lot without their fault.

Our golden hearted doctor, Aarzoo didn't leave any loops in Sudha's case. She asked an NGO to help Sudha and made arrangements of her stay and job. She also arranged the defence classes for her to fight the difficult situations when time comes. Flesh wounds heal as the time passes but wounds of soul may not heal so fast. We all helped her to come over that. Our IPS Preeti along with her smart police team found the culprits and threw them behind the bars within two months of mishap. Sudha was capable of handling herself alone by that time.

During these days, my case also saw some progress. Mansi started talking to me, although there wasn't any fire of physical relationship that I fantasised about her all the time. But I was happy to move a step ahead of few words a day from no words a day. On the other hand, our construction of township in the outskirts of the city had started with full flow of labour and finance. As Dad was busy with pending works of previous constructions, I was visiting the site along with Raju almost every day.

One fine day, Raju came to me with a young pretty girl. She belonged to a small village near the construction site. We went to the sales office, which we'd constructed before the towers. Raju introduced her to me 'Bhaiyya, she is Parvati. She is working in our site from last couple of months, yesterday she was about to jump off from our building, luckily I saw her and saved her!' he paused. 'What?' I uttered shockingly. Looking at the girl, 'Are you Mad? You know the consequences if you do that? Our whole work would have been kept on hold' I uttered again. 'Bhaiyya relax, there is more I want to say.' He pleaded. 'Go ahead!' I said sitting on my chair. 'This girl is just 15 years old. Her family has sent her to work here. They continuously tortured her for money. Her father is a hardcore drunkard and a landlord had always helped him fianancially, few days back the old landlord had come with a marriage proposal with her, and her father agreed in the greed of money.' Raju said. 'What! That sounds like an old movie!' I said mockingly. They both stood quietly. 'Ahh.. I am sorry…look girl, ahh…Parvati. It's wrong…and illegal, you go to the police. They will help you.' I said. She looked at Raju and he nodded his head and asked her to talk. She spoke in local Kannada language. 'Sir, I am just fourth class pass, poor girl, who will listen to me? I don't know any legal procedures. Moreover, I am afraid of everyone, my father, that landlord, and police. I don't know what to do.' She requested. 'You are a minor, this marriage is illegal. You just have to say that.' I said.

'Wait Bhaiyya, there is more,' Raju said. 'Ahh, now what?' I asked holding my head. Raju asked the girl to continue, 'Sir, My village is strugging with cultivation, we are completely dependent on the rain, and from past 2 years there has been no proper rain in our village. Farmers are struggling with debts, they leased their lands to the landlord, he has kept the lands for few hundreds, and many of the lands have been sold to the constructions like this. And our farmers are working as labourers to survive and some are just wasting their life like my father by drinking. This creepy landlord has spoiled many womens lives, he is fourty plus years old, he has married twice, nobody knows where his wives have gone. He spread the rumours that they ran away, but people say that he must have murdred them or sold them to an Arab after fullfiling his dirty needs. No one has guts to face him, most of the people are uneducated and superstitious, they believe more in Tantriks than real power of almighty, they go to this fraud Tantrik rather than a doctor, if someone falls sick! That Tantrik works for this man, he saw me one day while in the village, he controlled my father with his weakness of drinking and money, only to use me for his dirty needs. With that Tantrik, he has proved that I have some luck and if I marry him and give birth to a baby boy, all the bad luck of the village will vanish away. Now, after hearing that, all of a sudden the whole village is getting ready to sacrifice me to that monster, even after knowing the truth about him.' She paused and started crying.

I felt pity, thinking where are we heading, just few kilometres away there is a high-tech city of twenty-first century with all the modern lifestyle and this village is still in tenth century or even behind that! Believing all this bullshit, even after knowing the truth they are pushing this poor girl into hell. 'How could people do such things! Even if they are uneducated, they should atleast use their common sense! Village people...phew!' I said. 'It's not happening only in village bhaiyya, afterall those people are innocent undecucated villagers but in cities modern educated people are also falling in the traps of these fraud baba's and Mata's!! Everyday we see news like these...' Raju said the truth, which really opened my eyes. Yes, its happening allover our country, this trap has spread everywhere apart from all this next generation technology, people are going back with these frauds. 'Bhaiyya...' Raju woke me up from my thoughts. Parvati was still crying. I gave her some tissues from the table 'Parvati, calm down...I will help you. I can send them to jail, they will be punished for long time.' I consoled her. 'No sir, if you do something like that, they will harm you, they may spoil your work, or even physically hurt you or your family and they won't leave any proofs. They are monsters. You have to think some other way, where you can convince the villagers that this marriage should not be performed, his asset is the belief of villagers.' She explained the landlord's strength and weakness. 'Better, we can hide you somewhere?' Raju thought of a good shortcut. 'No, if you do that, then they will find someother girl in the village. That man has endless female desires in the village. He has raped many women but nobody complained about him in the fear of society.' She said. 'Knowing all that you were about to jump off the building?' Raju asked her. She felt ashamed and kept her head down. I understood her situation, 'Raju, we must appreciate the guts of this girl, even after going through all this she cares so much about her villagers.' I said. Looking at her 'Parvati, you don't worry. I will definetly try to do something to help you and your people. But till then you be normal, don't tell anybody that we met and DON'T DO ANYTHING SILLY like you did yesterday.' I warned her. She nodded and said 'The marriage is in four days!' That was shocking! Doing anything in just four days was really a difficult task. I nodded at her and asked Raju to drop her home safely.

I didn't go home, I called Preeti and Shaun who could help me in this case. The whole night we discussed it and made a trap to catch those culprits. Mansi called me twice in the meanwhile. Preeti and Shaun started teasing me on that, 'She still loves you man, it's just that anger.' Shaun said. 'I agree, why you don't try to get more close to her... You know what I mean? Afterall, she has a crush on you since childhood.' Preeti said winking her eye. I smiled biting my lips, looking at my teeth Shaun said 'Sandy! *Tumhare daant to motiyon jaise chamak rahe hain* (Your teeth are shining like pearls)!' Mocking the old hindi commercial. 'How can you remember the ad slogans, which are 10 years back of you?' I asked him wondering, as those ads were telecasted when we were just two or three. 'Those are classics man! I have all the collection... I can mock the movie stars and ads generations before us.' He said with pride. *'Hogaya* (Are we done?)? I have to go, I haven't come all the way to discuss the old ads here? Preeti said. 'No, you have come here to discuss about me and Mansi?' I said mockingly, reminding her that she started diverting the main discussion. 'I can spare any amount of time on you guys...but now, I seriously have to go. My parents are going to Europe trip, I have to see-off them at the airport. So let's come back to the point.' She said looking at her watch. We all got back to the discussion, we required Shaun's theatre troop's help in that plan. We called them and explained about our mission and made the full-proof plan to start from the coming day. It was a simple plan but was very difficult to execute.

TWENTY

I reached home at one in the midnight. Mansi and Mom were watching a movie together, basically they were waiting for me. Habitually, Mom waits for me whenever I get late but that day I was happy seeing Mansi along with her. Things were changing, which made me think about what Preeti suggested me that day. I was once a champ in that but with Mansi I didn't know why, I was always slow. 'What took you so long?' Mom asked. 'I was with friends Mom.' I said. 'I know that, but why so long…you have a wife waiting for you at home, have some responsibility for her as well.' Another expected dialogue came from Mom. Mansi went inside the kitchen when Mom was saying that. I stared her walk till she went inside. Mom looked at Mansi and me, she smiled 'Have your food and don't be late henceforth.' Saying, she went to her room to give us the privacy. 'OK' I smiled at her while she was going.

I washed my hands in the washbasin and sat on the dinning table. Mansi brought the food and served on the plate. She sat infront of me and didn't ask any questions. 'We were discussing on one problem.' I said to begin the conversation. 'You said that on phone, anything serious?' she asked. I explained her entire story. She was worried after hearing that. 'But as you said they seem like dangerous people, they may harm you and anybody in the gang, why are you doing that? You should have sent the girl to some NGO and filed a police complaint against them.' she said. I felt her concern in that. 'Is that a concern?' I asked staring at her. 'What…What do you mean by that? Ofcourse it's a concern and not only for you but for Preeti and Shaun as well.' She said wavering and pushing hair back her ears. My heart smiled with happiness, it was nothing but her love for me. I took a bite of roti with sabji and stared at her again, she was wearing a navy and orange combination dress. Day by day her bewitching beauty was mesmerising me. Artificial things which she does to show off that she doesn't care about me spoke loudly vice versa that she does care for me. 'Why did you wait for me tonight?' I asked. 'Mom was sitting alone, so to accompany her.' she said looking down. 'That's it?' I asked with my gaze. 'Listen, don't flatter yourself. I know what you are thinking but just to remind you that I …You have your food, I will bring water.' she muttered and went inside the kitchen. I imagined her reaction before saying that, it was similar to previous discussions on that matter, her behaviour made me go crazy about her. Sometimes, I felt going rebellious, hold her tightly, kiss her allover and make love to her but that wouldn't be me. I never forced any girl for anything, whatever I did that was all with the consent of opposite girls. Famous heartthrob of girls was struggling to win the heart of my love, pity!

The next morning I started early, I instructed Raju to look after the site job and call me only if anything was urgent. Dad was busy finishing the old projects as usual so wasn't aware of anything. I requested Mansi, not to disclose anything about my mission in the family and she agreed unwillingly. Shaun started with his theatre troop, they were about to do a sting operation of the main Tantrik that day. Preeti initiated enquiring about the background of the landlord, Mahadevaiyya. Soon, she enquired about his nephew. His name was Rudrappa, who left the family after knowing the awful operations of the baddie of our mission. He was working as waiter in a city hotel. Preeti went to meet him, I insisted her to take me along, she agreed but asked me to stay hidden as she wanted that to workout as legal as possible. She sat on the table of hotel with Rudrappa and started interrogating him, I sat as a customer next to their table. First he was hesitant to reply on anything she was asking him, but we had very less time so Preeti forced him to speak the truth. The guy revealed the dark side of the story. The landlord was involved in a flesh trade. He exports the poor village girls after using them for his needs. The girls were sent to some parts of North India, they were used as sex slaves. If anybody opposed that, they were murdered and buried in the back yard of the house by his men. He took charge of the poor farmers lands forcefully with dummy documents. He had accused Rudrappa and took his property as well, and abandoned him when he opposed. He threatened him for death if he opened his mouth infront of anybody. In the name of *Gramdevi* (Goddess of the village) he did many immoral things. He also had hidden his black money under the *Gramdevi* temple of village. That was a plus point for our plan, Preeti recorded the entire statement and asked Rudrappa to speak the truth in the court as well. Rudrappa asked for his security, Preeti assured him that.

With Rudrappa's statement, I got another special idea and I met Shreya. I requested her to show her love for art, I asked her to make a thick book which should look as composed in the ancient time. The words, design, paper everything should be shaped as an ancient epic book, I told her to write something which couldn't be understood or read by anybody. We bought all the items she required for that art and she started working on that. Everyone knew that it was silly but we all worked with heart on it. I called Shaun, he was on his mission but he didn't get any success till then, as the security wasn't allowing them to meet the Tantrik.

Two days passed and we had to proceed with plan B and spread the fishing net with beautiful girls from the theatre troop. The girls did the best job with their hidden cameras from their bags and shirt buttons, we saw the footage in the night. As the entire troop members were identified by Mahadevaiyya and his men, we needed a fresh face. I thought of adding Sumit into the plan, I called Sumit and gave him the note which he had to remember by-heart. Sumit belonged to Brahmin family and he had a look of an intellectual swamiji. He was good with stage shows and drama's since school time. We called Parvati and assured her that we would be coming next day. We were ready to proceed for the next day with our full proof plan for the fall of that demons kingdom.

The next morning, I got ready in a traditional dress. Shaun sent me Sumit's pictures! They transformed him into a traditional swamiji!! I laughed looking at his picture. While I was leaving, Mansi came and sat beside me in the car. I was amazed to see her in traditional green silk saree, fully dressed for the wedding, I stared her with no expression. 'What? I am coming with you.' she said. 'Hey…Hey…Easy…I am not going for a wedding OK! I am going to stop it! They are dangerous, I have no idea what's gonna happen there. I don't want to risk you in this…so please…get off the car!' I persuaded. 'I said I am coming with you. When everyone is joining, why do you want me to stay away from this?' She asked persistently. 'Aaa.. aa…Correction! Not everyone, Preeti is coming with her force accompanied by Sumit, even Shaun is staying away.' I tried to convince her. 'Whatever it may be but I am coming today.' She was certain with her decision. 'Mansi No! it's not safe there. Please.' I begged. 'I can't sit here the whole day worrying about you, so please take me with you.' she spoke her mind. 'What?' I was astounded to hear that, she was really concerned about me. 'I mean… I would be worried about all of you. So I want to come. In case if you need anything, I will be there.' She said hesitating a bit with her previous words. But I was sure that she had started caring for me just like old days. 'We have back up there. So just be at home, I will keep on calling you.' I tried once again to convince her. 'No…I am coming with you' she, locked the seat belt, knotted her hands across and sat in the car staring ahead. 'Ok, but you will not come out of the car.' I said and ignited the car.

We reached the the corner of *Gramdevi* temple, met Sumit and cops, who were all disguised as Sumitanada Swamiji's disciples. We all together started to go to the temple where the wedding was about to start. Preeti and her backup police force were ready around the temple in civil dress. Preeti was astonished to see Mansi. She came to us, staring at Mansi 'Why did you come here?' she muttered. 'I came to see the wedding drama.' Mansi said winking her eye. I looked at Preeti, so did she and we both nodded! I asked Mansi to stay inside the car and took out the big book which

Shreya created and moved in along with Preeti.

It was completely dramatic, the wedding was about to start as the innocent bride and the devil groom were ready to knot, we all entered uttering 'STOP!!'

Everyone looked at us, landlord Mahadevaiyya looked more dangerous than he was described by Parvati and Rudrappa. The whole *Gram Panchayat* (Village Authority) and all the villagers were present in the temple for wedding and free lunch. There were few lungi men inside-out, they were all bodyguards of landlord and Tantrik.

We all entered inside the temple and I proceeded saying '*Namaskar* (Hello), I am Sandeep Singh, you all must be knowing that there is a township construction going on just outside your village. My company is constructing that township. We are all here to give you some important news about your village. Few days back, while digging we got this ancient book which was hidden beneath the land of your village.' I paused showing everyone the epic book designed by Shreya and continued my approach 'I was curious about this book which looked so ancient. I took it to the archeology department and they confirmed that Swami Sumitanadaji can read this book as it's written in very rare language of *Halegannada* (Old Kannada language). We approached Swamiji, who lives in the Himalayas these days. He came all the way from there to here on our request.' Sumit waved his hands to everyone, by that time many villagers rushed ahead to touch his feet for his blessings. The cops who were disguised as his disciples instructed them 'Please don't touch the feet, take your blessings a foot distance away from Swamiji.'

The landlord, Mahadevaiyya and Tantrik along with his men were astonished and looked at me curiously for my next words. I continued 'Swamiji read the book, as you can see it's a big book and it took a month for him to read this book. Yesterday he completed it and came to me with the news and today we decided to meet you all and inform the important information about this village and near by villages. Swamiji will tell you all, everything written in this book.' I paused looking at Sumit to handle the rest of the drama practically. Since people will believe more on the words of Baba's, we decided that Sumit will tell the story of the book.

He started with strong voice 'Namaskar everyone!' people responded immedietly by joining hands infront of him and saying 'Namakara Swami'. Sumit continued with his serious expressions 'This book is written by a man called Bhairava, who lived in this place thousand years ago. He was a rich man and strong devotee of your *Gramdevi Kallamma*. One fine day, *Devi* appeared in his dream and instructed him some important things to write for the benefit of the people in the future. There are many things written in this book, praising the almighty, shlokas and many things. But more important things to be noted were-

Take care of woman in your house, never hurt any women and respect them, if you ill treat women it is as equal as ill treating your *Gramdevi* and problems will start arising in your life from there.

The illiterate landlord started scratching his head as he got irriated after that statement but in the fear of the public he kept quiet. Sumit continued,

Next point is no girl should be married before the age of 18!

Treat your female Child as equal as male Child as all the female Child have an ansh of *Gramdevi.*

All the people were listening to Swami Sumitanada by dropping their jaws.

If you take an oth of following these instructions then all your worries and problems will be resolved.

Most importantly, there is a hidden treasure under the temple. Just below the idol of *Gramdevi!* Which is meant for the development of you all and the village, it was hidden by Bhairava. The man who wrote this book.' And he rested his mouth.

'WHAT RUBBISH!! WHO THE HELL ARE YOU ALL? WHAT ALL YOU ARE UTTERING??' the angry landlord finally lost his temper and shouted at us, when Sumit spoke about the treasure which he saved from years under the idol of *Gramdevi.* Villagers looked at us, they were waiting for our response.

We expected this reaction. Sumit said '*Shaant bachcha* (Quiet son)! I am just informing you all about things written in this book. I will prove its true, just dig infront of the *Devi* idol, you will find the treasure.'

'NO…NOBODY MOVES! I WILL NOT LET ANYBODY GO NEAR THE IDOL. IT'S SACRED, NONE OF YOU SHOULD ENTER HERE WITH YOUR IMPURE BODIES!' The landlord uttered and stood infront of the entrance of the idol chamber. 'Let us check, we will come to know whether he is speaking the truth or not!' The *Sarpanch* (Head of village) opened his intelligent mouth. The landlord signalled the Tantrik and he uttered 'STOP! IT WILL BRING BAD LUCK IF ANY OUTSIDERS ENTER THE TEMPLE!' 'No problem, Sarpanch and his panch will dig and see, they are not outsiders and they are the head of this village.' I said calmly. People shouted, 'YES, WE WANT TO CHECK THE TRUTH.' Everyone requested all the panch to dig infront of the main idol. Landlord signalled his lungi army, they came ahead opposing. And then entered IPS

Preeti with her police force and CBI. 'Hello everyone, we got information of treasure in this place. Nobody opposes, as the temple comes under the government authority.' Everyone took a side when she raised her voice.

The panch started digging, I saw Mansi standing behind in the crowd watching everything quietly, avoiding my instruction of staying inside the car. I didn't speak to her as it was dangerous to show any relationship infront of the landlord and his lungi men. Within 2 feet they found 4 big pots filled with gold and currency. Every jaw in the temple dropped! Landlord had no option but to say that it was his money. But Tantrik opened his big mouth 'If it's old treasure then how come it has this era's currency?' Swami Sumitanada said 'It is written in this book that the amount will automatically turn as current era's notes!!' Nobody opened their mouth with that statement by Swamiji but Landlord and Tantrick got affended after that, they uttered 'IT ALL HAPPENED BECAUSE OF THIS MAN!' saying they enraged with stick and some local armours towards me, by that time Mansi came running at me, fearing she held my arm tightly and stood beside me. Immedietly, Preeti fired in the air and inculcated everyone that she had to arrest Landlord and Tantrick for their illegal activies. She revealed the villagers about the illegal activities of the landlord. She showed the video of Tantrik, who tried to seduce the women of the theatre troop. She came prepared with the arrest warrant of the landlord on the basis of video and Rudrappa's statement of raping and murdering many women and exporting the females outside the state in flesh trade.

CBI knew everything, they took charge of the amount and assured the villagers that the village will be benefited with that amount. Preeti arrested them along with their men. The landlord's dreadful look at me while going made Mansi's hold tighter, I didn't concentrate on landlord after that as her soft hands tight touch mesmerized me. 'We will soon take position on all the land papers which are kept under the custody of this man forcefully and return to you all.' said Preeti to everyone and left from there.

Meanwhile, Parvati ran towards me and fell on my feet. 'Thank you sir!! Thank you very much for saving my life from this monster. This all happened only because of you.' joining her palms she cried. I held her shoulder and raised her, 'No! It all happend only because of you! You took an initiative to reveal the truth of this man and not to forget Raju, who brought you to me. Now everything is fine. Don't ever do anything silly and live your life happily, study and do whatever you want, I am there to help you in any manner.' I said patting her shoulder. I went to her father 'What kind of man are you? You have such a wonderful girl and you are troubling her so much? Wasting your life just by drinking and doing nothing?'

I asked him knotting my hands against my chest. 'I am sorry sir, I will not do anything like that henceforth, financial worries and Parvati's mother's untimely death, turned me into a monster. I will follow the rules of Swamiji and live life peacefully. But we don't have any source of income to survive.' he solicited. 'You come to my site for work from tomorrow and send your daughter to school. And don't worry, I will pay all the expenses of her education.' I said, and by chance glanced at Mansi, who was staring at me.

People went to Swami Sumitanada seeking his blessings. We didn't reveal the truth of Swami Sumitanandaji because we wanted people to follow everything he said. Since, public will never give a damn for the words of Sumit the bank manager. They all requested Swami to stay with them. Our Swamiji denied their request saying 'I have to go to Himalaya and meet Lord Shiva! But my blessings will always be there with you, NEVER EVER FORGET WHATEVER I SAID! Respect women and girls, believe in your hard work and the true almighty, not the baba's like Tantriks or swami's like me, because we all are humans just like you. *Kallamma Devi* will bless you with all the happiness and prosperity. HARA HARA MAHADEV!!' he uttered to finish his speech and moved fast waving his hands to crowd. Mansi grinned appreciating his acting and unknowingly she held my hand, I felt happy to see her smile after a long time. I stared at her, she looked down, hesitating she took her hand back 'Shall we go now?' she asked. 'Ladies first…' I showed her the way and started walking with her.

In the meantime, the village authority came to us wiping their sweat after digging the treasure, 'We all knew about Mahadevaiyya's bad activities but had no proofs. We don't want to know what you did and how you did but we believe in everything you did, as a result, today all of a sudden our village experienced the much awaited justice, only because of you. We feel our *Gramdevi* sent you here to vanish out our sorrow. Thank you!' They joined their hands to show their gratitude. I joined my hands as well with smile and respect to the elders 'I did nothing, it is all your prayers…If you really want to thank me then please never ever allow any girl or women of your village to experience the pain by monsters like Mahadevaiyya and Tantrik.' They all held my hands with assurance and went back. That reminded Mansi something and she held my hand and took me to bow her head infront of the *Gramdevi*. The priest did special pooja in our name to the goddess. I poured all the money I had in my wallet in front of Devi. After seeking blessing of Goddess and taking leave from Parvati, her father as well as the villagers, we moved out from there with a strange satisfaction.

TWENTY ONE

I took Mansi to our site as she had never visited there. We got down from the car and Raju called me to check how the things are going on. He had called me in every half an hour to check the status as he was worried about the mission. I picked his call and informed him that we have reached the site. We went to my cabin. Raju came over running within few minutes. 'Namaste Bahbhi, how was it Bhaiyya? What happened with Parvati and villagers?' he wished Mansi and asked me breathlessly. 'Easy, everything went well. Mahadevaiyya and Tantrik are in police custody now. Obviously, the marriage has been stopped and villagers are free from all the demons.' I said. 'Wow, great! Was there any problem?' he asked again. 'No everything was fine.' I said sitting on the chair. Mansi sat before me smiling at Raju's curiousity. 'Yeah, just that the cuplrits came in rage to hit him.' Mansi spoke in the middle. I stared at her, she looked at the table ignoring me. 'What? Why?' Raju asked. 'Aah, it was nothing, everything got under control. Preeti arrested them before they could do anything.' I said chilling him. 'Thank god! And how's that girl Parvati?' he asked, which showed some special concern. 'Hmm...She is fine now. Why are you so much interested in knowing about her?' Mansi asked him with smile. 'Well, there nothing like that...its...its.. just...because she was so much worried... so...I asked.' he said trembling. 'She will be going to school from now on. However, its vacation time yet she won't be working here anymore. And yeah, she is just fifteen, keep that in mind OK!' I said to Raju reminding him not to take any further steps. 'Look who's talking!' Mansi muttered looking down. I stared her with fake anger, as I understood what she meant with that, a guy like me who dated as many girls as possible at Parvati's age was advicing Raju. 'Yeah...I am just saying that, without any girls approval, don't proceed for anything. However, her father will join to work in her place from tomorrow. Just keep a watch on that man, he seemed like a drunkard, I hope he won't do that here.' I said to Raju staring at Mansi, she was still watching the floor with her cute smile. Raju looked at both of us, he smiled as he knew our history and my love stories, after all he has been in the house since years and he was family. The guy was just 22 and less educated but has the finest heart. 'OK. I know Bhaiyya, I was just concerned about that poor girl, that's it.' he said looking at me. 'Hmm... That's it?' Mansi asked him again with her cute naughty smile, which used to make me crazy in the days when we used to date. I was desperate to see that look and that smile from months. That day, in the name of Parvati, I got a chance to see the naughty old Mansi again! 'C'mon Bhabhi, There's nothing like that! I will order something for you both.' Saying he walked out with his innocent smile.

'Oye wait! Kesar-pista milk shake for Madam and cold coffee for me, and you order whatever you want.' I said looking at Mansi. She looked here and there but her ears focussed all on my voice. That was the combination which we used to drink while in school, by sharing both together. 'I just had Tea, will order them for you.' he said and went outside. 'You remember!' she mumbled, after the exit of Raju. 'Every bit of it.' I said looking at her. 'You always had great memory! As it's difficult to remember each and everyones taste.' Sarcasm came out without any hestitation after a long time. I smiled in return 'Yup, everyone has different taste but some have different feelings, which always subsist deep in the heart.' I said. She looked at me, my eyes were straightly looking at hers, she couldn't look for long and turned her eyes outside the window 'Always an expert in impressing.' She whispered herself but I heard that. 'Glad to hear that! At last today I did it after 4 months of marriage!' I said.

There was a silence from her side. She was looking outside the window, it was end of May and the climate was hot outside. Rain was expected to be showering by the end of the month as per the whether reports, which are never accurate.

'Why were you bothered so much when they came to hit me?' I asked, to hear the truth hidden inside her, reminding the situation. She looked at me for a second and looked outside the window again, her hands were pressing her clutch tightly, 'I…I would have done the same if they went to hit Sumit or Preeti' she said, the words spoke less then the body language. I smiled in return, 'What? I mean that.' She said to make sure her words. 'Yeah, I know…and ofcourse you came along with the same intention.. right?' I said grinning. She looked here and there, hesitated and nervous. 'From where Raju will bring the drinks? I mean, it's a village…' She asked to change the topic. 'There is a dairy over here, everything is available in the dairy store.' I answered, without dragging the matter. I didn't want her to get uneasy, as she came out with me after a long time. She didn't speak more and took a magazine from the table and started reading that.

Meanwhile, I got a call from a vendor, and got busy talking to him. While talking, I couldn't resist my eyes from staring her. She was glacing at the magazine, she looked hot in that green saree, which bounded her body so perfectly, showing all her beautiful curves. Her pinkish waist was slightly peeking out in the gap between saree and the blouse, all her jewels made her look more bright. The scent of jasmine garland which she'd decorated in her hair was spread allover in the cabin. Sound of her bangles mesmerised my ears, I couldn't concentrate more on the vendor's speech, and I asked him to call later and kept the phone aside. I gazed at her face, the decorative bindi and sindhoor on her forehead enhanced her beauty; those pink soft lips were highlighted with maroon lipstick. Everytime I saw her, made me fall more in love with her. I was sure that she must have sensed my intent look but she wasn't taking her eyes off the magazine. Dadi was right, *No matter how long it takes, true love is always worth a wait because waiting is the sign of true love.* She has bewitched my soul, she was all over me, her presence made me go hypnotised in her love. Sometimes, I hated myself for hurting her, not valuing her feelings in school, dating the hot girls and not observing her inner beauty.

Sudden knock on the door woke me up from my thoughts. Mansi got up from her chair and opend the door. Raju came inside with the tray of 2 glasses filled with shake and cold coffee. 'I have to go to work Bhabhi, you both have these.' He kept the tray and went out. She added equal amount of sugar as I prefer in my coffee, and held the glass infront of me after couple of stirs, I took it with a smile, and she took her milk shake. At that moment her company gratified me, I wanted to ask her for sharing as we used to do back in school but the things which happened between us locked my lips. By that time my phone rang, it was Mom, I received the call saying 'Its Mom…' to Mansi and sipped the coffee. 'Me, Dadi and your Dad are going to Ramya's home now. She has planned 3 days tour to Alleppey, will be leaving with them today. Dad saying that you have to finish some legal documentation with vendor tomorrow, so you have to be here…Wait, Dadi wants to talk…' Mom said from the other side and gave the phone to Dadi. 'Hello, I decided not to take Mansi along with us. You both can have some quality time alone in the home, I am hoping something will work out.' experienced mind chuckled. I smiled. That news made me happy. I wished them happy journey and hung up the phone. 'Where they are going?' Mansi asked sipping the shake after hearing my wishes. 'They are all going to Alleppey with Ramya and family.' I said. 'What? All of a sudden?' she asked. 'Yeah, Ramya planned it.' I said. 'Oh' She sipped her shake. 'I have some important work tomorrow, so I can't go. If you want to go with them, then I will tell them now.' I said unwillingly as I didn't want her to be uncomfortable alone with me at home. 'No, its Ok. I am fine at home.' She said and those words flew all the butterflies in my stomach. 'What time they are leaving?' she asked after a pause. 'Now' I said and 'You want to see the site?' after a pause I asked. 'Yeah ok' she agreed.

I showed her the site and explained her how we are proceeding with work. After a tour of an hour at the site we left from there. I took her to a restaurant and we had nice lunch together then I dropped her at home. I had to go back to the site to prepare the documents for next day's meeting.

Later in the evening, I received calls from everyone but I was busy and kept all the calls on voice messages. It took till midnight for me to finish the documentation along with my legal adviser. Raju was about to wait in the site itself as he had to look after night workforce. I heard all the voice messages before leaving. Some were from work and whatsapp message from Ramya about their departure. And rest all from friends, read-

Sumit- Hello Rascal! *biwi sath mili toh dost ka award winning performance bhi bhool gaya!* (You forgot the award wining performance by friend when your wife came along!)No response! Anger and fist bang emojis. I saw the time, it was twelve, I called him and apologised for not calling back. I called Preeti as well and thanked her, she informed that the amount hidden was calculated and it was roughly around three crores and Rudrappa will be paid twenty percent of the amount. He said, he will use that amount for the development of the village. Rudrappa has become the next legal heir of Mahadevaiyya and he has agreed to handover all the papers of the villagers, which were forged by his uncle. That was good news, Preeti showed her interest in my special moments with Mansi that day, she asked how it went with Mansi later in the day, and I told her the story. She said that Mansi had called her, she was concerned about my safety. I felt happy hearing that. I called Shaun as well to ask him about the payment of his troop. Initially, he denied but when I forced him he said that he will take it later. Lastly, I called Mansi and informed her about my arrival at home.

I reached home at one thirty after midnight. Mansi was watching television and when I parked my car inside the garage, she opened the main door. 'You are still awake? I told that I would be late!' I asked showing my concern. 'Why your phone was switched off??' she asked anxiously. I understood that she was worried about me. 'Battery went off, but I called before leaving…Why didn't you sleep?' I asked looking at her while going inside the home. She took her eyes off me 'Yeah, I…I couldn't sleep so, was watching television.' She said wavering. I locked the door from inside and gazed at her, she wore purple colour night suit, her hair was open, her face was still bright like a full moon in those dim-lights of the house, and she looked stunning. I felt like grabbing her in my arms and kiss her. She cleared her throat and muttered 'Ahemm, you had your dinner?' I came out of my fascination 'I had some snacks' I said. 'You must be hungry, I will serve food for you…you get fresh and I will bring the food in the room itself.' she walked towards the kitchen. I went to the room and changed my clothes. By the time I came out of bathroom, she was keeping the tray on the teapoy.

'Why are you doing all this?' I asked her. 'What do you mean by that?' she asked. 'You know what I mean' I said with certainty. 'I'll bring the water' she said ignoring my question and started moving out. I held her arm and grabbed her close to me, pushing her against the wall, 'I want to know…why?' I asked with intensity. 'Please…leave me…there is nothing… As I said, I was just worried about you all…that's it…' she said strongly by making her point. 'That's it? C'mon Mansi…Whom are you fooling? You accompany me when I am going for a risky task, you get worried about me if I get late, you know how much sugar I take in my coffee, you know when I am hungry, you know all my needs and wants, you know hundreds of small things about me! You also know I am madly falling in love with you, you even know when I am staring at you! (Staring her lips) You know how much I desire you!' Whispering the last sentence, I went close to her, she smelled wonderful, my heartbeats were fast and I felt her fast heartbeats, we were breathing fast, I raised my hand and pushed her hair back her ears, and slowly caressed her face and held her waist from the other hand and pulled her more close to me, our bodies touched, she was shivering, her eyes were closed when I touched her, she melted, I caressed her lips with my finger and I kissed her pink lips. It lasted for few seconds and suddenly, she pushed me back and ran out of the room. 'MANSI…' I uttered to stop her but she didn't stop and I punched the wall in anger. 'SHITT!!' I shouted, ofcourse in pain, I hurt my hand by doing that.

I went out searching for her, pressing my injured hand with other. I searched down in the kitchen, she wasn't in there, and I came up and saw, guest room door was closed. I went close and knocked the door, she didn't open. 'Mansi, I am sorry, I flew with my heart…please open the door… ' I said pleading her. There was no sound from inside. 'Mansi, please…' I muttered again. She didn't respond. Waiting for a minute made me crazy 'Ok, you don't wanna talk to me…fine. But look inside yourself! Your heart still beats for me and I know you still love me! Why are you fooling yourself?' I uttered with strong voice and waited for some more time for her reply. But she didn't say a word. I got mad at her and walked from there. I banged the door of my room and sat on the bed biting my teeth. I was angry, hungry and hurt as well, I ate my food that she served for me. My anger calmed down after eating food, I kept the tray inside the kitchen and slept by applying pain relief balm on my hand, thinking about her closeness.

The next morning, I woke up at eleven. My hand was aching severely, it was puffed-up. I recalled the previous night punch on the wall. Nevertheless, I had to go for the meeting, I got fresh with all the difficulties in moving my painfully swollen right hand and came down searching for Mansi but I didn't see her anywhere in the house. Raju was home, he came an hour before to get fresh. Before I ask about Mansi, he told me that the breakfast has been served on the table and Mansi went to her mother's home. My temper hoisted with that message. She didn't even bother to inform me or talk to me after the last night scene. Afterall, I am her husband and have all the right on her, I didn't do anything wrong. My ego didn't allow me to call her and I went to office without having breakfast.

I met the vendor and completed the formalities, pain of my hand was rising as the day was passing, it was so painful that I couldn't even sign the papers comfortably. The vendor understood my situation and left early. After the meeting, I went to Aarzoo's hospital, which falls on the way to my home, it's a multi speciality hospital, so I consulted the bone specialist. He scanned my hand to check if there was any fracture, luckily I didn't hit so badly to break it. He dressed my hand with red-tape and gave pain killers after injecting. As I went there, thought of meeting Aarzoo as well but she was busy in a surgery. I left a message for her and drove back home with all the snags.

I reached home by five in the evening. Mansi was home when I went inside, my ego held my anger up. She was reading a magazine in the living room. I started hopping the steps to the room without looking at her. She saw me with dressing on my hand and ran towards me 'What happened to your hand?' worriedly she asked, she didn't know about my punch after her exit previous night. 'Why are you bothering about it?' I said with sarcasm, neglecting her, I raised the steps. '*Arey*! Let me see.' she said. I didn't stop and went inside the room hurriedly and took my clothes to change and went in the bathroom. She followed me 'Let me see it, please!' she begged on the bathroom door. I didn't respond to her, got fresh with a broken hand and changed the clothes with all the hitches. I opened the door and she was standing just before me. 'What happened?' she asked softly. Her behaviour resembled as nothing happened previous night. I was suffering from awful pain, and was feeling dizziness because of empty stomach and pain killer injection. I sat on the bed felt like collapsing. 'I will bring food for you.' she ran out of the room.

Within 15 minutes she came up with soup, roti's and sabji. I wasn't able to lift a single bite. She grabbed the stool and sat on it before me, holding the tray on her lap. She picked up soup in a spoon and held it infront of my mouth, I looked her, and she muttered 'Hmm' ordering me to open my mouth. My hunger lost the game against my ego and I opend my mouth. She fed me slowly one by one spoon of soup, later rotis with sabji. Every bite I ate from her hand was so pleasing. I kept on staring at her but she didn't make any eye contact. After feeding me, she collected all the empty utensils and went down. Within few minutes, she came with ice pack for my hand. My anger was suppressed a bit after tasty food she fed me. She slowly opened the red tape from my hand, and I screamed in pain 'Aahhhh'. She slowly kept my hand on her lap and started icing it, the touch of her hand and lap was so tender that I felt better in seconds. 'What happened?' she asked softly. 'I banged the wall.' I said. 'What? Why and when?' astonished she muttered looking at me. 'Last night, when you left the room….' I said looking straight into her eyes, our eyes met for seconds. Suddenly, she looked down and continued icing my hand without any word.

There was no conversation after that. She tied my hand with red-tape after icing it. 'You went to doctor?' While leaving she asked. 'Yeah' I said. 'Is it fine? I mean, I hope there isn't any fracture.' She said standing on the door. 'There is not.' I said. 'Any medicines?' she asked. That reminded me there was a tablet to be taken after food. 'Yeah, it is there in my pocket.' I said. She went inside the bathroom and took out tablet strips from the pocket of my shirt and gave me the medicines. 'You rest for some time.' saying she walked out of the room. I thought of asking her whether she had lunch or not but my ego hadn't rested yet. I laid on the bed and dozed off within few minutes.

By the time I woke up it was seven in the evening. I heard the voices from downstairs, I freshened up and went downstairs, saw Aarzoo was chatting with Mansi. 'Hi! How are you now?' she came to me and looked my hand by lifting it up. 'Ahh! much better now.' I reacted for lifting my hand up in that pain and replied. 'Hmm,' she checked and slowly let it down and asked me to sit. 'So, you lost your punching bag somewhere?' she asked mockingly. I looked at Mansi to check whether she said the truth, but her eyes didn't speak. Aarzoo looked at both of us, she doubted the situation, 'I got your message, so thought of visitng you.' to change the topic she said. 'Hmm, Thanks sweetheart!…so going home now?' I asked. 'No have to go back to hospital. I heard about your yesterday's chronicle! Mansi told me just now' she said. 'Hmm, I never imagined that it goes so easily.' I said sitting on the sofa. 'Nice.' She appreciated. We had a chit chat together for a while. After few minutes Sumit and Shaun came over. Aarzoo told Sumit about my hand. 'Hey man! What happened to your hand?' mockingly they both asked me.

'Wait for 2 days, I will show you practically on your faces.' I replied.

'So toh hai, abhi dusre hath se dikhata toh dhoneke waande hojayenge na!' (If you show now, it will be difficult to wash your back!) Shaun whispered in my ears and laughed. *'Tu baaz nahi ayega tere gande jokes se!'* (You will never stop cracking those dirty jokes). I said. 'By the way, *abhi left hath jagannath!*' He whispered again grinning at me. We both laughed as it was a joke on masturbation. Sumit understood that and he laughed as well, Aarzoo neglected it saying 'You guys are such cheapos!' Mansi did not understand our cheap jokes. She went inside the kitchen to bring snacks for everyone.

We all together had long time chat about the other day adventure and many more. 'They kept the Epic book of Shreya in the temple!' Sumit said unintentionally in the presence of Aarzoo. We usually didn't speak anything about Shreya when Aarzoo was around. We paused for a second, looking at us 'That's fine, you all made them believe that the book is epic and I am sure that the book would have looked exactly like an epic.' Aarzoo said appreciating the creativity of Shreya as she was the best judge of her art. Surprisingly, Shreya was standing on the door, hearing comments of her art from her best judge. It was always dramatic between those two. Mansi went and greeted Shreya with a hug and welcomed her. 'Hey! How are you?' she asked Mansi. 'I am fine. You tell me' Mansi said. 'I just dropped in to know how it was yesterday? Sorry, I couldn't call, as I went to Appa's home.' She came in asking, her son Akhil had started walking those days, and the moment she let him down, the liltle boy started exploring the house. 'Come in will tell you the whole story.' Sumit uttered. 'Oh my god! What happened to your hand Sandy?' astounded Shreya asked coming near to me. Whenever they asked about my hand Mansi looked down, I didn't wish to embarrass her by disclosing why it happened. So was avoiding the question with different funny answers. 'Nothing, I lost my punching bag...' I winked my eye looking at Aarzoo by recalling her satire. Shreya looked at both of us 'C'mon! What happened? Did you get injured in yesterday's drama?' she asked with a concern. 'No, Actually, I wasn't finding something I was looking, so hit the wall angrily.' I said without looking at Mansi, in the intention of not giving any idea to the guys about us. 'Oh! Hows it now?' she asked looking at me and Aarzoo. 'Ahh, much better.' I said. Aarzoo had to leave for work, she seemed like staying back because of Shreya but the work call made her to depart, Shreya seemed disappointed when Aarzoo left. We chatted for some more time, Mansi insisted everyone to stay back for dinner. Shreya went inside the kitchen to help Mansi, Sumit was also a good cook, and he joined them. I got busy chatting with Shaun. Shreya's son Akhil fell asleep when we were talking.

Meanwhile, Arjun came over looking for Shreya. His behaviour was little weird when he saw Shreya cooking inside the kitchen. He did not stay back even after insisting, he lifted the baby on his shoulder and asked Shreya to leave with him. Shreya went along with him without saying a word. I felt something fishy, Mansi seemed like knowing some secret. She looked dull since evening and I didn't speak to her much in the impact of my ego.

We all had dinner, I found it difficult to eat from left hand, Mansi made the rolls of the rotis filling sabji inside, which made it easy to eat and was tastier than any Labanese shawarma. Guys started pulling our leg for that, I didn't look at her as I was still angry and ignored their teasing. Mansi felt shy infront of the guys, she scolded them to keep quiet. We all had fun while having food, guys left after that.

It was again a time for us to be alone in the home but I was still under the influence of my ego, so didn't speak to her. Mansi got a call from her mother and she got busy talking to her and I went upstairs in the room. Meanwhile, I got a call from Mom and I didn't say anything about my hand to her, obviously I didn't want to spoil their fun. Dadi asked me about any improvement in our relationship but I ignored her question by changing the topic. She understood the situation 'You must know one thing, the beauty of love is not just loving someone, it is there in waiting for the love in return...' she said to cheer me. 'C'mon Dadi, you always say things like that but I have lost all the hopes!' Disappointed, I said. 'Don't lose it, I am thousand times sure that she loves you, it is just a matter a time...and that will definitely change one day.' The grey edge of the mind spoke. We spoke for a while and I hung up the phone and saw Mansi standing before me with an ice pack. 'It is not paining that much now' I said throwing the phone on the bed. 'But the swelling is still there, so I got the ice pack' she said keeping the tray on the teapoy.

'Stop it Mansi, why are you giving me fake hopes by doing all this?! I know you are living with me only to maintain the reputation of our families, let's deal with it now. I have spoiled your life and I am ready to take any type of punishment. But I can't handle this silence anymore...It hurts!' I uttered speaking my heart to break the silence. She sat silently on the couch. 'Great! Still you are silent...Talk to me damn it... I am the one who is expressing everything from months! OK, tell me... you don't want to live with me? Fine I will arrange something for that. I will face both the families, are you happy now? Tell me...atleast say something now!' I shouted.

'What should I say, you are deciding everything by yourself!' she said softly, and tears filled in her eyes.

'Based on your reactions' I said sarcastically.

'That's it? Are you done? Do you really know what I am going through?' she asked.

'How would I know, when you never say anything?' I asked.

'Yeah, how would you know? How would you know what others feel? You see everything only from your angle. It is always about you.' She said in bit louder voice.

'You really think that?' I asked.

'Yes, I do…it's always about you, how you feel, what you desire… what you want…Do you have any idea what am I going through?'

'I want to know…tell me what your problem is?'

'I am not like you Sandy…I can't express everything so easily like you do…I am suffering from months…there are lots of things going in my mind…and I ..I don't know how to say all that…' she muttered, tears fell out of her eyes.

'I want to know what's in your mind…please…this suspense is killing me…' I uttered.

She wiped her tears and started talking 'You know that my heart beated only for you, not for days or for months but from years. When you left me in school, I was broken! I cried everynight. Later, I accepted the situation. Coz, I always wanted you to be happy. I tried to move on but did not feel anything for anyone… My neighbours saw us together many times. After Papa's death, they spread the rumour on my character, they didn't hesitate once before saying that to my relatives! And slowly our relatives got detached from us. Only my uncle used to visit in the greed of our house. Mummy decided to get rid of everything with my marriage and uncle took a responsibility of my marriage, dressed with my character designed by the neighbours. As a result, I faced different kinds of wedding proposals like old age, widowers, divorcees…! People used to stare at me with terrible intentions…. Mummy cried everyday on our condition. That day, after your fight with my uncle, I made up my mind to fight the disdains by the people and not to get married in life. But the very next day, you came in my life, and I couldn't say no as it was my dream come true, everything changed, we got married. I was really happy but when you revealed the truth, I broke once again. I know you are guilty but I couldn't forget that you were the reason for my father's death and the problems I faced after his death! I am not able to make a decision on leaving you, it's not only the society or families, but its something inside me. I try to hate you but I can't, reason, years of love for you. I want to love you but I can't, since I see things I suffered. I don't know what to do! I really don't know!' She closed her face with her hands and started crying again.

My mind was simultaneously making visuals of everything she was saying, my fists got tight even in the pain, thinking about the scoundrels who kept their dirty eye on her, my eyes were slit and I grinded my teeth in anger, I wanted to bang those assholes who spread the rumours about her. How dare they? When they don't know her how can they bitch about her? Mansi is such a pious girl who never allowed me, her childhood love to touch her, not now, and not in the back when we were dating.

'Who spread the rumours about you? Who targeted you!? I want their names. Why didn't you tell me before? Bastards!' I uttered angrily.

'Calm down! I didn't tell you all this because of this anger of yours!' she said to tranquil my fury, after a pause 'I don't want to rage you against anybody, I said all that to explain what am I going through. Nevertheless, everyone's mouth got shut after our marriage.' She meant all that she said. I realised her pain, however, directly or indirectly I was responsible for everything. I had no words, I went outside the room leaving her alone.

TWENTY TWO

'*What the hell are you doing dude!! She has been with you since childhood, you are her life, everything happened and happening in her life is just because of you!! Even today she had taken care of you every minute and you are such a jerk that you didn't even bothered to know whether she had food or not! Now you left her crying! Selfish dog!!*' My inner voices yelled, I felt ashamed of myself and ran into Mansi, she was sitting on the couch, crying with no clue about the prospect.

I sat beside her, she wiped her eyes and looked otherside. 'I am sorry!' I said softly. I was mortified, I couldn't look at her, staring the floor I spoke, 'You were right, I always spoke about myself, my desires, and my feelings, I was selfish, and never thought how you feel? What you have gone through and what you are going through? Even today you took so much care of me and I was such an idiot that I didn't even bothered to know whether you ate or not?' I muttered. She didn't respond. I looked at her face, she was looking the other side, she was tired, that bright face was dull yet attractive as always, tears were still pouring out of her eyes, and she was wiping them. 'You know what, I have been so lucky to have you as my best friend, you always helped me since childhood, from homeworks, studies to my affairs, you always saved my ass from teachers and elders. And I, I am such an asshole that I can see the pain of those unknown girls out there but I never realised what my best friend is going through. I am Sorry! Sorry for everything.' Saying I went on my knees infront of her and I apologised by holding my ears. She wiped her tears, nodding her head, she took off my hands from ears. After a pause of few seconds, 'Don't be...' she said softly. Holding my hand, she gestured me to sit on the sofa. I sat beside her, holding her hand 'You know what? You deserve someone better...just like you, soft, caring and loving. Why you loved me?' I asked. She smiled, looking down 'You just answered that, you are as caring, helping and loving as I am or maybe more than me.' she said. I wondered after hearing that, 'How could you say that for me, who broke your heart so many times?' I asked her. 'Hmm, I am happy that I experienced the feeling of love and I never regretted that...Because I loved you how you are. Yeah, at times, I was sad when you were with other girls, but that's your nature, I didn't wished you to change your nature for being with me. I waited for you to come to me, only when you realise that you actually love me.' she said softly looking down. I kept staring her, till that day I never felt so close to her. It was other perceptive, till then it was always infatuation and desire, but that night, it was something more, I saw my soulmate sitting beside me. After all the pain I gave her, she had that feeling of pious love for me. I held her hand with my injured hand, looking at her, 'Mansi, look at me' I aksed. She didn't refuse my call and looked into my eyes. 'Till today, I have said hundreds of Sorrys and Thanks to you, they were all meant for some or other needs of mine. But today I am saying one SORRY for everything I did to hurt you! And one THANKS for coming in my life!' saying I took a long breath 'SORRY and THANKS !! And trust me, these words came from my heart.' I said staring her. She didn't know how to react, she had that mixed feeling after my mixed apology and gratitude, she smiled and started weeping again, I went more close to her and held her in my arms 'Shhhh....enough, please don't cry. From now onwords, I don't want to see tears in your eyes.' I muttered and lifted her face holding her chin 'Mansiii....I haaate tears' I said, mimicking Rajesh Khanna.

That brought a smile on her face, swiftly she realised that she is in my arms, she got separated quickly by sitting apart, and I got conscious about her feelings. 'Let's make a deal! Let us be friends again!! And this time only friendship, I won't complain and won't demand anything from you in our relationship...We will not hide anything, and ...whatever will be your decision... I will abide that by HEART! OK!' I said keeping my left hand on my heart and thumbs up with my injured hand. She looked at me and she agreed by nodding. 'And yeah, one more thing...you know my personality; it will be difficult for me to stop staring you sometimes, so, please bear with me....' I flirted to chill-out the serious atmosphere. She laughed lightly holding her hands on her mouth, nodding, she muttered 'Ok...'

'Thank you! By the way...ahh...leave it...' I stopped, scratching my head and squeezing my face. 'What?' She asked with curiosity. 'Nothing, it's not important...' I said. 'Just now you said that we'll not hide anything...' she reminded to open my mouth. I looked at her, gulping 'You look HOT in sarees!' I said, and waited for her reaction. She blushed after hearing that, she didn't look at me, hurriedly, she picked up the ice bowl 'The ice has melted, I will bring the fresh cubes.' she said and took the bowl 'Obviously, you are sitting infront of those cubes...' I flirted again, beaming at her. 'Shut up!' she said and walked out of the room. I smiled and whispered to myself 'Your heart has melted. Dadi is right, I am sure one day you will be mine, and I will wait for that day.' It was obvious that she was confused with situations that I had brought her into, I spoiled her life by breaking her heart again and again. She was angry on me but the love for me deep inside her, never allowed her for detestation. After all the mishaps, she wasn't sure to make justice for this relationship. Naturally, she needed time to sort out things going in her mind.

I followed her to the kitchen, 'It's fine, no need for ice now. It isn't paining that much and swelling is also down a bit. Let's go to sleep.' I said. She pushed her hair back her ears, she was uncomfortable remembering the last night incident. 'I have to clean the kitchen, you go to sleep.' She said holding the duster to clean the platform. 'You can do that in the morning, you must be tired. Let's go... And don't worry, I will not touch you...the promise is still on.' I assured her with a smile. She looked at the distance, she felt embarrassed, clearing her throat she stood there thinking. 'Please Madam!' I bowed infront of her. That brought a big smile on her face and she walked with me. As usual, we slept separate on the bed and couch.

I opened my eyes and it was eight in the morning. There wasn't any severe pain in my hand, I opened the red tape, and the swelling was down. I got fresh after all the natural calls and took bath, got ready for office and I was damn hungry. I went down, Mansi was preparing breakfast, she was wearing pink and white combination chudidaar, her hair was wet and the drops were falling on the floor. There wasn't any make up on the face apart from kumkum and sindhoor on the forehead, she looked sexy. Controlling my feelings, 'Good morning' I said smiling at her. She was shocked to hear my voice all of a sudden, 'Oh! Good morning...' she greeted holding her heart. I smiled 'Easy, I didn't mean to scare you.' I said. She smiled nodding her head 'No, that's fine. Actually, I just came in after tulsi pooja and the door is open, so I was shocked after hearing your voice. Anyways, how's your hand now?' she asked. 'Much better' I said, lifting my hand up. She glanced at my hand and said 'Good, sit I will bring the breakfast.' I sat on the chair, 'What time did you wake up?' I asked. 'Asusual, five.' She said bringing me Dosa and chatni. We had breakfast together. It is nothing better than tasty food when you are hungry. After the breakfast, I got ready to go to office. Raju was looking after the site, Dad wasn't in the town, and all the pending jobs ended on me.

While I was wearing my shoes, Mansi's mother walked in our house. She came to see my injured hand, previous night Mansi told her about it. She brought jawar roti's and moong sabji for me, one of my favourite dishes. During the school days, I regularly ate delicious food at Mansi's place. Mansi came over to greet her mother. 'What happened beta?' Mummy asked looking at my hand. An expected question, everyone asked the same in those two days. I looked at Mansi, she took the dishes from her mother's hand and went inside the kitchen with her head down, blushing and biting her lips, without looking at me. Whenever she gets mischievous, she bites her lips. Ofcourse, she must have remembered why I hit the wall. I got a tickle in my heart seeing her like that. Her mother was waiting for my reply. 'Nothing Mummy, I just banged on the wall…actually… I was angry on some phone call so…' I paused after a tiny lie. 'Oh! Don't be angry on small things. Try to be calm.' She adviced, I smiled in return. 'Last night Mansi told me about your hand, how is it now?' she asked. 'Yeah, it's fine now.' I replied promptly. 'I prepared your favourite rotis and sprouts sabji, also got peanuts chatni for you.' she named the mouth watering dishes. 'So sweet of you Mummy, Thank you! I will eat all in lunch.' I appreciated her effort. 'I have to go to work now, you please sit down.' Saying and I walked out. Mansi softly voiced, 'Wait, you forgot your mobile.' She came running towards me holding my mobile, I stared her without blinking my eyes. While giving the phone she noticed my gape and she blushed, the most powerful charm of her beauty. I smiled and left from there.

I reached office and called Raju, he reported the status of the site and I started following up Dad's job. After couple of hours two women came to my office searching for me. My staff wasn't allowing them to come inside. I noticed them from cabin and asked the receptionist to send them inside.

They were two ladies, one was middle aged and other was an old lady. They came inside joining their hands and greeted me, *'Namaskara,* (Hello)…' I gestured them to sit down and offered them water. They were villagers, wearing traditional sarees, big kumkums on their forehead, green bangles in the hand, completely dressed in village attire. *'Heli enagbekagittu?'* (Tell me, how can I help you) I asked politely. Middle aged lady started talking in local Kannada language 'We belong to the village where your construction is going on, the other day we saw you in the village and got the news that you were the one, who helped us to get rid of Mahadevaiyya. Yesterday we went to your site looking for you but some of your employees told that you didn't came there and gave this office address, we came here but you weren't here as well.' I was curious to know why they were searching me. I felt something fishy as I heard that Mahadevaiyya was a big player. Old lady continued 'Today we came again to see you. Actually, we are milk sellers in our village. We have an association and all together five nearby village people sells hundreds of litres milk everyday. There is a man named Indrappa, he is disciple of that Mahadevaiyya, an over-confident arrogant man, who takes all the milk from all 5 villages and sells them in the dairy at higher rates. In the fear of him and his goons we were afraid to raise our voice. We came here to check whether you can help us in this?'

My mind was trying to figure out the percentage of truth in their story. 'I am sorry, how can I help you out in this matter? I am not a social worker. I have this business to look after. It was just, I found that book and everything happened as it is. You people go to the police station.' I rejected courteously. 'Don't say that sir, the police isn't helping us. The other day, you got the city police so the local police quietly obeyed their senior authorities and arrested Mahadevaiyya without any cross questions. Otherwise, everyone is afraid of Mahadevaiyya and Indrappa in all five nearby villages. Indrappa also has connections in the politics. They are stealing our bread by doing this. Fifty percent of the villagers depend upon the milk business. Indrappa is also a rascal like Mahadevaiyya, he uses people for his needs. Please do something. Other day when we saw you, we found a hope in you. Please!' they begged joining their hands and they came to touch my feet. '*Arey*! Please don't do that. Ok, I will think on this and let you know.' I said by stopping them touching my feet. 'Can we come tomorrow?' they asked with a hope in their eyes. 'No-No, I will contact you, you people give me your number.' I said. 'This is my son's mobile number, you can call him.' the old lady took out a small chit and kept that on the table.

They left after submitting their issue infront of Mahaswami Sandy! I called Raju to check whether he sent them to me. He denied on that saying he knows how much I am busy and he can't send people repeatedly seeking my help, he doubted some of the workers must have opened their mouth, also assured me that he will check on that. There was truth in the eyes of those poor ladies. I was annoyed on the people like Mahadevaiyya and Indrappa. Why can't they earn from their own and leave the poor villagers. Why do they have to spread these traps to catch income of poor people? I thought of calling Preeti but I was sure that she would scold me if I take on this to her yet I had no choice and I called her.

'Yes, tell me? What's it now?' she answered the phone. 'How did you know?' I asked. 'It means you really called me for some work!? Go to hell man!' she grumbled. 'No it's not work, I just wanted to know, what's the status of Mahadevaiyya?' I asked to polish the situation before coming to the main point. 'He is behind the bars, I got him arrested with a non-bailable warrant, remember?' she asked mockingly. 'Nice, good job! Do you think he might be still playing games outside?' I slowly grabbed the point. 'Don't know but that son of a bitch can do anything but you don't worry, we have strong evidence against both of them and they can't get out of it. Why are you asking by the way? Are you afraid of him?' she asked with sarcasm. '*Darte toh hum uske baap se bhi nahi janeman!* (I am not even afraid of his father as well, darling!)' I said stylishly. 'Ha ha…then why are you asking all that?' she mocked as she smelled fishy at the first instance when I called her. A true police officer, who never stops doubting. 'Actually, two ladies have come to see me today...' saying I described the whole story to her. 'Have you started any social service side by side? What on earth happened to your family business?' she asked. 'It's running smoothly! Remember???' I said. 'Then why are you getting involved in all these?' she asked. 'I am a law abiding citizen yaar! It's my duty to inform police about these kind of illegal activities, your department staff is afraid of these ogres, so the people are looking for a second option for security...' I made my point. 'Hmm, I will look into this matter, but remember, don't get involved into these things. People will make you messiah one day and you may have to face adverse effects as well.' She warned me, which was right somehow, anybody would suggest the same. 'A police officer is saying that!' I mocked. 'No, a friend is saying that, to keep you on the safer side, I have taken all measures for not disclosing your name directly in the case of Mahadevaiyyah as well.' she said showing her care. 'Why you did that? You may need my witness or something like that in the court' I asked. 'I didn't want to tell you but yesterday morning Mansi called me and strictly instructed me not to involve you much in this case. She requested, not to tell you about this. But today you are getting involved in a new social work, so I couldn't resist myself. C'mon man, your wife is concerned so much about you and you are acting like ascetic, who has no family!' she said. That was surprising, she came to the village with me was explicable but she was so much worried that she called Preeti, amazed me. I was flattered after hearing that, why would she do that if she had small pinch of hatred for me, its nothing but love and she is not realising that.

'Hello!!! Are you there?' Preeti uttered from the other side. 'Yeah, Ok, I will try to stay away from all these.' I said. 'Good, how's your hand now? What happened by the way!' she asked the typical question, which I was tired of answering. 'I banged the wall! Duh!! It's fine now, ok bye...' I answered and hung up the phone before her reply. After all these years, I'd learnt to disconnect the phone before waiting for opposite side's reply.

TWENTY THREE

My family had come back after finishing their trip of Kerala. Dadi with her experienced eyes, noticed the difference in our behaviour for each other. She was happy to see the new beginning in my married life. Mom and Dad were in different mood, they seemed like they discovered the heavens in *Gods own country*. They were not even bothered to dig into our life. That was silently observed by everyone in the family, Ramya and Dadi were happy to explain their romance, after hearing that Mom used to pat Ramya for keeping her mouth shut, Dad disappeared from home due to shyness infront of all of us, especially, Mansi. For Mom, it was not less than any TV serial romance. Mansi enjoyed the funny side of the family after a long time. She was part of this during the school days. Couple of time, she had also witnessed the romance of my parents. She used come for taking her notes in morning hours, fortuitously, same hours were Dad's office going hours. Those days, that was little embarrassing for me and Ramya, but now when we have involved ourselves in love, we can understand their feelings and pursue their romance in our life.

It was more than a week after those village ladies visited my office. Preeti called me on one morning, she discovered that those ladies were saying the truth and she has solved their issue with the help of Gourav. 'Wow!!! Great!! Seriously proud of you yaar!! How did you solve that? How did you know that Gourav could help us in that...' I uttered eagerly. 'C'mon, he is a halwai! He knows the milkmen!' she laughed out louder, so did I. After a pause 'Actually, first I enquired about Indrappa, I got news from my informers that what you said was true. I was aware that Gourav knows the owner of that milk factory. I asked him to talk to the director. Those five villages send thirty percent of the milk to the factory, so the director didn't see any loss in sending private van from the company to those villages. And now onwards the villagers will sell the milk directly to the factory. Their bank accounts will be opened soon and payments will be credited to their accounts, based on daily delivery.' She rested her mouth. 'Brilliant!! I must appreciate that... If our country gets more officers like you, who work beyond their limits, then nobody could stop our country in becoming number one in the world.' Delightfully I appreciated. 'Ahh...stop it...There are so many officeres in our country who are working beyond their limits. It's just a matter of time and mission of their priority.' She said. 'Good, what about Indrappa?' I asked. 'He is a small fish, I informed my men in the village not to entertain these kind of people.' She replied. 'Great! And what happened to Mahadevaiyya? I mean, the case and all going on?' I asked. 'He is behind the bars, the case is strong against him. He has been shifted to Bangalore jail from village.' She said. 'I believe there are good officers in our country but I bet not as smart as you are…' I flattered her. '*Haay, maardala*! (Oh! Killed me!)You say so many things but why didn't you love me atleast once buddy!!' she moaned. 'I always loved you, deep in my heart!! But was afraid of your father's third degree treatment!' I laughed after flirting. 'Ha ha, very funny, by the way, it all happened because you, *mister law abiding citizen*! If we have more citizens like you then crimes would be completely vanished by the next five years in our country.' She appreciated my efforts. 'That is a wrong statement for me!' I said seriously, recalling Mansi's father's case. 'Look, No complaint! No case! Ha ha!' Smart officer got an idea of what I was thinking, 'Just kidding! Apart from all the mishaps you've done…I must say, you are a man of values! You are guilty that's enough, so don't think more. Anyways, how's Mansi, any progress between both of you?' She asked after consoling me. 'Yeah she is fine, it's still progressing.' I replied. I was getting a call from Gourav and I hung up the phone taking her leave. Gourav spoke to me about the milkmen and informed me that Mandar would be coming back from America. That was good news. I messaged everyone about Mandar.

A week later, we all met Mandar, he called us to a restaurant for lunch. It was a very delightful meeting him after years, he looked more handsome and he was well built, his looks weren't similar to skype, facebook and all the social networking video chats and pictures. He was different, looked more confident then school time shy Mandar. He was appointed as project manager in a well known IT Company of USA. Apart from his looks, we were all surprised to see a good looking foreign girl along with him. After greeting each other, he introduced us to her 'Hi everyone! Isabella Davis. My…my wife!' and that hit like a bomb to everyone! A guy like Mandar, who couldn't even take an extra breath without asking his mother, has married a foreign girl without informing her. We were surprised and everyone started asking different questions, base was obviously his marriage. 'Guys, Guys…Guys…relax. I will tell everything!' he asked everyone to calm down. 'Actually, we work together in US, and eventually friendship turned into love. I wanted to tell Maa, but before I could say anything about Bella (Isabella), she'd accepted the proposal of my uncle's daughter for marriage with me, without informing me. I didn't want to lose Bella, I knew if I came to India this time, she will get me married with the girl she chose for me. So, I had to make this decision and we got married before coming here. Bella doesn't have a family, her parents are no more, and I couldn't break her heart.' He paused. Isabella held his hand. She seemed like a shy and quiet girl, and we all saw genuine love in her eyes for Mandar.

'So, what was aunty's reaction?' Mansi asked him. 'As expected, she is not talking to both of us. She went to uncle's home.' He said sadly. 'What are you going to do now?' Sumit asked him. 'Trying to convince her, I want to take her along with us but….' He paused. 'Aunty has always been a strict lady. Woman with her vows, it's tough to convince her.' Shaun said. 'Yeah, yesterday there was full drama in home, my uncle made a scene shouting at both of us. Maa went along with him. This morning, I went to convince her but she didn't even look at me.' He repented. 'Do you want us to help?' Mansi asked him. 'No, she will not listen to anybody.' He said. 'How long are you here?' I asked him. 'Fifteen days, next week we are going to Agra and Delhi for couple of days.' he said. *'Oye hoye! Pardesi babu bangaya! Bahar jaake aate hi Taj Mahal dekhneki ichcha huyi!'* (Foriegner, after coming back from abroad, want to see Taj Mahal). Shaun taunted him. *'Teri bhabhi ko dekhna hai!'* (Your sister-in-law wants to see it.) He answered him looking at Isabella. 'He praises you all, it's really nice to meet you all!' Isabella said with a smile. 'Pleasure…' I said and everyone smiled. We all had lunch, Aarzoo, Preeti were busy at work, and they didn't join us. I wondered Shreya also didn't come, recalling Arjun's behaviour towards her a week back when she visited my home.

While on the way to home, I asked Mansi whether she spoke to Shreya in these days. Mansi seemed like she was hiding something, she looked at a distance with no reply. I stopped the car by the side of the road. 'What is the matter? The other day, I noticed that you are hiding something and today also you are quiet on this.' I asked her. There was too much sound of traffic, she asked 'Shall we go to some calm place?' I drove the car in the outskirts of the city, and we reached the calm place we were looking for. Hardly some vehicles were passing by and it was peaceful. There was platform of bridge beside the road, I parked the car near the bridge, river water was flowing below that. It was a bright cloudy day after couple of rains, everything smelled fresh and green. We got down from the car and sat on the bridge.

'Hmm' I muttered, reminding her to talk about Shreya. 'I don't know, from where to begin…' she looked confused to talk on that matter, I was waiting eagely to hear her out. After a pause she asked 'You know that Shreya and Arjun weren't together initially, and Arjun…forcefully…' she paused, it was discomforting for her to speak about thier sex life. Initially,

Arjun was very brutal and Shreya didn't launch complaint against him to spoil both the families reputation. We all knew that since Preeti saw bruises on Shreya's body once and she wanted to take action against Arjun but Shreya stopped her. 'Yeah, I know...' I said coming out of my thoughts. 'Hmm, Shreya told all of us that he has changed after Akhil but I think he has not changed.' She said. 'What?' I was shocked to hear that. 'Yeah, last year, after my office one day, accidentally I went to her home, and saw there were some marks on her face, and when she was breast-feeding Akhil, I saw some marks on her chest as well, those marks looked like ciggerette burns or something like that. And after that girl Sudha's case, I was very upset and went to talk to Shreya. That day, I saw some wounds near her neck. Remember, it was after Bindu's party and as we both know, she was with Aarzoo for couple of minutes in the washroom, Arjun was searching for her. And they left immediately when she came out of the washroom.' She reminded me. I was imagining about Shreya's bruises, my fist clenched, eyes were flashing and closing in slits, grinding my teeth, my mouth vibrated bad words for Arjun 'That's ridiculous! I am gonna tear apart that son of a...How could he?' I uttered in anger and went towards the car, to reach Shreya's home. Mansi held my hand and asked me to sit down. 'Realx, Please sit here, this is why I didn't tell you...we can't do anything unless we are sure on that. Because, Shreya is not ready to speak on this. We have to think on this and decide.' She said softly holding my hand, I calmed down bit after hearing her. I took a long breath 'I believe Aarzoo doesn't know about it.' I asked. 'Obviously, she would have acted long back if she did.' She made her point. 'I don't understand why Shreya is tolerating all this?' I questioned. 'Maybe, because of the families...and their reputation.' She said. Her statement made me think, over and over again. My mind was making pictures comparing situations of Shreya and Mansi.

Next day, we were waiting in the car outside Shreya's house. Her in-laws go to a garden every evening along with Akhil. Mansi was sure that they won't come back atleast for an hour. That time was sufficient for us to talk to her. The old couple left the home as per their schedule, we waited for them to disappear and taking the advantage we entered inside. Mansi pressed the door bell, Shreya took few minutes to open the door.

'Hi!' Mansi embraced her when Shreya opened the door. 'Hi! I saw you guys opening the gate...Anyways...What a surprise!' She replied. 'You saw us, still you took so long to open the door?' Mansi asked her mockingly. 'Yeah, I was busy with something in the kitchen...anyways...you tell... how come this side?' She looked nervous. 'We were passing by, thought of meeting you...' I said. We both observed that she wasn't pleased to see us suddenly at her home, her body language spoke out that there was something, which she was worried about.

After few minutes of chat and having glass of juice, Mansi came to the point. Shreya first denied everything. It was clear from her body language that she was lying. Her hands were shaking, she looked nervous and she was avoiding everything we asked her. 'Shreya, I know it's awkward, I will go out from here, and you can talk to Mansi freely. We all know, there is something wrong. Trust us, we are here to help you, don't drag all this for life.' Saying, I signalled Mansi that I will wait outside and got up from the sofa. 'Sandy, wait!' Shreya said with steady voice. 'I will tell everything.' For the first time she seemed to be decisive and she explained everything she has gone through all these years.

We all knew that initially she was dominated by her grandma and later the legacy was continued by Arjun and his mother. She explained us how Arjun is an over-possessive and strongly dominating man. If he needs something, then he will get that by hook or crook. He has been violent since marriage, she lied to all of us about his change of behaviour, which had never changed. And as expected by us he has been beating her whenever he was angry on her. The day, they left from Bindu's party he doubted that she was with someone inside the washroom, and took her to the hospital to verify his doubt whether she had sex with anybody! He needs explaination on every minute she spends outside the house. If she gets late in buying some stuff in supermarket, he takes her once again to the same super market buying all the things which she bought previously and finishes the shopping by keeping the time and asks her for an explaination, if she was late for even two or three minutes. The day they left from our house, he beated her, the reason she was inside the kitchen with Sumit. That moron didn't even thought that Mansi was also inside the kitchen along with them.

My muscles were tight and jaw was clenched, eyes turned red in anger. I felt like taking heckout of that man, who was ruining my friend's life. I picked my phone and dialled his number, within a fraction of second Shreya and Mansi ran to me and Mansi snatched the phone from my hand 'Wait, this is not the time.' She said. 'What are you saying! That man is ruining her life from years and still you want to wait for the time?' I uttered in anger. 'Sandy relax! Please sit sown.' Shreya said and she filled the water in a glass and gave in my hand. I didn't take the water, and sat on the chair facing the door. She kept the glass aside and sat before me, Mansi sat beside her. 'This is not his fault. I am the culprit. I knew how he is, yet pushed myself into this. I don't have guts to face the truth. This is my choice.' She said weeping. 'Are you out of your mind!? What are you saying?' I asked her astonished. She was quiet, 'He has been doing all the dreadful acts, and you are tolerating everything quietly!? WHY?' Mansi asked her. 'Yes! I chose this for me...' she said wiping her tears. 'Why?' Mansi asked her. 'There are reasons for that!' she replied. 'Name them please!' I asked in anger biting my teeth, holding my head with no clue of her foolish decision. She didn't speak for few seconds and later opened the curtain from the secret, which was killing us in that hour, 'In the fear of society.' She said. 'What?' I uttered. 'Yes, I don't have guts to face the society and families...' she expressed. I was speechless. My mind imagined my situation with Mansi. I started thinking that even Mansi is living with me in the fear of the same bitching society. The same society which never comes to help when the person is in bad circumstances but it will be always ready on one foot to comment on its state, thoughts covered my mind again. I didn't hear anything Shreya said after that for few minutes. I saw Mansi was argueing with her. My thoughts stopped when I saw Arjun on the door.

TWENTY FOUR

Shreya and Mansi turned around when they saw me paused on the door. Mercy subsided my anger for a while, but looking at Arjun the anger bursted again inside me, 'Oh! You call your friends here to bitch about us, when we are not home?!!' he uttered staring straight at Shreya.

Meanwhile, her in-laws entered the house along with baby Akhil. He paused looking at Akhil. Her mother-in-law understood the situation, she sent Akhil and her husband outside by whispering something in his ears. The old man left the house carrying Akhil in his arms. 'You people must have had juice and lots of talks, now you can leave.' She said looking at the juice glasses kept on the teapoy. 'We will leave but with Shreya and Akhil.' I said with strong voice. 'You leave now or you won't leave in single peace!' Arjun warned me. 'Try to do that!' I challenged him. 'Stop it guys! Sandy, please you leave now.' Shreya interfered in the middle. 'I ain't going out of here without you and Akhil.' I said.

'You son of a ....' Arjun raged towards me screaming, within a fraction of a second he held my collar. That bursted the volcano of anger inside me, I punched him on the face so hard that he fell on the floor. His mother rushed to him shouting 'Ajjuu...' Mansi and Shreya shouted 'No!!!' holding their hands on their mouth, Shreya went to him, her mother-in-law pushed her back saying 'Don't touch him! You are responsible for all this.' I held Shreya's shoulder and helped her in getting up. Arjun was staring at me with his red eyes, he got annoyed on that, biting his teeth he got up again and ran to hit me, I held his hand and punched once again on his face, this time he didn't leave my shirt and he tore a peace of it while holding it tightly. Mansi was pulling me back, Arjun's mother was pulling him back and Shreya was begging us to stop by coming in the middle, but we both were so angry that we weren't listening to anybody. I punched him on the face and stomach again and again. He punched me back on my stomach once. Meanwhile, Shreya's father-in-law entered the house hearing our voices and he made a call to police.

Arjun took a bat in his hand and said 'Now fight, if you are a real man!' and ran towards me to hit, he raised the bat Shreya came in the middle, I pushed her aside and before he could hit me I held my left palm to stop it. I grabbed the bat and threw it aside, holding his collar in both of my hands, I grabbed him and said 'I am a real man! I can crush you in minutes! But I don't want to, because you are not a man enough! If you were a real man you would have never hit a woman! I pity you, and your parent's up-brining! Shame on you all!!' I uttered on his face. His father dragged him back and stopped him by saying, 'Stop it, now police will come and teach him a lesson. Why you are wasting your energy.' I smiled and said 'Thank you for calling the police. Now we will see whom they will teach a lesson.' Shreya's mother-in-law took Shreya in the room, she instructed something to her, Shreya came out weeping. Mansi stood beside me, holding my hand. She seemed scared of everything that had happned in past few minutes.

Police came after twenty minutes, they took all of us along with them, I drove my car, a constable accompanied me. Arjun's mother started making a drama in the police station 'Its all his fault, he came to our house, these both husband and wife were pinning my daughter-in-law to leave my son, my daughter-in-law has an affair with one of her friends. And hearing all that my son begged to stop her, this man beat him like a street dog and tried to take my grand son and daughter-in-law with him. Beat him till he dies sir!!' she made the story infront of police and paused to weep. 'What are you saying aunty!? Atleast think before opening that dirty mouth!' Mansi jumped in between and said looking at her. I held her hand and signalled her to keep quiet. 'Mr. Sandeep, is that true?' the officer asked me, he knew about my reputation in the city and thus, he wanted to be sure on everything before taking any action. By that time my anger had calmed down, it was completely satisfied after hitting Arjun like a 'street dog' as explained by his mother. I smiled 'Yes, parts of it. But I don't want to give any explaination. I want you to hear the truth from Shreya.' I said confidently looking at Shreya. I imagined what Arjun's mother instructed to her and I was ready to face whatever Shreya decides. Mansi looked at Shreya, holding her hand she nodded. Shreya looked at both of us, she took a long breath, gulping her saliva she spoke the truth. Hearing which, Arjun and his parents jaws were dropped. They couldn't believe the courage she'd gained in that moment to explain everything. His mother uttered 'No way! We treated this woman like a queen and she is rewarding this to us!' and she started weeping. The officer asked lady sub-inspector to examine the truth inside the room, where Shreya can prove it with the scars on her body, which Arjun gifted her. Officer became sure on every bit of the truth Shreya said and they arrested them all on the complaint of Shreya. They released me, being a responsible citizen, they warned me not to indulge in any kind of violence. We took Shreya and Akhil to our home.

Akhil was asleep after having his food. We revealed the whole story to everyone in the house, Shreya was crying continuously on her situation, everyone in the home were consoling her. Mansi served food for everyone, no one was in a mood to eat anything. 'C'mon, lets have food first...will talk later.' Dadi said to cheer up everyone. I smiled 'Yeah, I am hungry and I am sure you must be!' I said to Shreya. 'She is! And today, Shreya and I will have food together in one plate, just like in school time' Mansi made a plate for Shreya, got it for her in the living room. Dad and Mom insisted her to eat. Shreya was hesitating and felt bashful, but Mansi convinced her to eat something. Rest of us went to the dining table.

We finished dinner for the name sake, as all of us were sad on her circumstances. 'What is all this? What have you done?!' Shreya's father came inside our house questioning her, it was ten thirty in the night. 'Come inside, please sit.' Dad greeted him going on the door and asked him to sit. He respected my father's approach and sat on the sofa. We exposed Arjun and his parents truth infront of him, he was shocked to hear that. 'Why didn't you tell me before? You didn't feel to share with me ever? Even today, after everything you came here! Am I dead?' her father asked her, 'No offence, Mister Singh. I really appreciate your concern for my daughter.' Poor fellow said joining his palms at my father. My father held his hands saying 'No, no...please...She is also like Ramya and Mansi to me.'

Shreya's grandma was bed-ridden in those days, she was admitted in the hospital due to kidney dialysis, her father was going through a tough time, he was retired and was living on his pension. Spending on the hospital and taking care of home was becoming tough for him. Arjun's family rarely allowed Shreya to visit her father or grandma. They visited grandma couple of times but with no financial support, whereas Shreya's father had helped Arjun in making his career. We weren't aware of grandma and Moorthy uncle's financial problem before that night.

After all the discussion Shreya's father requested her to take the case back, since they are a family and grandma will be very upset during her last days hearing all that. My family was against that but nobody said a word in due respect of her father. Shreya said 'I knew you will say this Appa. I will take the case back but on one condition...' she paused, 'What is that?' He asked her. 'I will tell tomorrow.' She said.

Shreya's father got ready to take Shreya and Akhil along with him to his house but we all insisted them to stay in our house, as it was late and she had to go to the police station in the morning. Unwillingly, he accepted our request and stayed at our house. Shreya came without packing any clothes, she wore Mansi's dress in the night. Kept her saree for washing, we had some clothes of Anvika at home, which fitted Akhil. She slept with Mansi in my bedroom, her father slept in the guest room. I went to sleep in Dadi's room. I couldn't sleep whole night, Shreya's words were haunting me. She was living with the man, who exploited her from years but she can't leave him in the fear of facing the society! My mind was connecting her story with Mansi, who was also living with me for the same reason! I was the culprit because of whom her father committed suicide. I am a murderer but she is not raising voice in the fear of society and respect of families. *'Oh God! Please help me! Show me the way to sort out everything once and for all!'* I begged the almighty. I went to the bar in the house, drunk few hot pegs to chill my mind. I slept in the living room, thinking over and over again the way to come out of the situation and finally found out the solution.

Mansi and I accompanied Shreya and her father to police station the next morning. Shreya went to meet Arjun and his parents inside the cell. After few minutes of discussions she came out and took the complaint off. They came out ashamed of their act, they weren't able to face Shreya's father. 'What was your condition?' her father asked, which created the same curiosity in us. 'I want a divorce from this man. And they agreed on that.' She said holding Akhil in her arm. 'What?' her father uttered. 'Yes, I told them that if he doesn't give divorce and settle this, I will drag them all to the court and send them to jail in domestic violence case. And they agreed immediately.' She rested her mouth. Surprised, Mansi and I stood still watching the new Shreya. Where was this will-power and strength a day before? Why didn't she take this step before? Why she tolerated everything so long? Many questions were arising in my mind.

She looked at us calmly and said, 'Thanks! Thanks for everything, I could have never done this without you guys.' We didn't react for a second because we were stunned after hearing whatever she said before. 'I love you sweety…you did a great job!' Saying, Mansi hugged her. 'Remember what I told you last night…' Shreya muttered at her. Mansi blushed.

Mansi asked her to meet in the afternoon at a well-known restaurant near her house, Shreya agreed and she went along with her father to his house. Meanwhile, Mansi called Aarzoo and asked her to come to the restaurant without any hint about Shreya. Aarzoo was busy but she agreed to come for half an hour. 'What are you doing?' I asked her with no clue. 'Last night I spoke to Shreya, she explained everything.' Mansi said calmly sitting in the car. 'Wha…What she said?' I asked eagerly.

I sat in the car and she spoke 'She accepted the marriage proposal in the fear of her grandma and society. As she knew nobody would accept her relationship with Aarzoo and she had no guts to face that. She knew that Arjun's family was greedy but after marriage she saw the devil inside Arjun, she tried to change him but was never successful, day by day he became worse to handle. Few days back after the fight for coming to our home, she made up her mind to leave him once it for all. But worrying about Akhil's future she stepped back. After yesterday's drama she had decided to leave him. She wants to live with self-esteem now onwards and she wants to start her career again. She wishes to be with her love of life but still she has that fear of society and she never wants to spoil Aarzoo's life, she thinks that, one day Aarzoo will marry someone and settle with her partner.' She explained, which left many questions in my mind.

'Then why did you call Aarzoo? Does she know about all this?' I asked. 'No, but she knows one thing clearly that she is madly in love with Shreya. So does Shreya. Aarzoo will never marry anybody other than Shreya!' She said looking at me. 'What are you talking? I...I... mean ... how do you know that?' I asked. 'I know that, because she said to me. I met Aarzoo as well after Bindu's party. I went to see that girl Sudha and spoke to Aarzoo about the party night. She told me that, after her M.D her parents were searching a groom for her but she has come up to her parents about her love interest. Her parents had gone mad initially with her decision, there was a lot of drama in her house. Afterall, they are doctors and more over her mother is a psychiatrist, in the end they accepted the truth. She said that she would never marry anybody in her life and spend her life in the love for Shreya. I know its very diffuclut in our country to accept all this but yet, I want them to be together. After all they are soulmates.' She said looking at me. I was speechless, I imagined everybit she told me and it was all like a movie for me, she waited for my reply. 'So what do you want to do now?...In the restaurant.' I asked. 'I am not doing anything.' She said. I looked at her twisting my eyebrows with a question. 'We are going there, hiding ourself disguised in one corner of the restaurant and will keep a check on them'. She said smiling. 'What?' I uttered. 'Yes Mr.James Bond! You did it many times in school and its time to do it again.' she said smiling.

TWENTY FIVE

We reserved the table for them and hid a microphone under the table. I am very much impressed with James Bond movies and keep on collecting the spy gadgets. We waited for the couple in the parking lot of the hotel, so that we can hear their conversation. It was awkward for me but I saw Mansi seemed to be very excited. I gave a strange look at her, she understood my feelings 'What? They are my friends! I want them to be together.' She said. 'So do I, but don't you feel this is all a bit... weird...I mean, hearing someones conversation like this...is...' I paused in confusion. 'Don't worry, everything is fair in love and war!' she consoled me by holding my hand. For the moment she didn't realise the meaning of her words and touch of my hand. Suddelnly, she took off her hands, gulping she looked here and there. I didn't react and looked out on the road and saw Shreya walking in with Akhil inside the restaurant.

'Aaah...Shreya is here.' I said and she looked hurriedly. She called Mansi in the meanwhile, to check when she is reaching; Mansi said that she is running late due to traffic and she will reach in half an hour and she also asked her to order the food and I switched on the speaker of the tape which we'd fixed under the table. Shreya ordered for soup for Akhil. We heard the voice of Akhil and Shreya, I tested the gadget for the first time and I was happy to notice that the sounds were clearly heard. Within few minutes, I saw Aarzoo getting down from her car and she entered the restaurant. There was a silence for couple of minutes, we heard voices of Akhil and Shreya, who was trying to feed him the soup. We imagined what must have gone through between them after seeing each other in such a surprising way. Aarzoo wasn't aware of Shreya's decision yet and Shreya wasn't aware that Aarzoo was also invited.

After a long pause, we heard the voice of waiter, 'What would you like to order Mam.'

'Aah, we are waiting for our friend, will order later, and now just get me some water please.' Aarzoo said. 'How are you my baby?' Aarzoo asked pampering Akhil. I imagined that she must have asked the question looking at Shreya. We heard some toddlings from Akhil. 'She is running late.' Shreya began the conversation by talking about Mansi. 'Oh...when did you come here?' Aarzoo asked her. 'Fifteen minutes ago.' She said. There was a pause after that. 'How are you?' Shreya asked her. 'Fine...and you?' she asked her. 'I am good.' Again there was a pause. 'How are all in the family?'

This time, Aarzoo began the conversation. I could imagine how someone feels to keep the conversation on, when he or she is in love with the opposite person. 'Yeah all are fine.' She replied. After a pause, 'You are looking beautiful' Aarzoo complimented her, she looked beautiful in purple dress. 'Thanks, and you are looking as pretty as usual.' She said the truth. Aarzoo has that charming face with her thick long hair and the curls in the end enhance her beauty, she dressed casual in jeans and yellow shirt. 'Thanks' Aarzoo said and she started playing with Akhil.

'Would you like to order something? Mansi asked me to order.' Shreya said.

'Yeah, order a soup.' She replied. Shreya ordered Aarzoo's all time favourite Chicken clear soup. 'You remember' Aarzoo asked.

'Yes…' Shreya said.

'I am going back to London…'

'Oh…that's…that's… great news…whe…when you will be back?' it was clear that she was nervous after hearing that. We got anxious after hearing that. Akhil started crying and the waiter took him along to play and keep him busy showing aquarium, as Mansi instructed the manager to take care of Akhil if he disturbs the couple in the middle.

'I got a good job there, as it is there is nothing left for me here, so…' Aarzoo said with a pinch of sarcasm.

'Congrats! Good…Happy for you…So…Whe...When are you leaving?'

'Next month…'

'Hmm, so, whats the next plan?'

'I don't know…'

'…'

'How's your grandma?'

'She is not well, admitted in the hospital, kidney dialysis.'

'Oh…Which hospital?'

'Dhanwantri'

'Hmm…ok. I will be shifting her to my hospital tomorrow.'

'No, that's very expensive and Appa can't afford that…'

'Did I ask you for money?'

'O…NO NO NO! I can't let you do that…'

'I am not asking your permission…'

'NO! Please Aarzoo...'

'Ssshhh…She will get good treatment so, keep quiet on this.'

'I know she will…but…Why are you doing this?'

'Shreya, because I…I am a doctor and I am doing my duty that's it.'

There was a silence after that between both of them. 'Why aren't they coming to the point? Why didn't you tell Aarzoo the truth?' I muttered at Mansi, as the suspense was killing me. 'Ssshhh, it takes time... wait!' Mansi said softly to calm me down and concentrated on the speaker. 'I am damn sure that Shreya will not tell her the truth. Wait I will do one thing, I will message Aarzoo...' I took the phone. 'Stop it! What are you doing? Have patience. I am sure they will come to the point.' Saying she took off the phone from my hand. I was irritated but kept calm.

'What's the plan about marriage?' Shreya asked her.

'You know what my plans are.' Aarzoo replied.

'How long can you take this Aarzoo? Our society will never accept it, forget the society, what your parents will think? Have you ever thought about that?' She asked.

'First of all, it was nice to hear my name from you after a long time...Second of all, I don't give a damn to the society! And lastly, my parents know everything and they accepted me as I am!'

'What?! Do they...do they know about us?'

'Yes'

'Oh my god!! What...what have you done?! What they'll think about me now?' embarrassed Shreya spoke.

'They imagined you as their daughter-in-law!' Aarzoo said with the funny tone.

'What! C'mon...please!!'

'Relax, I am just kidding...I never told your name to them.' Aarzoo said. Mansi was smiling hearing their conversation.

'Ah! Thank god! Thank you!! I got ghoosebumps! You haven't changed!'

'Sorry! I couldn't help...I wanted to see your anxious face...just like good old days...' Aarzoo said grinning at Shreya.

After a pause of few seconds, 'So, the girl...In your Facebook ...I mean...she still lives in London?' Shreya asked her.

'When did you see her in my Facebook?'

'I...I... was just looking through the Facebook recommendations and happened to see your profile.'

'So you need Facebook to recommend me to add in your friendslist.'

Shreya clearing the throat said 'No...I...I...'

'Aahhh...you are spying on me!'

'No...ofcourse not...I ...forget it!'

'She is still in London. I am going to see her...And she was my girlfriend…nice girl…'

'Oh!! Good for you…She is… She is beautiful? You…You both look cute together.'

'Hmm…Yes, indeed she is! But she is not good for me…and you know who is…'

'Aarzoo, please!'

'Ask yourself Shreya? Have you ever forgotten me?'

….

'Your silence speaks the truth!! How could you ruin your life by living with a person whom you never loved!'

'Ok! That's it…Don't wanna talk about this…'

'Fine…I am leaving.' Aarzoo said.

'Wait….I…I am divorcing him!' Shreya said, I imagined that she must have said that by closing her eyes tightly.

'Wha…What?' astonished Aarzoo asked.

'Yes, this morning, I decided that and he agreed for that. Now I am living with Appa.' And there she told her the whole story.

'How dare he? How dare him to beat you!! That son of a…I will drag him to jail!' furious Aarzoo spoke.

'Relax, its all over now…It wasn't fully his fault…I was punishing myself!'

'Wha…are you crazy? Why?'

'For leaving you…'

'Are you out of your mind? You chose to live with that psycho and tolerated everything for that… C'mon Shreya…its not a child's play… Luckily, it all ended when Akhil is young, have you ever imagined what impression that would have created in Ahkil's mind?' Aarzoo muttered.

'That's why I ended it. All thanks to Mansi and Sandy…I would have never made that decision without their support.'

'Hmm, that reminds me, where is Mansi? She is taking too long…' Aarzoo asked.

Within a few seconds Mansi's phone rang. She picked up the phone and said 'I am stuck in rain, I think I can't come, you guys carry on...ok bye.' She hung up the phone and continued the tradition of our group by disconnecting the phone without waiting for reply from opposite side. I stared at her, 'What, its not my time to enter, so have to say something…' She said looking at me and I didn't say anything.

'What she said?' Shreya asked her

'She is not coming…wait a minute…It was planned! To call us here…Are your sure she was coming?' Aarzoo caught our trap.

'I don't know, she said she wanted to talk to me personally about something.'

'She said the same to me.' Aarzoo said.

They paused for few seconds and started talking again.

'So, what's your plan now?' Aarzoo asked her.

'I will restart my career, look for a job and continue painting...'

'So you are saying you didn't paint all these years?'

'Mmm...I made an art piece for Sandy few days back...'

'That's it? By the way, why you left painting?'

'He never liked it...'

'Is he very much impressed with the movies like *Agnisakshi, Daraar* and *Sleeping with the enemy?*'

'Are you pulling my leg?'

'No! It all sounds like that...I am not going to leave that son of a...'

'I told you, its all over...why are you talking about him now...'

'I mean, I will send him to the *Psychiatrist*. People like him spoil the society, and as a doctor I can't let him out freely like that.'

Shreya kept quiet.

'Shreya, I know what you are going through right now...I just want you to know that I am always with you...'

'I know that but I want you to understand one thing for sure Aarzoo, we cannot get everything we desire in life.'

'Everything is possible, all we have to do is follow our heart, that's it.'

Hearing that Mansi looked at me, I smiled. She seemed to be thinking of something, I imagined she must be thinking on our relationship.

'Your family has understood, but mine will never? Appa and Ajji are very much afraid of the society...'

'They thought that Arjun and his family are perfect for you? Now, they must be regretting their decision.'

'That was different and this is different'

'Hmm, and can you tell me what is that 'difference'?

'....'

'Your eyes are telling, the difference is love...Regarless of whom, how and why? C'mon Shreya, stop fooling yourself, we both know that we still love each other, we never forgot each other! The society you are talking about, never came to help you when you were in trouble. The guys who helped you, wants us to be together, that's why they arranged this surprise meeting...Don't you understand that? I don't have any right to comment about your family's views, atleast you should understand where your happiness lies.'

'It is not possible Aarzoo! It never was...I wish I understood that back in school days...it would have never hurt this much, ever...'

'Stop repenting for living the happiest moments of your life... Shreya, all I can say is don't spoil your life. You have all the right to live your life according to your wish.'

'Appa and Ajji will never understand...What should I tell them?'

'Tell them the truth! They spoiled your life once...they may let you live your life happily...I know its tough for them to understand but there is nothing wrong in trying.'

'What about Akhil, one day he may ask questions...'

'He will grow up in a modern world, where all these things will be accepted normally...Everything is changing, things are getting accepted by people in our country and if they don't, we'll go to place where these things are normal...and moreover, it's all on the upbringing. Akhil will get love of two mothers.' Aarzoo said to convince her but Shreya was quiet. 'Shreya, people may or may not understand our love but we do. Follow your heart, that's all I can say. I may go away from here but my heart is always with you. Trust me, I will wait for you life long.'

After a pause of few seconds 'Have your sandwich...' Shreya said, to change the topic.

'I have to leave now. I will have sandwich on the way...I will drop you home. Ask the waiter to bring Akhil, I am sure Mansi must have tipped him to keep Akhil away from us while talking.' Aarzoo said, guessing that rightly.

'It's ok, I will catch an auto. You must be late.'

'C'mon, it's raining heavily outside. I will drop you, it hardly takes fifteen minutes.' Aarzoo insisted.

We saw them walking out of the restaurant sharing single umbrella. They both got into Aarzoo's car along with Akhil and left. After their departure, I went into the restaurant and collected my microphone hidden under the table. Mansi had already paid the bill of the hotel, manager was returing the balance amount to me while coming out from there but I tipped him that, after all he allowed me to spy on my friends in his hotel.

'So, that was it...I didn't see any progress...' I said to Mansi after sitting in the car.

'But I saw...' she said.

'What?'

'They came here separately and went out together...' she said looking out of the car.

'What? What was the progress in that?'

'You will see…' she said looking at me.

It was a confident look, she had strong belief that things will fall into place in their life. I was sure that Shreya will not come up to her father and she would not lie her father to go back to Aarzoo.

Coming to my case, no matter what, I was culprit of Mansi and her family's troubles. I wanted to end it as soon as possible, by going ahead with my decision which I made previous night. I drove the car and reached Mansi's home. 'Why did you stop here?' she asked. 'Will tell you.' I replied and got down from the car and opened the door for her and asked her to come out. She looked at me with knitted eyebrows, searching for the clue.

TWENTY SIX

Mansi's mother and grandmother came out of the house welcoming us, they saw our car from their window, and we entered the house. Before Mansi's mother hop into the kitchen for formalities, 'Mummy, please be seated, I don't want to have anything. I came here to talk to both of you, on an important matter.' I said. 'Can we talk a bit…?' Mansi asked staring at me, doubting my speech. 'Mansi please, let me do the talking first, you all please sit down.' All three ladies looked bewildered. 'I request you all, do not ask anything when I am talking, let me finish everything, I am ready to accept your decision, whatever it maybe...' I requested them. 'I want to talk to you, NOW! It's urgent…' Mansi came to me with wide open eyes and nodding, this time she was sure about what I was going to say. 'Mansi, please…let me do the talking…please sit.' I requested and she sat. 'I understand you all are worried on what am I going to say….' And there, I began my confession. Hearing which, all of them acted weird. Mansi sat holding her forehead, her grandma started crying as she was speechless. But her mother was sitting still, she didn't react, Mansi and I observed her, I sat on my knees infront of her, I didn't have the guts to hold her hands, which she kept knotted on her lap. Mansi held her shoulder from one hand and kept other hand on Mummy's hands.

'Mummy, I am sorry…I…I…' I begged apology with no words, joining my hands. She kept her hand on my head and said, 'I knew everything…' I was stunned after hearing that! Astound Mansi kept her hand on her mouth and Grandma looked at her in a shock. 'Me and Mansi's Papa searched for the bag all over the house, it was not under the bed even a day before his death. I saw the same bag in your hand, when you came for the funeral and it wasn't in your hand while your were leaving with your Grandma. Later, I found it in our bedroom after a month, I was sure that it must have been kept by you.' She paused. We were all shocked after hearing her.

'You knew everything and still your were quiet and moreover, you gave your daughter to him? Why?' Grandma asked her with strong voice. Mansi's head was down that time. I looked at her mother as I also wanted to know the answer. 'Yes, I didn't know why and how he did it, I didn't want to, because I saw guilt in his eyes, when he came on funeral and when he came with the wedding proposal, and it is still there, it requires lots of guts to say the truth and this boy has showed it. That is why, I didn't ask anything, and forgave him and accepted the proposal.' she said. I was still stunned and so was Mansi. 'What are you saying? Have you gone mad? You are forgiving the culprit, who was responsible for the death of your husband?' Grandma asked her, by turning her face towards her. 'My husband was a coward! I am sorry for saying that but I am assessing on it over and over again, since the day he left us all helpless. He had no guts to face the world and committed suicide for the crime, which he never did. But proved it true by suiciding! He was responsible solely for his death! People are suffering from so many problems, they never end up their lives, they fight and they succeed. He never thought about us atleast once before taking that harsh step. And you also know this truth very well.' She paused and started crying. Grandma didn't say a single word after that. Mansi started crying holding her mother. I was silent and helpless audience of everything which was going on in that house. I never saw Mummy so strong before infront of Grandma.

After couple of minutes, Mansi's mother stopped crying, she took a long breath and looked at me wiping her tears, she said 'Because of your immaturity, problems knocked our door, Mansi's father left us, and everyone left after him, few people gave helping hand unwillingly, adding lots of unwanted remarks, and we saw the real faces of our so called well-wishers. Our life was filled with storms! Everything was sinking in this broken boat, there was darkness everywhere, and later, only you came with your family, in our life as a light of hope and I couldn't refuse your proposal for Mansi. I was selfish on that, you know why? (I looked at her) because I knew that Mansi always liked you.' We were shocked more after hearing that. Holding Mansi's cheeks, she said 'I am your mother sweety, I always understood your feelings. I knew it since your school days, when you liked him quietly, often saw your notebooks with his designer names'. Mansi was embarrassed with mixed feelings of shyness, as her mother revealed her love infront of me. My heart smiled at that moment. 'I always wished you to be happy. No matter what, your wish was coming true, how could I reject the proposal on the grounds for which he was not solely responsible for.' We were all stunned, I still had no words. I was quietly sitting infront of her with my head down. Mansi and Grandma didn't know how to react, they were quiet.

'*Amma*, Mansi, I don't know about both of you but I forgive him. Not because he is my son-in-law, but he is genuinely guilty. You always said that there is no harsh punishment than guilt and self realisation.' Mummy said looking at Grandma. My head was still down, looking the floor, my eyes were filled with tears, and I questioned myself, what type of luck I was born with? Besides all my misdeeds and drama I create to hurt people, I am being forgiven. I was responsible for all the troubles in Mansi's family, if they forgive me then there is no looking back for me. I was happy and satisfied, and I thought why I didn't tell the truth to Mummy first before Mansi. Atleast, she would have understood the reality and some part of guilt would have been paid off early. Consecutively, thoughts were running in my mind. On the other side, I didn't see the reaction of Mansi and Grandma.

'Get up, you are the respect of this house, your place is not on the floor, it's in our heart...' saying that Grandma held my hand and made me seated on the sofa. I looked surprisingly at her and rest of the ladies. Wiping her tears, she was smiling at me, Mansi and her mother's eyes were on me, filled with tears. 'For the moment, I forgot what all you did to raise the standard of our family in the society. We couldn't have found a better person than you for our Mansi. You saved our house and life of our daughter, you solved all our problems in minutes, you took care of our health.' She was going on praising me, and I was feeling awkward. I stopped her by holding her hand. 'Please *Amma*, don't embarrass me, I did nothing compared to the thing I've done to spoil everything...Moreover, the wedding decision was taken by Dadi...' I said. 'We owe her, it's her maturity that we all are living together happily now. Without her vision and broad-mindedness it would have never been possible.' She said. 'Mansi, go and bring some juice for our beloved Son...' smiling she ordered Mansi. Mansi went inside the kitchen without any reaction. My battle was still on, I couldn't tell them about my relationship with Mansi. If I did, it would have been sounded like I went to complaint the old ladies about their daughter. Especially, after hearing that Mummy knew I was Mansi's secret love, my mouth was completely shut. We had a long chit chat, Mummy and Grandma regarded my family, and while talking, I consumed all the milkshake that Mansi prepared for me.

We left from there, Mansi didn't say a word. I received a call from Raju on the way back to home. I dropped Mansi at home and went to the site to hear the complaints of some workers, resolved the dispute between workers, which was raised on working shifts. Reached home in the midnight, Dad was waiting for me and he seemed angry, the first thought came in my mind was, *Did Mansi or her family exposed me?!* But the very next moment, positive side of my mind said that would never gonna happen! Mom served food for me on the dining table, I was staring at both Mom and Dad, they were quiet, my heartbeats increased, eye balls were rolling at both of them, within seconds the conversation between both the positive and negative inner voices turned into debate, until Mom asked me to have food. And then, I took a long breath of relief. Dad asked Mom to go inside the room and he interrogated me for not receiving any calls through out the day and not going to the site till evening. He kept on asking questions until my answers satisfied him. Meanwhile, Dadi came out saying, first let him have food, he ended the conversation with a common sentence of every parent, concentrate on work first rather than social service and friends! And he went to his room. It didn't surprise me to see that Mansi wasn't waiting for me.

I washed hands in the basin and sat on the dining table. I was starving, since I ate nothing through out the day other than a sandwich in the office and a milkshake at Mansi's house. Dadi dragged a chair before me and sat on it to accompany me. While having food, I told her the whole story of Aarzoo and Shreya first. She was happy to hear about Aarzoo and Shreya, she wished that they both should get together. 'I don't know about others, but for me, you are the only modern person alive on this earth.' I said. 'And I am not going to die before playing with your children!' she said laughing without any teeth in her mouth. 'Do you feel that would ever happen?' I asked smiling. 'You doubt on our family genes! Your great grand father had thirty children, your grand father had twelve, your father ended only with two of you but I want you to have at least four...' she laughed again. 'C'mon Dadi! Why you want me to contribute more in the population of our country?!' I said. 'Aahh, I was kidding! Atleast one should come out soon!' she said mocking. 'Hmm, I have to have sex with my wife for that to happen! Which seems to be impossible!' I said winking my eye. She patted me on shoulder saying 'Rascal!' she laughed 'Any progress?' she asked me after her cave mouth laugh. 'Nope!' I said jumping my shoulders.

'By the way, one more important news, I confessed all infront of Mansi's mother and grandma.' I said looking at her. Her jaw dropped and her dark cave mouth opened, she looked astonished. 'Nothing to worry, they didn't blame us for anything, on the contrary, they were praising you.' and I explained the whole story to her. She was happy to know that Mansi's mother and grandma forgave us 'It's their greatness. I will go to their home tomorrow and express my gratitude.' She said. 'Hmm, I am still feeling bad Dadi, I told everything thinking that they will punish me but that didn't happen. On the other side, Mansi hasn't spoken to me since then. I think this guilt will live with me, till the last breath of my life!' I muttered my pain looking at her. 'Don't worry, you are guilty from your heart and that is important, and you will never make any mistakes in life to hurt anyone. I am proud of you. People forgive you because of your humble nature. I am sure one day, Mansi will also understand you.' she consoled me keeping her hand on my shoulder. I smiled and finished my food.

While entering the room, I saw Mansi was alseep on the couch. I slowly took my clothes from the cupboard and went to the bathroom silently, I changed and came out. Mansi turned around from couch, she wasn't asleep and looked at me. I was feeling awkward to speak and so was she, I looked at her. The silence was odd, I went to her and she woke up and sat on the couch hurriedly covering herself with blanket. I showed hands to ease her down, clearing my throat I sat beside her 'Mmm, Mansi, I…I don't know what are you thinking on everything I did at your home today. I just want to say, I wanted to confess, it...it…it was killing me…I couldn't hide it for long…you remember what you said about Shreya that she must be living with Arjun because of the society…many things were going on in my mind comparing your situation on the same…I mean ours…our relationship…So I thought that the elders, I mean your Mummy and Grandma will decide what has to be done. As end of the day Dadi will think on my side… So...I...I…you know…you are also confused, so I….' I was stuck in between due to discomfort. I covered my face with my hands, resting the elbows on my knees, waiting for her reply but she was mutely staring the floor, covering herself under the blanket. I took a long breath 'Look, I am not expecting anything from you by doing all this. I didn't try to change your mind or anything like that. At the end of the day what matters for me is your decision. So, still the ball is in your court…I don't want you to compromise your life for the society. You take all the time you want to decide. Mummy and *Ajji* forgave me, that's enough for me.' Saying I gulped. She didn't reply, 'You had your food?' I asked after few seconds. She nodded saying 'Yes'. That was a relief and I went back to my bed and slept.

TWENTY SEVEN

It had been a week after the incident, Mansi rarely spoke to me all these days. That morning, I was busy working out in our gymnasium upstairs. Mansi came to pour water to the plants in the gym, she didn't look at me and got busy taking care of the plants. I was shirtless and felt it weird as she never comes around when I am half nude. My phone rang and I was running on the treadmill. Mansi picked the phone, it was Mandar, she spoke to him for a while and held the phone infront of me, looking otherside. I stopped the treadmill and got down from it, wiping my sweat, panting I took the phone from her hand 'Hey buddy, how are you?' He asked me. 'Fine, how are you? And…When did you come back from your honeymoon?' I asked him with fast breath, staring Mansi. She was busy with the plants, pushing her hair back her ears. Though, she was looking at the plants but her ears were on my conversation. She looked hot in her wine colour dress, her fair body was shining in that dark colour. She smelled wonderful and I was sweaty all over, my eyes were tracking her finely tonned figure. Those beautiful hands were busy touching the flowers, they looked so soft that even the plants may harm the softness of those delicate hands. I wished, I would have been one of the plant or flower which she was touching that time. Especially, after the workout, my testostrones were bursting all over my body, I wanted to hold her tightly in my arms, touch her curves and love her.

'Two days back, hello….HELLO! Can you hear me?' Voice of Mandar woke me up from my lust. He was saying it on the phone again and again, which my brain didn't take it in the hunger for my love. 'Yeah…I…I was lost in something…Ok…so what is the next plan?' I asked. Mansi was smart enough to notice that her beauty was distracting me, she blushed and started humming a song while spraying water to the plants. 'We are coming to your home in an hour, hope you are not busy. Actually, I have to go to the VISA office later and tomorrow I am going back, so can you take out some time for us?' he asked from the other side of the phone. '*Oh! Request! US jake kuch jyada hi formality kar raha hai!* (You have become more formal after going to USA), Yeah sure, you can hop in any time.' I said to Mandar and Mansi smiled hearing that. 'No...I thought you are a busy builder, so better to take appointment before.' he said mocking. 'I am never busy for you guys…we'll be waiting for you…*achcha sun…Bhabhi ko leke aana!* (Ok listen! Come along with your wife)' I said. 'Yeah, sure…*surprise bhi hai…*(There is a surprise) He said. 'Ok…I will wait for it.' I said and he hung up the phone.

Disconnecting the phone I gazed her, she was still humming an old Hindi song. I felt strange, as she wasn't like this a day before. 'Strange!' I said little louder so that she can hear my comment. She looked at me and went out from there, I noticed a touch of smile on her face. I'd fell in that trap of smile many times in those 7 months of marriage and had nothing rather than her confusion, so my heart lost the game over my mind. I went to take shower.

As informed, Mandar arrived at our home on time. It was a surprise to see his mother and his wife together, along with him. His foreigner wife was wearing saree and they all looked happy.

'Welcome, welcome' My Dadi, Mom and Mansi went ahead till the door greeting them, and I followed inviting them inside. After all the formalities, Mandar's mother stood up and gave a small box to Mansi, she called me ahead 'We couldn't come to your marriage, so this is a small gift for both of you from our side.' She said. I blushed as I never get that feeling of shilly-shally to receive gifts or eat and drink at others place. Mansi was sure about the expensive thing packed inside the box and hesitantly 'Aunty, why all this?' she asked. 'It's an order…' Mandar's Mom said strictly and everyone laughed. She opened it and as expected we all saw beautiful gold rings inside the box engraved with our names. Mandar's mother insited us to exchange the rings, starting from Mansi. She shyly took a ring of her name and softly placed it in my finger, followed by her I took residual ring and placed it in her finger. Everyone around clapped for us, which reminded me our engagement night before the day of wedding.

Meanwhile, Dadi asked Mansi to bring something from her room, she went inside and came with a bag. *Ladies are so fast in all these things, when do they get time to buy all this stuff? Super fast!* I thought myself. The thing surprised me more was, Mandar's Mom's changed behaviour. It was awkward to ask Mandar about that infront of everyone, I messaged him on the whatsapp and signalled him to check, he checked his message and smiled at me. Mom gave the big box to Mandar's mother and Dadi gave the small boxes to Mandar and his wife. And the history repeated, Dadi also presented the rings to Mandar and his wife Isabella, and a Mysore silk saree for Mandar's mother. It was Mandar's mother's time to hesitate and Dadi supposed 'It's my order now.' Everyone laughed again. Mandar and his wife exchanged the rings.

'Actually, we came here to express our gratitude to Mansi.' said Mandar toasting for Mansi, which surprised me. 'Yes, today we are all together only because of Mansi.' His Mom added. 'Mansi, I thank you from the bottom of my heart.' Isabella said in her US accent. 'Oh! Please you all are embarrassing me now, I did nothing.' said Mansi shyly. My Mom and Dadi were smiling, by which, it was clear that they knew everything and it was only me in the house, who knew nothing. And then Mandar's mother explained everything that how Mansi went to their home previous day and how she convinced his mother saying 'The entire life Mandar was an obedient son and for his single mistake it is not right to abandon him.' In the end, she convinced Aunty to accept her beloved son's marriage.

Mandar patted me on my shoulder and took me on the corner of the house 'I have something special for you ...' He opened a pack from his bag, there were two large bottles of *Black Dog* whisky. 'It's available in India as well!' I said with sarcasm. 'I know and I bought it here itself!' he replied. 'We are all joining tonight at Shaun's place. His parents are away from home, I am busy today can't carry through out the day. So you bring these tonight!' he finished his point. I grinned and took the packs from his hand. It was nice to get together and they left from home after having breakfast.

Dad was in the office, Raju and I went to the site to monitor the work. The hectic day kept me so busy that I didn't get a time to receive any calls from home or friends. Shaun messaged me to reach his home by 8. I sent him thumps-up emoji accepting his invitation. I was carrying the bottles in my car and before leaving for the party, I called home and Dadi answered it. I gave her my message saying that I was taking Raju along with me, she agreed immediately as she knew Raju don't drink and he can drive us home safely. I wanted to celebrate the joy with Raju, he was in the family from years and he was also there with me whenever I needed just like a buddy.

It was raining heavily outside, we reached Shaun's home an hour late. Sumit and Mandar were already present there. '*Booze lagi hai yaar! Kitna der! Jaldi nikal* ' (Thirsty for the drink, you are late. Open it) Sumit said loudly and snatched the packs out of my hand. '*Saale tharki! Humesha daaru!*' (Drunker! Always thinks about drinking) I said mocking, Sumit grinned. Raju was feeling awkward infront of all, he was never present in our booze party till that day. Shaun came ahead and said 'Come in Raju! Don't be shy, feel at home and enjoy the party.' he switched on the disco lights in his home and started the music. Smiling, Raju sat on the sofa. Sumit made drinks for everyone. 'Gourav is not coming?' I asked, 'Aah, his baby is not well, he went home from the shop.' Mandar said. It was all boys night out. Shaun ordered food from restaurant along with yummy starters.

We all started with loud CHEERS! After two pegs Raju slept on the sofa. Another two pegs made Mandar cry. He started uttering his family issues and thanking Mansi for resolving everything. With the name of Mansi, my heart beats increased, with shaking legs I mounted on the table and made a toast, saying 'I love you Mansi'. Looking at that Shaun accompanied me on the table and announced that he will be proposing his girlfriend soon. Later Sumit climbed the table wobbling by holding our hands and said something which we never expected, Sumit uttered loudly 'I am in love with Preeti!!' hearing that I didn't feel like I was drunk. Shaun and I tried to open our eyes widely, supporting each other we held Sumit and asked him to say that again. He uttered more loudly that he loves Preeti and in next second he fell on the floor, we bursted laughing on the floor and realised the happiness of falling in love. And then none of us remembered what we did.

I opened my eyes and looked around, it wasn't my bedroom. My head was bursting in hangover. Sumit was sleeping beside me with his open mouth, every stinky breath of his was blowed on me. I kicked him muttering 'Yuck! Go away you idiot.' That didn't affect his sleep and he did not move an inch from his position. It was Shaun's bedroom, I woke up holding my head. The pain was so sharp that I felt like someone is hammering my head from inside. I smelled horrible, just like Sumit. I went to the washroom and got fresh. Brushed my teeth with my finger and tried to vomit all the mess I filled inside my stomach previous night to get rid of the pounding headache, nothing came out. I used the mouth wash to gargle, and my breath was bareble after that.

I heard the voices of Raju and Shaun. I went in the living room, Raju and Shaun were clearing the mess. His living room was stinking. 'Hey buddy! Good morning!!' Shaun greeted in a fresh mood, as if he was enjoying his hangover. 'Bad morning for me! My head is bursting out of pain!' I said pulling the chair and perched on it holding my head. Shaun made a small peg, singing *'Zandu balm Zandu Balm peeda haari balm, sardi sardard peeda ko palme door kare...'* (An old TV commercial song of a pain relief balm) and said '*Yeh le Utaara!*' (Here for hangover), 'Man! I can't drink anymore!' I said. He went inside the kitchen and came out with a glass of Lemon juice, 'Here, have it...I prepared for everyone.' holding the glass before me he said. I took the glass from his hand saying 'Thanks buddy!' and drunk everydrop of it in one sip and kept the glass on the table.

'What happened here, why the room is stinking?' I asked looking around, the room looked clean yet it smelt bad. 'You don't remember?' Shaun asked, I nodded my head naively. 'Mandar blew up last night, he cleaned everything in the morning though. I was clearing all the food and mess we all did last night and Raju helped.' said Shaun, spraying the room-freshner all over. I asked Raju whether he called home or not? Obedient champ, Raju replied that he has done that job. It wasn't the first time that we were sleeping at Shaun's place. We did it many times while cheering the cricket team or football team, watching a movie or simply after the booze party, whenever his parents leave for their native to Goa. Drunken master, Sumit was once looted by some taxi driver while going back home! The driver threw him in the middle of the road after looting everything he had, and since then he is against of hiring the cabs while drunk and he never allowed us to hire one. So most of the time, we all sleep at Shaun's house to safeguard ourselves after drunk, either by driving or theifs.

Mandar left for home early in the morning, as he had last minute tasks to finish before flying back to US that night. Mandar's mother was about to join them in the coming month. As he married an US girl, he got a green card of US citizenship and he was taking his mother along with him there. After so many ifs and buts, his mother agreed for settling down with her son. Isabella was a nice girl, who insisted her Mother-in-law to accompany them for life time. It was surely not a case of using elders as maid in a foreign country. Mandar loved his mother, he worshipped her as God. He always wished his mother to be with him, his plans were never to settle down in India because of the cunning relatives he had, who never helped his mother when his father exprired years ego. His mother raised him single handedly and he remembered all the struggles she had gone through. When Mandar went to USA, the greedy relatives came to his mother for maintaining the relationship, with a marriage proposal of Mandar with their daughter by influencing his mother by their fake affection. Thanks to Mansi, who made his mother realise the truth. Mandar was arranging for his mother's VISA and rest of the admin works before leaving.

It was nine, my head ache subsided after a glass of lemon juice. Shaun prepared cereals for everyone. After eating a bowl of oatmeal, we all tried to wake up Sumit but he wasn't opening single eye, Shaun threw a glass of water on his face. He woke up shouting 'FUCK MAN!!!' and raged on Shaun to punch him, Shaun ran into the entire house laughing, followed by angrybird Sumit. 'Hi Preeti!' I uttered and Sumit stopped immediately to look at the door, no one was there. Shaun and I bursted out laughing, and Raju was grinning on the situation. 'Dude! You have to look at your face!' I said and laughed again. Dumbfounded Sumit stood still, with that innocent face no-one could make out that he was an obsessive asshole when it comes to booze. Stinky champ sat on the sofa wondering how come we knew about Preeti, as he did not remember that he admitted his love infront of all of us the previous night.

TWENTY EIGHT

We all sat together after Sumit got fresh, discussing his love and planning how and when he should propose Preeti. Sumit explained that after the incident of Mahadevaiyya, he started liking Preeti. Initially he felt it was an attraction but later he found out himself that its love. He met Preeti few times after that by making different excuses but could not express his feelings. He had another problem, caste of both the families. Sumit's family was vegetarian, where as Preeti belongs to a compulsory non-vegetarian family. Most important task was proposing Preeti, we all knew that Preeti was a strict girl when it comes to love, though she flirts but she never expressed her thought about love to anyone. We all decided that we will talk about this and if required will take a help of Mansi on this. On that note we dispersed from Shaun's house.

Traffic was normal on the double road. Speed of my car was on eighty kilometres per hour, a van on the road slowed its pace ahead of my car and I pressed the break to slow down but suddenly I realised that the break wasn't working! I turned the stearing wheel on the right immediately and took over the truck. 'Oh Shit!! Breaks aren't working Raju!' I uttered. 'What!?Why' he uttered in a shock. 'How would I know idiot!' I shouted and tried to slow down the speed by changing the gear. It was a busy road with continuous moving vehicles, I drove the car on first gear, but the speed wasn't coming under control, people blew horn and took over, some went shouting at me for changing lanes. I tried to apply the break many times but it didn't work. The traffic was an additional hurdle for me. It was dangerous to drive the car in that condition. Finally, with no option left, I asked Raju to fasten his seat belt and warned him to be prepared. I laid back trusting the car technology and aimed on the road side tree, turned the stearing wheel on the left, stone partition of the road bounced under the tires and at last my car dashed the tree. Immediately, the air bags flew on our faces and car alarm started blowing. Within seconds, people stopped by and some got down from their vehicles to help us.

It was one in the noon. 'What happened?' shouting, everyone rushed to us when we entered the house. We explained everything about how the accident happened and traffic police along with public helped us to move the car to garage after confirming that we weren't drunk. Thank goodness, I didn't drink the *utaara* (peg), which Shaun made for me to subside my hangover. 'Luckily we weren't injured, all thanks to bhaiyya's presence of mind' Raju appreciated. 'Nah…It is because of the car technology! We might have hit our head on the strearing and dashboard even after wearing seat belts if the airbags didn't blew on time!' I said.

'Will you shut up! We are all worried here and you both are discussing on the technology of the car?' Mom uttered, she paused and looked at Dadi and Dad 'Now will you talk to him or I do the job?' she asked them in her high tone.

Dadi showed her hand to Mom and gestured with her eyes to calm down. 'Both of you get fresh, we'll talk later.' Dadi said and sat on the couch of the living room. I looked around, everyone seemed to be worried, as it was natural. With my head down, I went into my room and Raju ran towards out-house where he lives. I rushed to the bathroom and brushed my teeth again, as I was stinking even after brushing at Shaun's house. I took bath twice by rubbing body wash. I got dehydrated after the double impact bath, I came out of the bathroom just by wrapping a towel, without wiping myself.

Mansi was roaming in the room, she was waiting for me to come out. Suddenly, she rushed at me, hugged me tightly and started crying. I saw her uneasy face downstairs but didn't think that she was worried this much for me. 'Hey! What happened?' Holding her shoulder, I asked her softly. She didn't reply and kept on crying. She hugged me so tight that I felt the warmth of her body. It was the first time after marriage that she was so close to me. She was wearing saree and smelled fantastic, I thanked myself for taking bath before that, I could never imagine Mansi to smell that nasty odour of mine in our first embrace. Before my lust start craving for her, I lifted her face holding her chin, wiping her tears 'I am fine, nothing happened.' I whispered. She looked into my eyes, so did I, and our eyes locked. I tucked her hair behind her ear and carrasing her cheek with my thumb I smiled. Her hands were on my bear chest, her body touched my body. Abruptly, she realised that she is in my arms, she pushed herself back and turned around. Wiping her tears with her saree, she stood still. I wasn't sure whether she was shy or she was embarrassed. 'Mansi' I called her name. 'I am sorry, I was very scared after hearing the news of that accident and couldn't control myself.' She muttered softly. 'It's ok, I am fine!' I said standing behind her, I felt awkward to go infront of her in towel. 'Your clothes are on the bed, you get ready and come down. Food is ready.' She said without looking at me and started walking out of the room. 'Mansi...' I called her and she stopped without turning. I was expecting to talk more with her, my heart felt that she has started developing feelings for me. 'What if something happened to me today?' I asked to check her reaction. Quickly, she turned around 'Are you nuts? How could you say that? Do you know what all I was going through when I got that call? I was crushed into pieces...' muttering she came close to me. I was smiling at her, and she realised what she was talking, hesitatingly she paused 'I....I...I...mean... WE...We were crushed into pieces...Mom, Dad and Dadi...all were worried...For the first time I saw that much of stress on everyones face...Dadi was praying all the time doing her *jaap*...before saying anything like that think about the people who care for you and Love....Love you so much...' she said staring at me.

I felt all the butterflies in my stomach hearing that. I was sure on every bit she said was true, as I know my family. But what was new to me, was her feelings that she expressed, the last lines she said, attracted me, with no single doubt, I was sure that once again her heart has started beating for me. I was on the top of the world, I wanted to shout her name loudly, hold her tight in my arms until she begs to leave her but I controlled my feelings, stayed gentle in the situation, 'Relax, I was just kidding, everything was under control.' I said and she looked at me, I stared her knotting my hands against my chest. She looked here and there, tucking her hair back her ears she went out of the room. While she was going out, I saw a touch of smile decorated with shyness on her face. *Haay! Kuch toh asar huwa accident ka*...(Some action happened after the accident.) I whispered and grabbed the clothes which, she'd neatly placed on the bed and got ready.

'Dad, you go to the meeting, I will send Raju to the garage to look after the car and I will take the bike today. However, bike has not been used from many days...' I said to Dad, while having my lunch, ignoring his stare and up coming interrogation. I knew that he will give lectures on *'do not drink', 'stop fooling around with friends', 'Be responsible, you are married now!'* blah blah blah! Mom and Mansi were busy in the kitchen, Dadi was having lunch with me. Dad was about to leave for the meeting with the registrar, he was waiting for me to come down so that he can finish his class with me. I wished, I would have waited some more minutes in the room. Raju was having lunch sitting on the sofa, away from Dad. He was running without eating in the fear of Dad, but Mom and Dadi forced him to eat first before going out.

'When are you going to be serious in life?' there he stricked his first question. 'I...I am serious Dad!' I said smiling, looking at Dadi. 'Shut up!' he shouted, 'Everytime I think that you have changed and now ready to take all the responsibility, you do something like this! Last night we were all waiting for you but you didn't come. You involved Raju as well in your shitty things!' he uttered again. Raju turned around and started eating fast to finish and run away from there, but he had to face Dad that day. Looking at Raju 'And you! Raju! I always thought that you are more mature than Sandy. I never expected this from you!' Dad said. Raju's head was down and he didn't say single word in defence in the respect of Dad. 'Let them eat first!' Dadi said to calm down Dad. 'Yeah, first let them get fresh, and then let them eat!! Let them do this, that!...Like this I will never talk to these idiots!! This is all because of you Maa. You always save him by taking his side. That's why they are becoming jerks!!' angrily he said to Dadi. Dadi patted her head slowly and nodded without any words.

Mansi came out with plate of rotis, she served me and Raju and went inside with her head down. 'Because of him, all the work has got delayed today! You know how much we were all worried? What was that poor girl's condition after receiving the call?' He asked me describing Mansi's state, who was quietly preparing rotis inside. 'And your Mom and Dadi were praying God every second! And our *mister serious* says *I am serious Dad.!* Listen to me carefully! I do not want you to repeat anything like this in the future! This is the final warning to you and you too, Raju!' He shouted looking at me and Raju and rested his mouth for seconds. We both nodded. 'Now finish your food and go back to work. Raju, I will see the car on the way while coming back, you go to the office, I need some papers, you bring them to the registrar office.' He paused, and looked at me, 'And you *mister serious*! You go to the CA office and check the accounts, and drop Raju to office on the way.' He said to me and went out of the house starting his XUV. Everytime he goes to the government offices and big clients, he takes his XUV. There were some giggling sounds from the kitchen, Mom and Mansi were enjoying everything silently, and that was not new for me to get Dad's scoldings infront of Mansi. She was familiar with these situations from school days. At times, Dad did his part of shouting at me infront of all my friends, sometimes even the boys shared my rebukes.

I showed fake angry look to Dadi, she laughed. 'But how were the breaks failed, has anybody thought about that? As far as I know the car had no problem with the breaks previously.' Mansi said from inside, and her question striked my mind. Raju and I looked at each other, the car was parked outside Shaun's home previous night and breaks were working perfectly when we parked it.

While on the way to office, 'Bhaiyya, I remember one thing, last night when we were driving the car to Shaun bhaiyya's home, one biker was following us from long distance. I saw him couple of times behind us.' Raju said remembering the incident. Immediately, I stopped the bike on the side and called the garage to clear the doubt, The mechanic told the truth, which was no more a surprise for us, he said that the break wires were purposely cut by someone. I called Shaun and asked him to check if he finds any evidence of tools, or people around, who saw someone near our car previous night. I did not tell anybody in the home to tense their fear more.

By the evening, Shaun called me and said, one of his neighbor saw a man from his window, near my car. He described that the man was wearing brown jacket and helmet, he couldn't see his face because of the helmet. But the Avenger bike was parked beside the car. With his statement and Raju's memory, I thought that it's a police case. Meanwhile, Dad checked car with mechanic and came to know about the truth and he called me. We both decided to go to the police and went to station along with Raju to launch a complaint. We called Shaun and his neighbour as witness for launching an FIR. The news spread to Sumit from Shaun and he called Mansi, Sumit couldn't resist anything and he called home to cross check and told her. He also took the credit of spreading the news to rest of the gang. And in seconds everyone started calling me. Mandar was leaving that night and he called while getting ready to go to the airport to confirm the news. Everyone asked me to be alert and not hop into any social welfare activities, as they all doubted that either Mahadevaiyya or Indrappa and their men must have done this to take a revenge on me.

I called Preeti to check the hold of Mahadevaiyya. But Preeti was sure that he may not have done that as he has nobody outside to accomplish his evil wishes. All his men were behind the bars. And if he does anything she will be the first to know before the task begins. I was also sure on that, because Shaun's neighbour had described that the man was wearing modern clothes and as far as I remembered, the people in village didn't wore modern clothes, and they were not so much far ahead to hire some modern guy for this task.

Suddenly, my mind hit the bullseye and I took everyone from police station to the place where we could find the same Avenger bike, police accompanied us. Shaun's neighbor described that the bike which was parked beside my car had big 'A' drawn on the number plate and helmet had tiger stripes.

TWENTY NINE

We reached the house, where the Avenger was parked. Immediately, after seeing the bike Shaun's neighbour identified the bike, and we went inside the house of a man. It was none other than Arjun, Shreya's husband, who tried to kill me!

Police found the brown jacket in the house and enquired his presence during previous night. His parents tried to save him, but with all the anxieties and frustration, Arjun and his family displayed his crime. Police arrested him on the benefit of doubt.

Within few minutes, Mansi reached the police station. Shreya and her father also came to the police station. In the meanwhile, Aarzoo reached there as well. Shreya and her father were embarrassed to face me and my family. Mansi was sitting with Shreya consoling her, as she wasn't able to stop crying after knowing the truth. I sat before her to ease her, looking at me 'I would have never forgiven myself if anything happened to you! This is all because of me!' She said while crying. 'Shreya!! Ssshhh... nothing happened. So relax, don't think about anything.' I said. 'Yes dear, and we know it's not your fault, why are you blaming youself?' Mansi said to comfort her. Akhil was crying restlessly looking his mother in pain, Aarzoo took him away with her and brought all the candy's and chocolates to calm the poor baby.

Arjun's parents were waiting outside cursing me and Shreya for getting him arrested. Every few minutes his mother was getting up from her bench and cursed us. At last, lady Constable shouted at her and then she kept quiet.

Those were the days when Shreya's grandma was getting good treatment in Aarzoo's hospital, credit goes to Aarzoo. The old lady had changed her mind during her last days and regretted hundreds of times for spoiling Shreya's life by forcing her to marry a monster.

Arjun was again behind the bars. Preeti was inside the cell with officers to spill the truth from Arjun, as that area was under her control. That psychopathic man, who possessed tough infront of helpless girl and her family, had very less strength to hold on to the truth in front of serious police grilling. He accepted that he cut the wires of my car break line and tried to kill me as he wanted to take revenge on me for separating him from Shreya.

Preeti came out with the news. Meanwhile, Aarzoo came inside the police station carrying Akhil in her arms, Shreya looked at her, wiping her tears she took a long breath and asked Preeti whether she can meet Arjun? Preeti nodded with permission. She held Aarzoo's hand and went inside, we all rushed behind her. That night was a crime free night in the area as only we were there to create all the drama in the station, we were all close to Preeti so none of the staff stopped us and that was an added advantage.

Arjun was sitting on the bench behind the bars, his body was full of sweat and there were some slap marks on his face, even after getting beaten so badly he had no guilt. Looking at Shreya he raged and came forward yelling 'You bitch! I will kill you!!' and he saw me in the crowd, pointing at me he shouted 'How dare you come here!' we all stared at him. Shreya looked straight into his eyes angrily 'Arjun, I am here to tell you something. I always thought that you will change one day but you don't deserve to be changed. Now, I will make sure that you die behind these bars!' Immediately, he tried to pull her neck but meanwhile Aarzoo hit him on his hand. He jumped off, jerking his hand to get rid of the pain, which was caused to him by black-belt Aarzoo. Shreya stood there still, pointing a finger at Arjun, she said 'You know what? I never loved you! I tolerated you only because of my family. You always doubted that I had an affair right? Today I am telling you! YES! I had an affair, I didn't choose my love fearing the society and chose the hell with you. You know who is my love? Aarzoo!' saying she held Aarzoo's hand. We were all stunned to hear that, Aarzoo was amused, her eyes didn't move from Shreya's face. Shreya's father muttered 'What are you saying?'

Meanwhile, Arjun started laughing by clapping his hands! He said 'You…you love that doctor!? You are a lesbian!! Ha ha ha…' he laughed loudly again. 'Yes, I love her and yes I …I am a lesbian.' she said this time looking at Aarzoo, who was smiling at her. That moment brought the smile on everyone's face but her father. All of a sudden, the shy girl, who never said those words to herself, said infront of the world within fraction of seconds. Arjun looked in the rage at Aarzoo, she smiled at Shreya and looking at Arjun 'Easy paper tiger! Don't you dare to think anything against us now on…Although, I am a doctor and cure wounds, but I can give horrific wounds that no doctors can cure in your lifetime!' She warned him, Arjun looked at his hand which was still paining. We grinned hearing that.

Preeti asked all of us to vacate that place and we all came out. It was raining heavily outside, we all stood inside the police station. Shreya's father perched on the bench, Mansi offered him water taking out the bottle from her bag. He waved his hand and muttered 'No' and sat quietly, keeping his head down. Shreya sat on her knees before him on the floor, holding his hands, 'I am sorry Appa, this is what I am… I...I can't help it, I can't change it…I never wanted to bring the truth infront of you. But today, Arjun crossed all the limits, so I had to say all that. But trust me Appa, I will not take any step beyond this. I have sacrificed my love long back, I have no expectations from anybody. All that matters to me is your happiness and Akhil's future.' She said softly. Aarzoo smiled, she was proud of her love. That day, what Shreya had done was impossible for any brave heart, we all were speechless.

Dad sat beside Shreya's father, 'Mr.Moorty, I can understand what you are thinking and going through. I don't know whether I have right to talk in this matter or not. Yet, I want to tell you something. All that I can say is, we as parents always accept our children's good and bad deeds with full of heart. In the end, we all want our children to be happy. As you know very well, your girl has sacrifised her life once for your happiness and ready to sacrifice it in the future as well... The time has changed and we have to move on with it. Coming to the society, every individual makes the society, when we change, society will also change one day. Rest the ball is in your court.' Dad said patting his shoulder. Shaun gave a cunning look at me after the speech of *Ball* and two old men's closeness in that queer moment. It was gay for all the boys but I knew my father and showed my tight fist to Shaun in fake anger, he grinned.

Meanwhile, Sumit rushed in the station. He came all wet on his bike, removing his jacket he looked at everyone. Knotting his eyebrows at all our tensed faces he asked 'What did I miss?' Preeti took him on the side and explained him what all happened, to make a prank with him she told that he was next target of Arjun. Sumit heard everything carefully but when he came to know about Arjun's thinking, his first reaction was 'What the Ffff…!!!' he paused looking at the elder's present there and uttered immediately 'Why the hell he thinks that! Where as I like you!' without his conciousness, he spoke his heart infront of Preeti, and bit his tongue! Tightly closing his eyes he punched the wall before him and muttered 'Shit!' And that was a surprise to everyone including Preeti.

The girl, infront of whom no boy had guts to say those words fearing her and her family, Sumit did it. Preeti was stunned with that ear-shot, her eyes were wide open and her jaw was dropped. Starting from Shaun, we all bursted into laughter, the entire serious atmosphere turned into laughter within seconds.

Dad understood the situation and asked Shreya's father 'There is a nice tea shop near this station, shall we go there Mr.Moorthy?' Shreya's father accepted his invitation and both the elders showed their maturity on time. Old men opened the umbrellas and walked out of the station, Dad patted Sumit's back while going out.

Preeti and Sumit stood still, embarrassed, confused. Sumit turned his face towards the wall, Preeti knotted her hands against her chest, she was clueless, thinking, how to react infront of her staff on that situation. The same staff, which gets scared when Preeti enters the station, the staff which thinks Preeti is the most strict and daring officer, ofcourse, she is with no doubt but the situation made her mortified infront of all. She looked at her staff, they all got back to work, grinning.

Sumit took long breath and looked at Preeti with his innocent face. He is the only man in our gang who creates all the mischief and has adorable innocent face like a child. Preeti gave final look at all of us seriously, we stopped laughing and pretended to look serious. She looked at Sumit with her lethal eyes and muttered 'Since when?' Sumit cleared his throat and said 'Af…af…After Sandy's village drama…when you took heck out of all the goons…I…I …I was impressed by your…your bravery and…I don't know... how and when I...I started…hmmm…I started liking you.' he finished his proposal hesitating. It was hard for all of us to control our laughter and I couldn't hold it any longer, I muttered 'Slap him Preeti!' and I laughed out louder and following me Shaun laughed so hard that he fell on the floor. Sumit's situation was very funny, everyone around and all the police started laughing looking at us, it was a treat to everyone after the hardcore drama by Arjun. All credit goes to our lover boy, Sumit.

My stomach started aching after laughing so hard and I stopped by taking fast breaths. I looked at the girls, they were smiling at Preeti. Akhil was happily walking around looking at all our happy faces. Preeti stood there elegantly, tying her hands against her chest. Her perfectly fitted police uniform suited her stature. Mansi walked at Preeti, as she noticed some shyness on the face of a strict police officer. My eyes followed Mansi, she stood beside Preeti and whispered something in her ears and they both giggled. Preeti stared at Sumit and the girls went inside the cabin. Sumit was standing with his head down, when the girls passed from there he rushed to us, punching me and Shaun, he said '*Saalon!! tum jaise dost ho toh dushmanon ki kya kami* (Why would someone need enemy if you can get friends like you!). We laughed again, Shaun teased him with an old Hindi TV commercial tag line '*Yeh bechara pyar ke boj ka maara…*' (This poor guy is stuck in love).

Within few seconds, Mansi came out of cabin and asked Sumit to get inside. We followed him seeking more entertainment. Sumit entered the cabin and we stood outside to listen to the conversation. 'Hmm…If

I find you saying this to any girl after this, I will straight away encounter you!' Preeti muttered. 'O..OK' said Sumit and started walking out. 'Idiot! Didn't you understand what she said?' Aarzoo muttered biting her teeth. We entered the cabin, the girls were giggling. Our stupid lover boy didn't get the signal of acceptance from his love. I whispered in his ears 'She said yes! Moron!' Sumit's eyes were wide open after hearing that and I pushed him towards Preeti, he was about to fall on her but he controlled himself. Cropping his hair with his fingers, he stood infront of her smiling, 'No, I won't say this to any girl except you!' He said and bent on his knee, offering his right hand to Preeti, he asked gently like a man, 'I Love You Preeti! And I want to grow old with you, spending my entire life saying these lines, only to you…Preeti, will you marry me?' he proposed with a smile. Instantly, Preeti covered her mouth with her hands, the strict police officer was shyly standing infront of her man. Girls started clapping, I glanced at Mansi, she was already staring at me and she took off her eyes, shyly she looked down. It was like back in school days again, the same old buddies and same old true love. 'My knees are hurting!' Sumit complained in pain, 'Do some workouts daily!' Aarzoo mocked. Preeti held his hand 'Yes!' softly she accepted raising him up.

We all clapped and my eyes were on Mansi, her eyes were still on the floor because she knew that I was staring her. Shaun said teasing all 'Great…congrats all the couples here. Please, pray for me!!' I patted his shoulder 'What happened to your neighbour's girl, she also dumped you?' I muttered. 'Shut up man! Nothing happened. I couldn't tell her…she is engaged!' Shaun complained. We both laughed, Sumit asked Preeti 'So… can I kiss you now?' Preeti slapped him lightly saying 'I have accepted your proposal on duty! That's enough!' and she hugged him. 'That's romantic!' Aarzoo muttered staring Shreya. New love birds got separated smiling. 'So…Now what?' Shaun asked them about the future. 'I don't know...and frankly I don't care for anything now.' Sumit said mocking. We all smiled. I was standing on the door, and meanwhile, saw Dad and Moorthy uncle coming inside the station. They both looked around for us, I waved my hand from inside the cabin, which had half door and Dad saw me. 'Dad and uncle are coming.' I said to all. Preeti and Sumit got apart.

'So do we have a plan to go home today? Good thing is that there is no crowd in the station but we fulfilled that emptiness. I think you all want to stay longer here?' teasing us, Dad said. 'No…No uncle, we all are leaving.' Sumit said 'I'll call you.' He whispered in Preeti's ears, joyfully she stared at him.

Aarzoo and Shreya were sad, they both looked at each other,

Moorthy uncle looked them with a pale expression. He picked up Akhil in his arm, who was roaming around all of us. 'I will drop you.' Aarzoo offered looking at Moorthy uncle. 'No Beta, we'll go by auto.' He said. 'It's raining heavily, I will drop you uncle. Please, I insist.' she insisted. Moorthy uncle quietly accepted her offer. Shreya showed her concern for me, she re-checked with Preeti about Arjun's custody. Preeti assured her that he won't be able to do anything. Aarzoo drove the car on front gate of the police station, Moorthy uncle sat on the back seat with Akhil, Shreya hugged all of us and sat on front seat of alongside Aarzoo. Dad gave me his car key, I drove it on the gate after Aarzoo's departure. Dad asked Mansi to sit in the front seat, denying that with a smile she opened the back seat door and sat behind asking him to sit in the front. Shaun and Sumit went on their bikes and we all left from there one by one.

I recalled what Dad said to Moorthy uncle about children's mistakes. 'Dad, would you forgive me if I ever did something… really wrong?' I asked him while driving. Mansi coughed 'It's raining heavily.' She said and gestured me aiming not to open my mouth about the past. 'I have always forgiven you, when you're guilty by heart. It's not the question of making mistakes, we all make mistakes in our life, it's a question of not repeating them.' He said gently by patting my shoulder. I sighed, and drove the car on third gear as the roads were empty. 'And yes *beta*, it is raining very heavily today but I am sure our hero will drive us home safely tonight.' He answered to Mansi, mocking at me. I smiled at him. While he was busy tuning the radio, I adjusted the rear mirror to take a glance of Mansi. She noticed that from the back seat, it was dark rainy night yet her face was shining like a full moon. She shyly pushed her hair back her ears and looked at the drizzling water on the glass of window with her smiling face.

Dadi and Mom were waiting for us when we entered the house. We explained complete drama that happened in the police station. Dadi was shocked to know about Arjun's intentions. She thanked Mansi for doubting on the car break fail.

THIRTY

It was ten in the night, we all had dinner. Dad was tired of entire day hustle-bustle, he went to sleep early after the dinner, followed by him Mom and Dadi also went to their respective rooms. Mansi was in the kitchen to clean up the mess. I was feeling sleepy but decided to stay back with Mansi down stairs. I switched on the TV and tuned into an English movie channel, which was telecasting my favourite James Bond movie. I have a complete collection of un-cut versions of 007 movies. It's no fun to watch the Hollywood movies on Indian television, as they edit all the special scenes from blood to kiss. It was '*Live and let die*' movie and I loved the scene when Bond (Roger Moore) with cards of love, convinces the tarrot reader bond girl Solitaire (Jane Seymour) that they are lovers. The same scene was live when I tuned into the channel. I was disappointed with the editing policy of the channel and switched off the television.

I went inside the kitchen, Mansi was clearing the utensils for maid, who comes early in the morning to wash the vessels. Staring her, I took out the water bottle from fridge and drank a sip, she was busy and didn't look at me yet, she sensed my presence. Her hair was coming on her face, her hands were dirty, and she was struggling to push her hair back with her arm. I went close to her, she stepped back and I moved forward, she had to stop when she touched the wall behind. She looked the floor in nervousness, I felt her fast breath in my imminence, I slowly raised my hand, she closed her eyes and her breathing got faster, my heartbeats also raised, I tucked her hair back her ear and caressed her beautiful fair neck with my fingers, closing her eyes she gulped but I controlled my desire of kissing that soft neck, those beautiful cheeks and pink soft lips.

Quickly, I stepped back and said 'Now you can do all the stuff with no trouble from your hair.' Astonished she looked at me and she was shy, she looked here and there 'Th...Thanks!' she said wavering. I stood infront of her, resting my back against the kitchen platfarm. She resumed her work of clearing the utensils. She was anxious in my presence, which was clear with the increased noise of utensils. I grinned.

'Do you need any help?' I asked. 'No...' she said, she was still trembling. 'So many things happened in past two days isn't it?' I changed the topic to comfort her. 'Hmm...Yeah' she said softly without looking at me. 'Finally, everything got sorted out.' I said. 'Hmm,' she mumbled. 'You didn't tell me, how did you convince Mandar's Mom? We all know that she doesn't listen to anybody so easily, she is a tough lady to handle.' I asked her in curiousity. 'Right, but I was sure that she will understand what I was going to tell her.' She replied politely. 'What? How?' I reacted. 'Because we both were sailing in the same boat, I saw the light house and I showed it to her as well.' She gave an example, which I hardly understood. 'I didn't understand.' I asked nodding.

She stood infront of me, looking straight into my eyes, 'It's simple, we both were in same confusion, and when I was clear, after everything that happened in past couple of months. I went to her, to clear her misunderstandings and uncertainties that happened between Mandar and her.' She said gracefully. 'And...what are those?' I asked her, with all the eagerness filled in my heart to heed those words from her that I wished to hear from months. She looked at me for couple of seconds and blushing she looked down, as she understood what I wanted to hear, 'Same that she said the other day.' she said. 'I wasn't paying attention that time, I want to know, which light house you saw and what are the confusions you cleared.' I asked her clearly. 'I wanted to say this to you yesterday itself but circumstances didn't allow me. First of all, one thing I want to make it clear! You know, when Mummy and Amma forgave you? That night you compared my situation with Shreya. No affence to Shreya but there is an infinite difference between you and Arjun. He is a rude, brutal, dirty man and can't even match your foot's dust. I recalled everything you did, over and over again, and there was a battle going on in mind. Finally, I realised whatever happened was our fate, we all were helpless in its hands. Sa..Sandy (Shyness filled on her face while saying my name) I want to forget everything, and start a new life with you.' She said, those last lines looking straight in to my eyes. Her eyes were shining and hearing that I was on the top of the world. I presumed her feelings with her hints but wanted to hear that from her. I got excited and I went close to her with all the happiness, I held her hands in my hands 'Really?' amused I looked in to her eyes. She nodded, she looked down blushing. 'Thank you!' I sighed, I waited for that moment from months and hugged her in happiness. I never cry but that moment my heart melted, controlling my tears 'Thanks' I said and walked out from there.

I rushed to my room in happiness and poured water again and again on my face in the basin to avoid crying. After few minutes, Mansi walked into the room, I was checking messages walking in the room. Without talking, she grabbed her night suit from the wardrobe and went inside the washroom. I observed some dampness on the floor, balcony slider was left open on one side. Heavy rain targeted the floor and the couch, which was close to the gallery. Drenched couch wasn't fit for sleeping, wicked romantic ideas flew in my mind in that situation. I hit my head smiling, as I didn't want to rush for anything without her consent. I grabbed some gunny bags from the store room and placed them carefully on the wet floor.

She came out and I glanced at her, purple night suit and her wet hair made her look more sensual. 'You washed your hair now?' I asked. 'Yeah, they were a mess due to rain and all'. She said wiping her hair with towel. 'You look hot!' I said immediately. Suddenly she looked at me, her towel fell on the floor, and hurriedly she grabbed the towel from the floor. *'That was fast, idiot!'* my inner voice barked, I bit my tounge. Shyly she walked infront of the dressing table and started drying her hair. 'You sleep on the bed tonight.' I said staring at her beauty in the mirror, she stopped drying her hair, and looked my image in the mirror with widening her eyes. Recalling my incomplete sentence, I bit my tounge again, 'Oh…I…I mean, the floor is wet and the rain has knocked the couch as well. Look, I placed some gunny bags on the floor but its all damp over here.' I said showing her the floor. 'Oh, how the water has logged inside?' wondering she said walking near couch. 'Slider was left open.' I said looking at her. 'Oh…My fault, morning I forgot to close it.' Remembering she said by holding her head. Mom and Dadi hardly come upstairs throughout the day. It is the duty of the maid who cleans the house in the morning and Mansi takes care of checking on everything throughout the day. 'It's alright. You sleep on the bed, I will go to the guest room.' I said like a gentle man, whereas from inside I was dying to sleep with her. I had to say that to maintain the promise of *not touching her without her permission.*

Meanwhile, our ears hit the sound of strong thunder storm. Suddenly, she ran into me and hugged me tightly as she got scared of that sound. The sound lasted for couple of seconds and her soft body was pressed against mine, her delicate hands were locked in my back. Looking up happily, I wishpered to myself *'What a filmy timing!'* Slowly, hesitatingly, I wrapped my arms around her, it was a hard moment for me to control my desires. When the sound stopped, she realised her presence in my arms and quickly, she pushed herself back, wavering 'I…I am sorry, it was so strong sound that I got scared.' she said and I smiled, she was looking the floor in an embarrassment. 'That's fine…' I said and took my mobile from the bed and started walking out of the room. In the meantime, some small thunderstorms struck back to back, 'WAIT!' she uttered, and I turned around. 'You, you sleep here only…I...I am getting scared of these sounds.' She said. Maybe that is why people say that rainy season is the most romantic season. I beamed 'Are you sure? I mean think again…that means we both will be sleeping on the same BED!' I teased her winking my eye. She thought of something and after a second she took out the load pillow from the cupboard and placed that in the middle of the bed 'Yes, I am sure now.' she said looking at me. 'Hm...that may be pushed on the floor in the mid of the night.' I said being naughty with an old friend, hiding all my desires for her. 'It won't, as someone promised me something.' She said smiling, biting her lips and staring at me. I sighed, and fell on my side of the bed, covering my face under the pillow, showing-off my fake anger. I heard her sound of chuckle and later she slept beside me, on the other side of the thick strong load.

Next morning, I went to play badminton in the common club of all my friends. Co-incidently, I saw Aarzoo while going to the court. She was coming out of squash court. 'Hey, good morning buddy! Good to see you here!' She said hugging me. 'Hi, yeah, I came after many days.' I said. 'Good...' she said and started packing her stuff into her bag 'So, what happened last night after that?' I asked her to know the reaction of Shreya's father in the car while dropping them to home. We sat together on the bench after my question. 'You know what? I am just happy that Shreya has come up infront of her family about our relationship. At last, that girl showed the guts and I am proud of her for that! We both know that our relationship is not easy. She won't live with me without acceptance of her family and her family won't accept it. So, I accepted the truth! My visa is processed and I am going back to London as planned. I think that is the end of our story.' She moaned. 'Did he say something last night?' I asked her. 'No. Infact, I told him not to worry about our relationship by informing him that I am going back to London.' She smiled and it was a fake one, hidden behind bunch of pain. 'You know what? Every story has a happy ending, and if its not, then *picture abhi baaki hai mere dost* (Still more to go, my friend)' I said mimicking Shahrukh Khan to cheer her up. She smiled and picked up her bag 'Our story is different from all yours, we are not as lucky as you guys are.' saying she left from there with a pale face.

My eyes followed her until she disappeared. I picked up my bat and went to Aarzoo's hospital, where Shreya's grandma was admitted. I saw the old lady, who was sleeping lifelessly on the bed. Looking at me she smiled, I was happy to notice that she recongnised me. Once, the strong and clear voice with long sentences of her's was turned into small whispers of one or two words. I sat beside her on a stool and spoke to her about other stuff for a while and came to the topic of Aarzoo and Shreya. I told her the entire story as I knew the person, who is counting her days, will surely understand the value of love and truth of life. Initially, it was difficult for her to digest such news. She couldn't believe it for the first instance but I tried everything to make her believe it. I explained her that the values of culture, tradition, religion which she possessed her entire life and made Shreya to follow, didn't give her peace, in her last days nothing came to save her, where as human being like Aarzoo was helping her to get back to her healthy life. I gave her the option for choosing either of Shreya's happiness with Aarzoo or her sorrow filled with the pain of remembering her life with Arjun. Her eyes were filled with tears. I held her hand and said 'It is all up to you, you are a mature person. Perhaps, you will take the right decision. And yes, I will not complain if you didn't agree with me.' and walked out from there.

When I started my bike for home, rain started pouring as usual. It never rains when I am indoors. Clouds started sprinkling immediately when I stepped out. That reminded me to check the status of the car, I called the mechanic to check whether the car was ready. He said it would take another two days. No matter how much you love the bikes but in rainy season you don't find anything more comfortable than a car. I always thanked god for providing me all the comforts than the people who struggle day and night travelling in public transports, bikes and cycles apart from all the hurdles. I waited for rain to subside and went home after that.

Dad was placing some luggage in his car, Mom, Dadi and Dad were ready to leave from home. I entered the house by knotting eyebrows, kept my bag on the sofa, wondering 'What's going on?' I asked Mom and Dadi. 'We are going to Vijaypur for two-three days.' Dadi said with a smile. 'What? In this heavy rainy season? Why?' I asked to both of them. 'There is no rain that side. I took an oath yesterday! After hearing your accident news, I prayed our *kuldevi* that if you come home safely and all your problems get resolved, I will visit her temple immediately!' Mom said holding my cheek. 'MOM! You and your oaths!' I said holding her hand with sarcasm. Mansi got a towel for me, as she observed my hair was wet after riding bike in that drizzle, I took it from her looking at Mom. 'Yes, because of that oath, all your problems got solved yesterday itself!' Mom defended with a smile. That reminded me about Mansi's change of mind as well. My eyes searched for her, she hid herself behind Dadi. I smiled wiping my hair 'Yeah, I think your gods are having fast forward service for you in this whole cynical world!' I mocked, remembering all good things happened previous day. They both grinned. Dad was busy calling someone. 'There is also a wedding of one of our relative's daughter tomorrow that is why we are going to finish both the works. Raju is busy at the site and you have office job, so only we are going. Mansi will be here to take care of you...

and you better take care of her, don't create anymore hurdles now and be at home in the evening soon, OK!?' Mom said to me, strictly. I heard her staring at Mansi, she blushed holding Dadi's hand by laying her head on Dadi's shoulder. When Mom was instructing me Do's and Don'ts. Dadi took Mansi aside and they whispered something to each other and giggled. 'But in this heavy rain how will Dad drive for such a long trip?' I asked Mom. 'Your Dad has booked a driver. He is talking to him.' Mom said, while checking her hand bag, and my eyes were on Mansi and Dadi. Meanwhile, Mansi covered her face with both of her hands when Dadi murmured something in her ear, and she hugged Mansi. I didn't give any importance to them at that time. Ignoring them with a smile, 'When is the driver coming?' I asked Dad, who was busy on his phone. And the driver got down from the auto infront of our gate, we said see-offs to our elders. I took bath, ate quick bites of breakfast and didn't get much time to talk to Mansi as the clients were continuously calling me. I went to work in a hurry as I was already late to meet the client.

THIRTY ONE

When I reached home, it was already nine in the night. The door was closed. I rang the bell many times but Mansi didn't open the door. I called on her mobile but she didn't pick up and that made me worried and I quickly searched the keys in my bag and opened the door. I searched for Mansi all over the house in downstairs but didn't find her. I got tensed and called on her mobile once again, and found it ringing on the teapoy. I hopped the stairs hurriedly and went to my room, the door was locked from inside. I heard the sound of shower from the bathroom, I knocked the door, she didn't open it. I assumed that she must be busy in the bathroom. I spoke to her in the evening around seven before an hour of leaving from the office, that time she was busy in a get-together at the corner house of the colony, where she was about to have her dinner after that.

I came downstairs, to my surprise, I saw a chit on the dining table. I read a note in her beautiful handwiring '*Sorry! I am busy, you get fresh. Your clothes are kept in Dadi's room....Food will be ready on the table once you come out.*' There was a fresh aroma of her cuisine around kitchen and dining table. I glanced at the dining table, it was clean but empty, I looked upstairs eagerly checking any sign of Mansi but she wasn't there. I threw my bag on the sofa, locked the main door and went to Dadi's room. My shampoo and soap were kept in Dadi's bathroom. I took bath and got fresh wearing my track pant and maroon t-shirt, which were neatly placed on the bed. When I came out, I saw the dining table was decorated with delicious dishes. The thali was garnished with all my favourite dishes along with desert and a sweet paan! I was hungry when I smelled the food immedietly after entering home. I was starving after looking at the yummy thali, and saw one more chit on the table, *Everything is on the table, please serve yourself...* I smiled but I doubted why she was hiding from me.

I went upstairs and knocked the door 'Mansi!...Mansi open the door.' I uttered. 'You had your dinner, so soon!' she asked from inside. 'No, What is all this? Why this *chit chat*? Come out. What are you doing inside from so long?' I uttered knocking the door. 'The...The floor is all filled with water, I forgot to close the balcony while going out in the evening for the function, so I am cleaning inside...Don't come inside right now...Have your dinner.' She said from inside. 'What? Mansi are you ok? I mean... all this...not sounding good to me? You had dinner?' I asked as I smelled something fishy. 'Yes, I told you na, I had my dinner in the function. And I am fine. It's just, I am messed up with all this cleaning stuff.' She said. 'We will clean it together, open the door.' I said. 'NO...NO... You finish your dinner.' She said quickly. I was worried about her 'Mansi, are you ok?' I asked, standing on the door, keeping my ear on the door to hear her out. 'Yes, I am fine...' She said softly. 'I mean, you just come out yaar, I want to see you...I just want to make sure that you are fine...' I demanded. Slowly she opened the door and came out closing the door immedietly after coming out 'I am fine...' she said softly, without facing me. She was in her pyjamas. Her hair was wet and tied up on head with towel. I stared at her for a while, she seemed mysterious to me 'Can I help you?' I asked staring her. 'Yes, you can, by having your dinner.' She said staring the floor. I smiled 'Ok, if you need anything, you call me.' I ordered showing my index finger. 'Yes...' she mumbled with her head down.

I stood there staring her, even after tying her hair with towel, drops were falling on the floor from her hair, her face looked pink and it was shining after taking bath without any make-up. *'Oh..man! I am madly in love with this girl'* my heart uttered. 'Will you stop staring me and go to have your dinner?' She asked mockingly. 'Yeah...yes...' I said blushing and walked down the steps. I had to resist my lust for Mansi. However, couldn't resist my starvation for food after looking at the delicious thali. I finished everything on the plate and served myself extra chapati's and rice, satisfied my hunger by garnishing it with moongdal halwa and eating the paan in the end. I cleaned the dining table and set aside all the left over food in the refrigerator and kept the used dishes in the basin. Saw television for few minutes in the living room, as I knew Mansi would take it long to clean the room, she wants everything to be perfect with no disturbance.

I heard the sound of bangles from upstairs. I looked up but did not see Mansi. I went upstairs and knocked the door but it was open, I pushed it and went inside. I was stunned to look at the complete make over of the room! My eyes couldn't believe what I was glancing at, lights were switched off and the entire room was illuminated with countless aromatic candles and diyas, various scented flower petals were decorated to form a heart shape on the bed. The room smelled fantastic with aroma's that my nostrils widened to smell. My eyes couldn't stop looking around the beauty of fully decorated room, which was not less than a five star honeymoon suite in Thailand. It was a treat to all my senses. Suddenly, I looked down the floor and there was no sign of water logging, the floor was dry and clean, balcony was closed from inside as it was raining out. Keeping my hands on my waist, I convinced my mind that it was all true, my heart was delighted by every bit of my sight, and it started beating fast. My eyes looked around for

Mansi but I didn't find her. I searched for her in the bathroom but she was not in there. I turned around to go out of the room to seek my love, who arranged this beautiful surprise for me. But I stopped looking at another note placed on the teapoy, two red roses were blossoming on it as paper weight. I tookoff the roses, smelling the scent, read the note with a smile.

'Dear Husband,

Since school days, I always thought that I am the one who understands you better than anyone else does. But I failed in last 7 months, I didn't see the man who took care of everyone around him. Wished for everyones happiness, struggled every bit and tried everything to bring smiles on the face of his wife and family, who kept his promise and never crossed his limits. My eyes were filled with the haze of confusions, they saw only the brat from the past. But now the mist passed and it's all clear. I realised my fault and request you to forgive me for my juvenile behaviour at times in past couple of months.

I AM SORRY! And, Thank you for being with me always, no matter what!

Sandeep, I have dedicated my soul to you, the only man whom I loved since I don't know from when! Everything that belongs to me is all yours from now on, I want to spend rest of my life in your arms.

I LOVE YOU SANDEEP, my dear SANDY.

Proud to be your wife,

Mansi.

My heart was delighted after reading it. I smiled and read the last lines again and again, my eyes were searching for Mansi. I turned around to look for my love and saw her standing on the door. She slowly walked inside, with her head down.

Staring at her beauty, I was stunned for few seconds, her hands were down, fingers were locked, and both the hands were designed with mehndi, which I didn't notice before when I met her outside the room, her wrists were full of red, white and golden bangles matching with her saree colour. She was wearing red and white combination saree, her perfect figure was looked spectacular to my eyes in that red hot saree. Her hair was wet styled and she kept it open, semi sleeve blouse was stitched in deep neck so nicely that her upper body looked seductive. My heartbeats increased, I walked towards her to gaze her beauty closely. She stepped back, I moved forward and she stepped back again and touched the edge of the door, which was half open, with my right hand I pushed the door, closing it I moved towards her, and she had to stop as her back touched the closed door of the dead end. Her head was still down in shyness. We were so close that we could hear each others heartbeats and sense the long breaths. She smelled awesome and I was not so bad at all after the bath and paan after the dinner. I was holding the rose and letter in one hand and my other hand was resting on the door beside her shoulder. She was so shy that she wasn't able to look up even for a second. I smiled and felt tons of butterflies in my stomach, I slowly lifted her face holding her chin, and she closed her eyes tightly. Even in those dim lights of candles and diyas, her face looked bright. She had applied dark lipstick on her natural pink lips, bright eyes looked highlighted with the eye liner, and face was delighted with light make-up. Overall, she looked like an angel from heaven. She stood still in shyness and that tickled my heart. Grinning, I took off my hand from the door and I ran my fingers through her slightly wet hair, pushing them back her ear, caressed her ear, which was beautifed with heart shaped ear ring. She was amazed with my touch, and shyly closed her face with her palms. I smiled, and caressed her hands with a rose in my hand. She was thrilled with that flowery soft touch. Grinning, 'You are looking so hot!' I whispered in her ear.

She shyly pushed me and ran inside the room, and stopped holding the curtains of closed balcony, opposite side. I turned around and watched her running towards balcony. My heart and mind believed what was happening was true. She stood near the curtains, shyly with her head still down, turning back towards me. I blushed and walked towards her in style with my hands in my pant pocket. Her deep neck blouse showed her sexy fair back. I raised my hand and carrassed her back, she got thrilled and quickly she turned towards me with her head down. I moved close to touch her waist, she moved aside, I moved with her, she moved again and this time I held her slim waist with one hand and pulled her close to me. She kept her hands against my chest and shyly placed her forehead on my chest 'Look at me…' I whispered. She nodded, both my hands were on her waist, I pressed her waist and she swiftly looked at me widening her eyes. I smiled and her heart melted, shyly she rested her forehead on my chest again. Her soft touch was amazing, even though, I'd experienced her touch many times before but that was something really special. 'By the way… beautiful surprise.' I whispered. She didn't reply, she hid her head in my chest. Although, I had experienced sex with other girls before but that was first time with Mansi and I was also feeling shy for the first time. I grinned at myself and took off my hand from her waist and held her face in my palms. Lifted her face 'Look at me…' I whispered seductively but she shook her head with closed eyes. 'Please…' I wishpered again and she slowly lifted her eyes up and looked at me. Our eyes met and they were locked, those beautiful deep brown eyes took away everything from me. I was mesmerised and surrendered myself to her. Passionately holding her face 'I love you Mansi! I love you so very much…' I said and caressed her lips and cheeks, gazed her beauty. 'I…I am nervous…' looking at me she said softly. Those innocent eyes looked down again. 'Frankly speaking, I am also nervous…because this is my first time!' I said grinning at her and she stared at me with fake anger! 'With you!' I chuckled. She hit me lightly on my chest, I grabbed her face towards me and kissed her. It lasted for few minutes, I moved my hands down around her waist, holding her tightly in my arms and she relaxed her hands from my chest and garlanded her arms around my neck. We surrendered our body and soul to each other that night.

THIRTY TWO

Preeti was always a rebel child of her family and Sumit was most pampered son in his family. Due to their nature and upbringing respectively, their marriage wasn't opposed by anybody in both the families, they got engaged in that same month.

Soon the day of separation arrived, Aarzoo was all set to go to London. We did everything to bring Aarzoo and Shreya together but things didn't work and we lost hope. Shreya wasn't ready to disappoint her family and Aarzoo didn't want to force her. Mansi hated the society for all its useless rules, which were not allowing the bond between true lovers. Mansi and I tried many ways to convince Aarzoo to stay back but she was stuck to her plan and flew to London. Before leaving, Aarzoo had secured of all the medical facilities for Shreya's grandmother. Aarzoo had a dream of building hospitals in various villages of India with all modern medical facilities and she was working on it along with her family.

Shreya started her course of painiting and lived with her father. Arjun went behind the bars for ten years in the cases of domestic violence on Shreya and attempt to my murder. Shreya's father realised his mistake of spoiling his daughter's life but sending her with Aarzoo was a taboo for him. A month passed and Shreya's grandma was taking her last breath, we all went to hospital to meet her the last time. The old lady called Moorthy uncle and made her last wish. It was *'Shreya's happiness! She specifically instructed him to send Shreya to her love of life, Aarzoo!'* And she died with that wish. Moorthy uncle was in pressure of facing the society. We all came to the solution that if Shreya can't live happily with Aarzoo in India, they can start new life in west, where their relation is not a taboo! It was a bit tough task but all was well in the end, and we all went to London in the month of October and united the true lovers. Shreya and Aarzoo got married in London and decided to live there until our society accepts their relationship.

Shaun was not a single bird anymore, he also chose his life partner. He met his ex-girlfriend in a pub and they fell in love again.

He got married as well by the end of the year. That wasn't the end, except for Aarzoo, Shreya and Mandar, we all attended Bindu's big-fat Punjabi-South Indian mix wedding in Punjab.

Thus, the year in search of a soulmate ended happily for us and we all stepped into the new beginning.

We get relatives by fate but we make friends by our own choice. Life is always beautiful when our friends are around. I got lucky with both friends and relatives. Wish you all the same luck, Good luck!

Love,
Sandy.